Julian Hawthorne

French Novels

Julian Hawthorne

French Novels

ISBN/EAN: 9783955630478

Auflage: 1

Erscheinungsjahr: 2013

Erscheinungsort: Bremen, Deutschland

@ Leseklassiker in Access Verlag GmbH, Fahrenheitstr. 1, 28359 Bremen. Alle Rechte beim Verlag und bei den jeweiligen Lizenzgebern.

Leseklassiker

Table of Contents

Victor Cherbuliez
Count Kostia   1

Paul Bourget
Andre Cornelis   184

Anonymous
The Last of the Costellos   308
Lady Betty's Indiscretion   329

Victor Cherbuliez

Count Kostia

I

At the beginning of the summer of 1850, a Russian nobleman, Count Kostia Petrovitch Leminof, had the misfortune to lose his wife suddenly, and in the flower of her beauty. She was his junior by twelve years. This cruel loss, for which he was totally unprepared, threw him into a state of profound melancholy; and some months later, seeking to mitigate his grief by the distractions of travel, he left his domains near Moscow, never intending to return. Accompanied by his twin children, ten years of age, a priest who had served them as tutor, and a serf named Ivan, he repaired to Odessa, and then took passage on a merchant ship for Martinique. Disembarking at St. Pierre, he took lodgings in a remote part of the suburbs. The profound solitude which reigned there did not at first bring the consolation he had sought. It was not enough that he had left his native country, he would have changed the planet itself; and he complained that nature everywhere was too much alike. No locality seemed to him sufficiently a stranger to his experience, and in the deserted places, where the desperate restlessness of his heart impelled him, he imagined the reappearance of the obtrusive witnesses of his past joys, and of the misfortune by which they were suddenly terminated.

He had lived a year in Martinique when the yellow fever carried off one of his children. By a singular reaction in his vigorous temperament, it was about this time that his somber melancholy gave way to a bitter and sarcastic gayety, more in harmony with his nature. From his early youth he had had a taste for jocularity, a mocking turn of spirit, seasoned by that ironical grace of manner peculiar to the great Moscovite nobleman, and resulting from the constant habit of trifling with men and events. His recovery did not, however, restore the agreeable manners which in former times had distinguished him in his intercourse with the world. Suffering had brought him a leaven of misanthropy, which he did not take the trouble of disguising; his voice had lost its caressing notes and had become rude and abrupt; his actions were brusque, and his smile scornful. Sometimes his bearing gave evidence of a haughty will which, tyrannized over by events, sought to avenge itself upon mankind.

Terrible, however, as he sometimes was to those who surrounded him, Count Kostia was yet a civilized devil. So, after a stay of three years under tropical skies, he began to sigh for old Europe, and one fine day saw him disembark upon the quays of Lisbon. He crossed Portugal, Spain, the south of France and Switzerland. At Basle, he learned that on the borders of the Rhine, between Coblenz and Bonn, in a situation quite isolated, an old castle was for sale. To this place he hurried and bought the antique walls and the lands which belonged to them, without discussing the price and without making a detailed examination of the property. The bargain concluded, he made some hasty and indispensable repairs on one of the buildings which composed a part of his dilapidated manor, and which claimed the imposing name of the fortress of Geierfels, and at once installed himself therein, hoping to pass the rest of his life in peaceable and studious seclusion.

Count Kostia was gifted with a quick and ready intellect, which he had strengthened by study. He had always been passionately fond of historical research, but above everything, knew and wished to know, only that which the English call "the matter of fact." He professed a cold scorn for generalities, and heartily abandoned them to "dreamers;" he laughed at all abstract theories and at the ingenuous minds which take them seriously. He held that all system was but logical infatuation; that the only pardonable follies were those which were frankly avowed; and that only a pedant could clothe his imagination in geometrical theories. In general, pedantry to his eyes was the least excusable of vices; he understood it to be the pretension of tracing back phenomena to first causes, "as if," said he, "there were any 'first causes,' or chance admitted of calculation!" This did not prevent him however from expending much logic to demonstrate that there was no such thing as logic, either in nature or in man.

These are inconsistencies for which skeptics never dream of reproaching themselves; they pass their lives in reasoning against reason. In short, Count Kostia respected nothing but facts, and believed that, properly viewed, there was nothing else, and that the universe, considered as an entirety, was but a collection of contradictory accidents.

A member of the Historical and Antiquarian Society of Moscow, he had once published important memoirs upon Slavonic antiquities and upon some of the disputed questions in the history of the Lower Empire. Hardly was he installed at Geierfels, before he occupied himself in fitting up his library, but a few volumes of which he had carried to Martinique. He at once ordered from Moscow most of the books he had left, and also sent large orders to German bookstores. When his "seraglio," as he called it, was nearly complete, he again became absorbed in study, and particularly in that of the Greek historians of the Byzantine Empire, of whose collective works he had the good fortune to possess the Louvre edition in thirty-six volumes folio; and he soon formed the ambitious project of writing a complete history of that Empire from Constantine the Great to the taking of Constantinople. So absorbed did he become in this great design, that he scarcely ate or drank; but the further he advanced in his researches the more he became dismayed by the magnitude of the enterprise, and he conceived the idea of procuring an intelligent assistant, upon whom he could shift a part of the task. As he proposed to write his voluminous work in French, it was in France this living instrument which he needed must be sought, and he therefore broached the project to Dr. Lerins, one of his old acquaintances in Paris. "For nearly three years," he wrote to the Doctor, "I have dwelt in a veritable owl's nest, and I should be much obliged to you if you would procure for me a young night bird, who could endure life two or three years in such an ugly hole without dying of ennui. Understand me, I must have a secretary who is not contented with writing a fine hand and knowing French a little better than I do: I wish him to be a consummate philologist, and a hellenist of the first order, – one of those men who ought to be met with in Paris, – born to belong to the Institute, but so dependent upon circumstances as to make that position impossible. If you succeed in finding this priceless being, I will give him the best room in my castle and a salary of twelve thousand francs. I stipulate that he shall not be a fool. As to character, I say nothing about it; he will do me the favor to have such as will suit me."

M. Lerins was intimate with a young man from Lorraine named Gilbert Saville, a savant of great merit, who had left Nancy several years before to seek his fortune in Paris. At the age of twenty-seven he had presented, in a competition opened by the Academy of Inscriptions, an essay on the Etruscan language, which took the prize and was unanimously declared a masterpiece of sagacious erudition. He had hoped for some time that this first success, which had gained him renown among learned men, would aid him in obtaining some lucrative position and rescue him from the precarious situation in which he found himself. Nothing resulted from it. His merits compelled esteem; the charm of his frank and courteous manner won him universal good will; his friends were numerous; he was well received and caressed; he even obtained, without seeking it, the entree to more than one salon, where he met men of standing who could be useful to him and assure him a successful future. All this however amounted to nothing, and no position was offered. What worked most to his prejudice was an independence of opinion and character which was a part of his nature. Only to look at him was to know that such a man could not be tied down, and the only language which this able philologist could not learn was the jargon of society. Add to this that Gilbert had a speculative, dreamy temperament and the pride and indolence which are its accessories. To bestir himself and to importune were torture to him. A promise made to him could be forgotten with impunity, for he was not the man to revive it; and besides, as he never complained himself, no one was disposed to complain for him. In short, among those who had been desirous of protecting and advancing him, it was said: "What need has he of our assistance? Such remarkable talent will make its own way." Others thought, without expressing it: "Let us be guarded, this is another Letronne, – once 'foot in the stirrup,' God only knows where he will stop." Others said and thought: "This young man is charming, – he is so discreet, – not like such and such a person." All those cited as not "discreet," were provided for.

The difficulties of his life had rendered Gilbert serious and reflective, but they had neither hardened his heart nor quenched his imagination. He was too wise to revolt against his fate, but determined to be superior to it. "Thou art all thou canst be," said he to himself; "but do not flatter thyself that thou hast reached the measure of my aspirations."

After having read M. Leminof's letter, Dr. Lerins went in search of Gilbert. He described Count Kostia to him according to his remote recollections, but he asked him, before deciding, to weigh the matter deliberately. After quitting his young friend he muttered to himself –

"After all, I hope he will refuse. He would be too much of a prize for that boyard. Of his very Muscovite face, I remember only an enormous pair of eyebrows, – the loftiest and bushiest I ever saw, and perhaps there is nothing more of him! There are men who are all in the eyebrows!"

II

A week later Gilbert was on his way to Geierfels. At Cologne he embarked on board a steamboat to go up the Rhine ten or twelve leagues beyond Bonn. Towards evening, a thick fog settled down upon the river and its banks, and it became necessary to anchor during the night. This mischance rendered Gilbert melancholy, finding in it, as he did, an image of his life. He too had a current to stem, and more than once a sad and somber fog had fallen and obscured his course.

In the morning the weather cleared; they weighed anchor, and at two o'clock in the afternoon, Gilbert disembarked at a station two leagues from Geierfels. He was in no haste to arrive, and even though "born with a ready-made consolation for anything," as M. Lerins sometimes reproachfully said to him, he dreaded the moment when his prison doors should close behind him, and he was disposed to enjoy yet a few hours of his dear liberty. "We are about to part," said he to himself; "let us at least take time to say farewell."

Instead of hiring a carriage to transport himself and his effects, he consigned his trunk to a porter, who engaged to forward it to him the next day, and took his way on foot, carrying under his arm a little valise, and promising himself not to hurry. An hour later he quitted the main road, and stopped to refresh himself at an humble inn situated upon a hillock covered with pine trees. Dinner was served to him under an arbor, – his repast consisted of a slice of smoked ham and an omelette au cerfeuil, which he washed down with a little good claret. This feast a la Jean Jacques appeared to him delicious, flavored as it was by that "freedom of the inn" which was dearer to the author of the Confessions than even the freedom of the press.

When he had finished eating, Gilbert ordered a cup of coffee, or rather of that black beverage called coffee in Germany. He was hardly able to drink it, and he remembered with longing the delicious Mocha prepared by the hands of Madame Lerins; and this set him thinking of that amiable woman and her husband.

Gilbert's reverie soon took another turn. From the bank where he was sitting, he saw the Rhine, the tow path which wound along by the side of its grayish waters, and nearer to him the great white road where, at intervals, heavy wagons and post chaises raised clouds of dust. This dusty road soon absorbed all of his attention. It seemed to him as if it cast tender glances upon him, as if it called him and said: "Follow me; we will go together to distant countries; we will keep the same step night and day and never weary; we will traverse rivers and mountains, and every morning we will have a new horizon. Come, I wait for thee, give me thy heart. I am the faithful friend of vagabonds, I am the divine mistress of those bold and strong hearts which look upon life as an adventure."

Gilbert was not the man to dream long. He became himself again, rose to his feet, and shook off the vision. "Up to this hour I thought myself rational; but it appears I am so no longer. Forward, then, – courage, let us take our staff and on to Geierfels!"

As he entered the kitchen of the inn to pay his bill, he found the landlord there busy in bathing a child's face from which the blood streamed profusely. During this operation, the child cried, and the landlord swore. At this moment his wife came in.

"What has happened to Wilhelm?" she asked.

"What has happened?" replied he angrily. "It happened that when Monsieur Stephane was riding on horseback on the road by the mill, this child walked before him with his pigs. Monsieur Stephane's horse snorted, and Monsieur Stephane, who could hardly hold him, said to the child: 'Now then, little idiot, do you think my horse was made to swallow the dust your pigs raise? Draw aside, drive them into the brush, and give me the road.' 'Take to the woods yourself,' answered the child, 'the path is only a few steps off.' At this Monsieur Stephane got angry, and as the child began to laugh, he rushed upon him and cut him in the face with his whip. God-a-mercy! let him come back, – this little master, – and I'll teach him how to behave himself. I mean to tie him to a tree, one of these days, and break a dozen fagots of green sticks over his back."

"Ah take care what thou sayest, my old Peter," replied his wife with a frightened air. "If thou'dst touch the little man thou'dst get thyself into a bad business."

"Who is this Monsieur Stephane?" inquired Gilbert.

The landlord, recalled to prudence by the warning of his wife, answered dryly: "Stephane is Stephane, pryers are pryers, and sheep are put into the world to be sheared."

Thus repulsed, poor Gilbert paid five or six times its value for his frugal repast, muttering as he departed: "I don't like this Stephane; is it on his account that I've just been imposed upon? Is it my fault that he carries matters with such a high hand?"

Gilbert descended the little hill, and retook the main road; it pleased him no more, for he knew too well where it was leading him. He inquired how much further it was to Geierfels, and was told that by fast walking he would reach that place within an hour, whereupon he slackened his pace. He was certainly in no haste to get there.

Gilbert was but a half a league from the castle when, upon

his right, a little out of his road, he perceived a pretty fountain which partly veiled a natural grotto. A path led to it, and this path had for Gilbert an irresistible attraction. He seated himself upon the margin of the fountain, resting his feet upon a mossy stone. This ought to be his last halt, for night was approaching. Under the influence of the bubbling waters, Gilbert resumed his dreamy soliloquy, but his meditations were presently interrupted by the sound of a horse's feet which clattered over the path. Raising his eyes, he saw coming towards him, mounted upon a large chestnut horse, a young man of about sixteen, whose pale thin face was relieved by an abundance of magnificent bright brown hair, which fell in curls upon his shoulders. He was small but admirably formed, and his features, although noble and regular, awakened in Gilbert more of surprise than sympathy: their expression was hard, sullen, and sad, and upon this beautiful face not any of the graces of youth appeared.

The young cavalier came straight towards him, and when at a step or two from the fountain, he called out in German, with an imperious voice: "My horse is thirsty, – make room for me, my good man!"

Gilbert did not stir.

"You take a very lofty tone, my little friend," replied he in the same language, which he understood very well, but pronounced like the devil, – I mean like a Frenchman.

"My tall friend, how much do you charge for your lessons in etiquette?" answered the young man in the same language, imitating Gilbert's pronunciation. Then he added in French, with irreproachable purity of accent: "Come, I can't wait, move quicker," and he began cutting the air with his riding-whip.

"M. Stephane," said Gilbert, who had not forgotten the adventure of the little Wilhelm, "your whip will get you into trouble some of these days."

"Who gave you the right to know my name?" cried the young man, raising his head haughtily.

"The name is already notorious through the country," retorted Gilbert, "and you have written it in very legible characters upon the cheek of a little pig-driver."

Stephane, for it was he, reddened with anger and raised his whip with a threatening air; but with a blow of his stick Gilbert sent it flying into the bottom of a ditch, twenty paces distant.

When he looked at the young man again, he repented of what he had done, for his expression was terrible to behold; his pallor became livid; all the muscles of his face contracted, and his body was agitated by convulsive movements; in vain he tried to speak, his voice died upon his lips, and reason seemed deserting him. He tore off one of his gloves, and tried to throw it in Gilbert's face, but it fell from his trembling hand. For an instant he looked with a scornful and reproachful glance at that slender hand whose weakness he cursed; then tears gushed in abundance from his eyes, he hung his head over the neck of his horse, and in a choking voice murmured:

"For the love of God, if you do not wish me to die of rage, give me back, – give me back – "

He could not finish; but Gilbert had already run to the ditch, and having picked up the riding-whip, as well as the glove, returned them to him. Stephane, without looking at him, answered by a slight inclination of the head, but kept his eyes fixed upon the pommel of his saddle, – evidently striving to recover his self-possession. Gilbert, pitying his state of mind, turned to leave; but at the moment he stooped to pick up his portmanteau and cane, the youth, with a well-directed blow of his whip, struck off his hat, which rolled into the ditch, and when Gilbert, surprised and indignant, was about to throw himself upon the young traitor, he had already pushed his horse to a full gallop, and in the twinkling of an eye he reached the main road, where he disappeared in a whirlwind of dust. Gilbert was much more affected by this adventure than his philosophy should have permitted. He took up his journey again with a feeling of depression, and haunted by the pale, distorted face of the youth. "This excess of despair," said he to himself, "indicates a proud and passionate character; but the perfidy with which he repaid my generosity is the offspring of a soul ignoble and depraved." And striking his forehead, he continued: "It just occurs to me, judging from his name, that this young man may be Count Kostia's son. Ah! what an amiable companion I shall have to cheer my captivity! M. Leminof ought to have forewarned me. It was an article which should have been included in the contract."

Gilbert felt his heart sink; he saw himself already condemned to defend his dignity incessantly against the caprices and insolence of a badly-trained child, – the prospect was not attractive! Plunged in these melancholy reflections, he lost his way, having passed the place where he should have quitted the main road to ascend the steep hill of which the castle formed the crown. By good luck he met a peasant who put him again upon the right track. The night had already fallen when he entered the court of the vast building. This great assemblage of incongruous structures appeared to him but a somber mass whose weight was crushing him. He could only distinguish one or two projecting towers whose pointed roofs stood out in profile against the starlit sky. While seeking to make out his position, several huge dogs rushed upon him, and would have torn him to pieces if, at the noise of their barking, a tall stiff valet had not made his appearance with a lantern in hand. Gilbert having given him his name, was requested to follow him. They crossed a terrace, forced to turn aside at every step by the dogs who growled fiercely, – apparently regretting "these amiable hosts" the supper of which they had been deprived. Following his guide Gilbert found himself upon a little winding staircase, which they ascended to the third story, where the valet, opening an arched door, introduced him into a large circular apartment where a bed with a canopy had been prepared. "This is your room," said he curtly, and having lighted two candles and placed them upon the round table, he left the room, and did not return for half an hour, when he reappeared bearing a tray laden with a samovar, a venison pie, and some cold fowl. Gilbert ate with a good appetite and felt great satisfaction in finding that he had any at all. "My foolish reveries," thought he, "have not spoiled my stomach at least."

Gilbert was still at the table when the valet re-entered and handed him a note from the Count, which ran thus:

"M. Leminoff bids M. Gilbert Saville welcome. He will give himself the pleasure of calling upon him to-morrow morning."

"To-morrow we shall commence the serious business of life," said Gilbert to himself, as he enjoyed a cup of exquisite green tea, "and I'm very glad of it, for I don't approve of the use I make of my leisure. I have passed all this day reasoning upon myself, dissecting my mind and heart, – a most foolish pastime, beyond a doubt" – then drawing from his pocket a note-book, he wrote therein these words: "Forget thyself, forget thyself, forget thyself," imitating the philosopher Kant, who being inconsolable at the loss of an old servant named Lamp, wrote in his journal: "Remember to forget Lamp."

He remained some moments standing in the embrasure of the window gazing upon the celestial vault which shone with a thousand fires, and then threw himself upon his bed. His sleep was not tranquil; Stephane appeared to him in his dreams, and at one time he thought he saw him kneeling before him, his face bathed in tears; but when he approached to console him, the child drew a poignard from his bosom and stabbed him to the heart.

Gilbert awakened with a start, and had some difficulty in getting to sleep again.

III

A great pleasure was in store for Gilbert at his awakening; he rose as the sun began to appear, and having dressed, hastened to the window to see what view it offered.

The rotunda which had been assigned to him for a lodging formed the entire upper story of a turret which flanked one of the angles of the castle. This turret, and a great square tower situated at the other extremity of the same front, commanded a view of the north, and from this side the rock descended perpendicularly, forming an imposing precipice of three hundred feet. When Gilbert's first glance plunged into the abyss where a bluish vapor floated, which the rising sun pierced with its golden arrows, the spectacle transported him. To have a precipice under his window, was a novelty which gave him infinite joy. The precipice was his domain, his property, and his eyes took possession of it. He could not cease gazing at the steep, wall-like rocks, the sides of which were cut by transverse belts of brush-wood and dwarf trees. It was long since he had experienced such a lively sensation, and he felt that if his heart was old, his senses were entirely new. The fact is that at this moment, Gilbert, the grave philosopher, was as happy as a child, and in listening to the solemn murmur of the Rhine, with which mingled the croaking of a raven and the shrill cries of the martins, who with restless wings grazed the abutments of the ancient turret, he persuaded himself that the river raised its voice to salute him, that the birds were serenading him, and that all nature celebrated a fete of which he was the hero.

He could hardly tear himself from his dear window to breakfast, and he was again engaged in contemplation when M. Leminof entered the room. He did not hear him, and it was not until the Count had coughed three times that he turned his head. Perceiving the enemy, Gilbert started, but quickly recovered himself. The nervous start, however, which he had not been able to conceal, caused the Count to smile, and his smile embarrassed Gilbert. He felt that M. Leminof would regulate his conduct to him upon the impression he should receive in this first interview, and he determined to keep close watch upon himself.

Count Kostia was a man of middle age, very tall and well made, broad-shouldered, with lofty bearing, a forehead stern and haughty, a nose like the beak of a bird of prey, a head carried high and slightly backwards, large, wide open gray eyes which shot glances at once piercing and restless, an expressive face regularly cut, in which Gilbert found little to criticise except that the eyebrows were a little too bushy, and the cheek bones a little too prominent; but what did not please him was, that M. Leminof remained standing while praying him to be seated, and as Gilbert made some objections the Count cut him short by an imperious gesture and a frown.

"Monsieur le Comte," said Gilbert mentally, "you do not leave this room until you have been seated too!"

"My dear sir," said the Count, pacing the room with folded arms, "you have a very warm friend in Dr. Lerins. He sets a great value upon your merit; he has even been obliging enough to give me to understand that I was quite unworthy of having such a treasure of wisdom and erudition in my house. He has also expressly recommended me to treat you with the tenderest consideration; he has made me feel that I am responsible for you to the world, and that the world will hold me to a strict account. You are very fortunate, sir, in having such good friends, they are among Heaven's choicest blessings."

Gilbert made no answer but bit his lips and looked at the floor.

"M. Lerins," continued the Count, "informs me also, that you are both timid and proud, and he desires me to deal gently with you. He pretends that you are capable of suffering much without complaint. This is an accomplishment which is uncommon nowadays. But what I regret is, that our excellent friend M. Lerins apparently considers me a sort of human wolf. I should be very unhappy if I inspired you with fear." Then, turning half round towards Gilbert: "Let us see, look at me well; have I claws at the ends of my fingers?"

Poor Gilbert inwardly cursed M. Lerins and his indiscreet zeal.

"Oh, Monsieur le Comte," replied he in his frankest tones and with the most tranquil air he could command, "I never suspect claws in a fellow-creature; – only when occasion makes me feel them, I cry out loudly and defend myself."

The sound of Gilbert's voice, and the expression of his face, struck M. Leminot. It was his turn if not to start (he seldom started) at least to be astonished. He looked at him an instant in silence, and then resumed in a more sardonic tone:

"This is not all; M. Lerins (ah! what an admirable friend you have there!) desires also to inform me that you are, sir, what is called nowadays, a beautiful soul. What is 'a beautiful soul?' I know nothing of the species." While thus speaking he seemed to be looking by turns for a fly on the ceiling and a pin on the floor. "I have old-fashioned ideas of everything, and I do not understand the vocabulary of my age. I know a beautiful horse very well or a beautiful woman; – but A BEAUTIFUL SOUL! Do you know how to explain to me, sir, what 'this beautiful soul' is?"

Gilbert did not answer a word. He was entirely occupied in addressing to Heaven the prayer of the philosopher: "Oh, my God! save me from my friends, and I will take care of my enemies." "My questions seem to you perhaps a little indiscreet," pursued M. Leminof; "but M. Lerins is responsible for them. His last letter caused me great uneasiness. He introduces you to me as an exceptionable being; it is natural that I should wish to enlighten myself, for I detest mysteries and surprises. I once heard of a little Abyssinian prince, who to testify his gratitude to the missionary who had converted him, sent to him, as a present, a large chest of scented wood. When the missionary opened the chest, he found in it a pretty living Nile crocodile. Fancy his delight! Experiences like this teach prudence. So when our excellent friend M. Lerins sends me a present of a beautiful soul, it is natural that I should unpack it with caution, and that before I install this beautiful soul in my house, I should seek to know what is inside of it. A beautiful soul!" he repeated, in a less ironical but harsher tone, "by dint of pondering upon it, I divine to be a soul which has a passion for the trumpery of sentiment. In this case, sir, suffer me to give you a piece of advice. Madame Leminof had a great fancy for Chinese ornaments, and she filled her parlors with them. Unfortunately, I am a little brusque, and it happened more than once that I overturned her tables laden with porcelain and other gewgaws. You can judge how well she liked it! My dear sir, be prudent, shut up your Chinese ornaments carefully in your closets, and carry the keys."

"I thank you for the advice," answered Gilbert gently; "but I am distressed to see that you have received a very false idea of me. Will you permit me to describe myself as I am?"

"I have no objection," said he.

"To begin then 'I am not a beautiful soul,' I am simply a good soul, or if you like it better, an honest fellow who takes things as they come and men as they are; who prides himself upon nothing, pretends to nothing, and who cares not a straw what others think of him. I do not deny that in my early youth I was subject, like others, to what a man of wit has called 'the witchery of nonsense;' but I have recovered from it entirely. I have found in life a morose and rather brutal teacher, who has taught me the art of living by severe discipline; so whatever of the romantic was in me has taken refuge in my brains, and my heart has become the most reasonable of all hearts. If I had the good fortune to be at the same time an artist and rich, I should take life as a play; but being neither the one nor the other I treat it as a matter of business."

M. Leminof commenced his walk again, and in passing Gilbert, gave him a look at once haughty and caressing, such as a huge mastiff would cast upon a spaniel, who fearing nothing, would approach his great-toothed majesty familiarly and offer to play with him. He growls loudly, but feels no anger. There is something in the eye of a spaniel which forces the big dogs to take their familiarity in good part.

"Ah, then, sir," said the Count, "by your own avowal you are a perfect egotist. Your great aim is to live, and to live for yourself."

"It is nearly so," answered Gilbert, "only I avoid using the word, it is a little hard. Not that I was born an egotist, but I have become one. If I still possessed the heart I had at twenty, I should have brought here with me some very romantic ideas. You may well laugh, sir, but suppose I had arrived at your castle ten years ago; it would have been with a fixed intention of loving you a great deal, and of making you love me. But now, mon Dieu! now I know a little of the world, and I say to myself that there can be no question between us but a bargain, and that good bargains should be advantageous to both parties."

"What a terrible man you are," cried the Count with a mocking laugh. "You destroy my illusions without pity, you wound my poetical soul. In my simplicity, I imagined that we should be enamored of each other. I intended to make an intimate friend of my secretary, – the dear confidant of all my thoughts, but at the moment when I was prepared to open my arms to him, the ingrate says to me in a studied tone: 'Sir, there is nothing but the question of a bargain between us; I am the seller, you are the buyer; I sell you Greek, and you pay me cash down.' Peste! Monsieur, 'your beautiful soul' does not pride itself on its poetry. As an experiment, I will take you at your word. There is nothing but a bargain between us. I will make the terms and you will agree without complaint, though I am the Turk and you the Moor."

"Pardon me," answered Gilbert, "it is naturally to your interest to treat me with consideration. You may give me a great deal to do, I shall not grudge my time or trouble, but you must not overburden me. I am not exacting, and all that I ask for is a few hours of leisure and solitude daily to enjoy in peace.

M. Leminof stopped suddenly before Gilbert, his hands resting upon his hips.

"You will sit down, you will sit down, Monsieur le Comte," muttered Gilbert between his teeth.

"So you are a dreamer and an egotist," said M. Leminof, looking fixedly at him. "I hope, sir, that you have the virtues of the class. I mean to say, that while wholly occupied with yourself, you are free from all indiscreet curiosity. Egotism is worth its price only when it is accompanied by a scornful indifference to others. I will explain: I do not live here absolutely alone, but I am the only one with whom I desire you to have any intimate acquaintance. The two persons who live in this house with me know nothing of Greek, and therefore need not interest you. Remember, I have the misfortune of being jealous as a tiger, and I intend that you shall be mine without any division. And as for your fantasies, should you think better of it, you will find me always ready to admire them; but you show them to no one else, you understand, to no one!"

Count Kostia pronounced these last words with a tone so emphatic that Gilbert was surprised, and was on the point of asking some explanation; but the stern and almost threatening look of the Count deterred him. "Your instructions, sir," answered he, "are superfluous. To finish my own portrait, I am not very expansive, and I have but little sociability in my character. To speak frankly, solitude is my element; it is inexpressibly sweet to me. Do you wish to try me? If so, shut me up under lock and key in this room, and provided you have a little food passed through the door to me daily, you will find me a year hence seated at this table, fresh, well and happy, unless perhaps," he added, "I should be unexpectedly attacked with some celestial longing, in which case, I could some fine day easily fly out of the window; the loss wouldn't be very great. Finding the cage empty, you would say, 'He has grown his wings, poor fellow – much good may they do him.'"

"I don't admit that," cried the Count, "Monsieur Secretary. You please me immensely, and for fear of accident, I will have this window barred."

With these words he drew a chair towards him, and seated himself facing Gilbert, who could have clapped his hands at this propitious result. Their conversation then turned upon the Byzantine Empire and its history. The Count unfolded to Gilbert the plan of his work, and the kind of researches he expected from him. This conversation was prolonged for several hours.

IV

A fortnight later, Gilbert wrote to his friends a letter conceived thus:

"Madame: – I have found here neither fetes, cavalcades, gala-days nor Muscovite beauties. What should we do, I beg to know, with these Muscovite beauties? or perhaps I ought to ask, what would they do with us? We live in the woods; our castle is an old, very old one, and in the moonlight it looks like a specter. What I like best about it, is its long and gloomy corridors, through which the wind sweeps freely; but I assure you that I have not yet encountered there a white robe or a plumed hat. Only the other evening a bat, who had entered by a broken pane, brushed my face with its wing and almost put out my candle. This, up to the present time has been my sole adventure. And as for you, sir, know that I am not obliged to resist the fascinations of my tyrant, for the reason that he has not taken the trouble to be fascinating. Know also that I am not bored. I am contented; I am enjoying the tranquility of mind which comes from a well-defined, well-regulated, and after all, very supportable position. I am no longer compelled to urge my life on before me and to show it the road; it makes its own way, and I follow it as Martin followed his ass. And then pleasures are not wanting for us, – listen! Our castle is a long series of dilapidated buildings, of which we occupy the only one habitable. I am lodged alone in a turret which commands a magnificent view, and I have a grand precipice under my window. I can say 'my turret,' 'my precipice!' Oh, my poor Parisians, you will never understand all there is in these two words: MY PRECIPICE! 'What is it then but a precipice?' exclaims Madame Lerins. 'It is only a great chasm.' Ah, yes! Madame, it is 'a great chasm'; but imagine that this morning this chasm was a deep blue, and this evening at sunset it was – stay, of the color of your nasturtiums. I opened my window and put my head out to inhale the odor of this admirable precipice, for I have discovered that in the evening precipices have an odor. How shall I describe it to you? It is a perfume of rocks scorched by the sun, with which mingles a subtle aroma of dry herbs. The combination is exquisite.

"The proud rock, of which we occupy the summit and which deserves its name of Vulture's Crag, is bounded at the north as you already know, at the west by a ravine which separates it from a range of hills higher and fantastically jagged, and following the windings of the river. This line of hills is not continuous; it is cut by narrow gorges, which open into the valley and through which the last rays of the sun reach us. The other evening there was a red sunset, and one of these gorges seemed to vomit flames; you might have supposed it the mouth of the furnace. Upon the east, from its heights and its terrace, Geierfels overlooks the Rhine, from which it is separated by the main road and a tow-path. At the south it communicates by steep paths with a vast plateau, of which it forms, as it were, the upper story, and which is clothed with a forest of beeches, and furrowed here and there with noisy streams. It is on this side only that our castle is accessible, – and here not to carriages, – even a cart could reach us but with difficulty, and all of our provisions are brought to us upon the backs of men or mules. Mountains, perpendicular rocks, turrets overhanging a precipice, grand and somber woods, rugged paths and brooks which fall in cascades, do not all these, Madame, make this a very wild and very romantic retreat? On the right bank of the Rhine which stretches out under our eyes, it is another thing. Picture to yourself a landscape of infinite sweetness, a great cultivated plain, which rises by imperceptible gradation to the base of a distant chain of mountains, the undulating outlines of which are traced upon the sky in aerial indentations.

"Directly in front of the chateau, beyond the Rhine, a market town, with neat houses carefully whitewashed and with gardens attached, spreads itself around a little cove, like a fan. Upon the right of this great village a rustic church reflects the sun from its tinned spire; on the left, some large mills show their lazily turning wheels, and behind these mills, the church and the market town, extends the fertile plain which I have just endeavored to describe to you, and which I cannot praise too much. Oh! charming landscape! This afternoon I was occupied in feasting my eyes upon it, when a white goat came to distract my attention, followed at a distance by a little girl whom I suspected of being very pretty; but I forgot them both in watching a steamboat passing up the river towing a flotilla of barges, covered with awnings and attended by their lighters, and a huge raft laden with timber from the Black Forest, manned by fifty or sixty boatmen, some of whom in front, and some in the rear, directed its course with vigorous strokes of the oar.

"But what pleases me above everything else is, that Geierfels, by its position, is a kind of acoustic focus to which all the noises of the valley incessantly ascend. This afternoon, the dull murmuring of the river, the panting respiration of the tug-boat, the vibration of a bell in a distant church tower, the song of a peasant girl washing her linen in a spring, the bleating of sheep, the tic tac of the mills, the tinkling bells of a long train of mules drawing a barge by a rope, the reverberating clamors of boatmen stowing casks in their boats – all these various sounds came to my ear in vibrations of surprising clearness, when suddenly a gust of wind mingled them confusedly together, and I could hear but a vague music which seemed to fall from the skies. But a moment afterwards all of these vibrating voices emerged anew from the whirlwind of confused harmony, and each, sonorous and distinct, recounted to my enraptured heart some episode in the life of man and nature. And then, when night comes, Madame, to all of these noises of the day succeed others more mysterious, more penetrating, more melancholy. Do you like the hooting of the owl, Madame? But first, I wonder if you have ever heard it. It is a cry – No, it is not a cry, it is a soft, stifled wail; a monotonous and resigned sorrow, which unbosoms itself to the moon and stars. One of these sad birds lodges within two steps of me, in the hollow of a tree, and when night comes, he amuses himself by singing a duet with the singing wind. The Rhine plays an accompaniment, and its grave, subdued voice furnishes a continuous bass, whose volume swells and falls in rhythmic waves. The other evening this concert failed; neither the wind nor the owl was in voice. The Rhine alone grumbled beneath; but it arranged a surprise for me and proved that it could make harmony of its own without other aid. Towards midnight a barge carrying a lantern on its prow had become detached from the bank and had drifted across the river, and I distinctly heard, or imagined that I heard, the wash of the waves upon the side of the boat, the bubbling of the eddy which formed under the stern, the dull sound of the oar when it dipped into the current, and still sweeter, when raised out of it the tender tears which dripped from it drop by drop. This music contrasted strongly with that I had heard the night before at the same hour. The north wind had risen during the evening, and near eleven o'clock it became furious; it filled the air with sad howlings, and increased to a rage that was inexpressible. The weathercocks creaked, the tiles ground against each other, the roof timbers trembled in their mortices, and the walls shook upon their foundations. From time to time a blast would hurl itself against my window with wild shrieks, and from my bed I imagined I could see through the panes the bloodshot eyes of a band of famished wolves. In the brief intervals when this outside tumult subsided, strange murmurs came from the interior of the castle; the wainscoting gave forth dismal creakings; – there was not a crack in the partitions, nor a fissure in the ceiling from which did not issue a sigh, or hoarse groans. Then again all this became silent, and I heard only something like a low whispering in the far off corridors, as of phantoms murmuring in the darkness as they swept the walls in their flight; then suddenly they seemed to gather up their forces, the floors trembled under their spasmodic tramping, while they clambered in confusion up the staircase which led to my room, throwing themselves over the threshold of my door and uttering indescribable lamentations.

"But enough of this, perhaps you will say; let us now talk a little of your patron: This terrible man, will you believe it, has not inspired me with the antagonism which you prophesied. But in the first place we do not live together from morning to night. The day after my arrival, he sent me a long list of difficult or mutilated passages to interpret and restore. It is a work of time, to which I devote all my afternoons. He has had some of his finest folios sent to my room, and I live in these like a rat in a Dutch cheese. It is true, I pass my mornings in his study, where we hold learned discussions which would edify the Academy of Inscriptions; but to my delight, after nightfall I can dispose of myself as I choose. He has even agreed that, after seven o'clock, I may lock myself in my room, and that no human being under any pretext whatever shall come to disturb me there. This privilege M. Leminof granted to me in the most gracious manner, and you can imagine how grateful I am to him for it. I do not mean to say by this that he is an amiable man, nor that he cares to be; but he is a man of sense and wit. He understood me at once, and he means to make me serviceable to him. I am like a horse who feels that he carries a skilful rider."

V

The next day was Sunday, and for Gilbert was a day of liberty. Towards the middle of the forenoon, he went out to take a walk in the woods. He had wandered for an hour, when, turning his head, he saw coming behind him a little troop of children, decked out in strange costumes. The two oldest wore blue dresses and red mantles, and their heads were covered with felt caps encircled by bands of gilt paper in imitation of aureoles. A smaller one wore a gray dress, upon which were painted black devils and inverted torches. The last five were clothed in white; their shoulders were ornamented with long wings of rose-tinted gauze, and they held in their hands sprigs of box by way of palm branches.

Gilbert slackened his pace, and when they came up with him, he recognized in the one who wore the san-benito the little hog- driver, so maltreated by Stephane. The child, who while marching looked down complacently on the torches and the devils with which his robe was decorated, advanced towards Gilbert, and without waiting for his questions, said to him, "I am Judas Iscariot. Here is Saint Peter, and here is Saint John. The others are angels. We are all going to R – – , to take part in a grand procession, that they have there every five years. If you want to see something fine, just follow us. I shall sing a solo and so will Saint Peter; the others sing in the chorus."

Upon which Judas Iscariot, Saint Peter, Saint John and the angels resumed their march, and Gilbert decided to follow them. The first houses of the village of R – – rise at the extremity of the wooded plain which extends to the south of Geierfels. In about half an hour, the little procession made its entry into the village in the midst of a considerable crowd which hastily gathered from the neighboring hamlets. Gilbert made his way along the main street, decorated with hangings and altars, and passed on to an open square planted with elms, of which the church formed one of the sides. Presently the bells sounded a grand peal; the doors of the church opened, and the procession came out. At the head marched priests, monks, and laymen of both sexes, bearing wax tapers, crosses, and banners. Behind them came a long train of children representing the escort of the Saviour to Calvary. One of them, a young lad of ten years, filled the role of Christ.

At a moment when Gilbert was absorbed in reflection, a voice which was not unknown to him murmured in his ear these words, which made him shudder:

"You seem prodigiously interested, Monsieur, in this ridiculous comedy!"

Turning his head quickly, he recognized Stephane. The young man had just dismounted from his horse, which he had left in the care of his servant, and had pushed his way through the crowd, indifferent to the exclamations of the good people whose pious meditations he disturbed. Gilbert looked at him a moment severely, and then fixed his eyes on the procession, and tried, but in vain, to forget the existence of this Stephane whom he had not met before since the adventure at the fountain, and whose presence at this moment caused him an indefinable uneasiness. The reproachful look which he had cast upon the young man, far from intimidating him, served but to excite his mocking humor, and after a few seconds of silence he commenced the following soliloquy in French, speaking low, but in a voice so distinct that Gilbert, to his great regret, lost not a word of it:

"Mon Dieu! how ridiculous these young ones are! They really seem to take the whole thing seriously; what vulgar types! what square, bony faces. Don't their low, stupid expressions contrast oddly with their wings? Do you see that little chap twisting his mouth and rolling his eyes? His air of contrition is quite edifying. The other day he was caught stealing fagots from a neighbor. . . . And look at that other one who has lost his wings! What an unlucky accident! He is stooping to pick them up, and tucks them under his arm like a cocked hat. The idea is a happy one! But thank God, their litanies are over. It's Saint Peter's turn to sing."

For a long time Gilbert looked about him anxiously, seeking an opportunity to escape, but the crowd was so compact that it was impossible to make his way through it. He saw himself forced to remain where he was and to submit, even to the end, to Stephane's amiable soliloquy. So he pretended not to hear him, and concealed his impatience as well as he could; but his nervousness betrayed him in spite of himself, and to the great diversion of Stephane, who maliciously enjoyed his own success. Fortunately for Gilbert, when Judas had stopped singing, the procession resumed its march towards a second station at the other end of the village, and this caused a general movement among the bystanders who hedged his passage. Gilbert profited by this disorder to escape, and was soon lost in the crowd, where even Stephane's piercing eyes could not follow him.

Hastening from the village he took the road to the woods. "This Stephane is decidedly a nuisance," thought he. "Three weeks since he surprised me at a bright fountain, where I was deliciously dreaming, and put my fancies to flight, and now by his impertinent babbling he has spoiled a fete in which I took interest and pleasure. What is he holding in reserve for me? The most annoying part of it is, that henceforth I shall be condemned to see him daily. Even to-day, in a few hours, I shall meet him at his father's table. Presentiments do not always deceive, and at first sight I recognize in him a strong enemy to my repose and happiness; but I shall manage to keep him at a distance. We won't distress ourselves over a trifle. What does philosophy amount to, if the happiness of a philosopher is to be at the mercy of a spoiled child!"

Thus saying, he drew from his pocket a book which he often carried in his walks: It was a volume of Goethe, containing the admirable treatise on the "Metamorphosis of Plants." He began to read, often raising his head from the page to gaze at a passing cloud, or a bird fluttering from tree to tree. To this pleasant occupation he abandoned himself for nearly an hour, when he heard the neighing of a horse behind him, and turning, he saw Stephane advancing at full speed on his superb chestnut and followed at a few paces by his groom, mounted on a gray horse. Gilbert's first impulse was to dart into a path which opened at his left, and thus gain the shelter of the copse; but he did not wish to give Stephane the pleasure of imagining that he was afraid of him, and so continued on his way, his eyes riveted upon the book.

Stephane soon came up to him, and bringing his horse to a walk, thus accosted him:

"Do you know, sir, that you are not very polite? You quitted me abruptly, without taking leave. Your proceedings are singular, and you seem to be a stranger to the first principles of good breeding."

"What do you expect, my dear sir?" answered Gilbert. "You were so amiable, so prepossessing the first time I had the honor of meeting you, that I was discouraged. I said to myself, that do what I would, I should always be in arrears to you."

"You are spiteful, Mr. Secretary," retorted Stephane. "What, have you not forgotten that little affair at the spring?"

"You have taken no trouble, it seems, to make me forget it."

"It is true, I was wrong," replied he with a sneer; "wait a moment, I will dismount, go upon my knees there in the middle of the road, and say to you in dolorous voice, 'Sir, I'm grieved, heart-broken, desperate,' – For what? I know not. Tell me, I pray you, sir, for what must I beg your pardon? For if I rightly remember, you commenced by raising your cane to me."

"I did not raise my cane to you," replied Gilbert, beside himself with indignation; "I contented myself with parrying the blow which you were about to give me."

"It was not my intention to strike you," rejoined Stephane, impetuously. "And besides, learn once for all, that between us things are not equal, and that even should I provoke you, you would be a wretch to raise the end of your finger against me."

"Oh, that is too much!" cried Gilbert, laughing loudly.

"And why so, my little friend?"

"Because – because – " stammered Stephane; and then suddenly stopped.

An expression of bitter sadness passed over his face; his brows contracted and his eyes became fixed. It was thus that terrible paroxysm had commenced which so alarmed Gilbert at their first meeting. This time, fortunately, the attack was less violent. The good Gilbert passed quickly from anger to pity; "there is a secret wound in that heart," thought he, and he was still more convinced of it when, after a long pause Stephane, recovering the use of his speech, said to him in a broken voice: "I was ill the other day, I often am. People should have some consideration for invalids."

Gilbert made no answer; he feared by a hard word to exasperate his soul so passionate, and so little master of itself; but he thought that when Stephane felt ill, he had better stay in his room.

They walked on some moments in silence until, recovering from his dejection, Stephane said ironically: "You made a mistake in leaving the fete so soon. If you had stayed until the end, you would have heard Christ and his mother sing; you lost a charming duet."

"Let us drop that subject," interrupted Gilbert; "we could not understand each other. Yours is a kind of pleasantry for which I have but little taste."

"Pedant!" murmured Stephane, turning his head, then adding with animation: "It is just because I respect religion that I do not like to see it burlesqued and parodied. Let a true angel appear and I am ready to render him homage; but I am enraged when I see great seraph's wings tied with white strings to the shoulders of wicked, boorish, little thieves, liars, cowards, slaves, and rascals. Their hypocritical airs do not impose on me, for I read their base natures in their eyes. I detest all affectations, all shams. I have the misfortune of being able to see through all masks."

"These are very old words for such very young lips," answered Gilbert sadly. "I suspect, my child, you are repeating a lesson you have learned."

"And what do you know of my age?" cried he angrily. "By what do you judge? Are faces clocks which mark the hours and minutes of life? Well, yes, I am but sixteen; but I have lived longer than you. I am not a library rat, and have not studied the world in duodecimos. Thank God! for the advancement of my education. He has gathered under my eyes a few specimens of the human race which have enabled me to judge of the rest, and the more experience I gain, the more I am convinced that all men are alike. On that account I scorn them all, – all without exception!"

"I thank you sincerely for myself and your groom," answered Gilbert smiling.

"Don't trouble yourself about my groom," replied Stephane, beating down with his whip the foliage which obstructed his path. "In the first place, he knows but little French; and it is useless to tell him in Russian that I despise him, – he would be none the worse for it. He is well lodged, well fed, and well clothed; what matters my scorn to him? And besides, let me tell you for your guidance, that my groom is not a groom, he is my jailer. I am a prisoner under constant surveillance; these woods constitute a yard, where I can walk but twice a week, and this excellent Ivan is my keeper. Search his pockets and you will find a scourge."

Gilbert turned to examine the groom, who answered his scrutinizing look by a jovial and intelligent smile. Ivan represented the type of the Russian serf in all his original beauty. He was small, but vigorous and robust; he had a fresh complexion, cheeks full and rosy, hair of a pale yellow, large soft eyes and a long chestnut beard, in which threads of silver already mingled. It was such a face as one often sees among the lower classes of Slavonians; indicating at once energy in action and placidity in repose.

When Gilbert had looked at him well, he said, "My dear sir, I do not believe in Ivan's scourge."

"Ah! that is like you bookworms," exclaimed Stephane with an angry gesture. "You receive all the monstrous nonsense which you find in your old books for Gospel truth, and without any hesitation, while the ordinary matters of life appear to you prodigious absurdities, which you refuse to believe."

"Don't be angry. Ivan's scourge is not exactly an article of faith. One can fail to believe in it without being in danger of hellfire. Besides, I am ready to recant my heresy; but I will confess to you that I find nothing ferocious or stern in the face of this honest servant. At all events, he is a jailer who does not keep his prisoners closely, and who sometimes gives them a relaxation beyond his orders; for the other day, it seems to me, you scoured the country without him, and really the use you make of your liberty – "

"The other day," interrupted Stephane, "I did a foolish thing.

For the first time I amused myself by evading Ivan's vigilance. It was an effort that I longed to make, but it turned out badly for me. Would you like to see with your own eyes what this fine exploit cost me?"

Then pushing up the right sleeve of his black velvet blouse, he showed Gilbert a thin delicate wrist marked by a red circle, which indicated the prolonged friction of an iron ring. Gilbert could not repress an exclamation of surprise and pity at the sight, and repented his pleasantry.

"I have been chained for a fortnight in a dungeon which I thought I should never come out of again," said Stephane, "and I indulged in a good many reflections there. Ah! you were right when you accused me of repeating a lesson I had learned. The pretty bracelet which I bear on my right arm is my thought-teacher, and if I dared to repeat all that it taught me – " Then interrupting himself:

"A lie!" exclaimed he in a bitter tone, drawing his cap down over his eyes. "The truth is, that I came out of the dungeon like a lamb, flexible as a glove, and that I am capable of committing a thousand base acts to save myself the horror of returning there. I am a coward like the rest, and when I tell you that I despise all men, do not believe that I make an exception in my own favor."

And at these words he drove the spurs into his horse's flank so violently that the fiery chestnut, irritated by the rude attack, kicked and pranced. Stephane subdued him by the sole power of his haughty and menacing voice; then exciting him again, he launched him forward at full speed and amused himself by suddenly bringing him up with a jerk of the rein, and by turns making him dance and plunge; then urging him across the road he made him clear at a bound, the ditch and hedge which bordered it. After several minutes of this violent exercise, he trotted away, followed by his inseparable Ivan, leaving Gilbert to his reflections, which were not the most agreeable.

He had experienced in talking with Stephane an uneasiness, a secret trouble which had never oppressed him before. The passionate character of this young man, the rudeness of his manners, in which a free savage grace mingled, the exaggeration of his language, betraying the disorder of an ill-governed mind, the rapidity with which his impressions succeeded each other, the natural sweetness of his voice, the caressing melody of which was disturbed by loud exclamations and rude and harsh accents; his gray eyes turning nearly black and flashing fire in a paroxysm of anger or emotion; the contrast between the nobility and distinction of his face and bearing, and the arrogant scorn of proprieties in which he seemed to delight – in short, some painful mystery written upon his forehead and betrayed in his smile – all gave Gilbert much to speculate upon and troubled him profoundly. The aversion he had at first felt for Stephane had changed to pity since the poor child had shown him the red bracelet, which he called his "thought- teacher," – but pity without sympathy is a sentiment to which one yields with reluctance. Gilbert reproached himself for taking such a lively interest in this young man who had so little merited his esteem, and more especially as with his pity mingled an indefinable terror or apprehension. In fact, he hardly knew himself; he so calm, so reasonable, to be the victim of such painful presentiments! It seemed to him that Stephane was destined to exercise great influence over his fate, and to bring disorder into his life.

Suddenly, he heard once more the sound of horse's hoofs and Stephane re-appeared. Perceiving Gilbert, the young man stopped his horse and cried out, "Mr. Secretary, I am looking for you."

And then, laughing, continued:

"This is a tender avowal I have just made; for believe me, it is years since I have thought of looking for anybody; but as in your estimation I have not been very courteous, and as I pride myself on my good manners, I wish to obtain your pardon by flattering you a little."

"This is too much goodness," answered Gilbert. "Don't take the trouble. The best course you can pursue to win my esteem is to trouble yourself about me as little as possible."

"And you will do the same in regard to me?"

"Remember that matters are not equal between us. I am but an insect, – it is easy for you to avoid me, whilst – "

"You are not talking with common sense," interrupted Stephane; "look at this green beetle crawling across the road. I see him, but he does not see me. But to drop this bantering – for it's quite out of character with me – what I like in you is your remarkable frankness, it really amuses me. By the way, be good enough to tell me what book that is which never leaves you for a moment and which you ponder over with such intensity. Do tell me," added he in a coaxing, childish tone, "what is the book that you press to your heart with so much tenderness."

Gilbert handed it to him.

"'Essay on the Metamorphosis of Plants.' So, plants have the privilege of changing themselves? Mon Dieu, they must be happy! But they ought to tell us their secret."

Then closing the volume, and returning it to Gilbert, he exclaimed:

"Happy man! you live among the plants of the field as if in your element. Are you not something of a plant yourself? I am not sure but that you have just now stopped reading to say to the primroses and anemones covering this slope, 'I am your brother!' Mon Dieu! I am sorry to have disturbed the charming conversation! And hold! your eyes are a little the color of the periwinkle."

He turned his head and looked at Gilbert with a scornful air, and had already prepared to leave him, when a glance over the road dispersed his ill-humor, for in the distance he saw Wilhelm and his comrades returning from the fete.

"Come quick, my children," cried he, rising in his stirrups. "Come quick, my lambs, for I have something of the greatest importance to propose to you."

Hearing his challenge, the children raised their eyes and recognizing Stephane, they stopped and took counsel together. The somewhat brutal impudence of the young Russian had given him a bad reputation, and the little peasants would rather have turned back than encounter his morose jesting or his terrible whip.

The three apostles and the five angels, after consulting together, concluded prudently to beat a retreat, when Stephane drawing from his pocket a great leather purse, shook it in the air crying, "There is money to be gained here, – come, my dear children, you shall have all you want."

The large, full purse which Stephane shook in his hand was a very tempting bait for the eight children; but his whip, which he held under his left arm, warned them to be careful. Hesitating between fear and covetousness, they stood still like the ass in the fable between his two bundles of hay; but Stephane at that moment was seized with a happy inspiration and threw his switch to the top of a neighboring tree, where it rested. This produced a magical effect, the children with one accord deciding to approach him, although with slow and hesitating steps. Wilhelm alone, remembering his recent treatment, darted into a path nearby and disappeared in the bushes.

The troop of children stopped a dozen paces from Stephane and formed in a group, the little ones hiding behind the larger. All of them fumbled nervously with the ends of their belts, and kept their heads down, awkward and ashamed, with eyes fixed upon the ground, but casting sidelong glances at the great leather purse which danced between Stephane's hands.

"You, Saint Peter," said he to them in a grave tone; "you, Saint John, and your five dear little angels of Heaven, listen to me closely. You have sung to-day very pretty songs in honor of the good Lord; he will reward you some day in the other world; but for the little pleasures people give me, I reward them at once. So every one of you shall have a bright dollar, if you will do the little thing I ask. It is only to kiss delicately and respectfully the toe of my boot. I tell you again, that this little ceremony will gain for each of you a bright dollar, and you will afterwards have the happiness of knowing that you have learned to do something which you can't do too well if you want to get on in this world."

The seven children looked at Stephane with a sheepish air and open mouths. Not one of them stirred. Their immobility, and their seven pairs of fixed round eyes directed upon him, provoked him.

"Come, my little lambs," he continued persuasively, "don't stretch your eyes in this way; they look like barn doors wide open. You should do this bravely and neatly. Ah! mon Dieu! you will see it done often enough, and do it yourselves again too in your lifetime. There must always be a beginning. Come on, make haste. A thaler is worth thirty-six silbergroschen, and a silbergroschen is worth ten pfennigs, and for five pfennigs you can buy a cake, a hot muffin, or a little man in licorice – "

And shaking the leather purse again, he cried:

"Ah, what a pretty sound that makes! How pleasantly the click, click of these coins sounds to our ears. All music is discordant compared to that. Nightingales and thrushes, stop your concerts! we can sing better than you. I am an artist who plays your favorite air on his violin. Let us open the ball, my darlings."

The seven children seemed still uncertain. They were red with excitement, and consulted each other by looks. At last the youngest, a little blond fellow, made up his mind.

"Monsieur HAS ONE CHEVRON TOO MANY," said he to his companions, which being interpreted means: "Monsieur is a little foolish with pride, his head is turned, he is crack-brained, and," added he laughingly, "after all, it's only in fun, and there is a dollar to get."

So speaking, he approached Stephane deliberately and gave his boot a loud kiss. The ice was broken; all of his companions followed his example, some with a grave and composed air, others laughing till they showed all their teeth. Stephane clapped his hands in triumph:

"Bravo! my dear friends," exclaimed he. "The business went off admirably, charmingly!"

Then drawing seven dollars from his purse, he threw them into the road with a scornful gesture:

"Now then, Messrs. Apostles and Seraphim," cried he in a

thundering voice, "pick up your money quick, and scamper away as fast as your legs can carry you. Vile brood, go and tell your mothers by what a glorious exploit you won this prize!

And while the children were moving off, he turned towards Gilbert and said, crossing his arms: "Well, my man of the periwinkles, what do you think of it?"

Gilbert had witnessed this little scene with mingled sadness and disgust. He would have given much if only one of the children had resisted Stephane's insolent caprice; but not having this satisfaction, he tried to conceal his chagrin as best he could.

"What does it prove?" replied he dryly.

"It seems to me it proves many things, and among others this: that certain emotions are very ridiculous, and that certain mentors of my acquaintance who thrust their lessons upon others – "

He said no more, for at this moment a pebble thrown by a vigorous hand whistled by his ears, and rolled his cap in the dust. Starting, he uttered an angry cry, and striking spurs into his horse, he launched him at a gallop across the bushes. Gilbert picked up the cap, and handed it to Ivan, who said to him in bad German:

"Pardon him; the poor child is sick," and then departed hastily in pursuit of his young master.

Gilbert ran after them. When he had overtaken them, Stephane had dismounted, and stood with clenched fists before a child, who, quite out of breath from running, had thrown himself exhausted at the foot of a tree. In running he had torn many holes in his San- benito, and he was looking with mournful eyes at these rents, and replied only in monosyllables to all of Stephane's threats.

"You are at my mercy," said the young man to him at last. "I will forgive you if you ask my pardon on your knees."

"I won't do it," replied the child, getting up. "I have no pardon to ask. You struck me with your whip, and I swore to pay

33

you for it. I'm a good shot. I sighted your cap and I was sure I'd hit it. That makes you mad, and now we're even. But I'll promise not to throw any more stones, if you'll promise not to strike me with your whip any more."

"That is a very reasonable proposition," said Gilbert.

"I don't ask your opinion, sir," interrupted Stephane haughtily, – then turning to Ivan: "Ivan, my dear Ivan," continued he, "in this matter you ought to obey me. You know very well the Count does not love me, but he does not mean to have others insult me: it is a privilege he reserves to himself. Dismount, and make this little rascal kneel to me and ask my pardon."

Ivan shook his head.

"You struck him first," answered he; "why should he ask your pardon?"

In vain Stephane exhausted supplications and threats. The serf remained inflexible, and during his talk Gilbert approached Wilhelm, and said to him in a low voice:

"Run away quickly, my child; but remember your promise; if you don't, you'll have to settle with me."

Stephane, seeing him escape, would have started in pursuit; but Gilbert barred his way.

"Ivan!" cried he, wringing his hands, "drive this man out of my path!"

Ivan shook his head again.

"I don't wish to harm the young Frenchman," replied he; "he has a kind way and loves children."

Stephane's face was painfully agitated. His lips trembled. He looked with sinister eye first at Ivan, then at Gilbert. At last he said to himself in a stifled voice:

"Wretch that I am! I am as feeble as a worm, and weakness is not respected!"

Then lowering his head, he approached his horse, mounted

him, and pushed slowly through the copse. When he had regained the wood, looking fixedly at Gilbert:

"Mr. Secretary," said he, "my father often quotes that diplomatist who said that all men have their price; unfortunately I am not rich enough to buy you; you are worth more than a dollar; but permit me to give you some good advice. When you return to the castle, repeat to Count Kostia certain words that I have allowed to escape me to-day. It will give him infinite pleasure. Perhaps he will make you his spy-in-chief, and without asking it, he may double your salary. The most profitable trade in the world is burning candles on the devil's shrine. You will do wonders in it, as well as others."

Upon which, with a profound bow to Gilbert, he disappeared at a full trot.

"The devil! the devil! he talks of nothing but the devil!" said Gilbert to himself, taking the road to the castle. "My poor friend, you are condemned to pass some years of your life here between a tyrant who is sometimes amiable, and a victim who is never so at all!"

VI

When Gilbert got back to the castle, M. Leminof was walking on the terrace. He perceived his secretary at some distance, and made signs to him to come and join him. They made several turns on the parapet, and while walking, Gilbert studied Stephane's father with still greater attention than he had done before. He was now most forcibly struck by his eyes, of a slightly turbid gray, whose glances, vague, unsteady, indiscernible, became at moments cold and dull as lead. Never had M. Leminof been so amiable to his secretary; he spoke to him playfully, and looked at him with an expression of charming good nature. They had conversed for a quarter of an hour when the sound of a bell gave notice that dinner was served. Count Kostia conducted Gilbert to the dining-room. It was an immense vaulted apartment, wainscoted in black oak, and lighted by three small ogive windows, looking out upon the terrace. The arches of the ceiling were covered with old apocalyptic paintings, which time had molded and scaled off. In the center could be seen the Lamb with seven horns seated on his throne; and round about him the four-and-twenty elders clothed in white. On the lower parts of the pendentive the paintings were so much damaged that the subjects were hardly recognizable. Here and there could be seen wings of angels, trumpets, arms which had lost their hands, busts from which the head had disappeared, crowns, stars, horses' manes, and dragons' tails. These gloomy relics sometimes formed combinations that were mysterious and ominous. It was a strange decoration for a dining-hall.

At this hour of the day, the three arched windows gave but a dull and scanty light; and more was supplied by three bronze lamps, suspended from the ceiling by iron chains; even their brilliant flames were hardly sufficient to light up the depths of this cavernous hall. Below the three lamps was spread a long table, where twenty guests might easily find room; at one of the rounded ends of this table, three covers and three morocco chairs had been arranged in a semi-circle; at the other end, a solitary cover was placed before a simple wooden stool. The Count seated himself and motioned Gilbert to place himself at his right; then unfolding his napkin, he said harshly to the great German valet de chambre:

"Why are not my son and Father Alexis here yet? Go and find them."

Some moments after, the door opened, and Stephane appeared. He crossed the hall, his eyes downcast, and bending over the long thin hand which his father presented to him without looking at him, he touched it slightly with his lips. This mark of filial deference must have cost him much, for he was seized with that nervous trembling to which he was subject when moved by strong emotions. Gilbert could not help saying to himself:

"My child, the seraphim and apostles are well revenged for the humiliation you inflicted upon them."

It seemed as if the young man divined Gilbert's thoughts, for as he raised his head, he launched a ferocious glance at him; then seating himself at his father's left, he remained as motionless as a statue, his eyes fixed upon his plate. Meantime he whom they called Father Alexis did not make his appearance, and the Count, becoming impatient, threw his napkin brusquely upon the table, and rose to go after him; but at this same moment the door opened, and Gilbert saw a bearded face which wore an expression of anxiety and terror. Much heated and out of breath, the priest threw a scrutinizing glance upon his lord and master, and from the Count turned his eyes towards the empty stool, and looked as if he would have given his little finger to be able to reach even that uncomfortable seat without being seen.

"Father Alexis, you forget yourself in your eternal daubs!" exclaimed M. Leminof, reseating himself. "You know that I dislike to wait. I profess, it is true, a passionate admiration for the burlesque masterpieces with which you are decorating the walls of my chapel; but I cannot suffer them to annoy me, and I beg you not to sacrifice again the respect you owe me to your foolish passion for those coarse paintings; if you do, I shall some fine morning bury your sublime daubings under a triple coat of whitewash."

This reprimand, pronounced in a thundering tone, produced the most unhappy effect upon Father Alexis. His first movement was to raise his eyes and arms toward the arched ceiling where, as if calling the four-and-twenty elders to witness, he exclaimed:

"You hear! The profane dare call them daubs, those incomparable frescoes which will carry down the name of Father Alexis to the latest posterity!"

But in the heart of the poor priest terror soon succeeded to indignation. He dropped his arms, and bending down, sunk his head between his shoulders, and tried to make himself as small as possible; much as a frightened turtle draws himself into his shell, and fears that even there he is taking up too much room.

"Well! what are these grimaces for? Do you mean to make us wait until to-morrow for your benediction?"

The Count pronounced these words in the rude tone of a

corporal ordering recruits to march in double-quick time. Father Alexis made a bound as if he had received a sharp blow from a whip across his back, and in his agitation and haste to reach his stool, he struck violently against the corner of a carved sideboard; this terrible shock drew from him a cry of pain, but did not arrest his speed, and rubbing his hip, he threw himself into his place and, without giving himself time to recover breath, he mumbled in a nasal tone and in an unintelligible voice, a grace which he soon finished, and everybody having made the sign of the cross, dinner was served.

"What a strange role religion plays here," thought Gilbert to himself as he carried his spoon to his lips. "They would on no account dine until it had blessed the soup, and at the same time they banish it to the end of the table as a leper whose impure contact they fear."

During the first part of the repast, Gilbert's attention was concentrated on Father Alexis. This priestly face excited his curiosity. At first sight it seemed impressed with a certain majesty, which was heightened by the black folds of his robe, and the gold crucifix which hung upon his breast. Father Alexis had a high, open forehead; his large, strongly aquiline nose gave a manly character to his face; his black eyes, finely set, were surmounted by well-curved eyebrows, and his long grizzly beard harmonized very well with his bronzed cheeks furrowed by venerable wrinkles. Seen in repose, this face had a character of austere and imposing beauty. And if you had looked at Father Alexis in his sleep, you would have taken him for a holy anchorite recently come out of the desert, or better still, for a Saint John contemplating with closed eyes upon the height of his Patmos rock, the sublime visions of the Apocalypse; but as soon as the face of the good priest became animated, the charm was broken. It was but an expressive mask, flexible, at times grotesque, where were predicted the fugitive and shallow impressions of a soul gentle, innocent, and easy, but not imaginative or exalted. It was then that the monk and the anchorite suddenly disappeared, and there remained but a child sixty years old, whose countenance, by turns uneasy or smiling, expressed nothing but puerile preoccupations, or still more puerile content. This transformation was so rapid that it seemed almost like a juggler's trick. You sought St. John, but found him no more, and you were tempted to cry out, "Oh, Father Alexis, what has become of you? The soul now looking out of your face is not yours." This Father Alexis was an excellent man; but unfortunately, he had too decided a taste for the pleasures of the table. He could also be accused of having a strong ingredient of vanity in his character; but his self-love was so ingenuous, that the most severe judge could but pardon it. Father Alexis had succeeded in persuading himself that he was a great artist, and this conviction constituted his happiness. This much at least could be said of him, that he managed his brush and pencil with remarkable dexterity, and could execute four or five square feet of fresco painting in a few hours. The doctrines of Mount Athos, which place he had visited in his youth, had no more secrets for him; Byzantine aesthetics had passed into his flesh and bones; he knew by heart the famous "Guide to Painting," drawn up by the monk Denys and his pupil Cyril of Scio. In short, he was thoroughly acquainted with all the receipts by means of which works of genius are produced, and thus, with the aid of compasses, he painted from inspiration, those good and holy men who strikingly resembled certain figures on gold backgrounds in the convents of Lavra and Iveron. But one thing brought mortification and chagrin to Father Alexis, – Count Kostia Petrovitch refused to believe in his genius! But on the other hand, he was a little consoled by the fact that the good Ivan professed unreserved admiration for his works; so he loved to talk of painting and high art with this pious worshiper of his talents.

"Look, my son," he would say to him, extending the thumb, index and middle fingers of his right hand, "thou seest these three fingers: I have only to say a word to them, and from them go forth Saint Georges, Saint Michaels, Saint Nicholases, patriarchs of the old covenant, and apostles of the new, the good Lord himself and all his dear family!"

And then he would give him his hand to kiss, which duty the good serf performed with humble veneration. However, if

Count Kostia had the barbarous taste to treat the illuminated works of Father Alexis as daubs, he was not cruel enough to prevent him from cultivating his dearly-loved art. He had even lately granted this disciple of the great Panselinos, the founder of the Byzantine school, an unexpected favor, for which the good father promised himself to be eternally grateful. One of the wings of the Castle of Geierfels enclosed a pretty and sufficiently spacious chapel, which the Count had appropriated to the services of the Greek Church, and one fine day, yielding to the repeated solicitations of Father Alexis, he had authorized him to cover the walls and dome with "daubs" after his own fashion. The priest commenced the work immediately. This great enterprise absorbed at least half of his thoughts; he worked many hours every day, and at night he saw in dreams great patriarchs in gold and azure, hanging over him and saying:

"Dear Alexis, we commend ourselves to thy good care; let thy genius perpetuate our glory through the Universe."

The conversation at length turned upon subjects which the Count amused himself by debating every day with his secretary. They spoke of the Lower Empire, which M. Leminof regarded as the most prosperous and most glorious age of humanity. He had little fancy for Pericles, Caesar, Augustus, and Napoleon, and considered that the art of reigning had been understood by Justinian and Alexis Comnenus alone. And when Gilbert protested warmly in the name of human dignity against this theory:

"Stop just there!" said the Count; "no big words, no declamation, but listen to me! These pheasants are good. See how Father Alexis is regaling himself upon them. To whom do they owe this flavor which is so enchanting him? To the high wisdom of my cook, who gave them time to become tender. He has served them to us just at the right moment. A few days sooner they would have been too tough; a few days later would have been risking too much, and we should have had the worms in them. My dear sir, societies are very much like game. Their supreme moment is when they are on the point of decomposition. In their youth they have a barbarous toughness. But a certain degree of corruption, on the contrary, imperils their existence. Very well! Byzantium possessed the art of making minds gamey and arresting decomposition at that point. Unfortunately she carried the secret to the grave with her."

A profound silence reigned in the great hall, uninterrupted except by the rhythmic sound of the good father's jaws. Stephane leaned his elbows on the table; his attitude expressive of dreamy melancholy; his head inclined and leaning against the palm of his right hand; his black tunic without any collar exposing a neck of perfect whiteness; his long silky hair falling softly upon his shoulders; the pure and delicate contour of his handsome face; his sensitive mouth, the corners curving slightly upwards, all reminded Gilbert of the portrait of Raphael painted by himself, all, except the expression, which was very different.

A profound melancholy filled Gilbert's heart. Nothing about him commanded his sympathies, nothing promised any companionship for his soul; at his left the stern face of a drowsy tyrant, made more sinister by sleep; opposite him a young misanthrope, for the moment lost in clouds; at his right an old epicure who consoled himself for everything by eating figs; above his head the dragons of the Apocalypse. And then this great vaulted hall was cold, sepulchral; he felt as though he were breathing the air of a cellar; the recesses and the corners of the room were obscured by black shadows; the dark wainscotings which covered the walls had a lugubrious aspect; outside were heard ominous noises. A gale of wind had risen and uttered long bellowings like a wounded bull, to which the grating of weathercocks and the dismal cry of the owls responded.

When Gilbert had re-entered his own room he opened the window that he might better hear the majestic roll of the river. At the same moment a voice, carried by the wind from the great square tower, cried to him:

"Monsieur, the grand vizier, don't forget to burn plenty of candles to the devil! this is the advice which your most faithful subject gives you in return for the profound lessons of wisdom with which you favored his inexperience to-day!"

It was thus Gilbert learned Stephane was his neighbor.

"It is consoling," thought he, "to know that he can't possibly come in here without wings. And," added he, closing his window, "whatever happens, I did well to write to Mme. Lerins yesterday – to-day I am not so well satisfied."

VII

This is what Gilbert wrote in his journal six weeks after his arrival at Geierfels:

A son who has towards his father the sentiments of a slave toward his master; a father who habitually shows towards his son a dislike bordering on hatred – such are the sad subjects for study that I have found here. At first I wished to persuade myself that M. Leminof was simply a cold hard character, a skeptic by disposition, a blase grandee, who believed it a duty to himself to openly testify his scorn for all the humbug of sentiment. He is nothing of the kind. The Count's mind is diseased, his soul tormented, his heart eaten by a secret ulcer and he avenges its sufferings by making others suffer. Yes, the misanthrope seeks vengeance for some deadly affront which has been put upon him by man or by fate; his irony breathes anger and hatred; it conceals deep resentment which breaks out occasionally in his voice, in his look and in his unexpected and violent acts; for he is not always master of himself. At certain times the varnish of cold politeness and icy sportiveness with which he ordinarily conceals his passions, scales off suddenly and falls into dust, and his soul appears in its nakedness. During the first weeks of my residence here he controlled himself in my presence, now I have the honor of possessing his confidence, and he no longer deems it necessary to hide his face from me, nor does he try any longer to deceive me.

It is singular, I thought myself entirely master of my glances, but in spite of myself, they betrayed too much curiosity on one occasion. The other day while I was working with him in his study, he suddenly became dreamy and absent, his brow was like a thundercloud; he neither saw nor heard me. When he came out of his reverie his eyes met mine fixed upon his face, and he saw that I was observing him too attentively.

"Come now," said he brusquely, "you remember our stipulations; we are two egotists who have made a bargain with each other. Egotists are not curious; the only thing which interests them in the mind of a fellow-creature, is in the domain of utility."

And then fearing that he had offended me, he continued in a softer tone:

"I am the least interesting soul in the world to know. My nerves are very sensitive, and let me say to you once for all, that this is the secret of all the disorders which you may observe in my poor machine."

"No, Count Kostia, this is not your secret!" I was tempted to answer. "It is not your nerves which torment you. I would wager that in despite of your cynicism and skepticism, you have once believed in something, or in some one who has broken faith with you," but I was careful not to let him suspect my conjectures. I believe he would have devoured me. The anger of this man is terrible, and he does not always spare me the sight of it. Yesterday especially, he was transported beyond himself, to such an extent that I blushed for him. Stephane had gone to ride with Ivan. The dinner-bell rang and they had not returned. The Count himself went to the entrance of the court to wait for them. His lips were pale, his voice harsh and grating, veiled by a hoarseness which always comes with his gusts of passion. When the delinquents appeared at the end of the path, he ran to them, and measured Stephane from head to foot with a glance so menacing that the child trembled in every limb; but his anger exploded itself entirely upon Ivan. The poor jailer had, however, good excuses to offer: Stephane's horse had stumbled and cut his knee, and they had been obliged to slacken their pace. The Count appeared to hear nothing. He signed to Ivan to dismount; which having done, he seized him by the collar, tore from him his whip and beat him like a dog. The unhappy serf allowed himself to be whipped without uttering a cry, without making a movement. The idea of flight or self-defense never occurred to him. Riveted to the spot, his eyes closed, he was the living image of slavery resigned to the last outrages. Indeed I believe that during this punishment I suffered more than he. My throat was parched, my blood boiled in my veins. My first impulse was to throw myself upon the Count, but I restrained myself; such a violent interference would but have aggravated the fate of Ivan. I clasped my hands and with a stifled voice cried: "Mercy! mercy!" The Count did not hear me. Then I threw myself between the executioner and his victim. Stupefied, with arm raised and immovable, the Count stared at me with flaming eyes; little by little he became calm, and his face resumed its ordinary expression.

"Let it pass for this time," said he at last, in a hollow voice; "but in future meddle no more in my affairs!"

Then dropping the whip to the ground, he strode away. Ivan raised his eyes to me full of tears, his glance expressed at once tenderness, gratitude, and admiration. He seized my hands and covered them with kisses, after which he passed his handkerchief over his face, streaming with perspiration, foam, and blood, and taking the two horses by the bridles, quietly led them to the stable. I found the Count at the table; he had recovered his good humor; he discharged several arrows of playful sarcasm at my "heresies" in matters of history. It was not without effort that I answered him, for at this moment he inspired me with an aversion that I could hardly conceal. But I felt bound to recognize the victory which he had gained over himself in abridging Ivan's punishment. After dinner he sent for the serf, who appeared with his forehead and hands furrowed with bloody scars. His lips bore their habitual smile, which was always a mystery to me. His master ordered him to take off his vest, turn down his shirt, and kneel before him; then drawing from his pocket a vial full of some ointment whose virtues he lauded highly, he dressed the wounds of the moujik with his own hands. This operation finished, he said to him:

"That will amount to nothing, my son. Go and sin no more."

Upon which the serf raised himself and left the room, smiling throughout. Ivan's smile is an exotic plant which I am not acquainted with, and which only grows in Slavonic soil, a strange smile, – real prodigy of baseness or heroism. Which is it? I am sure I cannot tell.

In spite of my trouble, I had been able to observe Stephane at the beginning of the punishment. At the first blow, a flash of triumphant joy passed over his face; but when the blood started he became horribly pale, and pressed one of his hands to his throat as if to arrest a cry of horror, and with the other he covered his eyes to shut out the sight; then not being able to contain himself, he hurried away. God be praised! compassion had triumphed in his heart over the joy of seeing his jailer chastised. There is in this young soul, embittered as it is by long sufferings, a fund of generosity and goodness; but will it not in time lose the last vestiges of its native qualities? Three years hence will Stephane cover his eyes to avoid the sight of an enemy's punishment? Within three years will not the habit of suffering have stifled pity in his breast? To-morrow, to-morrow perhaps, will not his heart have uttered its last cry!

Since you have no tender words for him, Count Kostia, would that I could close his ears to the desolating lessons that you give him! Do you not see that the life he leads is enough to teach him to hate men and life, without the necessity of your interference? He knows nothing of humanity, but what he sees through the bars of his prison; and imagines that there is nothing in the world but capricious tyrants and trembling, degraded slaves. Why thus kill in his heart every germ of enthusiasm, of hope, of manly and generous faith?

But may not Stephane be a vicious child, whose perverse instincts a justly provoked father seeks to curb by a pitiless discipline? No, a thousand times no! It is false, it is impossible; it is only necessary to look at him to be satisfied of this. His face is often hard, cold, scornful; but it never expresses a low thought, a pollution of soul, or a precocious corruption of mind. In his quiet moods there is upon his brow a stamp of infantile purity. I was wrong in supposing that his soul had lost its youth.

Alas! with what cruel harshness they dispute the little pleasures which remain to him. In spite of his jests over the periwinkles, he has a taste for flowers, and had obtained from the gardener the concession of a little plot of ground to cultivate according to his fancy. The Count, it appears, had ratified this favor; but this unheard-of condescension proved to be but a refinement of cruelty. For some time, every evening after dinner, Stephane passed an hour in his little parterre; he plucked out the weeds, planted, watered, and watched with a paternal eye the growth of his favorites. Yesterday, an hour after the sanguinary castigation, while his father was dressing Ivan's wounds, he had gone out on tiptoe. Some minutes after, as I was walking upon the terrace, I saw him occupied. with absorbing gravity, in this great work of watering. I was but a few paces from him, when the gardener approached, pickax in hand, and, without a word, struck it violently into the middle of a tuft of verbenas which grew at one end of the plot of ground. Stephane raised himself briskly, and, believing him stupid, threw himself upon him, crying out:

"Wretch, what are you doing there?"

"I am doing what his excellency ordered me to," answered the gardener.

At this moment the Count strolled toward us, his hands in his pockets, humming an aria, and an expression of amiable good humor on his face. Stephane extended his arms towards him, but one of those looks which always petrifies him kept him silent and motionless in the middle of the pathway. He watched with wild eyes the fatal pickax ravage by degrees his beloved garden. In vain he tried to disguise his despair; his legs trembled and his heart throbbed violently. He fixed his large eyes upon his dear, devastated treasures; two great tears escaped them and rolled slowly down his cheeks. But when the instrument of destruction approached a magnificent carnation, the finest ornament of his garden, his heart failed him, he uttered a piercing cry, and raising his hands to Heaven, ran away sobbing. The Count looked after him as he fled, and an atrocious smile passed over his lips! Ah! if this father does not hate his son, I know not what hatred is, nor how it depicts itself upon a human face. Meantime I threw myself between the carnation and the pickax, as an hour before between the knout and Ivan. Stephane's despair had rent my heart; I wished at any cost to preserve this flower which was so dear to him. The face of Kostia Petrovitch took all hope from me. It seemed to say:

"You still indulge in sentiment; this is a little too much of it."

"This plant is beautiful," I said to him; "why destroy it?"

"Ah! you love flowers, my dear Gilbert;" answered he, with an air of diabolical malice. "I am truly glad of it!"

And turning to the gardener, he added:

"You will carefully take up all these flowers and place them in pots – they shall decorate Monsieur's room. I am delighted to have it in my power to do him this little favor."

Thus speaking, he rubbed his hands gleefully, and turning his back upon me, commenced humming his tune again. He was evidently satisfied with his day's work.

And now Stephane's flowers are here under my eyes, they have become my property. Oh! if he knew it! I do not doubt that M. Leminof wishes his son to hate me; and his wish is gratified. Overwhelmed with respect and attentions, petted, praised, extolled, treated as a favorite and grand vizier, how can I be otherwise than an object of scorn and aversion to this young man? But could he read my heart! what would he read there, after all? An impotent pity from which his pride would revolt. I can do nothing for him; I could not mitigate his misfortunes or pour balm into his wounds.

Go, then, Gilbert, occupy yourself with the Byzantines! Remember your contract, Gilbert! The master of this house has made you promise not to meddle in his affairs. Translate Greek, my friend, and, in your leisure moments, amuse yourself with your puppets. Beyond that, closed eyes and sealed mouth; that must be your motto. But do you say, "I shall become a wretch in seeing this child suffer"? Well! if your useless pity proves too much of a burden, six months hence you can break your bonds, resume your liberty, and with three hundred crowns in your pocket, you can undertake that journey to Italy, – object of your secret dreams and most ardent longing. Happy man! arming yourself with the white staff of the pilgrim, you will shake the dust of Geierfels from your feet, and go far away to forget, before the facades of Venetian palaces, the dark mysteries of the old

Gothic castle and its wicked occupants.

VIII

As Gilbert rapidly traced these last lines, the dinner-bell sounded. He descended in haste to the grand hall. They were already at the table.

"Tell me, if you please," said Count Kostia, addressing him gayly, "what you think of our new comrade?"

Gilbert then noticed a fifth guest, whose face was not absolutely unknown to him. This newly invited individual was seated at the right of Father Alexis, who seemed to relish his society but little, and was no less a personage than Solon, the favorite of the master, one of those apes which are vulgarly called "monkeys in mourning," with black hair, but with face, hands, and feet of a reddish brown.

"You will not be vexed with me for inviting Solon to dine with us?" continued M. Leminof. "The poor beast has been hypochondriacal for several days, and I am glad to procure this little distraction for him. I hope it will dissipate it. I cannot bear melancholy faces; hypochondria is the fate of fools who have no mental resources."

He pronounced these last words half turning towards Stephane. The young man's face was more gloomy than ever. His eyes were swollen, and dark circles surrounded them. The indignation with which the brutal remark of his father filled him, gave him strength to recover from his dejection. He resolutely set about eating his soup, which he had not touched before, and feeling that Gilbert's eyes were fixed upon him, he raised his head quickly and darted upon him a withering glance. Gilbert thought he divined that he called him to account for his carnation, and could not help blushing, – so true is it that innocence does not suffice to secure one a clear conscience.

"Frankly, now," resumed the Count, lowering his voice, "don't you see some resemblance between the two persons who adorn the lower end of this table?"

"The resemblance does not strike me," answered Gilbert coldly.

"Ah! mon Dieu, I do not mean to say that they are identical in all points. I readily grant that Father Alexis uses his thumbs better; I admit, too, that he has a grain or two more of phosphorus in his brain, for you know the savants of to-day, at their own risk and peril, have discovered that the human mind is nothing but a phosphoric tinder-box."

"It is these same savants," said Gilbert, "who consider genius a nervous disorder. Much good may it do them. They are not my men."

"You treat science lightly; but answer my question seriously: do you not discover certain analogies between these two personages in black clothes and red faces?"

"My opinion," interrupted Gilbert impatiently, "is that Solon is very ugly, and that Father Alexis is very handsome."

"Your answer embarrasses me," retorted the Count, "and I don't know whether I ought to thank you for the compliment you pay my priest, or be angry at the hard things you say of my monkey. One thing is certain," added he, "that my monkey and my priest, – I'm wrong, – my priest and my monkey, resemble each other in one respect: they have both a passionate appetite for truffles. You will soon see."

They were just serving fowl with truffles. Solon devoured his portion in the twinkling of an eye, and as he was prone to coveting the property of others, he fixed his eyes, full of affectionate longing, on his neighbor's plate. Active, adroit, and watching his opportunity, he seized the moment when the priest was carrying his glass to his lips; to extend his paw, seize a truffle, and swallow it, was the work of but half a second. Beside himself with indignation, the holy man turned quickly and looked at the robber with flashing eyes. The monkey was but little affected by his anger, and to celebrate the happy success of his roguery, he capered and frisked in a ridiculous and frantic way, clinging with his forepaws to the back of his chair. The good father shook his head sadly, moved his plate further off, and returned to his eating, not, however, without watching the movements of the enemy from the corner of his eye. In vain he kept guard; in spite of his precautions, – a new attack, a new larceny – and fresh caperings of joy by the monkey. Father Alexis at last lost patience, and the monkey received a vigorous blow full in the muzzle, which drew from him a sharp shriek; but at the same instant the priest felt two rows of teeth bury themselves in his left cheek. He could hardly repress a cry, and gave up the game, leaving Solon to gorge himself to his beard in the spoils, while he busied himself in stanching his wound, from which the blood gushed freely.

The Count affected to be ignorant of all that passed; but there was a merry sparkle in his eyes which testified that not a detail of this tragic comedy had escaped his notice.

"You appear to distrust Solon, Father," said he, seeing that the priest pushed back his chair and kept at a distance from the baboon. "You are wrong. He has very sweet manners; he is incapable of a bad action. He is only a little sad now, but in his melancholy, he observes all the rules of good breeding; which is not the case with all melancholy people," added he, throwing a look at Stephane, who, taken with a sudden access of sadness, had just leaned his elbow upon the table and made a screen of his right hand to hide his tears from his father. Gilbert felt himself near stifling, and as soon as he could, left the table. Fortunately no one followed him onto the terrace. Stephane had no more flowers to cultivate, and went to shut himself up in his high tower. On his part, Father Alexis went to dress his wound; as to M. Leminof, he was displeased with the cool and, as he thought, composed air with which Gilbert had listened to his pleasantries, and he retired to his study, promising himself to give to Monsieur his secretary, whom, nevertheless, he valued very highly, that last touch of pliancy which he needed for his perfection. Count Kostia was of an age when even the strongest mind feels the necessity of occasional relaxation, and he would have been glad to have near him a pliant, agreeable companion, and enchanted could that companion have been his secretary.

Gilbert strode across the terrace, and, leaning over the parapet, gazed long and silently at the highroad. "Ten months yet!" said he to himself, and contracting his brows, he turned to look at the odious castle, where destiny had cast his lot. It seemed as if the old pile wished to avenge itself for his ill humor: never had it been clothed with such a smiling aspect. A ray of the setting sun rested obliquely upon its wide roof; the bricks had the warm color of amber, the highest points were bathed in gold dust, and the gables and vanes threw out sparks. The air was balmy; the lilacs, the citron, the jasmine, and the honeysuckle intermingled their perfumes, which the almost imperceptible breath of the north wind spread in little waves to the four corners of the terrace.

And these wandering perfumes mingled themselves, in passing, with other odors more delicate and more subtle; from each leaf, each petal, each blade of grass, exhaled secret aromas, mute words which the plants exchange with each other, and which revealed to Gilbert's heart the great mystery of happiness which animates the soul of things.

Gilbert was determined to drown his sorrows this evening in the divine harmonies of nature. To succeed the better, he called poetry to his aid, for the great poets are the eternal mediators between the soul of things and our feeble hearts of earth and clay. He recited the distichs where Goethe has related in a tongue worthy of Homer or Lucretius the metamorphosis of the plants. This was placed like a preamble at the beginning of the volume which he carried with him in his walks, and he had learned it by heart a few days before. The better to penetrate the sense of these admirable lines, he tried to translate them into French alexandrines, which he sometimes composed. This effort at translation soon appeared to him beyond his abilities; all the French words seemed too noisy, too brilliant or too vulgar, or too solemn to render these mute accents, these intonations veiled as if in religious mystery, by which the author of Faust intended to express the subtle sounds and even the silence of nature. We know that it is only in German poetry that we can hear the grass growing from the bosom of the earth, and the celestial spheres revolving in space.

Every language has its pedals and its peculiar registers; the Teutonic muse alone can execute these solemn airs which must be played with the soft pedal. For more than an hour Gilbert exhausted himself in vain attempts, and at last, disheartened, he contented himself with reciting aloud the poem which he despaired of translating. He uttered the first part with the fire of enthusiasm; but his voice fell as he pronounced the following passage:

"Every flower, my beloved, speaks to thee in a voice distinct and clear; every plant announces to thee plainly the eternal laws of life; but these sacred hieroglyphics of the goddess which thou decipherest upon their perfumed foreheads, thou wilt find everywhere hidden under other emblems. Let the caterpillar drag itself creeping along, and soon the light butterfly darts rapidly through the air; and let man also, with his power of self- development, follow the circle of his soul's metamorphoses. Oh! then wilt thou remember that the bond which united our spirits was first a germ from which sprang in time a sweet and charming acquaintance; friendship in its turn soon revealed its power in our hearts, until love came at last, crowning it with flowers and fruits."

At this place a light cloud of sadness passed over Gilbert's face; he felt a secret dissatisfaction at meeting in the verses of his favorite poet a passage which he could not apply to his own experience.

Meanwhile, night had come, a night like a softened and refreshed day. The radiant moon shone in the zenith; she inundated the fields of heaven with soft whiteness, she shook her torch over the Rhine, and made the crests of its restless waves scintillate; she poured over the tops of the trees a rain of silvery light; she suspended from their branches necklaces of sapphires and azure diamonds, which the breeze in passing sportively dashed together. The great slumbering woods thrilled at the touch of this dew of light which bathed their lofty brows; they felt something divine insinuating itself in the horror of their somber recesses.

From time to time a nightingale gave to the wind a few notes sonorous and sustained; it seemed the voice of the forest, speaking in its sleep, – its soul, carried away in ecstasy, exhaling its intoxication in a long sigh of love.

Gilbert had been sitting up very late recently, since he had decided to remain but a short time at Geierfels, and he had grown pale over the Byzantines, in the hope of advancing in his task so much, that Count Kostia would more easily consent to his departure. Robust as was his constitution, he finished by tiring himself out, and nature claiming its rights, sleep seized him at the moment when he was about leaving the bank to seek his room, and have a little nocturnal chat with Agathias and Procopius.

When he awoke, the moon had already declined towards the horizon, which discovery surprised him greatly, as he thought he had slept but a few moments. He rose and shook his limbs, stiff from the dampness. Fortunately, he was the only one at Geierfels who had free ingress and egress; the turret which he inhabited communicated with the terrace by a private staircase, to the entrance of which he had the key. Fortunately, too, the bulldogs had learned to know him, and never dreamed of disturbing his movements. He gained the little door without any difficulty, opened it, and having lit a candle which he drew from his pocket, commenced cautiously to ascend the winding staircase, the steps of which were broken in many places. He had just reached the first landing where terminated the spacious corridor, which extended along the principal facade parallel with the terrace, and was preparing to cross it, when he heard a long and painful groan, which seemed to come from the other end of the gallery. Starting, he remained motionless some moments, with neck extended and ears alert, peering into the obscurity from whence he expected to see some melancholy phantom emerge; but almost immediately a gust of wind driving through the broken square of a dormer window made it grind upon its hinges and give out a plaintive sound, which reverberated through the corridor. Gilbert then fancied that what he had taken for a sigh was only the moaning of the wind, counterfeiting in its melancholy gambols the voice of human grief. Resuming his ascent, he had already mounted some steps, when a second groan, still more dismal than the first, reached his ears, and froze the blood in his veins. He was sure he could not be deceived now; the wind had no such accents – it was a wail, sharp, harsh, and heartrending, which seemed as though it might come from the bosom of a specter.

A thousand sinister suppositions assailed Gilbert's mind, but he gave himself no time to reflect. Agitated, panting, his head on fire, he sprang with one bound down the staircase, and reaching the entrance of the gallery, cried out in a trembling voice, and scarcely knowing what he said:

"Who's there? Who wants assistance? I, Gilbert, am ready to come to his aid – "

His voice was swallowed up and lost in the somber arches of the corridor. No answer; the darkness remained dumb. In the rapidity of his movement, Gilbert had extinguished his candle; he prepared to relight it, when a hat flew by and struck his forehead with his wings. The start which this unforeseen attack gave him made him drop the candle; he stooped to pick it up, but could not find it. In spite of this accident, he walked on. A feeble ray of moonlight, which came in by the dormer window and shed through the entrance of the corridor a long thread of bluish light, seemed to guide him a few steps. Then he groped his way with arms extended and touching the wall. Every few steps he stopped and listened, and repeated in a voice hoarse with excitement:

"Who's there? You who are moaning, can I do anything to help you?"

Nothing answered him except the beating of his heart, and the murmur of the wind, which continued to torment the hinges of the dormer window.

The gallery into which Gilbert had entered was divided halfway in its length by two steps, at the bottom of which was a large iron door, always kept open during the day, but closed and double-locked as night set in. Approaching this, Gilbert saw a feeble light glimmering beneath the door. He descended the steps, and looking through the key-hole, from which the key had been withdrawn, saw what changed the frightful anguish he had just been suffering into surprise and terror.

At twenty paces from him he saw the appalling figure of a phantom standing erect; it was enveloped in a large white cloth wound several times round its body, passing under its left arm, and falling over the right shoulder. In one hand it held a torch and a sword, in the other an oval ebony frame of which Gilbert could only see the back, but which seemed to inclose a portrait. The face of this specter was emaciated, drawn, and of unusual length; its skin, withered and dry, seemed to be incrusted upon its bones, its complexion was sallow; a profuse perspiration trickled from its brows and glued the hair to its temples. Nothing could describe the expression of terror in its face. It seemed to Gilbert that its two burning eyeballs penetrated even through the door, though they saw nothing which surrounded them; their vision seemed turned within, and the invisible object which fastened their gaze, a heart haunted by specters.

Suddenly the lips of this nocturnal wanderer opened, and another groan more fearful than the first issued from them. It seemed as if his burdened breast wished to shake off by a violent effort a mountain of weariness, the weight of which was crushing it, or rather as though the soul sought to expel itself in this despairing cry. Gilbert was seized with inexpressible agitation, his hair stood on end. He started to fly; but a curiosity stronger than his terror prevented him from leaving the spot and kept him riveted to the door. By the eyebrows and cheekbones, in spite of the distortion of the face, he had recognized Count Kostia.

At length this sinister somnambulist stirred from his motionless position and advanced at a slow pace; he walked like an automaton. After taking a dozen steps he stopped, looked around him, and slightly bent forward. His strained features resumed their natural proportions, life re-animated his brow, the deathlike inertia of his face gave place to an expression of sadness and prostration. For a few seconds his lips moved, without saying a word, as if to become flexible, and fashioned anew to the use of speech: – then, in a soft voice which Gilbert did not recognize, and with the plaintive accents of a suffering child, he murmured:

"How heavy this portrait is! I can carry it no longer; take it out of my hands, it burns them. In mercy, extinguish this fire. I have a brand in my breast. It must be kept covered with ashes; when I can see it no more, I shall suffer less. It is my eyes that make me suffer; if I were blind, I could return to Moscow."

Then in a harsher voice:

"I could easily destroy this likeness, but THE OTHER, I cannot kill it, curses on me! it is the better portrait of the two. There is her hair, her mouth, her smile. Ah, thank God, I have killed the smile. The smile is no longer there. I have buried the smile. But there is the mole in the corner of the mouth. I have kissed it a thousand times; take away that mole, it hurts me. If that mole were gone I should suffer less. Merciful Heaven! it is always there. But I have buried the smile. The smile is no more. I have buried it deep in a leaden coffin. It can't come. . . ."

Then suddenly changing his accent, and in a tragical, but bitter voice, his eyes fixed upon the large rusty sword which he held in his right hand, he muttered:

"The spot will not go away. The iron will not drink it. It was not for this blood it thirsted. I shall find it in the other, it will drink that. Ah! we shall see how it will drink it."

Upon this, he relapsed into silence and appeared to be thinking deeply. Then raising his head, he cried in a voice so strong and vibrating that the iron door trembled upon its hinges:

"Morlof, then it was not thou! Ah! my dear friend, I was deceived. . . . Go, do not regret life. It is only the dream of a screech-owl. . . . Believe me, friend, I want to die, but I cannot. I must know . . . I must discover. Ah! Morlof, Morlof, leave thy hands in mine, or I shall think thou hast not forgiven me. . . . God! how cold these hands are . . . cold . . . cold . . ."

And at these words he shuddered; his head moved convulsively upon his shoulders, and his teeth chattered; but soon calming himself, he murmured:

"I want to know the name, I must know that name! Is there

no one who can tell me that name?"

Thus speaking, he raised the picture to a level with his face, and with bent head and extended neck, appeared to be trying to decipher upon the canvas some microscopic writing or obscure hieroglyphics.

"The name is there!" said he. "It is written somewhere about the heart, – at the bottom of the heart; but I cannot read it, the writing is so fine, it is a female hand; I do not know how to read a woman's writing. They have a cipher of which Satan alone has the key. My sight is failing me. I have flies in my head. There is always one of them that hides this name from me. Oh! in mercy, in pity, take away the fly and bring me a pair of pincers. . . . With good pincers I will seek that name even in the last fibers of this heart which beats no more."

He added with a terrible air:

The dead do not open their teeth. The one who lives will speak. You shall see how I will make him speak. You shall see how I will make him speak. . . . Tear off his black robe, stretch him on this plank. The iron boots! the iron boots! tighten the boots!"

Then interrupting himself abruptly, he raised his eyes and fixed them upon the door. An expression of fury mingled with terror swept over his face, as if he had suddenly perceived some hideous and alarming object. His features became distorted; his mouth worked convulsively and frothed; his eyes, unnaturally dilated, darted flames; he uttered a hollow moan, took a few steps backward, and suddenly dropping his torch to the ground, where it went out he cried in a frightful voice:

"There are eyes behind the door! there are eyes! there are eyes!"

Horror-struck, distracted, beside himself, Gilbert turned and took to flight. In spite of the darkness, he found his way as if by miracle. He crossed the corridor at a run, mounted the staircase in three bounds, dashed into his chamber and bolted the door. Then he hurriedly lighted a candle, and having glanced about to assure himself that the phantom had not followed him into his room, dropped heavily upon a chair, stunned and breathless. In a few moments he had collected his thoughts, and was ashamed of his terror; but in spite of himself his agitation was such that at every noise which struck his ear, he thought he heard the step of Count Kostia ascending the staircase of his turret. It was not until he had bathed his burning head in cold water that he recovered something like tranquillity; and determining by a supreme effort to banish the frightful images which haunted him, he seated himself at his worktable and resolutely opened one of the Byzantine folios. As he began to read, his eye fell upon an unsealed letter which had been left on his table during his absence; it ran thus:

"Man of great phrases, I write to you to inform you of the hatred with which you inspire me. I wish you to understand that from the first day I saw you, your bearing, your face, your manners, your whole person, have been objects of distrust and aversion to me. I thought I recognized an enemy in you, and the result has proved that I was not mistaken. Now I hate you, and I tell you so frankly, for I am not a hypocrite, and I want you to know, that just now in my prayers I supplicated St. George to give me an opportunity of revenging myself upon you. What do you want in this house? What is there between us and you? How long do you intend to torture me with your odious presence, your ironical smiles, and your insulting glances? Before your arrival I was not completely unhappy. God be praised, it has been reserved for you to give me the finishing stroke. Before, I could weep at my ease, with none to busy themselves in counting my tears; the man that makes me shed them does not lower himself to such petty calculations; he has confidence in me, he knows that at the end of the year the account will be there; but you! you watch me, you pry into me, you study me. I see very well that, while you are looking at me, you are indulging in little dialogues with yourself, and these little dialogues are insupportable to me. Mark me now, I forbid you to understand me. It is an affront which you have no right to put upon me, and I have the right to be incomprehensible if it pleases me. Ah! once a little while ago, I felt that you had your eyes fastened on me again. And then I raised my head, and looked at you steadily and forced you to blush. . . . Yes, you did blush; do not attempt to deny it! What a consolation to me! What a triumph! Alas! for all that, I dare not go to my own window any longer for fear of seeing you ogling the sky, and making declamations of love to nature with your sentimental air.

"Tell me, now, in a few words, clever man that you are, how you manage to combine so much sentimentality with such skillful diplomacy? Tender friend of childhood, of virtue and of sunsets, what an adroit courtier you make! From the first day you came here, the master honored you with his confidence and his affection. How he esteems you! how he cherishes you! what attentions! what favors! Will he not order us tomorrow to kiss the dust under your feet? If you want to know what disgusts me the most in you, it is the unalterable placidity of your disposition and your face. You know the faun who admires himself night and day in the basin upon the terrace; he is always laughing and looks at himself laugh. I detest this eternal laughter from the bottom of my soul, as I detest you, as I detest the whole world with the exception of my horse Soliman. But he, at least, is sincere in his gayety; he shows himself what he really is, life amuses him, great good may it do him! But you envelop your beatific happiness in an intolerable gravity. Your tranquil airs fill me with consternation; your great contented eyes seem to say: 'I am very well, so much the worse for the sick!' One word more. You treat me as a child – I will prove to you that I am not a child, showing you how well I have divined you. The secret of your being is, that you were born without passions! Confess honestly that you have never in your life felt a sentiment of disgust, of anger, or of pity. Is there a single passion, tell me, that you have experienced, or that you are acquainted with, except through your books? Your soul is like your cravat, which is always tied precisely the same way, and has such an air of repose and rationality about it, that it is perfectly insufferable to me. Yes, the bow of that cravat exasperates me; the two ends are always exactly the same length, and have an effect of INDERANGEABILITY which nearly drives me mad. Not that this famous bow is elegant. No, a thousand times no! but it has an exasperating accuracy. And in this, behold the true story of your soul. Every night when you go to bed you put it in its proper folds; every morning you unfold it carefully without rumpling it! And you dare to plume yourself on your wisdom! What does this pretended wisdom prove? Nothing, unless it be that you have poor blood, and that you were fifty years old when you were born. There is, however, one passion which no one will deny that you possess. You understand me, – man of the gilded tongue and the viper's heart, – you have a passion common to many others! But, hold, in commencing this letter, I intended to conceal from you that I had discovered everything. I feared it would give you too much pleasure to learn that I know. – Oh! why can't I make you stand before me now this moment! I should confound you! how I would force you to fall at my feet and cry for pardon!

"Oh, my dear flowers, my Maltese cross, my verbenas, my white starred fox, and you, my musk rosebush, and above all my beautiful variegated carnation, which ought to be opening to-day! Was it then for him, – was it to rejoice the eyes of this insolent parasite, that I planted, watered, and tended you with so much care? Beloved flowers, will you not share my hate? Send out from each of your cups, from each of your corollas, some devouring insect, some wasp with pointed sting, some furious horse-fly, and let them all together throw themselves upon him, harass him and persecute him with their threatening buzzing, and pierce his face with their poisoned stings. And you yourselves, my cherished daughters, at his approach, fold up your beautiful petals, refuse him your perfumes, cheat him of his cares and hopes, let the sap dry up in your fibers, that he may have the mortification of seeing you perish and fall to dust in his hands. And may he, this treacherous man, may he before your blighted petals and drooping stems, pine away himself with ennui, spite, anger, and remorse!"

IX

The castle clock had struck eight, when Gilbert sprang from his bed. Shall I confess that in dressing himself, when he came to tie his cravat, he hesitated for a moment? However, after reflection, he adjusted the knot as before, and would you believe it, he tied this famous, this regular knot without concentrating any attention upon it? His toilet finished, he went to the window. A sudden change had taken place in the weather; a cold, drizzly rain was falling noiselessly; very little wind; the horizon was enveloped in a thick fog; a long train of low clouds, looking like gigantic fish, floated slowly through the valley of the Rhine; the sky of a uniform gray, seemed to distill weariness and sadness; land and water were the color of mud. Gilbert cast his eyes upon his dear precipice: it was but a pit of frightful ugliness. He sank into an armchair. His thoughts harmonized with the weather; they formed a dismal landscape, over which a long procession of gloomy fancies and sinister apprehensions swept silently, like the trail of low clouds which wandered along the borders of the Rhine.

"No, a thousand times no!" mused he, "I can't stay in this place any longer; I shall lose my strength here, and my spirit and my health, too. To be exposed to the blind hatred of an unhappy child whose sorrows drive him to insanity; to be the table companion of a priest without dignity or moral elevation, who silently swallows the greatest outrages; to become the intimate, the complaisant friend of a great lord, whose past is suspicious, of an unnatural father who hates his son, of a man who at times transforms himself into a specter, and who, stung by remorse, or thirsting for revenge, fills the corridors of his castle with savage howlings – such a position is intolerable, and I must leave here at any cost! This castle is an unhealthy place; the walls are odious to me! I will not wait to penetrate into their secrets any further."

And Gilbert ransacked his brain for a pretext to quit Geierfels immediately. While engaged in this research, some one knocked at the door: it was Fritz, with his breakfast.

This morning he had the self-satisfied air of a fool who has worked out a folly by the sweat of his brow, and reached the fortunate moment when he can bring his invention to light. He entered without salutation, placed the tray which he carried upon the table; then, turning to Gilbert, who was seated, said to him, winking his eye:

"Good-morning, comrade! Comrade, good-morning!"

"What do you say?" said Gilbert, astonished, and looking at

him steadily.

"I say: Good-morning, comrade!" replied he, smiling agreeably.

"And to whom are you speaking, if you please?"

"I am speaking to you, yourself, my comrade, and I say to you, good-morning, comrade! good-morning."

Gilbert looked at him attentively, trying to find some explanation of this strange prank, and this excessive and astounding insolence.

"And will you tell me," he continued, after a few moments' silence, "will you be good enough to tell me, who gave you permission to call me comrade?"

"It was . . . it was . . ." answered Fritz, hemming and hawing. And he reflected a moment, as though trying to remember his lesson, that he might not stumble in its recital. "Ah!" resumed he, "it was simply his Excellency the Count, and I cannot conceive what you see astonishing in it."

"Have you ever heard the Count," demanded Gilbert, who felt the blood boiling in his veins, "call me your comrade?"

"Ah! certainly!" he answered with a long burst of laughter. "Every day, when I come from him, M. le Comte says to me: 'Well! how is your comrade Gilbert?' And isn't it very natural? Don't we eat at the same rack? Are we not, both of us, in the service of the same master? And don't you see. . . ."

He was not able to say more, for Gilbert bounded from his chair, and crying:

"Go and tell your master that he is not my master!" He seized the valet de chambre by the collar. He was at least a head shorter than his adversary, but his grasp was like iron; and in spite of appearances, great Fritz proved but a weak and nerveless body, and greatly surprised at this unexpected attack, he could only open his large mouth and utter some inarticulate sounds. Gilbert had already dragged him to the top of the staircase. Then Fritz, recovering from his first flurry, tried to struggle, but he lost his footing, stumbled, and fell headlong down the staircase to the bottom. Gilbert came near following him in his descent, but fortunately saved himself by clinging to the balustrade. As he saw him rolling, he feared that he had been too violent, but felt reassured, when he saw him scramble up, feel himself, rub his back, turn to shake his fist and limp away.

He returned to his chamber and breakfasted peaceably.

"Quite an opportune adventure," thought he. "Now, I shall be inflexible, unyielding, and if my trunks are not packed before night, I'm an idiot."

Gathering up under his arm a bundle of papers which were needed for the day's work, he left the room, his head erect and his spirits animated; but he had hardly descended the first flight of steps before his exaltation gave way to very different feelings. He could not look without shuddering at the place where he had stood like one petrified, listening to the horrible groans of the somnambulist. He stopped, and, looking at the packet which he held under his arm, thought to himself that it was with a specter he was about to discuss Byzantine history. Then resuming his walk, he arrived at M. Leminof's study, where he almost expected to see the formidable apparition of last night appear before his eyes, and hear a sepuchral voice crying out to him: "Those eyes behind the door were yours!" He remained motionless a few seconds, his hand upon his heart. At last he knocked. A voice cried: "Come in.

He opened the door and entered. Heavens! how far was the reality from his fancy.

M. Leminof was quietly seated in the embrasure of the window, looking at the rain and playing with his monkey. He no sooner perceived his secretary than he uttered an exclamation of joy, and after shutting up Solon in an adjoining room, he approached Gilbert, took both his hands in his and pressed them cordially, saying in an affectionate tone:

"Welcome, my dear Gilbert, I have been looking for you impatiently. I have been thinking a great deal since yesterday on our famous problem of the Slavonic invasions, and I am far from being convinced by your arguments. Be on your guard, my dear sir! Be on your guard! I propose to give you some thrusts that will trouble you to parry."

Gilbert, who had recovered his tranquillity, seated himself, and the discussion commenced. The point in dispute was the question of the degree of importance and influence of the establishment of the Slavonians in the Byzantine empire during the middle ages. Upon this question, much debated at present, Count Kostia had espoused the opinion most favorable to the ambitions of Muscovite policy. He affected to renounce his country and to censure it without mercy; he had even denationalized himself to the extent of never speaking his mother tongue and of forbidding its use in his house. In fact, the idiom of Voltaire was more familiar to him than that of Karamzin, and he had accustomed himself for a long time even to think in French. In spite of all this, and of whatever he might say, he remained Russian at heart: this is a quality which cannot be lost.

Twelve o'clock sounded while they were at the height of the discussion.

"If you agree, my dear Gilbert," said M. Leminof, "we will give ourselves a little relaxation. Indeed you're truly a terrible fellow; there's no persuading you. Let us breakfast in peace, if you please, like two good friends; afterwards we will renew the fight."

The breakfast was invariably composed of toast au caviar and a small glass of Madeira wine; and every day at noon they suspended work for a few moments to partake of this little collation.

"Judge of my presumption," suddenly said M. Leminof, underscoring, so to speak, every word, "I passed LAST NIGHT [and he put a wide space between these two words] in pleading against you the cause of my Slavonians. My arguments seemed to me irresistible. I beat you all hollow. I am like those fencers who are admirable in the training school, but who make a very bad figure in the field. I had prodigious eloquence LAST NIGHT; I don't know what has become of it; it seems to have fled like a phantom at the first crowing of the cock."

As he pronounced these words, Count Kostia fixed such piercing eyes on Gilbert, that they seemed to search through to the most remote recesses of his soul. Gilbert sustained the attack with perfect sangfroid.

"Ah! sir," replied he coolly, "I don't know how you argue at night; but I assure you by day you're the most formidable logician I know."

Gilbert's tranquil air dissipated the suspicion which seemed to weigh upon M. Leminof.

"You act," said he gayly, "like those conquerors who exert themselves to console the generals they have beaten, thereby enhancing their real glory; but bah! arms are fickle, and I shall have my revenge at an early day."

"I venture to suggest that you do not delay it long," answered Gilbert in a grave tone. "Who knows how much longer I may remain at Geierfels?"

These words re-awakened the suspicions of the Count.

"What do you mean?" exclaimed he.

Whereupon Gilbert related in a firm, distinct tone the morning's adventure. As he advanced in the recital, he became warmer and repeated with an indignant air the remark which Fritz had attributed to the Count, and strongly emphasized his answer:

"Go and tell your master that he is not my master."

He flattered himself that he would pique the Count; he saw him already raising his head, and speaking in the clouds. He was destined to be mistaken today in all his conjectures. From the first words of his eloquent recital, Count Kostia appeared to be relieved of a pre-occupation which had disturbed him. He had been prepared for something else, and was glad to find himself mistaken. He listened to the rest with an undisturbed air, leaning back in his easy-chair with his eyes fixed on the ceiling. When Gilbert had finished –

"And tell me, pray," said he, without changing his posture, "how did you punish this rascal?"

"I took him by the collar," replied Gilbert, "and flung him down head first."

"Peste!" exclaimed the Count, raising himself and looking at him with an air of surprise and admiration. "And tell me," resumed he, smiling in his enjoyment, "did this domestic animal perish in his fall?"

"He may perhaps have broken his arms or legs. I didn't take the trouble to inquire."

M. Leminof rose and folded his arms on his breast.

"See now, how liable our judgments are to be led astray, and how full of sense that Russian proverb is which says: 'It takes more than one day to compass a man!' Yesterday you had such a sentimental pathetic air, when I permitted myself to administer a little correction to my serf, that I took you in all simplicity for a philanthropist. I retract it now. You are one of those tyrants who are only moved for the victims of another. Pure professional jealousy! But," continued he, "there is one thing which astonishes me still more, and that is, that you Gilbert, you could for an instant believe – "

He checked himself, bent forward towards Gilbert, and looked at him scrutinizingly, making a shade of his two bony hands extended over his enormous eyebrows; then taking him by the arm, he led him to the embrasure of the window, and as if he had made a sudden change in his person which rendered him irrecognizable:

"Nothing could be better than your throwing the scoundrel downstairs," said he, "and if he is not quite dead, I shall drive him from here without pity; but that you should have believed that I, Count Leminof – Oh! it is too much, I dream – No, you are not the Gilbert that I know, the Gilbert I love, though I conceal it from myself – "

And taking him by both hands, he added:

"This man was silly enough to tell you that I was your master, and you replied to him with the Mirabeau tone: 'Go and tell your master – ' My dear Gilbert, in the name of reason, I ask you to remember that the true is never the opposite of the false; it is another thing, that is all; but to which I add, that in answering as you did, you have cruelly compromised yourself. We should never contradict a fool; it is running the risk of being like him."

Gilbert blushed. He did not try to amend anything, but readily changing his tactics, he said, smiling:

"I implore you, sir, not to drive this man away. I want him to stay to remind me occasionally that I am liable to lose my senses."

But what were his feelings when the Count, having sent for this valet de chambre, said to him:

"You have not done this on your own responsibility – you received orders. Who gave them?"

Fritz answered, stammering:

"Do please forgive me, your excellency! It was M. Stephane who, yesterday evening, made me a present of two Russian crowns on condition that every morning for a week I should say to M. Saville, 'good-morning, comrade.'"

A flash of joy shone in the Count's eyes. He turned towards Gilbert, and pressing his hand, said to him:

"For this once I thank you cordially for having addressed your complaints to me. The affair is more serious than I had thought. There is a malignant abscess there, which must be lanced once for all."

This surgical comparison made Gilbert shudder; he cursed his hasty passion and his stupidity. Why had he not suspected the real culprit? Why was it necessary for him to justify the hatred which Stephane had avowed towards him?

"And how happens it, sir," resumed Count Kostia, with less of anger in his tone, "that you have an opportunity of holding secret conversations with my son in the evening? When did you enter his service? Do you not know that you are to receive neither orders, messages, nor communications of any kind from him?"

Fritz, who in his heart blessed the admirable invention of lightning rods, explained as well as he could, that the evening before, in going up to his excellency's room, he had met Ivan on the staircase, going down to the grand hall to find a cap which his young master had forgotten. Apparently he had neglected to close the wicket, for Fritz, in going out through the gallery, had found Stephane, who, approaching him stealthily, had given him his little lesson in a mysterious tone, and as Ivan returned at this moment without the cap he said:

"Dost thou not see, imbecile, that it's on my head," and he drew the cap from his pocket and proudly put it on his head, while he ran to his rooms laughing.

When he had finished his story, Fritz was profuse in his protestations of repentance, servile and tearful; the Count cut him short, declaring to him, that at the request of Gilbert he consented to pardon him; but that at the first complaint brought against him, he would give him but two hours to pack. When he had gone out, M. Leminof pulled another bell which communicated with the room of Ivan, who presently appeared.

"Knowest thou, my son," said the Count to him in German, "that thou hast been very negligent for some time? Thy mind fails, thy sight is feeble. Thou art growing old, my poor friend. Thou art like an old bloodhound in his decline, without teeth and without scent, who knows neither how to hunt the prey nor how to catch it. Thou must be on the retired list. I have already thought of the office I shall give thee in exchange. . . . Oh! do not deceive thyself. It is in vain to shrug thy shoulders, my son; thou art wrong in believing thyself necessary. By paying well I shall easily find one who will be worth as much – "

Ivan's eyes flashed.

"I do not believe you," replied he, in Russian; "you know very well that you are not amiable, but that I love you in spite of it, and when you have spent a hundred thousand roubles, you will not have secured one to replace me, whose affection for you will be worth a kopeck."

"Why dost thou speak Russian?" resumed the Count. "Thou knowest well that I have forbidden it. Apparently thou wishest that no one but myself may understand the sweet things which thou sayest to me. Go and cry them upon the roof, if that will give thee pleasure; but I have never asked thee to love me. I exact only faithful service on thy part, and I answer for it that thy substitute, when his young master shall tell him 'go and find my cap, which I have left in the grand hall,' will answer him coolly: 'I am not blind, my little father, your cap is in your pocket.'"

Ivan looked at his master attentively, and the expression of his face appeared to reassure him, for he began to smile.

"Meantime," said the Count, "so long as I keep thee in thy office, study to satisfy me. Go to thy room and reflect, and at the end of a quarter of an hour, bring thy little father here to me; I want to talk with him, and I will permit thee to listen, if that will give thee pleasure."

As soon as Ivan had gone, Gilbert begged M. Leminof not to pursue this miserable business. "I have punished Fritz," said he, "with perhaps undue severity; you yourself have rebuked and threatened him; I am satisfied."

"Pardon me. In all this Fritz was but an instrument. It would not be right to allow the real culprit to go unpunished!"

"It is no trouble to me to pardon that culprit," exclaimed Gilbert, with an animation beyond his control, "he is so unhappy!"

M. Leminof gave Gilbert a haughty and angry look. He strode through the room several times, his hands behind his back; then, with the easy tempered air of an absolute prince, who condescends to some unreasonable fancy of one of his favorites, made Gilbert sit down, and placing himself by his side:

"My dear sir," said he to him, "your last words show a singular forgetfulness on your part of our reciprocal agreements. You had engaged, if you remember, not to take any interest in any one here but yourself and myself. After that, what difference can it make to you, whether my son is happy or unhappy? Since, however, you have raised this question, I consent to an explanation; but let it be fully understood, that you are never, never, to revive the subject again. You can readily perceive, that if your society is agreeable to me, it is because I have the pleasure of forgetting with you the petty annoyances of domestic life. And now speak frankly, and tell me what makes you conclude that my son is unhappy."

Gilbert had a thousand things to reply, but they were difficult to say. So he hesitated to answer for a moment, and the Count anticipated him:

"Mon Dieu! I must needs proceed in advance of your accusations, a concession which I dare to hope you will appreciate. Perhaps you reproach me with not showing sufficient affection for my son in daily life. But what can you expect? The Leminofs are not affectionate. I don't remember ever to have received a single caress from my father. I have seen him sometimes pat his hounds, or give sugar to his horse; but I assure you that I never partook of his sweetmeats or his smiles, and at this hour I thank him for it. The education which he gave me hardened the affections, and it is the best service which a father can render his son. Life is a hard stepmother, my dear Gilbert; how many smiles have you seen pass over her brazen lips! Besides, I have particular reasons for not treating Stephane with too much tenderness. He seems to you to be unhappy, he will be so forever if I do not strive to discipline his inclinations and to break his intractable disposition. The child was born under an evil star. At once feeble and violent, he unites with very ardent passions a deplorable puerility of mind; incapable of serious thought, the merest trivialities move him to fever heat, and he talks childish prattle with all the gestures of great passion. And what is worse, interesting himself greatly in himself, he thinks it very natural that this interest should be shared by all the world. Do not imagine that his is a loving heart that feels a necessity of spending itself on others. He likes to make his emotions spectacular, and as his impressions are events for him, he would like to display them, even to the inhabitants of Sirius. His soul is like a lake swept by a gale of wind that would drive a man-of-war at the rate of twenty-five knots an hour; and on this lake Stephane sails his squadrons of nutshells, and he sees them come, go, tack, run around, and capsize. He keeps his log-book very accurately, pompously registers all the shipwrecks, and as these spectacles transport him with admiration, he is indignant to find that he alone is moved by them. This is what makes him unhappy; and you will agree with me that it is not my fault. The regime which I prescribe for my invalid may appear to you a little severe, but it's the only way by which I can hope to cure him. Leading a regular, uniform life, – and sad enough I admit – he will gradually become surfeited with his own emotions when the objects of them are never renewed, and he will end, I hope, by demanding the diversions of work and study. May he be able some day to discover that a problem of Euclid is more interesting than the wreck of a nutshell! Upon that day he will enter upon full convalescence, and I shall not be the last to rejoice in it."

M. Leminof spoke in a tone so serious and composed, that for a few moments Gilbert could have imagined him a pedagogue gravely explaining his maxims of education; but he could not forget that expression of ferocious joy which was depicted on his face at the moment when Stephane fled sobbing from the garden, and he remembered also the somnambulist who, on the preceding night, had uttered certain broken phrases in regard to a LIVING PORTRAIT and a BURIED SMILE. These mysterious words, terrible in their obscurity, had appeared to him to allude to Stephane, and they accorded badly with the airs of paternal solicitude which M. Leminof had deigned to affect in the past few minutes. He had a show of reason, however, in his argument; and the picture which he drew of his son, if cruelly exaggerated, had still some points of resemblance. Only Gilbert had reason to think that the Count purposely confounded cause and effect, and that Stephane's malady was the work of the physician.

"Will you permit me, sir," answered he, "to tell you all that I have on my heart?"

"Speak, speak, improve the opportunity: I swear to you it won't occur again."

And looking at his watch:

"You have still five minutes to talk with me about my son. Hurry; I will not grant you two seconds more."

"I have heard it said," resumed Gilbert, "that in building bridges and causeways, the best foundations are those which HUMOR the waves of the sea. These are foundations with inclined slopes, which, instead of breaking the waves abruptly, check their movement by degrees, and abate their force without violence."

"You favor anodynes, Monsieur disciple of Galen," exclaimed M. Leminof. "Each one according to his temperament. We cannot reconstruct ourselves. I am a very violent, very passionate man, and when, for example, a servant offends me I throw him headforemost downstairs. This happens to me every day."

"Between your son and your valet de chambre, the difference is great," answered Gilbert, a little piqued.

"Did not your famous revolution proclaim absolute equality between all men?"

"In the law it is admirable, but not in the heart of a father."

"Good God!" cried the Count, "I do not know that I have a father's heart for my son; I know only that I think a great deal about him, and that I strive according to my abilities to correct in him very grave faults, which threaten to compromise his future welfare. I know also for a certainty that this whiner enjoys some pleasures of which many children of his age are deprived, as, for example, a servant for himself, a horse, and as much money as he wants for his petty diversions. You are not ignorant of the use which he makes of this money, neither in regard to the two thalers expended yesterday to corrupt my valet, nor of the seven crowns with which he purchased the delightful pleasure, the other day in your presence, of having his foot kissed by a troop of young rustics. And at this point, I will tell you that Ivan has reported to me that, on the same day, Stephane turned up his sleeve to make you admire a scar which he carried upon one of his wrists. Oblige me by telling me what blue story he related to you on this subject."

This unexpected question troubled Gilbert a little.

"To conceal nothing from you," answered he hesitatingly, "he told me, that for an escapade which he had made, he had been condemned to pass a fortnight in a dungeon in irons."

"And you believed it!" cried the Count, shrugging his shoulders. "The truth is, that, for a fortnight, I compelled my son to pass one hour every evening in an uninhabited wing of this castle; my intention was not so much to punish him for an act of insubordination, as to cure him of the foolish terrors by which he is tormented, for this boy of sixteen, who often shows himself brave even to rashness, believes in ghosts, in apparitions, in vampires. I ought to authorize him to guard himself at night by the best-toothed of my bulldogs. Oh what a strange compound has God given me for a son!"

At this moment the sound of steps was heard in the corridor.

"In the name of the kind friendship which you profess for me, sir," exclaimed Gilbert, seizing one of M. Leminof's hands, "I beg of you, do not punish this child for a boyish freak for which I forgive him with all my heart!"

"I can refuse you nothing, my dear Gilbert," answered he with a smiling air. "I spare him from his pretended dungeons. I dare hope that you will give me credit for it."

"I thank you; but one thing more: the flowers you deprived him of."

"Mon Dieu! since you wish it, we will have them restored to him, and to please you, I will content myself with having him make apologies to you in due form."

"Make apologies to me!" cried Gilbert in consternation; "but that will be the most cruel of punishments."

"We will leave him the choice," said the Count dryly. And as Gilbert insisted: "This time you ask too much!" added he in a tone which admitted of no reply. "It is a question of principles, and in such matters I never compromise."

Gilbert perceived that even in Stephane's interest, it was necessary to desist, but he understood also to what extent the pride of the young man would suffer, and cursed himself a thousand times for having spoken.

Someone knocked at the door.

"Come in," cried the Count in a hoarse voice; and Stephane entered, followed by Ivan.

X

Stephane remained standing in the middle of the room. He was paler than usual, and kept his eyes on the floor; but his bearing was good, and he affected a resolute air which he rarely displayed in the presence of his father. The Count remained silent for some time; he gazed with a cold eye on the supple and delicate body of his son, the exquisite elegance of his form, his fine and delicate features, framed in the slightly darkened gold of his hair. Never had the beauty of his child filled the heart of his father with keener bitterness. As for Gilbert, he had eyes only for a little black spot which he noticed for the first time upon the uniformly pale complexion of Stephane: it was like an almost imperceptible fly, under the left corner of his mouth.

"That is the mole," thought he, and he fancied he could hear the voice of the somnambulist cry:

"Take away that mole! it hurts me!"

Shuddering at this recollection, he felt tempted to rush from the room; but a look from the Count recalled him to himself; he made a strong effort to master his emotion, and fixing his eyes upon the window, he looked at the falling rain.

"As a preliminary question," suddenly exclaimed the Count,

speaking to his son; "do me the favor, sir, to tell me how much time you have passed in what you call a dungeon, for I do not remember."

Stephane's face colored with a vivid blush. He hesitated a moment and then answered:

"I was there in all fifteen hours, which appeared to me as long as fifteen days."

"You see!" said the Count, looking at Gilbert. "And now," resumed he, "let us come to the point; a scene of the greatest impropriety occurred in this house this morning. Fritz, my valet, in presenting himself to my secretary, who is my friend, permitted himself to say three times: 'Good-morning, comrade; comrade, good- morning!'"

At these words Stephane's lips contracted slightly, as if about to smile; but the smile was arrested on its way.

"My little story amuses you, apparently," pursued the Count, raising his head.

"It is the incredible folly of Fritz which diverts me," answered Stephane.

"His folly seems to me less than his insolence," replied the Count; "but without discussing words, I am delighted to see that you disavow his conduct. I ought not to conceal from you the fact, that this scoundrel wished to make me believe that he acted upon your orders, and I was resolved to punish you severely. I see now that he has lied, and it remains for me but to dismiss him in disgrace." Gilbert trembled lest Stephane's veracity should succumb under this temptation; the young man hesitated but an instant.

"I am the guilty one," answered he in a firm voice, "and it is I who should be punished."

"What," said M. Leminof, "was it then my son, who, availing himself of the only resources of his mind, conceived this truly happy idea. The invention was admirable, it does honor to your genius. But if Fritz has been but the instrument to carry out your sublime conceptions, why do you laugh at his stupidity?"

"Oh, poor soul!" replied Stephane, with animation, "oh! the donkey, how he spoiled my idea! I didn't order him to call M. Saville his comrade, but to treat him as a comrade, which is a different thing. Unfortunately I had not time to give him minute instructions, and he misunderstood me, but he did what he could conscientiously to earn his fee. The poor fellow must be pardoned. I am the only guilty one, I repeat it. I am the one to be punished."

"And might we know, sir," said the Count, "what your intention was in causing M. Saville to be insulted by a servant?"

"I wished to humiliate him, to disgust him, and to force him to leave this house."

"And your motive?"

"My motive is that I hate him!" answered he in a hoarse voice.

"Always exaggerations," replied the Count sneeringly. "Can you not, sir, rid yourself of this detestable habit of perpetual exaggeration in the expression of your thoughts? Can I not impress upon your mind the maxims upon this subject which two men of equal genius have given us: M. de Metternich and Pigault Lebrun! The first of these illustrious men used to say that superlatives were the seals of fools, and the second wrote these immortal words:

"'Everything exaggerated is insignificant.'" Then extending his arm:

"To hate! to hate!" exclaimed he. "You say the word glibly. Do you know what it is? Sorrow, anger, jealousy, antipathy, aversion, you may know all these; but hatred, hatred! – you have no right to say this terrible word. Ah! hatred is a rough work! it is ceaseless torture, it is a cross of lead to carry, and to sustain its weight without breaking down requires very different shoulders than yours!"

At this moment Stephane ventured to look his father in the

face. He slowly uplifted his eyes, inclining his head backward. His look signified "You are right, I will take your word for it; you are better acquainted with it than I."

But the Count's face was so terrible that Stephane closed his eyes and resumed his former attitude. A slight shudder agitated his whole frame. The Count perceived that he was near forgetting himself, and drove back the bitter wave which came up from his heart to his lips in spite of himself:

"Besides, my young friend here is the least detestable being in the world," pursued he in a tranquil tone. "Judge for yourself; just now he pleaded your cause to me with so much warmth, that he drew from me a promise not to punish you for what he has the kindness to call only a boy's freak. He even stipulates that I shall restore you your flowers, which he pretends give you delight, and within an hour Ivan will have carried them to your room. In short, two words of apology are all he requires of you. You must admit that one could not have a more accommodating disposition, and that you owe him a thousand thanks."

"Apologies! to him!" cried Stephane with a gesture of horror.

"You hesitate! oh! this is too much! Do you then wish to revisit a certain rather gloomy hall?"

Stephane shuddered, his lips trembled.

"In mercy," cried he, "inflict any other punishment upon me you please, but not that one. Oh, no! I cannot go back to that frightful hall. Oh! I entreat you, deprive me of my customary walks for six months; sell Soliman, cut my hair, shave my head, – anything, yes, anything rather than put my feet in that horrible dungeon again! I shall die there or go mad. You don't want me to become insane?"

"When one is unfortunate enough to believe in ghosts and apparitions at the age of sixteen," retorted the Count, "he should free himself as soon as possible from the ridiculous weakness."

Stephane's whole body trembled. He staggered a few steps, and falling on his knees before his father, clung to him and cried:

"I am only a poor sick child, have pity on me. You are still my father, are you not? and I am still your child? Mon Dieu! Mon Dieu! You do not, you cannot, want your child to die!"

"Put an end to this miserable comedy," cried the Count, disengaging himself from Stephane's clasp. "I am your father, and you are my son; no one here doubts it; but your father, sir, has a horror of scenes. This has lasted too long; end it, I tell you. You are already in a suitable posture. The most difficult part is done, the rest is a trifle!"

"What do you say, sir?" answered the child impetuously, trying to rise. "I am on my knees to you only. Ah! great God! I to kneel before this man! it is impossible! you know very well it is impossible!

The Count, however, pressing his hand upon his shoulder, constrained him to remain upon his knees, and turning his face to Gilbert:

"I tell you, you are kneeling before the man you have insulted, and we all understand it."

Was it, indeed thus, that Gilbert understood it? Quiet, impassible, his eyes fixed upon the window, he seemed a perfect stranger to all that passed around him.

A cry of anguish escaped Stephane, a frightful change came over his face. Three times he tried to rise, and three times the hand of his father weighed him down again, and kept him in a kneeling posture. Then, as if annihilated by the thought of his weakness and powerlessness, he yielded, and covering his eyes with both hands, he murmured these words in a stifled and convulsive voice:

"Sir they do me violence, – I ask pardon for hating you."

And immediately his strength abandoned him, and he fainted; as a lily broken by the storm, his head sank, and he would have fallen backward, if his father had not signed to Ivan, who raised him like a feather in his robust arms, and carried him hastily out of the room.

Gilbert's first care after returning to his turret, was to light a candle and burn Stephane's letter. Then he opened a closet and began to prepare his trunk. While engaged in this task, someone knocked at the door. He had only time to close the closet and the trunk when Ivan appeared with a basket on his arm. The serf came for the flowers, which he had orders to carry to the apartment of his young master. Having placed five or six in his basket, he turned to Gilbert and gave him to understand, in his Teutonic gibberish mingled with French, that he had something important to communicate to him. Gilbert answered in a tone of ill-humor, that he had not time to listen to him. Ivan shook his head with a pensive air, and left. Gilbert immediately seated himself at the table, and upon the first scrap of paper which came under his hand, hastily wrote the following lines:

"Poor child, do not distress yourself too much for the humiliation to which you have just submitted. As you said yourself, you yielded only to violence, and your apologies are void in my eyes. Believe me, I exact nothing. Why did I not divine, this morning, that Fritz spoke in your name! I should not have felt offended, for it is not to me that your insults are addressed, it is to some strange Gilbert of your imagination. I am not acquainted with him. But what can it avail you to provoke contests, the result of which is certain in advance? It is a hand of iron which lately weighed upon your shoulder. Do you hope then to free yourself so soon from its grasp? Believe me, submit yourself to your lot, and mitigate its rigors by patience, until the day when your eyes have become strong enough to dare to look him in the face, and your hand manly enough to throw the gage of battle. Poor child the only consolation I can offer you in your misfortune I should be a culprit to refuse. I have but one night more to pass here; keep this secret for me for twenty-four hours, and receive the adieus of that Gilbert whom you have never known. One day he passed near you and looked at you, and you read an offensive curiosity in his eyes. I swear to you, they were full of tears."

Gilbert folded this letter, and slid it under the facing of one of his sleeves; then taking the key of the private door in his hand, and posting himself at the head of the staircase, he waited Ivan's return. As soon as he heard the sound of his steps in the corridor, he descended rapidly and met him on the landing at the gallery.

"I do not know what to do," said Ivan to him. "My young master is not himself, and he has broken the first flower-pots I carried to him in a thousand pieces."

"Take the others too," replied Gilbert, taking care to let him see the key which he flourished in his hand. "You can put them in your room for the time being. When he becomes calmer he will be glad to see them again."

"But will it not be better to leave them with you until he asks for them?"

"I don't want to keep them half an hour longer," replied Gilbert quickly, and he descended the first steps of the private staircase.

"As you are going on the terrace, sir," cried the serf to him, "don't forget, I beg of you, to close the door behind you."

Gilbert promised this. "It works well," thought he; "his caution proves to me that the wicket is not closed." He was not mistaken. For the convenience of his transportation, the serf had left it half open, only taking the precaution to close and double-lock the door of the grand staircase. Gilbert waited until Ivan had reached the second story, and immediately remounting upon tiptoe, he darted into the corridor, followed its entire length, turned to the right, passed before the Count's study, turned a second time to the right, found himself in the gallery which led to the square tower, sprang through the wicket, and arrived without obstacle at the foot of the tower staircase. He found the steps littered with the debris of broken pots and flowers. As he began to descend, loud voices came to his ears; he thought for a moment that M. Leminof was with his son. This did not turn him from his project. He had nothing to conceal. "I will beg the Count himself," thought he, "to read my farewell letter to his son." Having reached the top of the staircase, he crossed a vestibule and found himself in a long, dark alcove, lighted by a solitary glass door, opening into the great room ordinarily occupied by Stephane.

This door was ajar, and the strange scene which presented itself to Gilbert, as he approached, held him motionless a few steps from the threshold. Stephane, with his back towards him, stood with his arms crossed upon his breast. He was not speaking to his father, but to two pictures of saints hanging from the wall above a lighted taper. These two paintings on wood, in the style of Father Alexis, represented St. George and St. Sergius. The child, looking at them with burning eyes, apostrophized them in a voice trembling with anger, at intervals stamping his foot and running his hands furiously through his long hair and tossing it in wild disorder. Illustrious Saints of the Eastern Church, heard you ever such language before?

Then he sprang on a chair, tore the two pictures from the wall, threw them to the ground, and seizing his riding whip, switched them furiously. In this affair, St. George lost half of his head and one of his legs, and St. Sergius was disfigured for the rest of his days. When he had satisfied his fury, Stephane hung them up again on their nails, turning their faces to the wall, and blew out the lamp; then he rolled upon the floor, twisting his arms and tearing his hair – but suddenly sitting up, he drew from his bosom a small, heart-shaped medallion which he gazed on fixedly, and as he looked the tears began to roll down his cheeks, and in the midst of his sobs, he cried out:

"Oh, my mother! I desire nothing from you! you could do nothing for me; but why did I have time to know you? To remember! to remember – what torment! Yes, I can see you now – Every morning you gave me a kiss, high on my forehead at the roots of my hair. The mark is there yet – sometimes it burns me. I have often looked in the glass to see if I had not a scar there – Oh, my mother! come and heal my wound by renewing it! To be kissed by one's mother, Great God! what happiness! Oh! for a kiss, for a single kiss from you, I would brave a thousand dangers, I would give my blood, my life, my soul. Ah! how sad you look! there are tears in your eyes. You recognize me, do you not? I am much changed, much changed; but I have always your look, your forehead, your mouth, your hair."

Then starting up suddenly, Stephane walked around the

room with an unsteady step. He held the medallion closely grasped in his right hand and kept his eyes upon it. Again he held it out at arm's length and looked at it steadily with half-closed eyes, or drawing it nearer to him, he said to it sweet and tender things, pressing it to his lips, kissing it a thousand times and passing it over his hair and his cheeks wet with tears; it seemed as though he were trying to make some particle of this sacred image penetrate his life and being. At last, placing it on the bed, he knelt before it, and burying his face in his hands, cried out sobbing, "Mother, mother, it is long since your daughter died. When will you call your son to you?"

Gilbert retired in silence. A voice from this room said to him: "Thou art out of place here. Take care not to meddle in the secret communion of a son and his mother. Great sorrows have something sacred about them. Even pity profanes them by its presence." He descended the staircase with precaution. When he had reached the last step, – extending his arm in the direction of the Count's room, he muttered in a low tone: "You have lied! Under that tunic of black velvet there is a beating heart!" Then advancing with a rapid step through the corridor, he hoped to pass out unseen; but on reaching the wicket, he found himself face to face with Ivan, who was coming out of his room, and who in his surprise dropped the basket he held in his hand.

"You here!" exclaimed he in a severe tone. "Another would have paid dearly for this – "

Then in a soft voice, expressing profound melancholy:

"Brother," said he, "do you want both of us to be killed? I see you do not know the man whose orders you dare to brave." And he added, bowing humbly: "You will pardon me for calling you brother? In my mouth, that does not mean 'comrade.'"

Gilbert gave a sign of assent, and started to leave, but the serf, holding him by the arm, said:

"Fortunately the barine has gone out; but take care; two days since he had one of his turns, he has one every year, and while they last, his mind wanders at night, and his anger is terrible during the day. I tell you there is a storm in the air, do not draw the thunderbolt upon your head."

Then placing himself between Gilbert and the door, he added with a grave air:

"Upon your conscience, what have you been doing here? Have you seen my young father? Has he been talking to himself? You could understand what he said, for he always talks in French. He only knows enough Russian to scold me. Tell me, what have you heard? I must know."

"Don't be alarmed," answered Gilbert. "If he has secrets he has not betrayed them. He was engaged in complaining to himself, in scolding the saints and weeping. Neither must you think that I came hither to spy upon him, or to question him. As he had met with sorrow, I wanted to console him by imparting the agreeable news of my near departure; but I had not the courage to show myself to him, and besides, I am not quite certain now what I shall do."

"Yes, you will do well to go," eagerly answered the serf; "but go secretly, without warning anyone. I will help you, if you wish it. You are too inquisitive to remain here. Certain suspicions have already been excited on your account, which I have combated. Then, too, you are imprudent!" Thus saying, he drew from his pocket the candle which Gilbert had dropped in the corridor, the preceding night.

"Fortunately," said he, returning it to him, "it was I who found it, and picked it up, and I wish you well, you know why. But before going from here," added he in a solemn tone, "swear to me, that during the time you may yet remain in this house, you will not try to come into this gallery again, and that you will not ramble in the other any more in the night. I tell you your life is in danger if you do."

Gilbert answered him by a gesture of assent, and passing the wicket, regained his room, where alternately standing at the window, or stretched upon an easy-chair, he passed two full hours communing with his thoughts. The dinner-bell put an end to his long meditations. There was but little conversation during the repast. M. Leminof was grave and gloomy, and seemed to be laboring under a great nervous excitement which he strove to conceal. Stephane was calmer than would have been expected, after the violent emotions he had experienced, but there was something singular in his look. Father Alexis alone wore his everyday face; he found it very good, and did not judge it expedient to change it. Towards the end of the repast, Gilbert was surprised to see Stephane, who was in the habit of drinking only wine and water, fill his glass with Marsala three times, and swallow it almost at a single draught. The young man was not long in feeling the effect of it; his face flushed, and his gaze became vacant. Towards the close of the meal, he looked a great deal at the Apocalyptic frescoes of the vaulted ceiling: then turning suddenly to his father, he ventured to address him a question. It was the first time for nearly two years, – an event which made even Father Alexis open his eyes.

"Is it true," asked Stephane, "that living persons, supposed to be dead, have sometimes been buried?"

"Yes, it has sometimes happened," replied the Count.

"But is there no way of establishing the certainty of death?"

"Some say yes, others no. I have been told of a frozen man who was dissected in a hospital. The operator, in opening him, saw his heart beating in his breast; he took flight and is running yet."

"But when one dies a violent death – poisoned, for example?"

"My opinion is, that they can still be mistaken. Physiology is a great mystery."

"Oh! that would be horrible," said Stephane in a penetrating voice; "to awaken by bruising one's forehead against the cover of a coffin."

"It would certainly be a very disagreeable experience, answered the Count. And the conversation dropped. Stephane appeared very much affected by his father's answers. He gazed no more at the ceiling, but fixed his eyes on his plate. His face changed color several times, and as if feeling the need of stupefying himself, he filled his glass with wine for the fourth time, but he could not empty it, and had hardly touched it with his lips before he set it on the table with an air of disgust.

Tea was brought in. M. Leminof served it; and leaving his cup to cool, rose and walked the floor. After making two or three turns, he called Gilbert, and leaning upon his arm continued his walk, talking with him about the political news of the day. Stephane saw them come and go; he was evidently deeply agitated. Suddenly, at the moment when they turned their backs, he drew from his sleeve a small packet, which contained a pinch of yellow powder, and unfolding it quickly, held it over his still full cup; but as he was about emptying it, his hand trembled, and at this moment, his father and Gilbert returning to his side, he had only time to conceal the paper in his hand. In an instant he raised it again, but at the decisive moment his courage again failed him. It was not until the third trial that the yellow powder glided into the cup, where Stephane stirred it with his spoon. This little scene had escaped Gilbert. The Count alone had lost nothing of it; he had eyes at the back of his head. He reseated himself in his place and drank his tea slowly, continuing to talk with Gilbert, and apparently quite unconscious of his son; but not a movement escaped him. Stephane looked at his cup steadily, his agitation increased, he breathed heavily, he shuddered, and his hand trembled with feverish excitement. After waiting several minutes, the Count turned to him and, looking him full in the eyes, said:

"Well! you do not drink? Cold tea is a bad drug."

The child trembled still more; his eyes had a glassy brightness. Turning his head slowly, they wandered over everything about him, the table, the chairs, the plate, and the black oak wainscoting. There are moments when the aspect of the most common objects stirs the soul with solemn emotion. When the condemned man is led out to die, the least straw on the floor of his cell seems to say something to his heart. Finally, gathering all his courage, Stephane raised the cup and carried it to his mouth; but before it had touched his lips, the Count took it roughly from his hands.

Stephane uttered a piercing cry and fell back in his chair with closed eyes. M. Leminof looked at him for a moment with a sarcastic and scornful smile; then bending over the cup he examined it with care, smelt of it, and dipping his spoon in it, drew out two or three yellow grains which he rubbed and pulverized between his fingers. Then in a tone as tranquil and as indifferent as if speaking of the rain, or of the fine weather, he said:

"It is phosphorus, a sufficiently active poison, and phosphorus matches have been the death of a man more than once. But I saw your little paper some time before. If I am not mistaken the dose was not strong enough." And dipping his finger in the cup, he passed it over his tongue, and curled his lip disdainfully. "I was not mistaken," continued he, "it would only have given you a violent colic. It was very imprudent in you; you do not like to suffer, and you know we have only fresh-water physicians in this neighborhood. Why didn't you wait a few hours? Doctor Vladimir Paulitch will be here to-morrow evening." And then he went on in a more phlegmatic tone. "It should be a first principle to do thoroughly whatever you undertake to do at all. Thus, when a man wants to kill himself according to rule, he should not begin by exciting suspicions in talking of the cemetery. And as these affairs require the exercise of coolness, he should not try to get intoxicated. The courage which a person finds at the bottom of a glass of Marsala is not of a good quality, and the approach of death always sobers one. Finally, when a man has seriously resolved to kill himself, he does not do this little thing at the table, in company, but in his room, after having carefully bolted the door. In short, your little scene has failed in every point, and you do not know the first rudiments of this fine art. I advise you not to meddle with it any more."

At these words he pulled the bell for Ivan.

"Your young master wanted to kill himself," said he; "take him to his room and prepare him a composing draught that will put him to sleep. Watch with him to-night, and in future be careful not to leave any phosphorus matches in his rooms. Not that I suspect him of entertaining any intense desire of killing himself, – but who knows? Wounded vanity might drive him to try it. As his nerves are excited, you will see that for some days he takes a great deal of exercise. If the weather is fine tomorrow, keep him in the open air all day, and in the evening walk him on the terrace; he must get his blood stirred up."

From the moment that his father had taken the poisoned cup from him, Stephane had remained petrified on his chair, with livid face and arms hanging over his knees, giving no sign of life. When Ivan approached to take him away, he rose with a start, and leaning upon the arm of the serf, he crossed the room without opening his eyes. When he had gone, the Count heaved a long sigh of weariness and dejection.

"What did I tell you?" exclaimed he, throwing upon Gilbert a scrutinizing look; "this boy has a theatrical turn of mind. I would wager my life that he hadn't the faintest desire to kill himself: he only aimed at exciting us; but certainly if it was the sensitive heart of Father Alexis which he took for a target, he has lost the trouble." And he directed Gilbert's attention to the worthy priest, who, as soon as he had emptied his cup, had fallen sound asleep on his stool, and smiled at the angels in his dreams. Gilbert gave the Count a lively and agreeable surprise by answering him in the steadiest tone:

"You are entirely right, sir; it was only a very ridiculous affectation. Fortunately, we may consider it pretty certain that our young tragedian will not regale us a second time with his little play. Where courage is required, it is good to have an opportunity of seeing to the bottom of one's sack; nothing is more likely to cure a boaster of the foolish mania for blustering."

"Decidedly my secretary is improving," thought the Count; "he has a tender mouth and feels the curb." And in the joy which this discovery gave him, he felt that he entertained for him sentiments of real friendship, of which he would not have believed himself capable. His surprise and pleasure increased still more when Gilbert resumed:

"But apropos, sir, do you persist in believing that, according to Constantius Porphyrogennatus, all Greece became Slavonian in the eighteenth century? I have new objections to present to you on that subject. And first this famous Copronymus of whom he speaks. . . ."

They did not rise from the table until eleven o'clock. It was necessary to awaken Father Alexis, who slept during the whole time, his right arm extended over his plate, and his head leaning upon his elbow. The Count having shaken him, he rose with a start and exclaimed:

"Don't touch it! The colors are all fresh; Jacob's beard is such a fine gray!"

The compliant secretary retired humming an aria. M. Leminof followed him with his eyes, and, pointing after him, said to his serf in a confidential tone:

"Thou seest that man there; just fancy! I feel friendship for him. He is at least my most cherished – habit. My suspicions were absurd, thou wert right in combating them. By way of precaution, however, make a tour of the corridor between midnight and two o'clock. Now come and double-lock me in my room, for I feel a paroxysm coming on. To-morrow at five o'clock thou wilt come to open it for me."

"Count Kostia!" murmured Gilbert, when he found himself in his room, "fear no longer that I shall think of leaving you. Whatever happens, I remain here. Count Kostia, understand me, you have buried the smile: I take heaven to witness that I will resuscitate it."

XI

The day following the one on which Gilbert had resolved to remain at Geierfels, Father Alexis rose at an early hour, and betook himself as usual to his dear chapel; he entered with a slow step, bowed back, and anxious face; but when he had traversed the nave and stood before the main entrance to the choir, the influence of the holy place began to dissipate his melancholy; his thoughts took a more serene turn, and his face brightened.

For several days Father Alexis had been occupied in painting a group of three figures, Abraham, Isaac, and Jacob, and their posterity on their knees. It was the exact copy of a picture in the Convent of Lavra. These patriarchs were gravely seated upon a grassy bank, separated from each other by little shrubs of a somewhat fantastic shape. Their venerable heads were crowned with aureoles; their abundant hair, combed with the greatest care, fell majestically upon their shoulders, and their thick beards descended to the middle of their breasts.

Father Alexis worked for nearly an hour, when he heard a step in the court, and turning his head quickly, perceived Gilbert coming towards the chapel. The priest thrilled with joy, as a fisherman might, who after long hours of mortal waiting sees a fish of good size imprudently approaching his net. Eager for his prey, he threw aside his brush, quickly descended the ladder with the agility of a young man and ran to place himself in ambuscade near the door, where he waited with bated breath. As soon as Gilbert appeared, he rushed upon him, seized him by the arm, and looked upon him with eyes which seemed to say: "You are caught, and you won't escape from me either."

When he had recovered from his first excess of joy, "Ah, my son," exclaimed he, "what happy inspiration brings you hither?"

"M. Leminof is not well to-day," answered Gilbert, "and I thought I could make no better use of my leisure than to pay my respects to you."

"Oh! what a charming idea," said the priest, looking at him with ineffable tenderness. "Come, come, my son, I will show you all, yes all."

This word ALL was pronounced with such an energetic accent, that Gilbert was startled. It may be readily believed that it was not exactly about Byzantine pictures that he was curious at this moment. Nevertheless, he entered with great good-nature into a minute examination of the images of the choir and the nave; he praised all which appeared praiseworthy, kept silent upon the prominent defects which offended the delicacy of his taste, and allowed himself to criticise only some of the details.

At last he announced to the priest that he wished to talk with him of a serious matter.

"A serious matter?"

And the face of the good father became grave. "Have you anything to confess to me? What am I saying? You are not orthodox, my child, – would to God you were."

"Let us descend, let us descend," said Gilbert, putting his foot upon the ladder.

They descended and seated themselves upon the end of a white marble step, which extended the entire width of the nave, at the entrance of the choir.

"My son," began the priest timidly, "yesterday evening – "

"That is precisely what I want to talk to you about," said Gilbert.

"Ah! you are a good, generous child. You saw my embarrassment, and you wished, – I confess it, a slight drowsiness, – flesh is weak, – ah, it is good in you. Favors do not turn your head. Speak, speak, I am all attention."

"It is understood that you will keep the secret, father, for you know – "

"I understand! we should be lost if it were known that we talked of certain things together. Oh! you need not be afraid. If Kostia Petrovitch alludes to this matter, I shall appear to know nothing, and I shall accuse myself of having violated the precept of the great Solomon, who said, 'When thou sittest down to eat with a prince, consider attentively what is done before thee.'

"Speak with confidence, my child, and rest assured that this mouth has an old tongue in it which never says what it does not want to."

When Gilbert had finished his recital, Father Alexis burst forth in exclamations accompanied by many signs of the cross.

"Oh! unhappy child!" cried he; "what folly is thine! He has then sworn his own destruction? To wish to die in mortal sin! A spirit of darkness must have taken possession of him. Then he invokes St. George no longer every morning and evening? He prays no more, – he no longer carries on his heart the holy amulet I gave him. Ah! why did I fall asleep yesterday evening? What beautiful things I would have said to him! I would have commenced by representing to him – "

"I do not doubt your eloquence; but it is not remonstrance, nor good counsel that this child wants: a little happiness would answer the purpose far better."

"Happiness! Ah, yes! his life is a little sad. There are certain maxims of education – "

"It is not a question of maxims of education, but of a father who betrays an open hatred to his son."

"Holy Virgin!" exclaimed the priest with a gesture of terror, "you must not say such things, my child. These are words which the good God does not like to hear. Never repeat them, it would be neither prudent nor charitable."

Gilbert persisted; announcing the conjectures which he had formed as certainties, and even exaggerating his suspicions in the hope that the priest, in correcting him, would furnish the explanations which he desired. The success of this little artifice surpassed his expectation.

"I know for a certainty," said he, "that M. Leminof loved his wife, – that she was unfaithful to him – that he finished by suspecting her, and that he revenged himself – "

"False! false!" cried the priest with deep emotion. "To hear you one would believe that Count Kostia killed his wife. You have heard lying reports. The truth is, that the Countess Olga poisoned herself, and then feeling the approach of death, became terrified and implored aid. It was useless: they could not counteract the effects of the poison. She then sent in haste for me. I had but just time to receive her confession. Oh! what a frightful scene, my child! Why recall it to me? And above all, whose calumnious tongue – "

"I have been told, also," pursued the inflexible Gilbert, "that after this deplorable event M. Leminof, holding in abhorrence the localities which witnessed his dishonor, quitted Moscow and Russia, and went to Martinique. Having arrived there, he lost, after some months' residence, one of his two children, a daughter if I am not mistaken, and this death may have been hastened by – "

"A fresh calumny!" interrupted the priest, looking steadily at Gilbert. "The young girl died of yellow fever. Kostia Petrovitch never raised a finger against his children. Ah! tell me what viper's tongue – "

"It is not a calumny, at least, to state that he has two good reasons for not loving his son. First, because he is the living portrait of his mother, and then because he doubts, perhaps, if this child is really his son."

"An impious doubt, which I have combated with all my strength. This child was born nine years before his mother committed her first and only fault. I have said it, and I repeat it. It has been objected that he was born after six years of a marriage which seemed condemned by Heaven to an eternal sterility: – fatal circumstance, which appeared proof positive to a vindictive and ulcerated heart. But again, who could have told you – "

"One more word: before leaving for Martinique, M. Leminof did everything he could to discover the lover of his wife. His suspicions fell upon one of his intimate friends named Morlof. In his blind fury he killed him, but nevertheless Morlof was innocent."

"Did they tell you that he assassinated him?" said Father Alexis, who became more and more agitated. "Another calumny! he killed him in a regular duel. Holy Virgin! the sin was grave enough; but the police hushed up the matter, and absolution has been granted him."

"Alas!" resumed Gilbert, "if the church has pardoned, the conscience of the murderer persists in condemning; it curses that rash hand which shed innocent blood, and by a strange aberration it exhorts him to wash out this fatal mistake in the blood of the real offender. This offender, after six years' fruitless search, he has not given up the hope of discovering; he will go into the very bowels of the earth to find him, if he must, and if by chance there is some heart upon which the name is written, he will open that heart with the point of his sword to decipher those letters of blood and of fire!"

Gilbert pronounced these last words in a vibrating voice. He had suddenly forgotten where he was and to whom he was speaking. He thought he again saw before him the scene of the corridor, and could again hear those terrible words which had frozen the blood in his veins. The priest was seized with a convulsive trembling; but he soon mastered it. He raised himself slowly and stood up before Gilbert, his arms crossed upon his breast. Within a few moments his face became dignified, and at the same time his language. Now the transformation was complete; Gilbert had no longer before him the timid, easy soul who trembled before a frown, the epicure in quest of agreeable sensations, the vain artist ingeniously begging eulogies. The priest's eyes opened wide and shone like coals of fire; his lips, wreathed in a bitter smile, seemed ready to launch the thunders of excommunication; and a truly sacerdotal majesty diffused itself as if by miracle over his face. Gilbert could scarcely believe his eyes; he looked at him in silence, incapable of recognizing this new Father Alexis, who had just been revealed to him.

Then, said the priest, speaking to himself:

"Brother! what simplicity is yours! A few caresses, a few cajoleries, and your satisfied vanity silences your distrust and disarms your good sense! Did you not know that this young man is the intimate friend of your master?"

Then bowing towards Gilbert:

"They thought then that you could make me speak. And you imagined yourself that a coarse artifice and some threatening talk would suffice to tear from me a secret I have guarded for nearly seven years. Presumptuous young man, return to him who sent you, and repeat faithfully what I am about to say to you: One day at Martinique, in a remote house some distance from the outskirts of the town of St. Pierre, – let me speak, my story will be short. – Picture to yourself a great dark hall, with a table in the center. – They shut me in there near noon; the next day at evening I was there still, and for thirty hours I neither ate nor drank. The night came, – they stretched me upon a table, – bound me and tied me down. Then I saw bending over me a face more terrible than thou wilt ever see, even in thy dreams, and a mouth which sneered as the damned must sneer, approached my ear and said to me: 'Father Alexis, I want your secret – I will have it.' I breathed not a word; they tightened the cords with a jack, and I did not speak; they piled weights on my chest, and I spoke not; they put boots upon me which I hope never to see upon thy feet, and I spake not; my bones cracked, and I spake not; I saw my blood gush out, and I did not speak. At length a supreme anguish seized me, a red cloud passed over my eyes, I felt my heart freezing, and I thought myself dying. Then I spoke and said: 'Count Leminof, thou canst kill me, but thou shalt not tear from me the secrets of the confessional.'" And at these words, the priest stooping, laid bare his right foot and showed Gilbert the bruised and withered flesh, and bones deformed by torture; then covering it again he recoiled, as if from a serpent in his path, and cried in a thundering voice, extending his arms to Heaven:

"God curse the vipers who take the form of doves! Oh, Solomon, hast thou not written in thy Proverbs: 'When he shall speak graciously, do not believe him, for he has seven abominations in his heart'?"

As he listened to the recital of the priest, Gilbert was reminded of some incoherent phrases of the somnambulist, which he had not been able to explain: "STRETCH HIM ON THIS TABLE! THE BLACK ROBE! TIGHTEN THE IRON BOOTS!"

"That black robe then," said he to himself, "was Father Alexis."

He rose and looked at the priest in surprise and admiration; he could not take his eyes from that face which he believed he saw for the first time, and he murmured in a low voice:

"My God! how complex is the heart of man. What a discovery I have just made!"

Then he tried to approach him; but the priest, still recoiling and raising his arms threateningly above his head, repeated:

"Cursed be the vipers who come in the form of doves!"

"And I say," cried Gilbert, "blessed forever be the lips which have touched the sacred coal, and keep their secrets even unto death!"

And rushing upon him he took him in his arms, and kissed three times the scar which the cruel bite of Solon had left.

Father Alexis was surprised, stupefied, and confounded. He looked at Gilbert, then at Abraham, then at Jacob. He uttered disjointed phrases. He called upon Heaven to witness what had happened to him, gesticulated and wept until, overcome by emotion, he dropped on the marble step, and hid his face, bathed in tears, in his hands.

"Father," said Gilbert respectfully, seating himself near him, "pardon me for the agitation I have caused you. And if by chance some distrust of me remains, listen to what I am about to tell you, for I am going to put myself at your mercy, and by betraying a secret it will depend upon you to have me expelled from this house the day and hour you please."

He then related to him the scene of the corridor.

"Judge for yourself what impression the terrible words I heard produced upon me! For some days my mind has been at work. I ceaselessly tried to picture to myself the details of this lamentable affair; but fearing to stray in my suspicions, I wished to make a clean breast of it, and came to find you. I have grieved you sorely, father; once more, will you pardon my rash curiosity?"

Father Alexis raised his head. Farewell to the saint! farewell to the prophet! His face had resumed its habitual expression; the sublime tempest which had transfigured it had left but a few almost invisible traces of its passage. He looked at Gilbert reproachfully.

"Ah!" said he, "it was only for this that you sought me? My dear child, you do not love the arts then?"

XII

That day Gilbert passed an entire hour at his window. It was not the Rhine which fixed his attention, nor the precipice, the mountains nor the clouds. The narrow space within which he confined his gaze was bounded on the west by the great square tower, on the south by a gable, on the north by a spout; I mean to say that the object of his contemplations was a very irregular, very undulating roof, or to speak more accurately, two adjacent and parallel roofs, one higher than the other by twelve feet, and both inclining by a steep slope towards a frightful precipice.

As he closed the window, he said to himself:

"After all, it is less difficult than I thought; two rope ladders will do the business, with God's help!"

M. Leminof finding himself too much indisposed to leave his room, Gilbert dined alone in his turret; after which he went out for a walk on the borders of the Rhine. As he left the path for the main road, he saw Stephane and Ivan within twenty paces of him. Perceiving him, the young man made an angry gesture, and turning his face, started his horse off at full speed. Gilbert had scarcely time to leap into the ditch to avoid being run down. As Ivan passed, he looked at him sadly, shook his head, and carried his finger to his forehead, as if to say: "You must pardon him; his poor mind is very sick." Gilbert returned to the castle without delay, and as he reached the entrance to the terrace, he saw the serf leaning against one of the doors, where he seemed to be on guard.

"My dear Ivan," said he, "you appear to be waiting for someone."

"I heard you coming," answered he, "and I took you for Vladimir Paulitch. It was the sound of your step which deceived me; you haven't such a measured step generally."

"You are a keen observer," replied Gilbert smiling; "but who, I pray, is this Vladimir Paulitch?"

"He is a physician from my country. He will remain two months with us. The barine wrote to him a fortnight since, when he felt that he was going to be ill; Vladimir Paulitch left immediately, and day before yesterday he wrote from Berlin, that he would be here this evening. This Vladimir is a physician who hasn't his equal. I am waiting for him to arrive."

"Tell me, good Ivan, is your young master in the garden?"

"He is down there under the weeping ash."

"Very well, you must permit me to speak to him a moment. You will even extend the obligation by saying nothing about it to Kostia Petrovitch. You know he cannot see us, for he keeps his bed now, and even if he should rise, his windows open on the inner court."

Ivan's brow contracted. "Impossible, impossible!" he murmured.

"Impossible? Why? Because you will not?

"Ivan, my good Ivan, it is absolutely necessary for me to speak to your young master. I have made him submit to a humiliation against my will. He mistakes my sentiments and credits me with the blackest intentions, and it will be torture to him in future to be condemned to sit at the same table with me daily. Let me explain myself to him. In two words I will make him understand who I am, and I wish him no harm."

The discussion was prolonged some minutes, Ivan finally yielding, but on the condition that Gilbert should not put his good will to the proof a second time. "Otherwise," said Ivan, "if you still attempt to talk with him secretly, I cannot permit him to go out, and, of course, he could only blame you, and would then have the right to consider you an enemy."

Upon his side, the serf promised that the Count should know nothing of the interview.

"Recollect, brother," continued he, "that this is the last improper favor that you will obtain from me. You are a man of heart, but sometimes I should say that YOU HAD BEEN EATING BELLADONNA."

Stephane had left the circular bank where he had been sitting, and stood, with his back against the parapet of the terrace, his arms hanging dejectedly, and his head sunk upon his breast. His reverie was so profound that Gilbert approached within ten steps of him without being perceived; but suddenly rousing himself, he raised his head quickly, and stamped his foot imperiously.

"Go away!" cried he, "go away, or I will set Vorace on you!"

Vorace was the name of the bulldog that kept him company at night, and was crouching in the grass some paces distant. Of all the watchdogs of the castle, this one was the strongest and most ferocious.

"You see," said Ivan, retaining Gilbert by the arm, "you have nothing to do here."

Gilbert gently disengaged himself and continued to advance.

"Get out of my sight," screamed Stephane. "Why do you come to trouble my solitude? Who gives you the right to pursue me, to track me? How dare you look me in the face after – "

He could say no more. Excitement and anger choked his voice. For some moments he looked alternately at Gilbert and the dog; then changing his purpose, he moved as if to fly, but Gilbert barred the way.

"Listen to me but a minute," said he in a gentle and penetrating voice, "I bring you good news."

"You!" exclaimed Stephane, and he repeated, "You! you! good news!"

"I!" said Gilbert, "for I come to announce to you my near departure."

Stephane stared with wide-open eyes, and recoiled slowly to

the wall, where, leaning back again, he exclaimed:

"What! are you going? Ah! certainly the news is excellent, as well as unexpected; but you are giving yourself unnecessary trouble, there was no need to forewarn me. Your departure! Great God! I should have been notified of it in advance by the clearness of the air, by the more vivid brightness of the sun, by some strange joy diffused through all my being. Oh! I understand, you are not able to digest the outrage done to you by the excellent Fritz at my order. You consider the reparation insufficient. You are right, I swear it by St. George, my heart made no apologies to you. I upon my knees to you! Horror and misery! As I told you yesterday, I yielded only to force. It was the same as if I should make my bulldog drag you down at my feet now!"

Gilbert made no answer; he contented himself with drawing from his pocketbook the letter which he had written the day before, and presenting it to Stephane.

"What have I to do with this paper?" said Stephane with a gesture of disdain. "You have told me your news, that is sufficient for me. Anything more you could add would spoil my happiness."

"Read!" said Gilbert. "I have granted you such a great favor that you can well afford to grant me a small one." - Stephane hesitated a moment, but the habitual tediousness of his life was so great that the want of diversion overcame his hatred and scorn.

"This letter is not bad!" said he as he read. "Its style is eloquent, the penmanship is admirable too. It involuntarily suggests to me the tie of your cravat. Both are so correct that they are insufferable."

Gilbert, smiling, untied the cravat and let the ends hang down upon his vest.

"It is not worth while to incommode yourself," pursued Stephane, "we have so short a time to live together! Pray do not renounce your most cherished habits for me. The bow of your cravat as well as your writing, harmonize wonderfully with your whole person. I do not suppose, however, that to please me you would reconstruct yourself from head to foot. The undertaking would be considerable."

"Permit me to speak," answered Gilbert. "I have made a little change in my programme: I shall not leave tomorrow. I have granted myself a week's delay."

Stephane's face darkened, and his eyes flashed.

"I swear to you here, upon my honor," continued Gilbert, "that in a week I will leave, never to return, unless you yourself beg me to remain."

"What baseness! and how cleverly this little plot has been contrived; I see it all. By force of threats and violence they hope to compel me a second time to bend my knees to you and cry with clasped hands, 'Sir, in the name of Heaven, continue us the favor of your precious presence!' But this act of cowardice I shall never commit! Rather death! rather death!"

"A word only," resumed Gilbert, without being discouraged. "Submit me to some proof. Have you no caprice which it is in my power to satisfy?"

"Throw yourself at my feet," cried he impetuously; "drag yourself in the dust, kiss the ground before me, and demand pardon and mercy of me! At this price I will grant you, not my affection certainly, but my indulgence and pity."

"Impossible!" answered Gilbert, shaking his head. "I am like you; I should not know how to kneel, unless someone stronger than myself constrained me by violence. Oh, no! in such a performance I should lose even the hope of being some day esteemed by you. The more so as in the trial to which I wish you would subject me, I should desire to have some danger to brave, some difficulty to surmount."

Stephane could not conceal his astonishment. Never in all his life had he heard language like this. Nevertheless, distrust and pride triumphed still over every other feeling.

"Since you wish it!" said he, sneering . . . and he drew a kid glove from one of his pockets, rubbed it between his hands and threw it to the bulldog, who caught in his teeth and kept it there. "Vorace," said he to him, "keep your master's glove between your teeth, watch it well; you will answer to me for it."

Then turning to Gilbert, – "Sir, will you please restore my glove to me? I should be infinitely obliged to you for it."

"Ah! this is then the trial to which you will subject me?" answered Gilbert with a smile upon his lips.

Stephane looked him in the face. For the first time, he could not avoid being struck by its noble expression and the clearness and purity of his glance.

Stephane was involuntarily moved, and strove in vain to conceal it by the jocular tone in which he replied:

"No, sir, it is not a test of your sincerity, but a jest which we shall do well not to push further. This animal is not amiable. Should you be unfortunate enough to irritate him, it would be impossible even for me, his master, to calm his fury. Be good enough then to leave my glove where it is, and return peaceably to your study to meditate upon some important problem in Byzantine history. That will be a trial less perilous and better proportioned to your strength. Good-evening, sir, good-night."

"Oh! permit me," replied Gilbert. "I am resolved to carry this adventure to its conclusion!"

And gently repulsing Stephane, who sought to restrain him, he walked straight toward the bulldog.

"Take care," cried the young man, shuddering, "do not trifle with that beast, or you are a dead man!"

"Take care," repeated Ivan, who, not having understood half of what had been said, hardly suspected Gilbert's intention. "Take care, this dog is a ferocious beast."

Meantime Gilbert, crossing his arms upon his breast, advanced slowly towards the bulldog, keeping his eyes steadily fixed on those of the animal, and when he thought he had disconcerted him by his undaunted gaze sufficiently to make him relax his grip upon the prize, he suddenly tore the glove from him and waved it in the air with his right hand. At the same moment Vorace, with a howl of rage, bounded up to leap at the throat of his despoiler. Gilbert sprang back, covering himself with his left arm, and the dog's jaws only grazed his shoulder. Yet when he touched the ground again, he held between his teeth a long strip of cloth, a scrap of linen, and a morsel of bloody flesh. Mad with fury the bulldog rolled over on the grass with this prize which he could hardly devour, and then suddenly, as if seized with a paroxysm of frenzy, he moved towards the castle doubling upon himself; but reaching the foot of the turret, he looked for his enemy and returned like an arrow, to pounce upon him again.

"Throw down the glove," cried Ivan, "and climb the ash."

"I will surrender the glove only to him who asked me for it," answered Gilbert.

And hiding it in his bosom, he drew a knife from his pocket. He had not time to open it. The dog, with bristling hair and foaming jaws, was already within three steps of him, gathering himself to spring upon him; but he had scarcely raised himself from the ground when he fell back with his head shattered. The hatchet which Ivan carried at his girdle had come down upon him like a flash. The terrible animal vainly attempted to rise, rolled writhing in the dust, and breathed out his life with a hoarse and fearful howl.

XIII

Doctor Vladimir Paulitch arrived at the castle just in time to take care of Gilbert. The wound was wide and deep, and in consequence of the great heat which prevailed, it might easily have proved serious; fortunately, Doctor Vladimir was a skillful man, and under his care the wound was soon healed. He employed certain specifics, the uses of which were known only to himself, and which he took care to keep a secret from his patient. His medicine was as mysterious as his person.

Vladimir Paulitch was forty years of age; his face was striking but unattractive. His eyes had the color and the hard brightness of steel; his keen glances, subject to his will, often questioned, but never allowed themselves to be interrogated. Well made, slender, a slight and graceful figure, he had in his gait and movements a feline suppleness and stealthiness. He was slow, but easy of speech, and never animated; the tone of his voice was cold and veiled, and whatever the subject of conversation might be, he neither raised nor lowered it; no modulations; everyone of his sentences terminated in a little minor cadence, which fell sadly on the ear. He sometimes smiled in speaking, it is true, but it was a pale smile which did not light up his face. This smile signified simply: "I do not give you my best reason, and I defy you to divine it."

One morning when Ivan had come by order of the doctor to dress Gilbert's wound, our friend questioned him as to the character and life of Vladimir Paulitch. Of the man Ivan knew nothing, and confined himself to extolling the genius of the physician; he expressed himself in regard to him in a mysterious tone. The imposing face of this impenetrable personage, the extraordinary power of his glance, his impassible gravity, the miraculous cures which he had wrought, it needed no more to convince the honest serf that Vladimir Paulitch dealt in magic and held communications with spirits; and he felt for his person a profound veneration mingled with superstitious terror. He told Gilbert that since the age of twenty-five, Vladimir had been directing a hospital and private asylum which Count Kostia had founded upon his estates, and that, thanks to him, these two establishments had not their equals in all Russia.

"Last year," added the serf, "he came to attend the barine, and told him that his malady would return this year, but more feebly, and that this would be the last. You will see that all will come to pass as he has said. Kostia Petrovitch is already much better, and I wager that next summer will come and go without his feeling his nerves."

As Ivan prepared to go, Gilbert detained him to ask news of Stephane. The serf had been very discreet, and had related the adventure upon the terrace to his master without compromising anyone. The only trouble he had had was in persuading him that it was not on a sign from Stephane that the dog had attacked Gilbert.

The next day Gilbert dined in the great hall of the castle with M. Leminof and Father Alexis.

"Do not disturb yourself because Stephane does not dine with us," said the Count to him. "He is not sick; but he has a new grievance against you; you have caused the death of his dog. I ask your pardon, my dear Gilbert, for the irrational conduct of my son. I have given him three days for the sulks. When that time has passed, I intend that he shall put on his good looks for you, and that he shall take his place at the table opposite you without frowning."

"And how is it that Doctor Vladimir is not with us?"

"He has begged me to excuse him for a time. He finds himself much fatigued with the care he has given me. A magnetic treatment, you understand. I should inform you that every year, some time during the summer, I am subject to attacks of neuralgia from which I suffer intensely. By the way, you have seen our admirable doctor several times. What do you think of him?"

"I don't know whether he is a great savant, but I am inclined to think he is a first-class artist."

"You cannot pay him a finer compliment; medicine is an art rather than a science. He is also a man capable of the greatest devotion. I am indebted to him for my life, it was not as physician that he saved me either. A pair of stallions ran away within twenty paces of a precipice; the doctor, appearing from behind a thicket, darted to the heads of the horses and hung on to them by their nostrils, which he held in an iron grip. You have the whole scene from these windows. What was amusing in it was, that having thanked him, with what warmth you can imagine, he answered, in a tranquil tone, and wiping his knees – for the horses in falling had laid him full length in the dust – 'It is I who am obliged to you; for the first time I have been suspended between life and death, and it is a singular sensation. But for you I should not have known it.' This will give you an idea of the man and his sangfroid!"

"I am not surprised at his having the agility of a wildcat," replied Gilbert; "but I suspect the sangfroid is feigned, and that his placidity of face is a mask which hides a very passionate soul."

"Passionate is not the word, or at least the doctor knows only the passions of the head. There was a time when he thought himself desperately in love; an unpardonable weakness in such a distinguished man; but he was not long in undeceiving himself, and he has not fallen into such a fatal error since."

The night having come, Gilbert, who had inquiries to make, crossed the yard of which the chapel formed one side, and gaining the rear by a private door, went in search of Father Alexis. It was not long before he discovered him, for the priest had left his shutters open, and he was seated in the embrasure of the window, peaceably smoking his pipe, when he perceived Gilbert.

"Oh, the good boy!" cried he, "let him come in quickly! My room and my heart are open to him."

Gilbert showed him his arm in a sling, on account of which he could not climb the window.

"Is that all, my child?" said Father Alexis. "I will hoist you up here."

Gilbert raised himself by his right arm, and Father Alexis drawing him up, they soon found themselves seated face to face, uniting to their heart's content the blue smoke of their chibouques.

"Have you not noticed," said Father Alexis, "that Kostia Petrovitch has been in a charming humor to-day? I told you that he had his pleasant moments! Vladimir Paulitch has already done him much good. What a physician this Vladimir is! It is a great pity that he does not believe in God; but some day, perhaps, grace will touch his heart, and then he will be a complete man."

"If I were in your place, father, I should be afraid of this Vladimir," said Gilbert. "Ivan pretends that he is something of a sorcerer. Aren't you afraid that some fine day he may rob you of your secret?"

Father Alexis shrugged his shoulders.

"Ivan talks foolishly," said he. "If Vladimir Paulitch were a sorcerer, would he not have long since penetrated the mystery which he burns to fathom? for he does more than love Count Kostia; he is devoted to him even to fanaticism. It is certain that having discovered that the Countess Olga was enceinte, he had the barbarity to become her denouncer; and that letter which announced to Count Kostia his dishonor, that letter which made him return from Paris like a thunder-clap, that letter in short which caused the death of Olga Vassilievna, was written by him – Vladimir Paulitch."

"And Morlof," said Gilbert, "was it this Vladimir who denounced him to the unjust fury of the Count?"

"On the contrary, Vladimir pleaded his cause; but his eloquence failed against the blind prejudices of Kostia Petrovitch. This Morlof was, unfortunately for himself, a fashionable gentleman, well known for his gallantries. A man of honor, however, incapable of betraying a friend; this reputation for gallant successes, of which he boasted, was his destruction. When Count Kostia interrogated his wife, and she refused to denounce her seducer, it occurred to him to name Morlof, and the energy with which she defended him confirmed the Count's suspicion. To disabuse him, it needed but that tragic meeting of which I was informed too late. In breathing his last sigh, Morlof extended his hand to his murderer and gasped 'I die innocent!' And in these last words of a dying man, there was such an accent of truth that Count Kostia could not resist it: light broke in upon his soul."

As the darkness increased, Father Alexis closed the shutters and lit a candle.

"My child," said he, refilling and lighting his pipe, "I must tell you something I learned to-day, a few moments before dinner, which appeared to me very strange. Listen attentively, and I am sure you will share in my astonishment."

Gilbert opened his ears, for he had a presentiment that Father Alexis was about to speak of Stephane.

"It is a singular fact," resumed the priest, "and one that I should not wish to relate to the first-comer, but I am very glad to impart it to you, because you have a serious and reflective mind, though unfortunately you are not orthodox; would to God you were. Know then, my child, that to-day, Saturday, I went according to my custom to Stephane to catechize him, and for reasons which you know, I redoubled my efforts to impress his unruly head with the holy truths of our faith. Now it appears that without intending it, you have caused him sorrow; and you can believe that such a character, far from having pardoned you, has taken the greatest pains to get me to espouse his side in the difficulty. However he, who will usually fly into a passion and talk fiercely if a fly tickles him, recited his griefs to me with an air of moderation and a tranquillity of tone which astonished me to the last degree. As I endeavored to discover a reason for this, I happened to raise my eyes to the images of St. George and St. Sergius which decorate one of the corners of his room, and before which he was in the habit of saying his prayers every morning. What was my surprise, my grief, when I perceived that the two saints had suffered shameful outrages. One had no legs, the other was disfigured by a horrible scar. With hands raised to Heaven, I threatened him with the thunder of God. Without being excited, without changing countenance, he left his chair, came to me and placed his hand on my mouth. 'Father,' said he, with an air of assurance which awed me, 'listen to me. I have been wrong, if you wish it so, and still, under the same circumstances, I should do it again, for since I have chastised them, the two saints have decided to come to my aid, and the very day after their punishment, without any change in my life, all at once I felt my heart become lighter; for the first time, I swear to you, a ray of celestial hope penetrated my soul.' What do you say to that, my child? I had often heard similar things related, but I did not believe them. Little boys may be whipped, but as for saints! – Ah! my dear child, the ways of God are very strange, and there are many great mysteries in this world."

Father Alexis had such an impressive air in speaking of this great mystery, that Gilbert was tempted to laugh; but he controlled himself; he was too grateful for his obliging narrative, and could have embraced him with all his heart.

"Good news!" said he to himself. "That heart has become lighter; that 'ray of celestial hope.' Ah! God be praised, my effort has not been thrown away. St. George, St. Sergius, you rob me of my glory, but what matters it? I am content!"

"And what reply did you make to Stephane?" said he to the priest. "Did you reprimand him? Did you congratulate him?"

"The case was delicate," said the good father, with the air of a philosopher meditating on the most abstruse subject; "but I am not wanting in judgment, and I drew out of the affair with honor."

"You managed admirably," cried I, looking at him with admiration; then immediately putting on a serious face, "but the sin is enormous."

The third day after, Gilbert didn't wait for the bell to ring for dinner before going down to the great hall. He was not very much surprised to find Stephane there. Leaning with his back against the sideboard, the young man, on seeing him appear, lost his composure, blushed, and turned his head towards the wall. Gilbert stopped a few steps from him. Then in an agitated manner, and with a voice at once gentle and abrupt, he said:

"And your arm?"

"It is nearly well. To-morrow I shall take off my sling."

Stephane was silent for a moment. Then in a still lower voice:

"What do you mean to do?" murmured he; "what are your plans?"

"I wait to know your good pleasure," replied Gilbert.

The young man covered his eyes with both hands, and, as Gilbert said no more, he seemed to feel a thrill of impatience and vexation.

"His pride demands some mercy," thought Gilbert. "I will spare him the mortification of making the first advances."

"I should like very much to have a conversation with you," said he gently. "This cannot be upon the terrace, Ivan will not leave you alone there. Does he keep you company in your room in the evening?"

"Are you jesting?" answered Stephane, raising his head. "After nine o'clock Ivan never comes near my room."

"And his room, if I am not mistaken," answered Gilbert, "is separated from you by a corridor and a staircase. So we shall run no risk of being overheard."

Stephane turned towards him and looked him in the face. "You think of everything," said he, with a smile, sad and ironical. "Apparently, to reach me, you will be obliged to mount a swallow. Have you made your arrangements with one?"

"I shall come over the roofs," said Gilbert quietly.

"Impossible!" cried Stephane. "In the first place, I do not wish you to risk your life for me again. And then – "

"And then you do not care for my visit?"

Stephane only answered him by a look.

At this moment steps sounded in the vestibule. When the Count entered, Gilbert was pacing the further end of the hall, and Stephane, with his back turned, was attentively observing one of the carved figures upon the wainscoting. M. Leminof, stopping at the threshold of the door, looked at them both with a quizzical air.

"It was time for me to arrive," said he, laughing. "This is an embarrassing tete-a-tete."

XIV

At about ten o'clock Gilbert began to make preparations for his expedition. He had no fear of being surprised; his evenings were his own – that was a point agreed upon between the Count and himself. He had also just heard the great door of the corridor roll upon its hinges. On the side of the terrace the thick branches of the trees concealed him from the watchdogs which, had they suspected the adventure, could have given the alarm. There was nothing to fear from the hillock below the precipice; it was frequented only by the young girl who tended the goats and who was not in the habit of allowing them to roam so late among the rocks. Besides, the night, serene and without a moon, was propitious; no other light than the discreet glistening of the stars which would help to guide him, without being bright enough to betray or disturb him; the air was calm, a scarcely perceptible breeze stirred at intervals the leaves of the trees without agitating the branches. Thanks to this combination of favorable circumstances, Gilbert's enterprise was not desperate; but he did not dream of deceiving himself in regard to its dangers.

The castle clock had just struck ten when he extinguished his lamp and opened the window. There he remained a long time leaning upon his elbows: his eyes at last familiarized themselves with the darkness, and favored by the glimmering of the stars, he began to recognize with but little effort the actual shape of the surrounding objects. The window was divided in two equal parts by a stone mullion, and had in front a wide shelf of basalt, surrounded by a balustrade. Gilbert fastened one of two knotted ropes with which he had supplied himself securely to the mullion; then he crept upon the ledge of basalt and stood there for a few moments contemplating the precipice in silence. In the gloomy and vaporous gulf which his eyes explored, he distinguished a wall of whitish rocks, which seemed to draw him towards them, and to provoke him to an aerial voyage. He took care not to abandon himself to this fatal attraction, and the uneasiness which it caused him disappearing gradually, he stretched out his head and was able to hang over the abyss with impunity. Proud at having subdued the monster, he gave himself up for a moment to the pleasure of gazing at a feeble light which appeared at a distance of sixty paces, and some thirty feet beneath him. This light came from Stephane's room; he had opened his window and closed the white curtains in such a way that his lamp, placed behind this transparent screen, could serve as a beacon to Gilbert without danger of dazzling him.

"I am expected," said Gilbert to himself.

And immediately, bestriding the balustrade, he descended the swaying rope as readily as if he had never done anything else in his life.

He was now upon the roof. There he met with more difficulty. Partly covered with zinc and partly with slate, this roof – the whole length of which he must traverse – was so steep and slippery that no one could stand erect on it. Gilbert seated himself and remained motionless for a moment to recover himself, and the better to decide upon his course. A few steps from this point, a huge dormer window rose, with triangular panes of glass, and reached to within two feet of the spout. Gilbert resolved to make his way by this narrow pass, and from tile to tile he pushed himself in that direction. It will readily be believed that he advanced but slowly, much more so on account of his left arm, which, as it still pained him, required to be carefully managed; but by dint of patience and perseverance he passed beyond the dormer window, and at length arrived safely at the extremity of the roof, just in front of Stephane's window.

"God be praised, the most difficult part is over," he said to himself, breathing freely.

But he was far from correct in his supposition. It is true he had now only to descend upon the little roof, cross it, and climb to the window, which was but breast-high; but before descending it was necessary to find some support – stone, wood or iron, to which he could fasten the second rope, which he had brought wound about his neck, shoulders, and waist. Unfortunately he discovered nothing. At last, in leaning over, he perceived at the outer angle of the wall a large iron corbel, which seemed to sustain the projecting roof; but to his great chagrin, he ascertained at the same time, that the great roof passed three feet beyond the line of the small one, and that if even he should succeed in attaching his second rope to the corbel, the other end of it would float in empty space. This reflection made him shudder; and turning his eyes from the precipice, he examined the ridge-pole, where he thought he saw a piece of iron projecting. He was not mistaken: it was a kind of ornamental molding, which formed the pediment of the ridge. It was not without great effort that he raised himself even there, and when he found himself seated astride the beam, he rested a few moments to breathe, and to study the strange spectacle before him. His view embraced an immense extent of abrupt, irregular roofing, from every part of which rose turrets of every kind, in the shape of extinguishers, pointed gables, corners, retreating or salient angles, bell-towers, open to the daylight, profound depths where the gloom thickened, grinning chimneys, heavy weathercocks cutting the milky way with their iron rods and feathered arrows; from the top of the chapel steeple a great cross of stone, seeming to stretch out its arms; here and there the whitish zinc, cutting the dark blue of the slates; in spots an indistinct glittering and flashes of pale light enveloped in opaque shadows, and then the tops of three or four large trees which extended beyond the eaves, as if prying into the secrets of the attic. By the glittering light of the stars, the slightest peculiarity in the architecture assumed singular contours, fantastic figures were profiled upon the horizon like Chinese shadows; everywhere an air of mystery, of curiosity, of wild surprise. All these shadows leaned towards Gilbert, examined him, and interrogated him by their looks.

When he had recovered breath, Gilbert approached the projecting ornament from which he proposed to suspend his rope; he had been greatly deceived; he found that this ovolo of sheet iron, for a long time roughly used by the elements, held only by a wretched nail, and that it would inevitably yield to the least strain.

"It is decided," said he. "I must go by the iron corbel!" And although it cost him an effort, his mind was soon resolutely fixed. Impatient at the loss of so many steps and at the waste of so much precious time in vain efforts, he redescended the roof much more actively than he had mounted it. Arriving below, and by the power of his will conquering a new attack of vertigo with which he felt himself threatened, he lay down upon his face parallel with the spout, and advancing his head and arm beyond the roof he succeeded, not without much trouble, in tying the cord firmly to the iron corbel. This done, without loitering to see it float, he swung himself slowly round, and let himself glide over the edge of the roof as far as his armpits, resting suspended by the elbows. Critical moment! If but a lath, but a nail should break – He had no time to make this alarming reflection; he was too much occupied in drawing towards him with his feet the rope, and when at length he succeeded, detaching his left arm from the roof, he seized the corbel firmly, and soon after, his right hand removing itself in its turn, firmly grasped the rope.

"That's not bad for a beginner," thought he.

He then began to descend, giving careful attention to every movement. But at the moment when his feet had reached the level of the small roof, having had the imprudence to look down into the space beneath him, he was suddenly seized with a dizziness a thousand times more terrible than he had yet experienced. The whole valley began to be agitated, and rolled and pitched terribly. By turns it seemed to rise to the sky or sink into the bowels of the earth. Presently the motion was accelerated, trees and stones, mountains and plains were all confounded in one black whirlwind, which struggled with increasing fury, and from which came forth flashes of lightning and balls of fire. Restored to himself after a few minutes, to dispel the emotion which his frightful nightmare caused him, he had recourse to old Homer, and recited in one breath that passage of the Iliad where the divine bard describes the joy of a herdsman contemplating the stars from a craggy height. Gilbert never, in after life, read these verses without recalling the sweet but terrible moment when he recited them suspended in mid-air; above his head the infinite smile of starry fields, and under his feet the horrors of a precipice. As soon as he felt more calm, he commenced the task of effecting his descent upon the small roof, less steep than the other, and covered with hollow tiles which left deep grooves between them. To crown his good fortune, the spout was surmounted from place to place by iron ornaments imbedded in the wall and rolled up in the form of scrolls. Gilbert imparted an oscillating motion to the rope, and when it had become strong enough to make this improvised swing graze the gutter, choosing his time well, he disengaged his right foot and planted it firmly in one of the grooves, loosening at the same time his right hand and quickly seizing one of the scrolls. Midnight sounded, and Gilbert was astonished to find that he had spent two hours upon his adventurous excursion. To mount the roof halfway, cross it, and climb into the window was but a slight affair, after which, turning the curtains aside with his hand, he called in a soft voice: "Am I expected?" and leaped with a bound into the room.

With his chin upon his knees and his head buried in his hands, Stephane was crouching at the feet of the holy images. Hearing and perceiving Gilbert, he started, raised himself quickly and remained motionless, his hands crossed above his head, his neck extended, his lips quivering and opening with a smile, lightnings and tears in his eyes. How paint the strangeness of his countenance? A thousand diverse emotions betrayed themselves there. Surprise, gratitude, shame, anxiety, long expectation at last satisfied; a remnant of haughtiness which felt its defeat certain; an obstinate incredulity forced to surrender; the disorder of an imagination, enchanted, rapt, distracted, the delights of hope and the bitterness of memory; all these appeared upon his face, and formed a melange so confused that to see him thus laughing and crying at once, it seemed as if it was his joy which wept and his sadness which smiled. His first agitation dispelled, the predominating expression of his face was a dreamy and startled sweetness. He moved backwards from Gilbert and fell upon a chair at the end of the room.

"Do I intrude? Must I go away?" asked Gilbert, still standing. Stephane made no answer.

"Evidently my face does not please you," continued Gilbert, half turning towards the window.

Stephane contracted his brows.

"Do not trifle, I beg of you," said he, in a hollow voice. "We have serious matters between us to discuss."

"The seriousness which I prefer is that of joy."

Stephane passed his thin and taper hands nervously through his hair.

"Joy?" said he. "It will come, perhaps, in its time, through speaking to me about it, who knows? Now I seem to be dreaming. The disorder of my thoughts frightens me. Ask me no questions, for I should not know how to answer you. And then the sound of my voice mortifies me, irritates me. It is like a discord in music. Let me be silent and look at you."

And approaching a long table which stood in the middle of the room, he signalled to Gilbert to place himself at one side of it and seated himself at the other.

After a long silence, he began to express his thoughts audibly, as if he had become reconciled to the sound of his voice:

"This bold, resolute air, so much pride in the look, so much goodness in the smile. It is another man. Ah! into what contempt have I fallen. I have seen nothing, divined nothing. I despised him, I hated him, – this one whom God has sent to save me from despair. See what was concealed under this simple unaffected air; this serene face, whose calmness irritated me; this gentleness which seemed servile; this wisdom which I thought pedantry; this pliancy of disposition which I took for the meanness of a crouching dog. All this I can it really be the same man!" He was silent for a moment and then continued in a more assured voice:

"How did you manage to reach here? Ah! my God! that great roof is so steep! Only to think of it makes me shudder and sets my head to whirling. While waiting I prayed to the saints for you. Did you feel their aid? I should like to know whether they stood by me in this. They have so often broken faith."

Silence again, during which Stephane looked at Gilbert with a steadiness sufficient to disconcert him.

"So you have risked your life for me!" continued the young man; "but are you quite sure that I am worth the trouble? Come now, be frank. Has anyone spoken to you of me? Or have you, by studying my character, made some interesting discovery? Answer, and be careful not to lie. My eyes are upon you, they will readily discover if you are sincere."

"Really, you astonish me," answered Gilbert tranquilly; "and what have I to conceal from you? All I know resolves itself into two points. In the first place, I know that you belong to the race, to the brotherhood of noble souls; I know, besides, that you are unhappy. – Pardon me, I know another thing still. I know beyond a doubt that I have conceived a lively and tender friendship for you, and that I should be very unhappy, too, if I could not expect any return from you."

"You feel friendship for me? How can that be?"

"Ah! a strange question! Who has ever been able to answer it? It is the mystery of mysteries. I love you, because I love you: I know of no other explanation. You have certainly never made any very flattering advances to me. I think I have sometimes even had cause to complain of you.

"Ah, well! in spite of your scorn, of your haughtiness, of your injustice, I loved you. Ask the secret of this anomaly of Him who created man, and who planted in his heart that mysterious power which is called sympathy."

"Why," said Stephane, "was not this sympathy reciprocal? As for me, from the first day I saw you I hated you. I do not know with what eyes I looked at you, but I thought that I recognized an enemy. Alas! suspicion and distrust invaded my heart long ago. And mark, even at this moment I still doubt, I fear I may be the dupe of some illusion: I believe and I do not believe, and I am tempted to exclaim with one of the Holy Evangelists, 'My patron, my brother, my friend, I believe, help thou mine unbelief!'"

"Your incredulity will cure itself, and be sure, a day will come when you will say with confidence: there is in this world a soul, sister of my own, into which I can fearlessly pour all my cares, all my thoughts, all my sorrows and all my hopes. There is one who occupies himself unceasingly about me, to whom my happiness is of great moment, of supreme interest, a being to whom I can say all, confess all; a being who loves me because he knows me, and who knows me because he loves me; a being who sees with me, who sees in me, and who would not hesitate, if necessary, to sacrifice everything, even his life, upon the holy altar of friendship. And then could you not cry out in the joy of your heart: 'God he praised! I possess a friend! By the blessing of God I have learned what it is to love and to be loved."

Stephane began to weep:

"To be loved!" said he. "It is a great word and I hardly dare to pronounce it. To be loved! I have never been. I believe, though, that my mother loved me, – what do I say? I am sure of it, but it was a long time ago. My mother, – it is like a legend to me. It seems to me I was not born when I knew her. I remember that she often took me upon her knees and covered me with kisses. Such joys are not of this world; I must have tasted them in some distant star, where hearts are less hard than here, and where I lived some time, a sojourn of peace and innocence. But one day my mother dropped me from her arms, and I was thrown upon this earth where hatred expected me and received me in her bosom. Oh, hatred! I know her! This second mother cradled me in her arms, nourished me with her milk, lavished upon me her careful lessons and watched over me night and day. Ah! hatred is a marvelous providence. It sees everything, thinks of everything, notices everything, is omnipresent, always on the alert, unconscious of fatigue, ennui, or sleep. Hatred! she is the mistress of this castle, she governs it; these great corridors are full of her. I cannot take a step without meeting her; even here in this solitary room I see her image floating upon the paneling, upon the tapestry, about the curtains of this bed, and often at night in my sleep, she comes and sits upon my breast and peoples my dreams with specters and terrors. To be hated without knowing wherefore, – what torment! And remember, too, that in my early infancy, this father who hates me was then a father to me. He rarely caressed me and I feared him; he was imperious and severe; but he was a father after all, and occasionally he took the trouble to tell us so. Often in our presence his gravity relaxed, and I recollect that he sometimes smiled upon me. But one day, a cursed day, – I was then ten years old; my mother had been dead a month. – He was shut up in his room while a week passed, during which I did not see him. I said to my governess: 'I want to see my father.' I knocked at his door, entered, and ran to him. He repelled me with such violence that I fell and struck my head against the leg of a chair. I got up bleeding, and he looked at me with scorn, laughed, and left the room. My mind wandered, all my ideas were thrown into confusion; I thought the sun had gone out and that the world had come to an end. A father who could laugh at the sight of the blood gushing from his child! And what a laugh! He has made me hear it often since, but I have not been able to accustom myself to it yet. A fever attacked me, and I became delirious. They put me to bed, and I cried to those who took care of me: 'I am cold, I am cold, make me warm.' And in that icy body I felt a heart that seemed on fire, which consumed itself. I could have sworn that a red-hot iron had been passed into it."

Stephane dried his tears with a curl of his hair, and then, leaning with his elbows upon the table, he resumed in a feeble voice: "I do not want you to be deceived. You entertain friendship for me and you ask a return; that is very simple, friendship lives by exchange. If I had nothing to give you, you would soon cease to love me. Listen to me then. Yesterday, for the first time in my life, I went into myself, – a singular fancy, which you alone have been able to inspire in me; for the first time I examined myself seriously, I laid hold of my heart with both hands, and examined it as a physician does his patient; I carried my researches even to the very bottom, and I recognized there a strange barrenness and blight, which frightened me. It has been suffering a long time, – this poor heart; but within a year a fearful crisis has passed within me, which has killed it. And now there is nothing in this breast but a handful of ashes, good for nothing but to be thrown out of the window and scattered in the air.

"What! you are orthodox," said Gilbert, in a tone of authority; "you believe in the saints after your own fashion, and nevertheless you have yet to learn that death is but a word, or better, a respite, a pause in life, a fallow time followed by fresh harvests. You are ignorant of the fact, or you forget, that there are no ashes so cold but that when the wind of the spirit breathes upon them, they will be seen to start, rise up, and walk. You have left to me the care of teaching you that your soul is capable of rejuvenescence, of unexpected regeneration; that upon the sole condition that you wish and desire it, you will feel unknown powers awakened in your breast, and that without changing your nature, but by transforming yourself from day to day, you will become to yourself an eternal novelty!

Stephane looked at him, smiling.

"So you have crossed the roofs to come and preach conversion to me, like Father Alexis!"

"Conversion! I don't know. I don't undertake to work miracles; but the metamorphosis – "

"You speak to me much about my soul; but my life, my destiny, will you also find the secret of transforming them?"

"That secret we will seek together. I have already some light upon it. Only let us not press it. Before undertaking that great work, it is essential that your heart should recover its health and strength."

"Ingrate that I am!" cried Stephane. "My destiny! It has changed from to-day. Yes, from this moment I am no longer alone in the world. Frightful void in which I consumed myself, despair who with your frightful wings made it night for an abandoned child, it is all over now, I am delivered from you; the instrument of torture is broken. Henceforth, I believe, I hope, I breathe! But think of it, my friend, for me to live will be to see you, to hear you, to speak to you. Could you come here often?"

"As often as prudence will permit, – two or three times a week. We will choose our days well; we will consult the sky, the wind, the stars. On other days, at propitious hours, we will place ourselves at our windows, and communicate by signs which we will agree upon, for it seems that you, like me, are long-sighted. And besides, I know the sign language. I will teach it to you, and if you ever send me such a message as this upon your fingers: 'I am sad, I am sick, come this evening at any risk' – Well, whatever the winds and stars may say – "

"To expose your life foolishly!" interrupted Stephane, "I would rather die. Curses upon me if ever by a caprice – But away with such a thought! And how long, if you please, will this happiness, which you promise me, last? Some day, alas! retaking your liberty – "

"I have two, perhaps three years to pass here; it will even depend upon me whether I stay longer or not. Whatever happens, be assured, that before I leave this house, your destiny will have changed. I have told you to believe in the seen; believe also in the unforseen."

"The unforeseen!" exclaimed Stephane, "I believe in it, since I have seen it enter here by the window."

And suddenly carrying his hand to his heart, he closed his eyes, became pale, and uttered a piteous moan. Gilbert sprang towards him, but repulsing him gently:

"Fear nothing," said he; "joy has come, I feel it there, it burns me. Let me enjoy a suffering so new and so sweet." He remained some minutes with his eyes closed; then reopening them, and shaking his beautiful head with its long curls, he said sportively:

"Sit down there quick, and teach me the deaf mute language."

"Impossible," replied Gilbert; "the hour for going has already struck."

Stephane impatiently stamped his foot.

"Teach me at least the first two letters; if I don't know a and b, I shall not be able to close my eyes to-night."

Gilbert, taking him by the arm, led him to the window, where, drawing aside the curtain, he pointed out to him the stars already paling and a vague whiteness which appeared at the horizon. Then suddenly changing his tone, but still carried away by his impetuous nature, which stamped upon all the movements of his mind the character of passion, Stephane became much excited at the idea of the dangers which his friend was about to brave.

"I will go with you," said he, "I want to know what risks you run in coming here. To descend from the large roof to the small one, you must have had a ladder. I want to see this ladder, I want to assure myself that it is strong."

"Do not be afraid, I have attended to that."

"When I tell you that I wish to see it! I will believe only my own eyes and hands. Where is this ladder? I positively must see it."

"And I forbid you to climb this window. Take my word, my rope ladder is entirely new and very strong."

"Ah!" exclaimed Stephane, struck with a sudden idea. "I will bet that you have fastened it to that great iron corbel, which stretches its frightful beak up there at the angle of the wall. And just now you were suspended in space on this treacherous floating cord. Monstrous fool that I was not to understand it."

And to Gilbert's great astonishment, he added:

"You do not yet love me enough to have the right to run such risks."

"Do be a little calmer," said Gilbert. "You displayed just now a gentleness and wisdom which enchanted me. Take care; Ivan might wake and come up."

"These walls are deafened, the flagging is thick; between this room and the staircase there is an alcove, a vestibule, and two large closed doors; and between the rail of this staircase and the cage of my jailer, there is a long corridor. Besides, he is capable of everything but rambling at night round my apartment; but what matters it? – Let him come to surprise us, this hateful Ivan! I will resign myself to everything rather than see you put your feet upon that horrible ladder again. And take my word for it, if you violate my injunction, – at that very moment before your eyes, I will throw myself headlong down the precipice."

"You are extremely unreasonable," replied Gilbert, in a severe tone; "I must leave here at any cost. Since my ladder displeases you, instead of uttering a thousand follies, try rather to discover – "

Stephen struck his forehead.

"Here is my discovery," interrupted he; "opposite this window, on the other side of the roof, there is another, which, if you can only open it, will certainly let you into some empty lofts. Where these lofts will take you I don't exactly know, for Ivan told me once when he wanted to store some broken furniture there, that he had not been able to find the entrance; but you will no doubt discover some window near, by which you can get out upon the great roof, half-way from your turret, and so you will be spared a great deal of trouble and danger. Ah! if this proves so, how proud I shall be of finding it out."

"Now you are as I like to see you," said Gilbert; "instead of prancing like a badly-bitted horse, you are calm, and you reason."

"So to reward me you will permit me to accompany you."

"God forbid! and if you presume to go without my permission, I swear to you that I will never come here again."

And as Stephane resisted and chafed, Gilbert took his head between his hands, and drawing him to his breast, pressed a paternal kiss on his forehead, just at the roots of his hair. This kiss produced an extraordinary effect, which alarmed him; Stephane shuddered from head to foot, and a cry escaped him.

"Awkward fellow that I am," said Gilbert in an uneasy tone; "I have wounded you without intending it."

"No," murmured he, "it is of no consequence; but that was the place where my mother used to kiss me. May the saints be with you. I love you. Good-bye!"

And thus speaking he covered his face which was on fire, with both hands.

Ah! if Gilbert had understood! But he divined nothing; he descended to the roof, crossed it, and discovered as he groped about, a window, all the panes of which were broken; which saved him the trouble of opening it. When he found himself in the lofts, he lighted the candle which he had taken the precaution to bring in his pocket. The place which he had just entered was a wretched garret, three or four feet wide. In front of him he noticed four or five steps, ascended them, and opened an old door without any fastening. This let him into a vast corridor, which had no visible place of exit at the other end; it was infested by spiders and rats, and encumbered with dilapidated old furniture. Gilbert discovered, on raising his eyes, that he was in the mansard, lighted by the great dormer window. The bolt which held the shutter was so high up that he could not reach it with his hand. An old rickety table stood in the corner, buried under a triple coating of dust. Having reached the window by its aid, Gilbert drew the bolt; he mounted upon the roof and, supporting himself by one of the projecting timbers of the pediment, restored the shutter to its embrasure and fastened it as well as he could; after which he made his way once more towards the small roof; for, before returning to his lodging, it was necessary at any cost to detach and draw up the rope, an unimpeachable witness which would have testified against him. While Gilbert was extended at length, fully occupied in this delicate operation, Stephane, standing at his window and trembling like a leaf, was tearing his handkerchief with his beautiful teeth. The ladder withdrawn, Gilbert cried out to him:

"Your lofts are admirable. Hereafter, coming to see you will only be a pleasure trip."

When he found himself again upon his balcony, dawn began to break, and a screech owl, returning from his hunt after field mice, passed before him and regained his hole. Gilbert waved his hand to this nocturnal adventurer whose confrere he felt himself, and leaping lightly into his room, was sleeping profoundly in five minutes. At the same moment Stephane, raising his eyes to the holy images to which he had given such terrible blows, exclaimed with a passionate gesture: "Oh! St. George, St. Sergius, help me to keep my secret."

XV

Yesterday evening I returned to Stephane by the dormer window and the lofts; the journey took me but twenty minutes. There was a slight wind, and I was glad to have nothing to do with the iron corbel. Arriving at ten o'clock I returned half an hour after midnight. On leaving the young man, I felt terrified and overjoyed at the same time, – frightened at the impulsive ardor of his temperament and at the efforts it will cost me to moderate his impetuosity; but overjoyed, astonished at the quickness and grasp of his mind, at his vivid imagination, and the truly Slavonian flexibility of his naturally happy disposition. It is certain that the sad and barren existence he has led for years would have shattered the energies of a soul less finely tempered than his; the vigor and elasticity of his temperament have saved him. But I arrived just in time, for he confessed to me that the idea of suicide had taken possession of him since that unlucky escapade punished by fifteen hours' imprisonment.

"My first attempt was unfortunate," said he, "but I was resolved to try again; I had sounded the ford; another time I should have crossed the stream."

I hastened to turn the conversation, especially as he was not in the humor to weary himself with such a gloomy subject. How happy he appeared to see me again; how his joy expressed itself upon his ingenuous face, and how speaking were his looks! We occupied ourselves at first with the language of signs. Nothing escaped his eager intellect; he complained only of my slow explanations.

"I understand, I understand," he would cry; "something else, my dear sir, something else, I'm not a fool."

I certainly had no idea of such quickness of apprehension. "The Slavonians learn quickly," said I, "and forget quickly too."

To prove the contrary, he answered me by signs:

"You are an impertinent fellow."

I was confounded. Then all at once:

"Extraordinary man," said, he, with a gravity which made me smile, "tell me a little of your life."

"Extraordinary I am not at all," said I.

"And I affirm," answered he, "that humanity is composed of tyrants, valets, and a single and only Gilbert."

"Nonsense! Gilberts are abundant."

"There is but one, there is but one," cried he, with a fire and energy that enchanted me.

I must own I am not sorry that for the time being he looks upon me as an exceptional being; for it is well to keep him a little in awe of me. To satisfy him I gave him the history of my youth. This time he reproached me for being too brief, and not going enough into detail.

As his questions were inexhaustible, I said: "After today do not let us waste our time upon this subject. Besides, the top of the basket shows the best that's in it."

"There may perhaps be something to hide from me?"

"No; but I will confess that I do not like to talk about myself too much. I get tired of it very soon."

"What?" said he, in a tone of reproach, "are we not here to talk endlessly about you, me, us?"

"Certainly, and our favorite occupation will be to entertain ourselves with ourselves; but to render this pastime more delightful, it will be well for us to occupy ourselves sometimes with something else."

"With something else? With what?"

"With that which is not ourselves."

"And what do I care for anything which is neither you nor me?"

"But at all events you sometimes work, you read, you study?"

"At Martinique, Father Alexis gave me two or three hours of lessons every day. He taught me history, geography, and among other stuff of the same kind, the inconceivable merits and the superhuman perfections of his eternal Panselinos. The dissertations of this spiritual schoolmaster diverted me very little, as you may well suppose, and I was furious that in spite of myself his tiresome verbiage rooted itself in my memory, which is the most tenacious in the world."

"And did he continue his instructions to you?"

"After our return to Europe, my father ordered him to teach me nothing more but the catechism. He said it was the only study my silly brain was fit for."

"So for three years you have passed your days in absolute idleness."

"Not at all; I have always been occupied from morning till night."

"And how?"

"In sitting down, in getting up, in sitting down again, in pacing the length and breadth of my room, in gaping at the crows, in counting the squares of these flagstones, and the tiles of the little roof, in looking at the iron corbel and the water-spout on top of it, in watching the clouds sailing through the empty air, and then in lying down there in that recess of the wall, to rest quiet, with my eyes closed, ruminating over the problem of my destiny, asking myself what I could have done to God, that he chastised me so cruelly, recalling my past sufferings, enjoying in advance my sufferings to come, weeping and dreaming, dreaming and weeping, until overcome with lassitude and exhaustion I ended by falling asleep; or else, driven to desperation by weariness, I ran down to Ivan's lodging, and there gave vent to my scorn, fury, and despair, at the top of my lungs."

These words, pronounced in a tone breathing all the bitterness of his soul, troubled me deeply. I trembled to think of this desolate child, whose griefs were incessantly augmented by solitude and idleness, of that soul defenselessly abandoned to its gloomy reveries, of that poor heart maddened, and pouncing upon itself as upon a prey; self-devouring, constantly reopening his wounds and inflaming them, without work or study to divert him a single instant from his monotonous torment. Oh! Count Kostia, how refined is your hatred!

"I have an idea," I said at last. "You love flowers and painting. Paint an herbarium."

"What's that?"

"See this large paper. You will paint on it, in water colors, a collection of all the flowers of this region, of all those, at least, that you may find in your walks. If you don't know their names, I will teach them to you, or we will seek for them together."

"Provided that books take no part in it."

"We will dispense with them as much as possible. I will muster up all my knowledge to tell you the history of these pretty painted flowers; I will tell you of their families; I will teach you how to classify them; in short, will give you little by little, all I know of botany."

He made a hundred absurd objections, – among others, that he found in all the flowers of the fields and the woods in this country a creeping and servile air; then this, and then that, expressing himself in a sharp but sportive tone.

"I shall teach you botany, my wild young colt," I said to myself, "and not let you break loose."

I have not been able, however, to draw from him any positive promise.

July 14th.

Victory! By persistent hammering I have succeeded in beating the idea of the painted herbarium into this naughty, unruly head.

But he has imposed his conditions. He consents to paint only the flowers that I will gather myself, and bring to him. After some discussion I yielded the point.

"Ah!" said I, "take care to gather some yourself, for otherwise Ivan..."

Sunday, July 15th.

This afternoon I took a long walk in the woods. I had succeeded in gathering some labiates, the dead nettle, the pyramidal bell-flower and the wild thyme, when in the midst of my occupation, I heard the trot of a horse. It was he, a bunch of herbs and flowers in his hand. Ivan, who according to his custom, followed him at a distance of ten paces, regarded me some way off with an uneasy air; he evidently feared that I would accost them; but having arrived within a few steps of me, Stephane, turning his head, started his horse at full gallop, and Ivan, as he passed, smiled upon me with an expression of triumphant pity. Poor, simple Ivan, did you not hear our souls speak to each other?

July 16th.

Yesterday I carried my labiates to him. After some desultory talk, I endeavored to describe as best I could the characters of this interesting family. He listened to me out of complaisance. In time, he will listen to me out of curiosity, inasmuch as, to tell the truth, I am not a tiresome master; but I dare not yet interrogate him in a Socratic way. The SHORT LITTLE QUESTIONS would make our hot-headed young man angry. The lesson finished, he wished to commence his herbarium under my eyes. The honor of precedence has been awarded to the wild thyme; its little white, finely cut labias and the delicate appearance of the stem pleased him, whilst he found the dead nettle and the bell flower extremely common, and pronounced by him the word "extremely" is most expressive. While he made pencil sketches, I told him three stories, a fairy tale, an anecdote of Plutarch and some sketches of the life of St. Francis of Assisi. He listened to the fairy tale without uttering a word, and without a frown; but the other two stories made him shake his head several times.

"Is what you are telling me really true?" said he. "Would you wager your life upon it?" And when I came to speak of St. Francis embracing the lepers –

"Oh! now you're exaggerating." Then speaking to St. George: "Upon your conscience now, would you have done as much?"

He ended by becoming sportive and frolicsome. As he begged me to sing him a little song, I hummed Cadet Roussel, which he did not know; the "three hairs" made him laugh till the tears ran down his cheeks, but he paid dearly for this excess of gayety. When I rose to leave he was seized with a paroxysm of weeping, and I had much trouble in consoling him. I repent having excited him so much. I must humor his nerves, and never put him in that state of mind which contrasts too strongly with the realities of his life. At any cost I must prevent certain AWAKINGS.

July 19th.

I admire his conduct at the table. Seated opposite me, he never appears to see me, whilst you, grave Gilbert, do not know at times what to do with your eyes; but the other day he crossed the great hall with such a quick and elastic step that the Count's attention was drawn to him. I must caution him to be more discreet. I am also uneasy because in our nocturnal tete-a-tetes he often raises his voice, moves the furniture, and storms round the room; but he assures me there is nothing to fear. The walls are thick, and the foot of the staircase is separated from the corridor by a projection of masonry which would intercept the sound. Then the alcove, the vestibule, the two solid oak doors! These two doors are never locked. Ivan, he told me, is far from suspecting anything, and the only thing which could excite his distrust would be excessive precaution.

"And besides," added he, "by the mercy of God he is beginning to grow old, his mind is getting dull, and he is more credulous than formerly. So I have easily persuaded him that I will never forgive you, as long as I live, for the death of my dog. Then again, he is growing hard of hearing, and sleeps like a top. Sometimes to disturb his sleep, I amuse myself by imitating the bark of Vorace but I have the trouble of my pains. The only sound which he never fails to hear, is the ringing of my father's bell. I admit, however, that if anyone presumed to touch his great ugly oak door, he would wake up with a start. This is because his door is his property, his object, his fixed idea: he has a way of looking at it, which seems to say: 'you see this door? it is mine.' I believe, that in his eyes there is nothing lovelier in the world than a closed door. So he cherishes this horrible, this infamous door: he smiles on it benignly, he counts its nails and covers them with kisses."

"And you say that after nine o'clock he never comes up here?"

"Never, never. I should like to see him attempt it!" cried he, raising his head with an indignant air.

"You see then, that he is a jailer capable of behaving handsomely. I imagine that you do not like him much; but after all, in keeping you under lock and key, he is only obeying orders."

"And I tell you he is happy in making me suffer. The wicked man has done but one good action in his whole life, – that was in saving you from the fury of Vorace. In consideration of this good action, I no longer tell him what I think of him, but I think it none the less, and it seems to me very singular that you should ask me to love him."

"Excuse me, I do not ask you to love him, but to believe that, at heart, he loves you."

At these words he became so furious, that I hastened to change the subject.

"Don't you sometimes regret Vorace?"

"It was his duty to guard me against bugaboos, but I have had no fear of them, since one of them has become my friend.

"I am superstitious, I believe in ghosts; but I defy them to approach my bed hereafter."

He blushed and did not finish the sentence. Poor child! the painful misery of his destiny, far from quenching his imagination, has excited it to intoxication, and I am not surprised that he shapes friendship to the romantic turn of his thoughts.

"You're mistaken," I said to him, "it is not my image, it is botany which guards you against spirits. There is no better remedy for foolish terrors than the study of nature."

"Always the pedant," he exclaimed, throwing his cap in my face.

July 23rd.

Vladimir Paulitch appeared yesterday at the end of dinner. The presence of this man occasions me an indefinable uneasiness. His coldness freezes me, and then his dogmatic tone; his smile of mocking politeness. He always knows in advance what you are going to say to him, and listens to you out of politeness. This Vladimir has the ironical intolerance characteristic of materialists. As to his professional ability there can be no doubt. The Count has entirely recovered; he is better than I have ever seen him. What vigor, what activity of mind! What confounds me is, that in our discussions, I come to see in him, in about the course of an hour, only the historian, the superior mind, the scholar; I forget entirely the man of the iron boots, the somnambulist, the persecutor of my Stephane, and I yield myself unreservedly to the charm of his conversation. Oh, men of letters! men of letters!

July 27th.

He said to me:

"I do not possess happiness yet; but it seems to me at moments, that I see it, that I touch it."

July 28th.

To-day, Doctor Vladimir appeared again at dessert. He aimed a few sarcasms at me; I suspect that I do not please him much. Will his affection for the Count go so far as to make him jealous of the esteem which he evinces for me? We talked philosophy. He exerted himself to prove that everything is matter. I stung him to the quick in representing to him that all his arguments were found in d'Holbach. I endeavored to show him that matter itself is spiritual, that even the stones believe in spirit. Instead of answering, he beat about the bush. Otherwise, he spoke well, that is to say, he expressed his gross ideas with ingenuity. What he lacks most, is humor. He has something of the saturnine in his mind; his ideas have a leaden tint. The Count, prompted by good taste, saw that he held out too obstinately, without taking into account that Kostia Petrovitch himself detests the absolute as much in the negative as in the affirmative. He thanked me with a smile when I said to the doctor, in order to put an end to the discussion:

"Sir, no one could display more mind in denying its existence;" and the Count added, alluding to the doctor's meagerness of person:

"My dear Vladimir, if you deny the mind what will be left of you?"

July 30th.

Yesterday, to my great chagrin, I found him in tears.

"Let this inexorable father beat me," said he, "provided he tells me his secret. I prefer bad treatment to his silence. When we were at Martinique he had attacks of such violence that they made my hair stand on end. I would gladly have sunk into the earth; I trembled lest he should tear me in pieces; but he at least thought about me. He looked at me; I existed for him, and in spite of my terrors I felt less unhappy than now. Do not think it is my captivity which grieves me most. At my age it is certainly very hard and very humiliating to be kept out of sight and under lock and key; but I should be very easily resigned to that if it were my father who opened and closed the door. But alas! I am of so little consequence in his eyes that he deputes the task of tyrannizing over me to a serf. And then, during the brief moments when he constrains himself to submit to my presence – what a severe aspect, what threatening brows, what grim silence! Consider, too, the fact that he has never entered this tower; no, has never had the curiosity to know how my prison was made. Yet he cannot be ignorant of the fact that I lodge above a precipice. He knows, too, that once the idea of suicide took possession of me, and he has not even thought of having this window barred."

"That is because he did not consider your attempt a serious one."

"Then how he despises me!"

I represented to him that his father was sick, that he was the victim of a nervous disorder which deranges the most robust organizations, that Doctor Vladimir guaranteed his cure, that once recovered, his temper would change, and that then would be the moment to besiege this citadel thus rendered more vulnerable.

"We must not, however, be precipitate," said I, "let us have courage and patience."

I reasoned so well that he finally overcame his despondency. When I see him yield to my reasoning, I have a strong impulse to embrace him; but it is a pleasure I deny myself, as I know by experience what it costs him. A moment afterwards, I don't know why, he spoke to me of his sister who died at Martinique.

"Why did God take her from me?"

"Alas!" said I, "she could not have supported the life to which you have been condemned."

"And why not, pray?"

"Because she would have suffered ten times as much as you. Think of it, – the nerves and heart of a woman!"

He looked at me with a singular expression; apparently he could not understand how anyone could suffer more than he. After this he talked a long time about women, who are to him, from what he said, an impenetrable mystery, and he repeated eagerly:

"You do not despise them, as HE does?"

"That would be impossible, I remember my mother."

"Is that your only reason?"

"Some day I will tell you the others."

As I left and was already nearly out of the window, he seized me impetuously by the arm, saying to me:

"Could you swear to me that you would be less happy if you

did not know me?"

"I swear it."

His face brightened, and his eyes flashed.

August 8th.

And you too are transformed, my dear Gilbert; you have visibly rejuvenated. A new spirit has taken possession of you. Your blood circulates more quickly; you carry your head more proudly, your step is more elastic, there is more light in your eyes, more breath in your lungs, and you feel a celestial leaven fermenting in your heart. My old friend, you have emerged from your long uselessness to give birth to a soul! Oh, glorious task! God bless mother and daughter!

August 9th.

Stephane is painfully astonished at the friendship which his father displays towards me.

"He has the power of loving then, and does not love me? It is because I am destestable!"

Poor innocent! It is certain that in spite of himself, the Count has begun to like me. Good Father Alexis said to me the other evening:

"You are a clever man, my son; you have cast a spell upon Kostia Petrovitch, and he entertains an affection for you, which he has never before manifested for anyone."

August 11th.

His painted herbarium is enriched every day. He already enumerates twenty species and five families. Yesterday Stephane so far forgot himself as to look at it with an air of satisfied pride. How happy I was! I kept my joy to myself, however. He further delighted me by deciding to write from memory at the bottom of each page the French and Latin names for each plant. "It is a concession I have made to the pedant," said he; but this did not prevent him from being proud of having written these forty names without a mistake. Last time I carried to him some crowsfeet and anemones. He took the little celandine in his hand, crying:

"Let me have it; I am going to tell you the history of this little yellow fellow."

And he then gave me all the characteristics with marvelous accuracy. What a quick and luminous intellect, and what overflowing humor! His hands trembled so much that I said to him:

"Keep cool, keep cool. It requires a firm and steady hand to raise the veil of Isis."

I contented myself with explaining in a few words who Isis was, which interested him but moderately. His masterpiece, as a faithful reproduction of nature, is his marsh ranunculus, which I had introduced to him under the Latin name of ranuncula scelerata. He has so exquisitely represented these insignificant little yellow flowers that it is impossible not to fall in love with them.

"This little prisoner has inspired me," said he. "By dint of practicing Father Alexis, I begin to wish good to the rascals."

I rebuked him sharply, but he was not much affected by my rating.

August 13th.

The Count's conduct is atrocious, and yet I understand it. His pride, his whole character, despotic; the horror of having been deceived.... And besides, is he really Stephane's father? ... These two children born after six years of marriage, and a few years later to discover.... Suspicions often have less foundation. And then this fatal resemblance which keeps the image of the faithless one constantly before his eyes! The more decided the resemblance, the greater must be his hatred. Even his smile, that strange smile which belongs to him alone, Stephane according to Father Alexis, must have inherited from his mother. "I HAVE BURIED THE SMILE!" Frightful cry which I can hear still! Finally, I believe that in the barbarous hatred of this father there is more of instinct than of system. It lives from day to day. I am sure that Count Kostia has never asked himself: "What shall I do with my son when he is twenty?"

August 14th.

Ivan, of whom I asked news of Stephane, said to me:

"Do not be uneasy about him any more. He has become much better within the past month, and he grows more gentle from day to day; this is the result of seeing death so near."

M. Leminof greatly astonished me this morning.

"My dear Gilbert," said he unreservedly, "I do not claim that I am a perfect man; but I am certainly what might be called a good sort of fellow, and I possess, in the bargain, a certain delicacy of conscience which sometimes inconveniences me. Without flattery, you are, my dear Gilbert, a man of great merit. Very well! I am using you unjustly, for you are at an age when a man makes a name and a career for himself; and these decisive years you are spending in working for me, in collecting, like a journeyman, the materials of a great work which will bring neither glory nor profit to you. I have a proposition to make to you. Be my coadjutor; we will compose this monumental work together; it shall appear under our two names, and I give you my head upon it, shall make you famous. We agree upon nearly all questions of fact, and as to our difference in ideas. . . Mon Dieu! we are neither of us born quibblers; we shall end in agreeing, and even supposing we do not agree, I will give you carte blanche; for, to speak frankly, an idea is not just the thing I should be ready to die for. What say you to it, my dear Gilbert? We will not part until the task is finished, and I fancy that we shall lead a happy life together."

In spite of his persuasions, I have not consented; he has only drawn from me a promise that I will give him an answer within a month. Stephane, Stephane, how awkward I shall be, if I do not make this happy incident instrumental in accomplishing your deliverance! The day will come when I can say to your father: For the sake of your health, for the sake of your repose, of your studies, of the work we have undertaken together, send this child away from your house; his presence troubles and irritates you. Send him to some school or college. By a single act you will make two persons happy. Gracious Heaven, the stronghold will be hard to take! But by dint of patience, skill and vigilance . . . have I not already carried a fortress by storm – Stephane's heart? No, I do not despair of success. But it will cost me dear, this success that I hope for! To see him leave this house, to be separated from him forever! At the very thought my heart bleeds.

August 16th.

Doctor Vladimir will leave us during the early part of next month. I shall not be sorry. Decidedly this man does not please me. The other day at the table, he looked at Stephane in a way that alarmed me.

August 18th.

The sky is propitious for my nocturnal excursions. Not a drop of rain has fallen for six weeks. The north wind, which sometimes blows violently in the daytime, abates regularly in the evening. As to the vertigo, no return of it. Oh! the power of habit!

August 19th.

What a misfortune! Day before yesterday Stephane, in crossing a vestibule in front of the great hall, impelled by some odd motive, gave vent to a loud burst of laughter. The Count started from his chair and his face became livid. To-day Soliman was sold. A horse dealer is coming directly to take him away. Ivan, whom I just met, had great tears in his eyes. Poor Stephane, what will he say?

August 20th.

It is very singular! Yesterday I expected to find him in a state of despair. He was gay, smiling.

"I was sure," said he, "that I should pay dearly for that unlucky burst of laughter.

"My father is mistaken; it was not a burst of gayety, but purely nervous spasm which seized me while thinking of certain things, and at a moment when I was not at all merry. However, besides life, there were but two things left to take from me, my horse and my hair, and thank God, he was not happily inspired in his choice, and has not struck me in the most sensitive place."

"What! between Soliman and your hair."

"Isn't it beautiful?" said he quickly.

"Magnificent without any doubt!" I answered, smiling.

"I've always been a little vain of it," continued he, waving his curls upon his shoulders; "but I value it more since I know it pleases you."

"Oh! for that matter," I replied, "if you had your head shaved, I should not love you any the less."

This answer, I don't know why, seemed to affect him deeply. During the rest of the evening he was thoughtful and gloomy.

August 24th.

I thought it glorious to be able to communicate to him the overtures which his father has made me, and the project they suggested to me. I said to him:

"What a joy it would be to me to release you from this prison, and yet with what bitter sadness this joy would be mingled! But wherever you go, we will find some means of writing and of seeing each other. The friendship between us is one of those bonds which destiny cannot break."

"Oh, yes!" replied he in a sarcastic tone, "you will come to see me once a year, upon my birthday, and will be careful to bring me a bouquet."

He burst into a fit of laughter which much resembled that of the other day.

August 30th.

How he made me suffer yesterday! I have not recovered from it yet. What! was it he – was it to me? God! what bitterness of language; what keen irony! Count Kostia, you make a mistake – this child is really yours. He may have the features and smile of his mother, but there is a little of your soul in his. What grievances can he have against me? I can imagine but two. Sunday last, near three o'clock, we were both at the window. He commenced a very animated speech by signs, and prolonged it far beyond the prudential limits which I have prescribed to him. He spoke, I believe, about Soliman, and of a walk which he had refused to take with Ivan. I did not pay close attention, for I was occupied in looking round to see that no one was watching us. Suddenly I saw on the slope of the hill big Fritz and the little goat girl, to whom he is paying court, seated on a rock. At the moment I was about to answer Stephane, they raised their eyes to me. I began then to look at the landscape, and presently quitted the spot. Stephane could not see them from his window, and of course did not understand the cause of my retreat. The other grievance is, that for the first time three days have passed without my paying him a visit; but day before yesterday the wind was so violent that it overthrew a chimney nearby, . . . and it was to punish me for such a grave offense that he allowed himself to say that I was no doubt an excellent botanist, an unparalleled philanthropist, but that I understood nothing of the refinements of sentiment.

"You are one of those men," said he, "who carry the whole world in their hearts. It is useless for you to deny it. I am sure you have at least a hundred intimate friends."

"You are right," I replied; "it is even for the hundredth one that I have risked my life."

September 7th.

During the last week, I have seen him three times. He has given me no cause for complaint; he works, he reflects; his judgment is forming, not a moment of ill-humor; he is calm, docile, and gentle as a lamb. Yes, but it is this excess of gentleness which disturbs me. There is something unnatural to me, in his condition, and I am forced to regret the absence of those transports, and the childishness of which I have endeavored to cure him. "Stephane, you have become too unlike yourself. But a short time since, your feet hardly touched the ground; lively, impetuous, and violent, there came from your lips by turns flashes of merriment or of anger, and in an instant you passed from enthusiasm to despair; but in our recent interviews I could scarcely recognize you. No more freaks of the rebellious child; no more of those familiarities which I loved! Your glances, even, as they meet mine, seem less assured; sometimes they wander over me doubtfully, and from the surprise they express, I am inclined to believe that my figure must have grown some cubits, and you can no longer take it in at a glance. And then those sighs which escape you! Besides, you no longer complain of anything; your existence seems to have become a stranger to you. It must be that without my knowledge – " Ah! unhappy child, I will know. You shall speak; you shall tell me. . . .

September 10.

Heavens! what a flood of light! Father Alexis, you did not tell me all! The more I think of it. . . . Ah! Gilbert, what scales covered your eyes! Yesterday I carried him that copy of the poem of the Metamorphoses, which I had promised him. A few fragments that I had repeated to him had inspired him with the desire of reading the whole piece, not from the book, but copied in my hand. We read it together, distich by distich. I translated, explained, and commented. When we arrived at these verses: "May you only remember how the tie which first united our souls was a germ from which grew in time a sweet and charming intimacy, and soon friendship revealed its power in our hearts, until love, coming last, crowned it with flowers and with fruit – " At these words he became agitated and trembled violently.

"Do not let us go any further," said he, pushing the paper away. "That is poetry enough for this evening."

Then leaning upon the table, he opened and turned the leaves of his herbarium; but his eyes and his thoughts were elsewhere. Suddenly he rose, took a few steps in the room, and then returning to me:

"Do you think that friendship can change into love?"

"Goethe says so; we must believe it."

He took a flower from the table, looked at it a moment and dropping it on the floor, he murmured, lowering his eyes:

"I am an ignoramus; tell me what is this love?"

"It is the folly of friendship."

"Have you ever been foolish?"

"No, and I do not imagine I ever shall be."

He remained motionless for a moment, his arms hanging listlessly; at length, raising them slowly, he crossed his hands over his head, one of his favorite attitudes, raised his eyes from the ground, and looked steadily at me. Oh! what a strange expression! His wild look, a sad and mysterious smile wandering over his lips, his mouth which tried to speak, but to which speech refused to come! That face has been constantly before me since last night; it pursues me, possesses me, and even at this moment its image is stamped in the paper I am writing on. This black velvet tunic, then, may be a forced disguise? Yes, the character of Stephane, his mind, his singularity of conduct, – all these things which astonished and frightened me are now explained. Gilbert, Gilbert! what have you done? into what abyss. . . And yet, perhaps I am mistaken, for how can I believe – There is the dinner bell. . . I shall see HIM again!

XVI

Some hours later, Gilbert entered Stephane's room, and struck by his pallor and with the troubled expression of his voice, inquired about him anxiously.

"I assure you I am very well," Stephane replied, mastering his emotion. "Have you brought me any flowers?"

"No, I have had no time to go for them."

"That is to say, you have not had time to think of me."

"Oh! I beg your pardon! I can think of you while working, while reading Greek, even while sleeping. And last night I saw you in my dreams: you treated me as a pedant, and threw your cap in my face."

"That was a very extravagant dream."

"I am not so sure about that. It seems to me that one day – "

"Yes, one day, two centuries ago."

"Is it then so long since our acquaintance commenced?"

"Perhaps not two centuries, but nearly. As for me, I have already lived three lives: my first I passed with my mother. The second – let us not speak of that. The third began upon the night when, for the first time, you climbed into this window. And that must have been a long time ago, if I can judge of it by all which has passed since then, in my soul, in my imagination, and in my mind. Is it possible that these two centuries have only been two months? How can it be that such great changes have been wrought in me, in so short a time, for they are so marvelous that I can hardly recognize myself?"

"One of these changes, of which I am proud, is that you no longer throw your cap at my head."

"That was a liberty I took only with the pedant."

"And are you at last reconciled to him?"

"I have discovered that the pedant does not exist. There is a hero and a philosopher in you."

"That is a discovery I did not expect from you, and one that astonishes as much as it flatters me."

"When I tell you that I am changed throughout, and that I no longer recognize myself – "

"And I, in spite of your transformation, recognize you very easily. My dear Stephane has preserved his habit of exaggerating all his impressions. Once I was a man who ought to be smothered; now I am an extraordinary being who passes his life in executing heroic projects. No, my poet, I am neither a scoundrel nor a knight errant, and the best that can be said of me is that I am not a blockhead, that I do not lack heart, and that I run over the roofs with remarkable agility."

"No, I exaggerate nothing," he said. "I speak of things as they are, and the proof that you are an extraordinary man is, that in all you do, you appear perfectly simple and natural."

And as Gilbert shrugged his shoulders and smiled:

"Ah! you need not laugh!" he continued. "Feel my pulse, you will see I have no fever. And have you not noticed how calm I have been for several days?"

I confess that your quietness surprises me; but is it really a calm? I suspect that you have only covered the brazier, and that the fire smoulders under the ashes."

"And you stir up the ashes to draw out the sparks. As you please, but I forewarn you, that you will not succeed, and that I shall remain insensible to all your efforts."

"So for a week, you have felt more tranquil in heart and mind?"

"Yes, and I have a good reason for it. There was a great fomenter of seditions in me, a great stirrer up of rebellion. It was my pride."

Stephane hid his face in his hands; then after a long silence:

"No," said he, "I have not the courage to speak yet. Besides, before making my revelation, which you will perhaps consider extravagant, I want to prove to you more thoroughly that my senses have been restored, and that I have become wise in your school. Know then, that before I became acquainted with you, religion was in my eyes, but a coarse magic in which I believed with passionate irrationality. I considered prayer as a kind of sorcery, and attributed to it the power of compelling the divine will; every day I called upon Heaven to perform a miracle in my favor, and, finding myself refused, my ungranted prayers fell back like lead upon my heart. Then I rebelled against the celestial intelligences which refused to yield to my enchantments, or else I sought in anguish to ascertain to what error in form, to what neglected precaution, to what sin of omission I could attribute the impotence of my operations in magic and my formulas.

"And now am I nothing but a charmed dreamer, a half-crazy child, a sick brain feeding on crochets, an incorrigible, wrong-headed fellow? No, you admit that I have profited by your lessons; that a grain of wisdom has fallen into my brain, and that without having seen the bottom of things, I have at least lucid intervals. If this be so, my Gilbert, believe what I am going to say as you would the Holy Bible. You have worked with all your strength to cure my soul, and there is not a more skillful physician in the world than you. But all of your trouble would have been lost, if you had not had by your side an all-powerful ally, whom you don't know, and whom I am about to reveal to you. Ah! tell me, when you came into this room the first time, did you not feel that a celestial spirit followed in your track and entered with you? You went, he remained, and has not left me, and never will. Look, do not these walls speak of him? Do not these saints move their lips to murmur his name to you? And the air we breathe here, is it not full of those delicious perfumes which these envoys of Heaven scatter in their earthward journeys? How strange this spirit appeared to me at first! His face was all unknown to me, it had never appeared to me in my dreams. Startled and bewildered, I said to him: Who then art thou? What is thy name? And, one day, Gilbert, one day, it was through your mouth that he answered me. Gilbert, Gilbert, oh! what a singular company you have introduced to me in his person. Sometimes he seated himself near me, pale, melancholy, clothed in mourning, and breathed into my heart a venomous bitterness, such as I had never dreamed of. And feeling myself seized with an inexpressible desire to die; I cried out 'I know you, you must be the brother of death!' But all at once transforming himself, he appeared to me holding a fool's cap in his hand. He shook the bells and sang to me songs which filled my ears with feverish murmurings. My head turned, smoke floated before me, my dazzled eyes were intoxicated with visions, and it seemed to me, poor child, nourished with gall and tears, that life was an eternal fete, upon which Heaven looked down smiling. Then I said to the spirit: 'Now I know you better, you are the brother of folly.' But he changed himself again, and suddenly I saw him standing erect before me folded in the long white wings of the seraphim; at once serious and gentle, divine reason shone in his deep eyes and the serenity on his brow announced an inhabitant of Heaven. In these moments, my Gilbert, his voice was more penetrating and more persuasive than yours; he repeated your words and gave me strength to believe in them; he engraved your lessons on my mind; he instilled your wisdom into my folly, your soul in my soul; and know that if the lily has drunk the juices of the earth, if the lily has grown, if the lily should blossom one day, it shall not be from the impotent sun rays which you brought to me in your breast, to which thanks must be rendered; but to him, the celestial spirit, to him who lighted in my heart a divine flame with which, may it please God that yours too may be illuminated!" And rising at these words, he almost gasped: "Have I said enough? Do you understand me at last?"

"No!" answered Gilbert resolutely, "I do not understand this celestial spirit at all."

Stephane writhed his arms.

"Cruel! you do not wish then to divine anything!" murmured he distractedly. And going to the window, he stood some moments leaning against it. When he turned towards Gilbert, his eyes were wet with tears; but by one of those rapid changes which were familiar to him, he had a smile upon his lips, "What I dare not say to you, I have just now written," resumed he, drawing a letter from his bosom.

"It was a last resort which I hoped you would not force me to call to my aid. Oh! hard heart! to what humiliations have you not abased my pride!" He presented the letter, but changing his mind, he said:

"I wish to add a few words to it."

And ran and seated himself at the table. His pen had fallen on the floor, and not being able to find it, he quickly sharpened a pencil with a keen-edged poniard which he drew from the depths of a drawer.

"What a singular penknife you have there," said Gilbert, approaching him.

"It is a Russian stiletto of Toula manufacture. It belongs to Ivan, he lent it to me day before yesterday, when we were out walking, to uproot a plant with. He has forgotten to take it back."

"You will oblige me by returning it to him," answered Gilbert; "it is a plaything I don't like to see in your hands."

Stephane gave a sign of assent, and bent over the paper. The letter which he had written was as follows:

"My Gilbert, listen to a story. I was eleven years old when MY BROTHER STEPHANE died. Scarcely was he buried when my father called me to him. He held in his hand a suit of clothes like these I wear now, and he said to me: 'Stephane, understand me clearly. It was my daughter that just died, my son lives still.' And as I persisted in not understanding him, he had a coffin brought in, placed on a table and he laid me in it; and closing the cover by degrees, he said, 'My daughter, are you dead?' When it was entirely closed, I decided to speak, and I cried out, 'Father, your daughter is dead. It shall be as you desire.' Then he drew me out of the coffin half dead with fear and horror, and exclaimed, 'Stephane, remember that my daughter is dead. Should you ever happen to forget it' . . . He said no more, but his eyes finished the sentence. Gilbert, at this moment the daughter of my father comes back to life to tell you that she loves you with an unconquerable love which she can no longer conceal. In my simplicity, I thought at first that I loved you as you loved me; but you yourself have taken care to undeceive me. One day you spoke of our approaching separation, and you said to me: 'We shall see each other sometimes!' And you did not hear the cry of my heart which answered you; to pass a day without seeing you! What a hell!

"When I had fairly comprehended that your friendship was a devotion, a virtue, a wisdom, and that mine was a folly, then the daughter of my father thought of dying, so bitter were the torments which her rebellious pride inflicted upon her. Ah! what would I not have given, my Gilbert, if divining who I was, you had fallen at my feet crying: 'I too know how to love madly!'

"But no; you have understood nothing, suspected nothing. My hair, the resemblance to my mother imprinted on my face, the smile, which they tell me, passed from her lips to mine. . . . Oh! blindest of men! how I have hated you at moments! But it does not really seem that a fatality pursues me? That hand with its iron grip fastened on my shoulder, and forcing me to prostrate myself before you, I feel no longer, with its nails pressing into my flesh; and yet my knees, trembling, powerless, bend under me, and again you see me fall at your feet. Yes, my poor pride is dead indeed. The thunder growled when it gave up its last breath. You remember that stormy night. Glued at the window pane, I tried to pierce the darkness with my eyes, to discern you in the midst of the tempest. All at once the heavens were ablaze, and I saw you standing upon the ledge of your window, bending proudly over the abyss, at which you seemed to hurl defiance. Enveloped in flashing light, you appeared to me like a blissful spirit, and I exclaimed to myself: 'This is one of the elect of God! I can ask of him without shame for indulgence and mercy!' And now, my Gilbert, do not presume to tell me that my love is a malady, which needs only careful attention. Oh, God! all that would be useless; the saints themselves have refused to cure me. Do not try to terrify me, either, or speak to me of insurmountable obstacles to our union; of dangers which threaten us. The future! We will talk of that hereafter. Now, I want to know but one thing; that is, if you are capable of loving me as I love you? Friend, if hatred can change to love, would it be impossible for friendship? . . . Gilbert, Gilbert, forget what the refined barbarity of my father has made of me; forget my gusts of passion, my violence, the unruliness of a badly educated child; forget the vehemence of my language, the rudeness of my actions; forget the fountain; my whip raised to you; forget those young villagers I compelled to kiss my feet; forget even the cap which I threw in your face, for, Heaven is my witness, I feel a woman's heart awakened in my bosom; it shakes off its long sleep, it stirs, it sighs, it speaks, and the first name it utters, the only one it ever wants to know, is yours! . . .

"What more shall I say? I would like to appear to you in your dreams decked as if for a fete: clothed in white, a smile upon my lips, pearls about my neck, around my head the flowers you love – white anemones and blue gentians. Only take care, some of the henbane flowers have slipped into my crown. Tear them from my hair yourself, lest their perfume instill a deadly poison into my heart. But no, I do not wish to frighten you. Stephane is wise; she is reasonable; she does not ask the impossible; she gives you time to breathe; to recover yourself. Wait, if you wish it, a week, a fortnight, a month, before coming here again; until that blessed day dawns when you can say with your adored poet; 'In its turn, friendship revealed its power to my heart, and at length love, coming last, crowned it with flowers and fruit.'"

To this letter Stephane added these words: "And if that day, Gilbert, if that day should never come – "

But here she hesitated; her hand trembled; she looked alternately at Gilbert and the knife; then rising –

"I do not know how to finish my letter," she said. "You can easily supply what is lacking. But you must not read it here; carry it to your turret; you will meditate upon it there more at leisure."

And at these words, having returned the paper to him, she burst into a fit of laughter.

"Again that same laugh, which I detest," said Gilbert, trying to hide the anguish which was consuming him.

"Do you want to know what it means?" said the young girl, looking him in the face. "When we were at Baden-Baden, three years ago, Father Alexis had a fancy to take me to a gambling house, and in entering I heard a burst of laughter much resembling those which shock you so. 'Who is laughing in that way?' said I to the good father. He found on inquiring that it was a man who had just gained enormous sums, and who was preparing to play double or quits.

"Double or quits!" added she; "to play double or quits! If I should lose – "

All at once her eyes dilated, and shot fire; she turned her head backward, and raising her arm towards Gilbert, she exclaimed:

"You know who I am, and you have condemned me in your heart. Ah! think twice; you have my life in your hands." And recoiling a few steps she suddenly turned, fled across the room, threw open a small side-door, and disappeared.

How did Gilbert manage to reach his turret?

All he knows himself is, that on coming out of the dormer window, beside himself, forgetting all idea of danger, he committed, for the first time, the signal imprudence of walking erectly over the roof, which ordinarily he found difficult to cross even in crawling; seeing and hearing nothing, entirely absorbed in a single thought, he started forward at a quick pace. From his gait and carriage, the moon, which shone brightly in the sky, must have taken him for a madman, or a somnambulist. He reached the end of the roof, when a broken slate slipped under his feet. He lost his balance, fell heavily, and it would have been all over with him, if, in falling, his hand had not by a miracle encountered the trailing end of his ladder, by which he had strength enough to hold himself. Slates are brittle, and when hurled against a hard substance break in a thousand pieces. The one which Gilbert had just precipitated into space met a point of rock which scattered it into fragments, one of which struck, without wounding, the hand of a man who happened to be rambling on the border of the ravine.

As fate would have it, this evening M. Leminof had an important letter to forward by the mail; and near nine o'clock, contrary to all the usages and customs of his house, he had sent Fritz to a large town about a league distant, where the courier passed during the night. Unluckily, upon his return, Fritz saw a light shining in the cottage of his Dulcinea. Appetite, the opportunity, some devil also urging him, he left the road, walked straight to the cabin, opened the door, which was only closed by a latch, entered with stealthy tread, and surprised his beauty seated upon a stool and mending her linen. He drew near her, said gallant things to her, and soon began to take liberties. The damsel, frolicsome and forward, instead of awakening her father, who slept in the neighboring room, rushed to the door, darted out and gained upon a run the serpentine path which ran along the edge of the ravine. A hundred times more active than Fritz, she kept in advance of him; then halted, called him, and the moment when he thought he was going to seize her, she escaped and ran on faster. She continued this game until becoming weary she hid herself behind a bush, and laughing in her sleeve, saw the amorous giant pass her, continue to ascend, reeking with sweat, slipping frequently, and constantly fearing he would fall down the precipice.

At length, by dint of scrambling, he arrived at the place where the path ended at the perpendicular fall of the precipice, a height of forty feet. By what means had his fantastic princess scaled this wall? All at once he heard a silvery voice which called him below. In his rage he struck his forehead with his fist; but at the moment he was about to descend, a singular noise struck his ear – a piece of slate grazed his hand and drew from him an exclamation of surprise. Raising his head quickly, and favored by the light of the moon, he saw upon his right a shadow suspended in the air. It mounted, stopped upon the ledge of a window, stooped down and soon disappeared.

"Oh! oh!" said he, much astonished, "here's something odd! Monsieur secretary goes out at night, then, to make the rounds of the roofs? And for this we have provided ourselves with rope ladders. I am much mistaken if his Excellency, the Count, will relish this little amusement. Peste, the jolly fellow has a good foot and a good eye. There must be a great deal to gain to risk his skin this way. Faith! these demure faces are not to be trusted."

The great Fritz was so stupefied with his discovery that he seated himself a moment upon a stone to collect his thoughts. The fine idea which his thick skull brought forth was that the secretary belonged to the illustrious brotherhood of ambidexters, and that his nocturnal circuits had for their object the search for hidden treasure. Proud of his sagacity, and delighted with the opportunity to satisfy his resentment, he descended the path, not without trouble, and deaf to the voice and the laughter of his enchantress, who challenged him to new trials, he regained the road and strode on to the castle.

"Oh! then, Mr. Secretary," said the knave to himself with a wicked smile, "you threw me down a staircase, and thought you'd get me turned out of doors. What will you say if I make you go out by the window?"

XVII

The next day – it was the second Sunday of September – Gilbert went out at about ten o'clock in the morning, and directed his steps to a wild and solitary retreat. It was a narrow glade upon the borders of a little pond dried up by the summer heat, near which he had often gathered plants for Stephane. Among groups of trees which straggled up on all sides, under a patch of blue sky, a ground of blackish clay, cracked and creviced, herbage, dried rushes; here and there some patches of stagnant water, the surface of which was rippled by the gambols of the aquatic spider; further on a large tuft of long-plumed reeds, which shivered at the least breath and rocked upon their trembling stems drowsy red butterflies and pensive dragonflies; upon the steep banks of the pond, sad flowers, pond weed, the marsh clover, the sand plantain; in a corner, a willow with roots laid bare, which hung over the exhausted pool as if looking for its lost reflection; around about, nettles, briars, dry heather, furze, stripped of its blossoms; that damp and heavy atmosphere which is natural to humid places; the light of day thinly veiled by the exhalations from the earth; an odor of decaying plants, long silence interrupted by dull sounds; an air of abandonment, of idleness, of lassitude, the melancholy languor of a life departing regretfully; the recollection of something which was, and will never reappear, never! Such was the word which this wild solitude murmured to Gilbert's ear. Never! repeated he to himself, and his heart was oppressed by a sense of the irretrievable. He seated himself upon the sward, a few steps from the willow, his elbows upon his knees, and his head in his hands, and lost himself in long and painful meditation. I shall tell all; he felt at intervals in the depths of his being, in the very depths, the agitation of a secret joy which he dared not confess to himself; but it was a passing movement of his soul which he did not succeed in defining in the midst of the whirlwind which shook him. And then, in such a moment, he thought but little of asking himself what he could or could not feel. His mind was elsewhere. Sometimes he sought to picture to himself all the successive phases of this unhappy existence, of which, henceforth, he held the key; sometimes he felt a tender admiration for the energy and elasticity of this young soul which unparalleled misfortunes had not been able to crush. And now to abandon him, to break such close and sweet ties, was it not to condemn him to despair, to deliver him up a victim to the violence of his passions rendered more violent by unhappiness? Ought he not at least to attempt to draw from his impulsive heart this fatal arrow, this baleful love which to his eyes was a danger, an extravagance, a calamity? And from reflection to reflection, from anxiety to anxiety, he always returned to deplore his own blindness. The eccentricities of Stephane's conduct, certain salient points in his character, the passionate ABANDON of his language; his face, his hair, his glances, the charm of his smile; how was it that so many of his indications had escaped him? And this want of penetration which resulted from the rather unromantic character of his mind, he attributed to bluntness of sensibility and charged himself with it as a crime. He was profoundly absorbed in his reverie when the cry of a raven aroused him. He opened his eyes, and when he had lost sight of the croaking bird, which crossed the glade in rapid flight, he looked for a moment at a handsome variegated butterfly which fluttered about the willow; then noticing in the grass, within reach of his hand, a pretty little marsh flower, he drew it carefully from the soil with its root and set about its examination with an attentive eye. He admired the purple tint of its pistil and the gold of its stamens, which contrasted charmingly with the brilliant whiteness of the petals, and said unconsciously: "There is a lovely flower which I have not yet shown to my Stephane: I must carry it to him."

But instantly recollecting himself, and throwing away the innocent flower spitefully, he exclaimed:

"Oh, fortune, what singular games you play!"

"Yes, fortune is singular!" answered a voice which was not unknown to him; and before he had time to turn, Dr. Vladimir was seated beside him.

Vladimir Paulitch had employed his morning well. Scarcely out of bed, he had given a private audience to Fritz, who, not daring to address his master directly, for his frowns always made him tremble, had come to ask the doctor to receive his revelations and obligingly transmit them to his Excellency. When in an excited and mysterious tone he had disclosed his important secret:

"There is nothing astonishing in that," replied Vladimir

coldly ."This young man is a somnambulist, and the conclusion of your little story is, that his window must be barred. I will speak to Count Kostia about it."

Upon which Fritz slunk away discomfited and much confused at the turn the adventure had taken.

After his departure, Vladimir Paulitch concluded to take a walk upon the grassy hillock, and on his way said to himself: "Have my suspicions, then, been well founded?"

He had passed an hour among the rocks, studying the spot, examining the aspect of the castle from this side, and particularly the irregularities of the roof. As his eyes rested on the square tower which Stephane occupied, he saw him appear at the window, and remain there some minutes, his eyes fixed upon Gilbert's turret.

"Aha! Now we see how matters stand!" said he, "but to risk his head in this way, our idealist must be desperately in love. And he'll carry it through! We must find him and have a little chat."

In reascending to the castle, Vladimir had seen Gilbert turn into the woods, and without being perceived, had followed him at a distance.

"Yes, fortune is singular!" repeated he, "and we must resist it boldly and brave it resolutely, or submit humbly to its caprices and die. This is but reasonable; half measures are expedients of fools. As for me, I have always been the partisan of sequere Deum, which I interpret thus: 'Take luck for your guide, and walk on blindly.'"

And as Gilbert made no answer, he continued:

"May I presume to ask you what caused you to say, just now, that fortune plays us odd tricks?"

"I was thinking," replied Gilbert, tranquilly, "of the emperor, Constantine the Great, who you know – "

"Ah! that is too much," interrupted Vladimir. "What! on a

beautiful morning, in the midst of the woods, before a little dried-up pond, which is not without its poetry, seated in the grass with a pretty white flower in your hand – the emperor, Constantine, the subject of your meditations? As for me, I have not such a well-balanced head, and I will confess to you that just now, in rambling among the thickets, I was entirely occupied with the singular games of my own destiny, and what is more singular still, I felt the necessity of relating them to someone."

"You surprise me," replied Gilbert; "I did not think you so communicative."

"And who of us," resumed Vladimir, "never contradicts his own character? In Russia the duties of my position oblige me to be reserved, secret, enveloped in mystery from head to foot, a great pontiff of science, speaking but in brief sentences and in an oracular tone; but here I am not obliged to play my role, and by a natural reaction, finding myself alone in the woods with a man of sense and heart, my tongue unloosens like a magpie's. Let us see; if I tell you my history do you promise to be discreet?"

"Undoubtedly. But if you must have a confidant, how happens it that intimate as you are with Count Kostia – "

"Ah, precisely! when you know my history you will understand for what reason in my interviews with Kostia Petrovitch I speak often of him, but rarely of myself."

And at these words Vladimir Paulitch turned up his sleeves, and showing his wrists to Gilbert; "Look!" he said. "Do you see any mark, any scar?"

"No, I cannot detect any."

"That is strange. For forty years, however, I have worn handcuffs, for such as you see me – I, Vladimir Paulitch; I, one of the first physicians of Russia; I, the learned physiologist, I am the refuse of the earth, I am Ivan's equal; in a word, I am a serf!"

"You a serf!" exclaimed Gilbert, astonished.

"You should not be so greatly surprised; such things are common in Russia," said Vladimir Paulitch, with a faint smile.

"Yes, sir," he resumed, "I am one of Count Kostia's serfs, and you may imagine whether or not I am grateful to him for having had the goodness to fashion from the humble clay of which nature had formed one of his moujiks, the glorious statue of Doctor Vladimir Paulitch. However, of all the favors he has heaped upon me the one which troubles me most is, that, thanks to his discretion, there were but two men in the world, himself and myself, who knew me for what I am. Now there are three.

"My parents," continued he, "were Ukraine peasants, and my first profession was taking care of sheep; but I was a born physician. The sick, whether men or sheep, were to my mind the most interesting of spectacles. I procured some books, acquired a slight knowledge of anatomy and chemistry, and by turns I dissected, and hunted for simples, the virtues of which I tried with indefatigable ardor. Poor, lacking all resources, brought up from infancy in foolish superstitions, from which I had the trouble in emancipating myself; living in the midst of coarse, ignorant men degraded by slavery, nothing could repulse me or discourage me. I felt myself born to decipher the great book of nature, and to wring from it her secrets. I had the good fortune to discover some specifics against the rot and tag sore. That rendered me famous within a circuit of three leagues. After quadrupeds, I tried my hand on bipeds. I effected several happy cures, and people came from all parts to consult me. Proud as Artaban, the little shepherd, seated beneath the shade of a tree, uttered his infallible oracles, and they were believed all the more implicitly, as nature had given to his eyes that veiled and impenetrable expression calculated to impose upon fools. The land to which I belonged was owned by a venerable relative of Count Kostia. At her death she left her property to him. He came to see his new domain; heard of me, had me brought into his presence, questioned me, and was struck with my natural gifts and precocious genius. He had already proposed to found a hospital in one of his villages where he resided during the summer, and it occurred to him that he could some day make me useful there. I went with him to Moscow. Concealing my position from everyone, he had me instructed with the greatest care. Masters, books, money, I had in profusion. So great was my happiness that I hardly dare to believe in it, and I was sometimes obliged to bite my finger to assure myself that I was not in a dream. When I reached the age of twenty, Kostia Petrovitch made me enter the school of medicine, and some years later I directed his hospital and a private asylum which he founded by my advice. My talents and success soon made me known. I was spoken of at Moscow, and was called there upon consultations. Thus I was in a fair way to make a fortune, and what gratified me still more, I was sought after, feted, courted, fawned upon. The little shepherd, the moujik, had become King and more than King, for a successful physician is adored as a god by his patients; and I do not believe that a pretty woman gratifies her lovers with half the smiles which she lavishes freely upon the magician upon whom depend her life and her youth. At this time, sir, I was still religious. Imagine the place Count Kostia held in my prayers, and with what fervor I implored for him the intercession of the saints and of the blessed Mary. Prosperity, nevertheless, has this much of evil in it; it makes a man forget his former self.

"Intoxicated with my glory and success, I forgot too soon my youth and my sheep, and this forgetfulness ruined me. I was called to attend a cavalry officer retired from service. He had a daughter named Pauline; she was beautiful and charming. I thought myself insensible to love, but I had hardly seen her before I conceived a violent passion for her. Bear in mind that I had lived until that time as pure as an ascetic monk; science had been my adored and lofty mistress. When passion fires a chaste heart, it becomes a fury there. I loved Pauline with frenzy, with idolatry. One day she gave me to understand that my folly did not displease her. I declared myself to her father, obtained his consent, and felt as if I should die of happiness. The next day I sought Count Kostia, and telling him my story, supplicated him to emancipate me. He laughed, and declared such an extravagant idea was unworthy of me. Marriage was not what I required. A wife, children, useless encumbrances in my life! Petty delights and domestic cares would extinguish the fire of my genius, would kill in me the spirit of research and vigor of thought. Besides, was my passion serious? From what he knew of my disposition, I was incapable of loving. It was a fantastic trick which my imagination had played me. Only remain a week without seeing Pauline, and I would be cured. My only answer was to throw myself at his feet. I glued my mouth to his hands, watered his knees with my tears, and kissed the ground before him. He laughed throughout, and asked me with a sneer, if to possess Pauline it were necessary to marry her. My love was an adoration. At these insulting words anger took possession of me. I poured forth imprecations and threats. Presently, however, recovering myself, I begged him to forgive my transports, and resuming the language of servile humility, I endeavored to soften that heart of bronze with my tears. Trouble lost; he remained inflexible. I rolled upon the floor and tore my hair; and he still laughed – That must have been a curious scene. Recollect that at this epoch I was quite recherche in my costume. I had an embroidered frill and very fine ruffles of point d'Alencon. I wore rings on every finger, and my coat was of the latest style and of elegant cut. Fancy, also, that my deportment, my gait, my air breathed of pride and arrogance. Parvenus try it in vain, they always betray themselves. I had a high tone, an overbearing manner. I enveloped myself in mysterious darkness, which obscured at times the brightness of my genius, and as I had accomplished several extraordinary cures, strongly resembling miracles, or tricks of sorcery, my airs of an inspired priest did not seem out of place, and I had devotees who encouraged these licenses of my pride by the excess of their humility. And then, behold, suddenly, this man of importance, this miraculous personage, flat upon his face, imploring the mercy of an inexorable master, writhing like a worm of the earth under the foot which crushed his heart! At last Kostia Petrovitch lost patience, seized me in his powerful hands, set me upon my feet, and pushing me violently against the wall, cried in a voice of thunder, 'Vladimir Paulitch, spare me your effeminate contortions, and remember who I am and who you are. One day I saw an ugly piece of charcoal in the road. I picked it up at the risk of soiling my fingers, and, as I am something of a chemist, I put it in my crucible and converted it into a diamond. But just as I have set my jewel, and am about to wear it on my finger, you ask me to give it up! Ah! my son, I do not know what keeps me from sending you back to your sheep. Go, make an effort to conquer your passion; be reasonable, be yourself again. Wait until my death, my will shall emancipate you; but until then, even at the risk of your displeasure, you shall be my THING, my PROPERTY. Take care you do not forget it, or I will shatter you in pieces like this glass;' and, seizing a phial from the table, he threw it against the wall, where it broke in fragments.

"Sir, Count Kostia displayed a little too much energy at the time, but at bottom he was right. Was it just that he should lose all the fruits of his trouble? Think what a gratification it was to his pride, to be able to say to himself, 'The great doctor, so feted, so admired, is my thing and my property.' His words were true; he wore me as a ring upon his finger. And then he foresaw the future. For two consecutive years it has only been necessary for him to move the end of his forefinger, to make me run from the heart of Russia to soothe his poor tormented nerves. You know how the heart of man is made. If he had had the imprudence to emancipate me, I should have come last year out of gratitude; but this time – "

While Vladimir spoke, Gilbert thought to himself, "This man is truly the compatriot of Count Leminof."

And then recalling the amiable and generous Muscovite with whom he had once been intimate, he justly concluded that Russia is large, and that nature, taking pleasure in contrasts, produces in that great country alternately the hardest and the most tender souls in the world.

"One word more," continued Vladimir: "Count Kostia was right; but unfortunately passion will not listen to reason. I left him with death in my heart, but firmly resolved to cope with him and to carry my point. You see that upon this occasion I observed but poorly the great maxim, Sequere fatum. I flattered myself I should be able to stem the current. Vain illusion! – but without it would one be in love? Pauline lived in a small town at about two leagues from our village. Whenever I had leisure, I mounted a horse and flew to her. The third day after the terrible scene, I took a drive with this amiable girl and her father. As we were about to leave the village, I was seized with a sudden trembling at the sight of Count Kostia on the footpath, holding his gold-headed cane under his arm and making his way quietly toward us. He recognized us, smiled agreeably, and signed to the coachman to stop and to me to descend.

"Plague upon the thoughtless fellow! whip up, coachman!" cried Pauline gayly.

But I had already opened the door.

"Excuse me," said I, "I will be with you in a moment." And while saying these words I was so pale that she became pale, too, as if assailed by a dark presentiment. Kostia Petrovitch did not detain me long. After saluting me with ceremonious politeness, he said in a bantering tone:

"Vladimir, faith she is really charming. But I am sorry to say that if your engagement is not broken off before this evening, tomorrow this pretty girl will learn from me who you are."

After which, saluting me again, he walked away humming an aria.

"Money, sir, had always appeared to me so small a thing compared with science and glory; and besides, my love for Pauline was so free from alloy, that I had never conceived the idea of informing myself in regard to her fortune, or the dowry which she might bring to me. That evening, as we took tea together in the parlor of my expected father-in-law, I contrived to bring up this important question for consideration, and expressed views of such a selfish character, and displayed such a sordid cupidity, that the old officer at last became indignant. Pauline had a proud soul; she listened to us some time in silence, and then rising, she crushed me with a look of scorn, and, extending her arm, pointed me the door. That devil of a look, sir, I have not forgotten; it has long pursued me, and now I often see it in my dreams.

"Returning home, I tried to kill myself; but so awkwardly that I failed. There are some things in which we never succeed the first time. I was prevented from renewing the attempt by the Sequere fatum, which returned to my memory. I said to the floods which beat against my exhausted breast: 'Carry me where you please; you are my masters, I am your slave.'

"And believe me, sir, this unhappy adventure benefited me. It led me to salutary reflection. For the first time I ventured to think, I eradicated from my mind every prejudice which remained there, I took leave of all chimeras, I saw life and the world as they are, and decided that Heaven is a myth. My manners soon betrayed the effect of the enlightenment of my mind. No more arrogance, no more boasting. I did not divest myself of pride, but it became more tractable and more convenient; it renounced ostentation and vain display; the peacock changed into a man of good breeding. This, sir, is what experience has done for me, assisted by Sequere fatum. It has made me wise, an honest man and an atheist. So I said a little while afterwards to Count Kostia:

"'Of all the benefits I have received from you, the most precious was that of delivering me from Pauline. That woman would have ruined me. Ah, Count Kostia, how I laugh to myself when I recall the ridiculous litanies with which I once regaled your ears. You knew me well. A passing fancy – a fire of straw. Thanks to you, Kostia Petrovitch, my mind has acquired a perspicuity for which I shall be eternally grateful to you.

"This declaration touched him; he loved me the more for it. He has always had a weakness for men who listen to reason. Until then, notwithstanding the marks of affection which he lavished upon me, he had always made me feel the distance between us. But from that day I became intimate with him; I participated in his secrets, and, what cemented our friendship still more, was that one day I had an opportunity of saving his life at the risk of my own."

"And Pauline?" said the inquisitive and sympathetic Gilbert.

"Ah! Pauline interests you! Comfort yourself. Six months after our rupture she made a rich marriage. She still lives in her little town; she is happy, and has lost none of her beauty. I meet her sometimes in the street with her husband and children, and I have the pleasure of seeing her turn her head always from me. And I, too, sir, have children; they are my pupils. They are called in Moscow THE LITTLE VLADIMIRS, and one of them will become some of these days a great Vladimir. I have revealed all my secrets to him, for I do not want them to die with me, and my end may be near. I have yet an important work to accomplish; and when my task is finished, let death take me. The life of the little shepherd of Ukraine has been too exciting to last long. 'Short and sweet,' is my motto."

And at these words, leaning suddenly towards Gilbert, and looking him in the eye:

"Apropos," said he, "were you really thinking of Constantine, the emperor, when you exclaimed: 'Oh, fortune! what strange tricks you play?'"

Gilbert was nearly disconcerted by this sudden attack, but promptly recovered himself.

"Ah! ah!" thought he, "it was not for nothing, then, that you told me your history; you had a purpose! Who knows but that Count Leminof has sent you to get my confidence?"

Vladimir employed all the skill he possessed to make Gilbert speak; his insidious questions were inexhaustible: Gilbert was impenetrable. From time to time they looked steadily at each other, each seeking to embarrass his adversary, and to surprise his secret, but in vain; they fenced with glances, but they were both so sure in the parries, that not a thrust succeeded. At last Vladimir lost patience.

"My dear sir," exclaimed he, "I have the weakness to put faith in dreams, and I had one the other night which troubled me very much. I dreamed that Count Kostia had a daughter, and that he made her very unhappy, because she had the twofold misfortune of not being his daughter, and of resembling in a striking manner a woman whose remembrance he did not cherish. You see that dreams are as singular as the tricks of fortune. But the most serious matter was, that the unhappiness and beauty of this child had strongly touched your heart and that you had conceived an ardent passion for her.

"'What must I do?' you said to me one day.

"Then I related my story to you, and said: 'You know the character of Kostia Petrovitch. Do not hope to move him, it would be an amusement for him to break your heart. If I had been as much in love as you are, I should have carried off Pauline and fled with her to the ends of the world. An elopement! – that is your only resource. And mark (it was in my dream that I spoke thus), and mark – if you perform this bold stroke successfully, the Count, at first furious to see his victim escape him, will at last be reconciled to it. The sight of this child is a horror to him; even the tyranny which he exercises over her excites him and disorders his nerves. After she has left him, he will breathe more freely, will enjoy better health, and will pardon the ravisher, who will have relieved his life of the ferment of hatred which torments him. Then you can treat with him, and I shall be much mistaken if it is long before your dear mistress becomes your wife.' It was thus I repeat, that I spoke to you in my dream, and I added: 'Do not lose an instant; there is danger in remaining here. Kostia Petrovitch has suspicions; to-morrow perhaps it will be too late!'"

"And then you awoke," interrupted Gilbert, laughing.

Then rising, he continued:

"Your dreams have no common sense, my dear Doctor; for without taking into consideration that M. Leminof has no daughter, the faculty of loving has been denied to me by nature, and the only abduction of which I am capable is that of ink spots from a folio. With a little chlorine you see – "

He took a few steps to pick up the little flower which he had thrown away, and continued as he retraced with Vladimir the path which led to the castle. "Let us speak of more serious things. Do you know the family of this pretty flower?"

Thus walking on they conversed exclusively upon botany, and having arrived at the terrace, separated amicably. Vladimir saw Gilbert move away, and then muttered between his teeth:

"Ha! you won't speak, you refuse me your confidence, and you only take off spots of ink! Then let your fate work itself out!"

Shall I describe the feelings which agitated Gilbert's heart?

They will readily be divined. In addition to the anxiety which preyed upon him, a further and greater source of uneasiness was the fear that all had been discovered. "In spite of my precautions," thought he, "some spy stationed by the Count may have seen me running over the roof, but it is very improbable.

"I am inclined to believe rather, that the lynx eyes of Vladimir Paulitch have read Stephane's face. At the table he has watched her narrowly. Perhaps, too, my glances have betrayed me. This mind, coarse in its subtilty, has taken for a common love the tender and generous pity with which a great misfortune has inspired me. Doubtless he has informed the Count, and it was by his order that he attempted to force my confidence and to draw out my intentions. Stephane, Stephane, all my efforts then will have but resulted in heaping upon your head new misfortunes!" He was calmed a little, however, by the reflection that she had authorized him of her own accord to remain away from her for at least two weeks. "Before that time expires," thought he, "I shall have devised some expedient. It is, first of all, important to throw this terrier, who is upon our track, off the scent. Fortunately he will not be here long. His departure will be a great relief to me, for he is a dangerous person. If only Stephane will be prudent!"

Dinner passed off well! Vladimir did not make his appearance. The Count was amiable and gay. Stephane, although very pale, was as calm as on the preceding days, and her eyes did not try to meet those of Gilbert, who felt his alarm subsiding; but when they had risen from the table, Kostia Petrovitch having left the room first, his daughter had time, before following him, to turn quickly, draw from her sleeve a little roll of paper, and throw it at Gilbert's feet; he picked it up, and what was his chagrin when, after having locked himself in his room, he read the following lines. "The spirit of darkness has returned to me! I could not close my eyes last night. My head is on fire. I fear, I doubt, I despair. My Gilbert, I must at any cost see you this evening, for I feel myself capable of anything. Oh, my friend! come at least to console me – come and take from my sight the knife which remains open on my table."

Gilbert passed two hours in indescribable anguish. Whilst

day lasted, he stood leaning upon his window sill, hoping all the time that Stephane would appear at hers, and that he could communicate to her by signs; but he waited in vain, and already night began to fall. He deliberated, wavered, hesitated. At last, in this internal struggle, one thought prevailed over all others. He imagined he could see Stephane, pale, disheveled, despair in her eyes; he thought he could see a knife in her hands, the slender blade flashing in the darkness of the night. Terrified by these horrible fancies, he turned a deaf ear to prudential counsels, suspended his ladder, descended, crossed the roofs, clambered up the window, and sprang into the room. Stephane awaited him, crouching at the feet of the saints. She rose, bounded forward, and seized the knife lying upon the table with a convulsive motion, turned the point towards her heart, and cried in a vibrating voice:

"Gilbert, for the first and last time, do you love me?"

Terrified, trembling, beside himself, Gilbert opened his arms to her. She threw the poniard away, uttered a cry of joy, of delirium, leaped with a bound to her friend, threw her arms about him, and hanging upon his lips she cried:

"He loves me! he loves! I am saved."

Gilbert, while returning her caresses, sought to calm her excitement; but all at once he turned pale. From the neighboring alcove came a sigh like that he had heard in one of the corridors of the castle.

"We are lost!" gasped he in a stifled voice. "They have surprised us."

But she, clinging to him, her face illuminated by delirious joy, answered:

"You love me! I am happy. What matters the rest?"

At this moment the door of the alcove opened and Count Kostia appeared upon the threshold, terrible, threatening, his lips curling with a sinister smile. At this sight his daughter slowly raised her head, then took a few steps towards him, and for the first time dared to look that father in the face, who for so many years had held her bowed and shuddering under his iron hand. Then like a young lion with bristling mane, her hair floating in disorder upon her shoulders, her body quivering, her brows contracted, with flashing eyes and in a thrilling voice, she cried:

"Ah! it really is you then, sir!

"You are welcome. You here, great God! Truly these walls ought to be surprised to see you. Yes, hear me, deaf old walls: the man you see there upon the threshold is my father! Ah, tell me, would you not have divined it by the tenderness in his face, by that smile full of goodness playing about his lips?" And then she added: "Unnatural father, do you remember yet that you once had a daughter? Search well, you will find her, perhaps, at the bottom of your memory. Very well! this daughter whom you killed, has just left her coffin, and he who resuscitated her is the man before you." Then more excitedly still: "Oh, how I love him, this divine man! and in loving him, obedient daughter that I am, what have I done but execute your will? for was it not you yourself who one day threw me at his feet? I have remained there."

At these words, exhausted by the excess of her emotion, her strength deserted her. She uttered a cry, closed her eyes, and sank down. Gilbert, however, had already sprang towards her; he raised her in his arms and laid her inanimate form in an armchair; then placing himself before her, made a rampart of his body. When he turned his eyes upon the Count again, he could not repress a shudder, for he fancied he saw the somnambulist. The features of Kostia Petrovitch were distorted, his eyes bloodshot, and his fixed and burning pupils seemed almost starting from their sockets. He bent down slowly and picked up the knife, after which he remained some time motionless without giving any signs of life except by passing his tongue several times over his lips, as if to assuage the thirst for blood which consumed him. At last he advanced, his head erect, his arm holding the knife suspended in the air, ready to strike. As he drew near, Gilbert recovered all his composure, and in a clear, strong voice, cried out:

"Count Leminof, control yourself, or you will lose your reason."

And as the frightful phantom still advanced, he quickly uncovered his breast, and exclaimed in a still louder voice:

"Count Kostia, strike, here is my heart, but your blows will not reach me, – the specter of Morlof is between us."

At these words the Count uttered a cry like a fallow deer, followed by a long and plaintive sigh. A terrible internal struggle followed; his brow contracted; the convulsive movements which agitated his body, and the flakes of foam which stood upon his lips, testified to the violence of the effort he was making. Reason at length returned; his arms fell and the knife dropped, the muscles of his face relaxed, and his features by degrees resumed their natural expression. Then turning in the direction of the alcove, he called out:

"Ivan, come and take care of your young mistress, she has fainted."

Ivan appeared. Who could describe the look which he threw upon Gilbert? Meanwhile the Count had reentered the alcove; but returned immediately with a candle, which he lighted quietly, and then, with an easy gesture, said to Gilbert:

"My dear sir, it seems to me we are in the way here. Be good enough to leave with me by the staircase; for please God, you do not return by the roof. If an accident should happen to you, the Byzantines and I would be inconsolable!"

Gilbert was so constituted, that at this moment M. Leminof inspired him more with pity than anger. He obeyed, and preceding him a few steps, crossed the alcove and the vestibule and descended the stairs. When at the entrance of the corridor, he turned, and placing his back against the wall, said sadly:

"I have a few words to say to you!"

The Count, stopping upon the last step, leaned nonchalantly over the balustrade and answered, smiling:

"Speak, I am ready to hear you; you know it always gives me pleasure to talk with you."

"I beg you, sir," said Gilbert, "to pardon your daughter the bitterness of her language. She spoke in delirium. I swear to you that at the bottom of her heart, she respects you, and that you have only to wish it to have her love you as a father."

M. Leminof answered only by a shrug of the shoulders, which signified – "What matters it to me?"

"I am bound to say further," resumed Gilbert, "that your anger ought to fall upon me alone. It was I who sought this child, who hated me; and I constrained her to receive me. I pressed my attentions upon her and had no peace or rest until I had gained her affection."

The Count shrugged his shoulders again, as much as to say: "I believe you, but how does that change the situation?"

"As for me," continued Gilbert, "I assure you, upon my honor, that it was only yesterday I drew from your daughter her secret."

The Count answered:

"I believe you readily; but tell me, if you please, is it true that you now love this little girl as she loves you?"

Gilbert reflected a moment; then considering only the dignity and interests of Stephane, he replied:

"Yes, I love her with a pure, deep love."

A sarcastic joy appeared upon the Count's face.

"Admirable!" said he; "that is all I wish to know. We have nothing more to say."

Gilbert raised his head: "One word more, sir!" he exclaimed. "I do not leave you until you have sworn to me that you will not touch a hair of your daughter's head, and that you will not revenge yourself upon her for my well-meant imprudence."

"Peste!" said the Count, laughing, "you are taking great airs; but I owe you some gratitude, inasmuch as your coolness has saved me from committing a crime which would have been a great folly, for only fools avenge themselves with the knife. So I shall grant you even more than you ask. Hereafter, my daughter shall have no cause to complain of me, and I will interest myself paternally in her happiness. It displeases her to be under Ivan's charge; he shall be only her humble servant. I intend that she shall be as free as air, and all of her caprices will be sacred to me. I will begin by restoring her horse, if he is not already sold. I will do more: I will permit her to resume the garments of her sex. But for these favors I exact two conditions: first, that you shall remain here at least six months; second, that you will try neither to see, speak, nor write to my doll, without my consent."

Gilbert breathed a deep sigh.

"I swear it, on my honor!" replied he.

"Enough! Enough!" resumed M. Leminof, "I have your promise, and I believe in it as I do in the Gospels."

When the Count reentered his study, Doctor Vladimir, who was patiently awaiting him, examined him from head to foot, as if seeking to discover upon his garments or his hands some stain of blood, then controlling his emotion:

"Well," said he coolly, "how did the affair terminate?"

"Very well," said the Count, throwing himself in a chair. "I have not killed anyone. This young man's reason restored mine."

Vladimir Paulitch turned pale.

"So," said he, with a forced smile, "this audacious seducer gets off with a rating."

"You haven't common sense, Vladimir Paulitch! What are you saying about seduction? Gilberts are an enigma to you. They are not born under the same planets as Doctors Vladimir and Counts Leminof. There is a mixture in them of the humanitarian, the knight-errant, the gray sister, and the St. Vincent de Paul, added to all which, our philanthropist has a passion for puppets, and from the time of his arrival he has forewarned me that he intended to make them play. He must have wanted, I think, to give himself a representation of some sacramental act, of some mystery play of the middle ages. The piece began well. The principal personages were faith, hope, and charity. Unfortunately, love got into the party, and the mystery was transformed into a drama of cloak and sword. I am sorry for him; these things always end badly."

"You are mistaken, Count Kostia!" replied Vladimir ironically; "they often end with a wedding."

"Vladimir Paulitch!" exclaimed the Count, stamping his foot, "you have the faculty of exasperating me. Today you spent an hour in kindling the fire of vengeance in my soul. You hate this young man. I believe, on my honor, that you are jealous of him. You are afraid, perhaps, that I may put him in my will in place of the little shepherd of Ukraine? Think of it as you please, my dear doctor; it is certain that if I had had the awkwardness to kill this admirable companion of my studies, I should lament him now in tears of blood, for I know not why, but he is dear to me in spite of all. But who loves well, chastises well, and I cannot help pitying him in thinking of all the sufferings which I shall make him undergo. Now go to bed, doctor. To-morrow morning you will go on your nimble feet, three leagues from here, on the other side of the mountain, to a little inn, which I will direct you how to find. I will follow on horseback. I need exercise and diversion. We will meet there and dine together. At dessert we will talk physiology, and you will exert yourself to entertain me."

"But what are you thinking of?" exclaimed Vladimir, surprised to the last degree. "Will you permit these two lovers – "

"Oh! you have but a dull mind, in spite of your wisdom," interrupted the Count. "In matters of vengeance, you only know the calicoes and cottons. Mine I prefer to weave of silk and threads of gold."

On returning to his room, Vladimir Paulitch said to himself:

"These two men are too rational. The piece moves too slowly. I must hasten the denouement."

XVIII

Early in the morning Ivan entered Gilbert's room. The face of the poor serf was distressing to see. His eyes were red and swollen, and his features bloated. The bloody marks of his nails were visible on his face; forehead and cheeks were furrowed with them. He informed Gilbert that towards noon Count Kostia would go out with Vladimir Paulitch and would be absent the rest of the day.

"He left me here to watch you and to render an account to him upon his return of all I should see and hear. I am not ugly; – but after what has passed, you would be foolish to expect the least favor from me. My eyes, ears, and tongue will do their duty. You must know, too, that the barine is in a very gloomy mood to-day. His lips are white, and he frequently passes his left hand over his forehead, a sure sign that a storm is raging within."

"My dear Ivan," answered Gilbert, "I also shall be absent all day; so you see your task of watching will be easy."

Ivan breathed a sigh of relief. It seemed as if a mountain had been taken from his breast.

"I see with pleasure," said he, "that you repent of your sin, and that you promise to be wiser in the future; ah, if my young master would only listen to reason, like you."

"Your young master, as you call him, will be as rational as myself. But do me the favor to tell me – "

"Oh! don't be alarmed; his fainting fit was not long. I had hardly got to him, when he opened his eyes and asked me if you were still alive. On hearing my answer he exclaimed: 'Ah! my God! how happy I am! He lives and loves me!' Then he tried to rise, but was so weak that he fell back. I carried him to his bed and he said to me: 'Ivan, for four nights I have not closed my eyes,' and at these words he smiled and fell asleep, smiling, and he is asleep yet."

"In order to be wise, Stephane must be occupied. She must work with her mind and her hands. Here, take this little white flower," added he, handing him the one he had plucked the day before; "ask her, for me, to paint it in her herbarium to-day."

And as Ivan examined the plant with an air of distrust, he added:

"Go, and fear nothing. I've not hidden a note in it. I am a man of honor, my dear Ivan, and never break my word."

Ivan hid the flower in one of his sleeves and went out muttering to himself:

"How is all this going to end? Ah! may the Holy Trinity look down in pity upon this house. We are all lost!"

Gilbert went out. Leaving upon his right the plateau and its close thickets, he gained the main road and followed the bank of the Rhine for a long distance. A thousand thoughts crowded in confusion through his mind; but he always came to the same conclusion:

"I will save this child, or lose my life in the attempt."

As the sun began to sink towards the horizon, he returned to the castle. He went in search of Father Alexis and found him in the chapel. The good father had learned from Ivan what had happened the night before. He reproached Gilbert severely, but nevertheless, after hearing his explanations, softened considerably, and in a tone of grumbling indulgence, repeated the old proverb, "Everyone to his trade." "Oxen," added he, "are born to draw the plow, birds to fly, bees to make honey, Gilberts to read and make great books, and Father Alexis to edify and console his fellow-creatures. You have encroached upon my prerogatives. You wanted to walk in my shoes. And what has been the result of your efforts? The spoiling of my task! Have you not observed how much better this child has been for the last two months, how much more tranquil, gentle, and resigned? I had preached so well to her, that she at last listened to reason. And you must come to put in her head a silly love which will cost both of you many tears."

Upon which, seizing him rudely by the arm, he continued:

"And what need had we of your assistance, the good God and I? Have you forgotten? Open your eyes and look! To-day, my child, even to-day I have put the finishing touch to my great work."

Then he pointed his finger to two long rows of sallow faces, surmounted by golden halos, which two lamps suspended from the ceiling illuminated with a mysterious light. Like a general enumerating his troops, he said:

"Look at these graybeards. That is Isaac, this Jeremiah, and this Ezekiel. On the other side are the holy warrior martyrs. Then St. Procopius, there St. Theodore, who burnt the temple of Cybele. His torch may yet be relighted. And these archangels, do you think their arms will be forever nerveless and their swords always asleep in their scabbards?"

Then, falling upon his knees, he prayed aloud:

"And thou, holy mother of God, suffer thy unworthy servant to summon thee to keep thy promise. Let thy august power at last be made manifest. At the sight of thy frowning brows let there be accomplished a mystery of terror and tears in hardened hearts. Let the neck of the proud be broken, and let his haughty head, bent down by the breath of thy lips, as by the wind of a tempest, bow to the very earth and its hair sweep the dust of this pavement."

Just then they heard a voice calling:

"Father Alexis, Father Alexis, where are you?"

The priest turned pale and trembled. He tried in vain to rise, his knees seemed nailed to the ground.

"Ah! my child, did you not hear a divine voice answer me?"

But helping him to his feet, Gilbert said with a sad smile:

"There is nothing divine in that voice. It has a strongly-marked Provencal accent, and if I am not mistaken, it belongs to Jasmin the cook, who is there in the court with a lantern in his hand, and is calling you."

"Perhaps you are right," answered the good father, shaking his head and passing his hand over his forehead, which was bathed in perspiration. "Let us see what this good Jasmin wants. Perhaps he brings my dinner. I had notified him, however, that I proposed to fast to-day."

Jasmin no sooner saw them come out of the chapel than he ran towards them and said to the priest:

"I don't know, father, what has happened to Ivan, but when I went into his room to carry him his dinner, I found him stretched on his bed. I called him and shook him, but couldn't wake him up."

A shudder ran through Gilbert's whole body. Seizing the lantern from Jasmin he darted off on a run; in two seconds he was with Ivan. Jasmin had told the truth; the serf slept heavily and profoundly. By dint of pulling him by the arm, Gilbert succeeded in making him open his eyes; but he soon closed them again, turned towards the wall, and slept on.

"Someone must have given him a narcotic," said Gilbert, whispering to Father Alexis who had just joined him.

And addressing Jasmin, who had followed the priest.

"Has anyone been here this afternoon?"

"I ask your pardon," said the cook. "Doctor Vladimir returned from his walk at about five o'clock. This surprised me very much, as Count Kostia told me before he left, that M. Stephane would dine here alone to-day."

"The doctor is at the table then, now."

"Pardon, pardon! He didn't wish any dinner. He told me in a joking way, that he would shortly go to a grand dinner in the other world."

"But where is he then? In his study?"

"Two hours afterwards, he went out with M. Stephane."

"Which way did they go?" cried Gilbert, shaking him violently by the arm.

"Ah! pardon, sir, take care, you'll put my arm out of joint," answered the huge Provencal.

"Jasmin, my good Jasmin, answer me: which way did they go?"

"Ah! I remember now, they took the road to the woods."

Gilbert darted off instantly. Father Alexis cried after him in vain:

"Wait for me, my child, I will accompany you. I am a man of good judgment." As if carried by the wind, Gilbert was already in the woods. His head bare, pale, out of breath, he ran at the top of his speed. Night had come, and the moon began to silver over the foliage which quivered at every breath of wind. Gilbert was blind to the moon's brightness, deaf to the sighing of the wind. He heard nothing but the diminishing sound of steps in the distance, he saw nothing but a cloud of blood which floated before his eyes and indicated the path; the sole thought which shed any light upon his mind, filled with gloomiest apprehensions, was this:

"I did not understand this man! It was an offensive alliance which he proposed to me yesterday. I refused to avenge him: he is going to revenge himself, and a Russian serf seeking vengeance is capable of anything."

On he ran with unabated speed, and would have run to the end of the world if, in an elbow of the road, some steps before him, he had not suddenly perceived Stephane. Standing in the moonlight erect and motionless, Gilbert stopped, held out his arms, and uttered a cry. She trembled, turned, and running to him, cried:

"Gilbert, do you love me?"

He answered only by pressing her to his heart; and then perceiving Doctor Vladimir, who was sitting on the edge of a ditch, his head in his hands, he stammered:

"This man here with you!"

"I do not know," said she in a trembling voice, "whether he is a mad man or a villain; but it is certain that he is going to die, for he has poisoned himself."

"What have you to say?" said Gilbert, looking wildly at the dejected face of the doctor, upon which the moon was shining full. "Explain I beg of you."

"What do I know?" said she; "I think I have been dreaming since yesterday evening. It seems to me, however, that this man came to my room for me. He had taken the precaution to drug Ivan. I was dying with melancholy. He persuaded me that you, my Gilbert, were waiting for me in one of the paths of this forest, to fly with me to a distant country. 'Let us go, let us go,' I cried; but on the way I began to think, I grew suspicious, and at this turning of the road I said to my gloomy companion: 'Bring my Gilbert to me here; I will go no further.' Then he looked at me with frightful eyes, and I believe said to me: 'What is your Gilbert to me? Follow me or you die;' and then he fumbled in his bosom as if to find a concealed weapon; but if I am not mistaken, I looked at him steadily, and crossing my arms, said to him: 'Kill me, but you shall not make me take another step.'"

Vladimir raised his head.

"How deceptive resemblances are," said he in a hollow voice. "I once knew a woman who had the same contour of face, and one evening, by the sole power of my eye, I compelled her to fall at my feet, crying: 'Vladimir Paulitch, do with me what you will.' But your young friend has a soul made of different stuff. You can believe me if you wish, sir; but the fact is that her charming face suddenly struck me with an involuntary respect. It seemed to me that her head was adorned with a royal diadem. Her eyes glowed with a noble pride; anger dilated her nostrils, and while a scornful smile flitted over her lips, her whole face expressed the innocence of a soul as pure as the rays of the moon shining upon us. At this sight I thought of the woman of whom I spoke to you yesterday, and I felt a sensation of horror at the crime I had premeditated, and I, Doctor Vladimir, I prostrated myself at the feet of this child, saying to her: 'Forgive me, I am a wretch;' after which I swallowed a strong dose of poison of my own composition, whose antidote I do not know, and in two hours I shall be no more."

Gilbert looked steadily at him.

"Ah! great God," thought he, "it was not the life but the honor of Stephane which was in danger! But the promised miracle has been wrought, only this is not the one which Father Alexis expected, since it has been the work of the God of nature."

Stephane approached him, and taking his hands murmured:

"Gilbert, Gilbert, let us fly – let us fly together! There is yet time!"

But he only muttered:

"I see through it all!" Then turning to Vladimir he said in a tone of authority, "Follow me, sir! It is right that Count Kostia should receive your last breath."

Vladimir reflected for a moment, then rising, said:

"You are right. I must see him again before I die; but give me your arm, for the poison begins to work and my legs are very weak."

They began to walk, Stephane preceding them a few steps. At intervals, Vladimir would exclaim:

"To die – to breathe no more – no more to see the sun – no more to remember – to forget all!" And then he added, "One thing disturbs my happiness. I am not sufficiently revenged!"

At last his voice died upon his lips and his legs failed him. Gilbert was obliged to carry him on his shoulders, and was nearly giving out under the burden when he saw Father Alexis coming towards them breathless. He gave him no time to recover breath, but cried:

"Take this man by the feet. I will support his shoulders. Forward! my good father, forward! We have no time to lose."

Father Alexis hastened to comply with Gilbert's request, and they continued on their way with bowed heads and in gloomy silence. Stephane alone, with her cap drawn over her eyes, occasionally uttered disconnected words and alternately cast a furtive glance at Gilbert, or gazed sadly at the moon. Arriving at the castle, they crossed the court and ascended the stairs without meeting anyone; but entering the vestibule of the first story, in which all the lamps were lighted, they heard a noise of steps in the corridor which led to the square tower.

"M. Leminof has returned," said Gilbert, trembling. "Father Alexis, carry this man to his room. I will go and speak to the Count, and will bring him to you in a moment."

Then taking Stephane by the arm, he whispered to her:

"In the name of Heaven, keep out of the way. Go down on the terrace and conceal yourself. Your father must not see you until he has heard me."

"Do you think I am afraid, then?" she replied, and escaping from him, darted off in the direction of the corridor.

Meanwhile Father Alexis had entered the room of Vladimir Paulitch, whom he sustained with difficulty in his trembling arms. At the moment he laid him upon his bed, a voice, which reached even to them, uttered these terrible words:

"Ah! this is braving me too much! Let her die!" Then a sharp cry pierced the air, followed by the dull noise of a body falling heavily upon the floor.

Father Alexis looked at Vladimir with horror. "The mother was not enough," cried he, "thou hast just killed the daughter!"

And he sprang out of the room distracted.

Vladimir sat up. An atrocious joy gleamed in his face; and recovering the use of his speech, he murmured, "My vengeance is complete!"

But at these words a groan escaped him – the poison began to burn his vitals. Nevertheless he forgot his sufferings when he saw the Count appear, followed by the priest, and holding in his hand a sword, which he threw in the corner.

"Count Kostia," cried the dying man, "what have you done with your daughter?"

"I have killed her," answered he sternly, questioning him with his eyes.

Vladimir remained silent a moment.

"My good master," resumed he, "do you remember that Pauline whom I loved? Do you also remember having seen me crouched at your feet crying, 'Mercy! Mercy! for her and for me'? My good master, have you forgotten that corner of the street where you said to me one day: 'This woman is charming; but if your marriage is not broken off before evening, to-morrow she will learn from me who you are'? That day, Count Kostia Petrovitch, you had a happy and smiling air. Say, Kostia Petrovitch, do you recollect it?"

The Count answered only by a disdainful smile.

"Oh! most simple and most credulous of men," continued Vladimir, "how could you think that I would empty the cup of sorrow and of shame to the very dregs, and not revenge myself upon him who smiled as he made me drink it."

"Six months later, you saved my life," said the Count, slightly shrugging his shoulders.

"Because your days were dear to me. You do not know then the tenderness of hatred! I wished you to live, and that your life should be a hell."

And then he added, panting:

"The lover of the Countess Olga, . . . was I."

The Count staggered as if struck by lightning. He supported himself by the back of a chair, to avoid falling; then springing to the table, he seized a carafe full of water and emptied it in a single draught. Then in a convulsed voice, he exclaimed:

"You lie! The Countess Olga could never have given herself

to a serf!"

"Refer to your memory once more, Kostia Petrovitch. You forget that in her eyes I was not a serf, but an illustrious physician, a sort of great man. However, I will console you. The Countess Olga loved me no more than I loved her. My magnetic eyes, my threats had, as it were, bewitched her poor head; in my arms she was dying with fear, and when at the end of one of these sweet interviews, she heard me cry out, 'Olga Vassilievna, your lover is a serf,' she nearly perished of shame and horror."

The Count cast upon his serf a look of indescribable disgust, and, making a superhuman effort to speak, once more exclaimed: "Impossible! That letter which you addressed to me at Paris – "

"I feared that your dishonor might be concealed from you, and what would life have been to me then?"

M. Leminof turned to the priest who remained standing at the other end of the room. "Father Alexis, is what this man says true?"

The priest silently bowed.

"And was it for this, foolish priest, that you have endured death and martyrdom – to prolong the days of a worm of the earth?"

"I cared little for his life," answered the priest, with dignity, "but much for my conscience, and for the inviolable secrecy of the confessional."

"And for two years in succession you have suffered my mortal enemy to lodge under my roof without warning me?"

"I was ignorant of his history and of the fact that he had reasons for hating you. I fancied that a mad passion had made him a traitor to friendship, and that in repentance he sought to expiate his fault, by the assiduous attentions which he lavished upon you."

"Poor fellow!" said the Count, crushing him with a look of pity.

Then Vladimir resumed in a voice growing more and more feeble:

"Since that cursed hour, when I crawled at your feet, without being able to soften your stony heart with my tears, I became disgusted with life. To feel that I belonged to you was every instant a torment. But if you ask me why I have deferred my death so long, I answer that while you had a daughter living my vengeance was not complete. I let this child grow up; but when the clock of fate struck the hour I waited for, courage suddenly failed me, and I was seized with scruples, which still astonish me. But what am I saying? I bless my weakness, since I brought home a victim pure and without stain, and since her virginal innocence adds to the horror of your crime. Ah! tell me, was the steel which pierced her heart the same that silenced Morlof's? Oh, sword, thou art predestinated!"

Count Kostia's eyes brightened. He had something like a presentiment that he was about to be delivered from that fatal doubt which for so many years had poisoned his life, and he fixed his vulture-like eyes upon Vladimir.

"That child," said he, "was not my daughter."

Vladimir opened his vest, tore the lining with his nails and drew out a folded paper, which he threw at the Count's feet:

"Pick up that letter!" cried he, "the writing is known to you. I meant to have sent it to you by your dishonored daughter. Go and read it near your dead child."

M. Leminof picked up the letter, unfolded it, and read it to the end with bearing calm and firm. The first lines ran thus: "Vile Moujik. Thou hast made me a mother. Be happy and proud. Thou hast revealed to me that maternity can be a torture. In my ignorant simplicity, I did not know until now it could be aught else than an intoxication, a pride, a virtue, which God and the church regard with favor, and the angels shelter with their white wings. When for the first time I felt my Stephan and my Stephane stir within me, my heart leaped for joy, and I could not find words enough to bless Heaven which at last rewarded six years of expectation; but now it is not a child I carry in bosom, it is a crime...."

This letter of four pages shed light, and carried conviction into the mind of Count Kostia.

"She was really my daughter," said he, coolly... "Fortunately I have not killed her."

He left the room, and an instant after re-appeared, accompanied by Gilbert, and carrying in his arms his daughter, pale and disheveled, but living. He advanced into the middle of the room. There, as if speaking to himself, he said:

"This young man is my good genius. He tore my sword from me. God be praised! he has saved her and me. This dear child was frightened, she fell, but she is unhurt. You see her, she is alive, her eyes are open, she hears, she breathes. To-morrow she shall smile, to-morrow we shall all be happy."

Then drawing her to the head of the bed and calling Gilbert to him, he placed his hands together, and standing behind them, embracing their shoulders in his powerful arms, and thrusting his head between theirs, he forced them, in spite of themselves, to bend with him over the dying man.

Gilbert and Stephane closed their eyes.

The Count's and Vladimir's were wide open devouring each other. The master's flamed like torches; the serf's were sunken, glassy, and filled with the fear and horror of death. He seemed almost petrified, and murmured in a failing voice:

"I am lost. I have undone my own work. To-morrow, to-morrow, they will be happy."

One last look, full of hatred, flashed from his eyes, over which the eternal shadow was creeping, his features contracted, his mouth became distorted, and, uttering a frightful cry, he rendered up his soul.

Then the Count slowly raised himself. His arms, in which he held the two young people as in a living vice, relaxed, and

Stephane fell upon Gilbert's breast. Confused, colorless, wild-eyed, intoxicated with joy and terror at the same time, clinging to her friend as the sailor to his plank of safety, she said in an indistinct voice:

"In the life to which you condemn me, my father, the joys are as terrible as the sorrows."

The Count said to Gilbert:

"Console her, calm her emotion. She is yours. I have given her to you. Do not fear that I shall take her back again." Then, turning again to the bed, he exclaimed: "What a terrible thorn death has just drawn from my heart!"

In the midst of so many tragic sensations, who was happy? Father Alexis was, and he had no desire to hide it. He went and came, moved the furniture, passed his hand over his beard, struck his chest with all his might, and presently in his excess of joy threw himself upon Stephane and then upon Gilbert, caressing and embracing them. At last, kneeling down by the bed of death, under the eyes of the Count, he took the head of the dead man between his hands and kissed him upon the mouth and cheeks, saying:

"My poor brother, thou hast perhaps been more unfortunate than guilty. May God, in the unfathomable mystery of his infinite mercy, give thee one day, as I have, the kiss of peace! Then raising his clasped hands, he said: "Holy mother of God: blessed be thy name. Thou hast done more than I dared to ask."

At that moment Ivan, roused at last from his long lethargy, appeared at the threshold of the door. For some minutes he remained paralyzed by astonishment, and looked around distractedly; then, throwing himself at his master's feet and tearing his hair, he cried:

"Seigneur Pere, I am not a traitor! That man mixed some drug in my tea which put me to sleep. Seigneur Pere, kill me, but do not say that I am a traitor."

"Rise," returned the Count gayly, "rise, I say. I shall not kill thee. I am not going to kill anybody. My son, thou'rt a rusty old tool. Dost know what I shall do with thee? I shall slip thee in among the wedding presents of Madame Gilbert Saville."

Paul Bourget

Andre Cornelis

I

I was nine years old. It was in 1864, in the month of June at the close of a warm, bright afternoon. I was at my studies in my room as usual, having come in from the Lycee Bonaparte, and the outer shutters were closed. We lived in the Rue Tronchet, near the Madeleine, in the seventh house on the left, coming from the church. Three highly-polished steps (how often have I slipped on them!) led to the little room, so prettily furnished, all in blue, within whose walls I passed the last completely happy days of my life. Everything comes back to me. I was seated at my table, dressed in a large black overall, and engaged in writing out the tenses of a Latin verb on a ruled sheet divided into several compartments. All of a sudden I heard a loud cry, followed by a clamor of voices; then rapid steps trod the corridor outside my room. Instinctively I rushed to the door and came up against a man-servant, who was deadly pale, and had a roll of linen in his hand. I understood the use of this afterwards. I had not to question this man, for at sight of me he exclaimed, as though involuntarily:

"Ah! M. Andre, what an awful misfortune!"

Then, regaining his presence of mind, he said:

"Go back into your room – go back at once!"

Before I could answer, he caught me up in his arms, rather threw than placed me on the upper step of my staircase, locked the door of the corridor, and walked rapidly away.

"No, no," I cried, flinging myself against the door, "tell me all; I will, I must know." No answer. I shook the lock, I struck the panel with my clenched fists, I dashed my shoulder against the door. Vain was my frenzy! Then, sitting upon the lowest step, I listened, in an agony of fear, to the coming and going of people outside, who knew of "the awful misfortune," but what was it they knew? Child as I was, I understood the terrible signification which the servant's exclamation bore under the actual circumstances. Two days previously, my father had gone out after breakfast, according to custom, to the place of business which he had occupied for over four years, in the Rue de la Victoire. He had been thoughtful during breakfast, indeed for some months past he had lost his accustomed cheerfulness. When he rose to go out, my mother, myself, and one of the habitual frequenters of our house, M. Jacques Termonde, a fellow student of my father's at the Ecole de Droit, were at table. My father left his seat before breakfast was over, having looked at the clock, and inquired whether it was quite right.

"Are you in such a hurry, Cornelis?" asked Termonde.

"Yes," answered my father, "I have an appointment with a client who is ill – a foreigner – I have to call on him at his hotel to procure some important papers. He is an odd sort of man, and I shall not be sorry to see something of him at closer quarters. I have taken certain steps on his behalf, and I am almost tempted to regret them."

And since then, no news! In the evening of that day, when dinner, which had been put off for one quarter of an hour after another, was over, and my father, who was always so methodical, so punctual, had not come in, my mother began to betray increasing uneasiness, and could not conceal from me that his last words dwelt upon her mind. It was a rare occurrence for him to speak with misgiving of his undertakings!

The night passed, then the next morning and afternoon, and once more it was evening. My mother and I were once more seated at the square table, where the cover laid for my father in front of his empty chair gave, as it were, a form to our nameless dread.

My mother had written to M. Jacques Termonde, and he came after dinner. I was sent away immediately, but not without my having had time to remark the extraordinary brightness of M. Termonde's eyes, which were blue, and usually shone coldly in his thin, sharp face. He had fair hair and a beard best described as pale. Thus do children take note of small details, which are speedily effaced from their minds, but afterwards reappear, at the contact of life, just as certain invisible marks come out upon paper when it is held to the fire.

While begging to be allowed to remain, I was mechanically observing the hurried and agitated turning and returning of a light cane – I had long coveted it – held behind his back in his remarkably beautiful hands. If I had not admired the cane so much, and the fighting centaurs on its handle – a fine piece of Renaissance work – this symptom of extreme disturbance might have escaped me. But, how could M. Termonde fail to be disturbed by the disappearance of his best friend? Nevertheless, his voice, a soft voice which made all his phrases melodious, was quite calm.

"To-morrow," he said, "I will have every inquiry made, if Cornelis has not returned; but he will come back, and all will be explained. Depend on it, he went away somewhere on the business he told you of, and left a letter for you to be sent by a commissionaire who has not delivered it."

"Ah!" said my mother, "you think that is possible?"

How often, in my dark hours, have I recalled this dialogue, and the room in which it took place – a little salon, much liked by my mother, with hangings and furniture of some foreign stuff all striped in red and white, black and yellow, that my father had brought from Morocco; and how plainly have I seen my mother in my mind's eye, with her black hair, her brown eyes, her quivering lips. She was as white as the summer gown she wore that evening. M. Termonde was dressed with his usual correctness, and I remember well his slender and elegant figure.

I attended the two classes at the Lycee, if not with a light, at least with a relieved heart. But, while I was sitting upon the lower step of my little staircase, all my uneasiness revived. I hammered at the door again, I called as loudly as I could; but no one answered me, until the good woman who had been my nurse came into my room.

"My father!" I cried, "where is my father?"

"Poor child, poor child," said nurse, and took me in her arms.

She had been sent to tell me the awful truth, but her strength failed her. I escaped from her, ran out into the corridor, and reached my father's bedroom before anyone could stop me. Ah! upon the bed lay a rigid form covered by a white sheet, upon the pillow a bloodless, motionless face, with fixed, wide-open eyes, for the lids had not been closed; the chin was supported by a bandage, a napkin was bound around the forehead; at the bed's foot knelt a woman, still dressed in her white summer gown, crushed and helpless with grief. These were my father and my mother.

I flung myself madly upon her, and she clasped me passionately, with the piercing cry, "My Andre, my Andre!" In that cry there was such intense grief, in that embrace there was such frenzied tenderness, her heart was then so big with tears, that it warms my own even now to think of it. The next moment she rose and carried me out of the room, that I might see the dreadful sight no more. She did this easily, her terrible excitement had doubled her strength. "God punishes me! God punishes me!" she said over and over again taking no heed of her words. She had always been given, by fits and starts, to mystical piety. Then she covered my face, my neck, and my hair with kisses and tears. May all that we suffered, the dead and I, be forgiven you, poor mother, for the sincerity of those tears at that moment!

II

When I asked my mother, on the instant, to tell me all about the awful event, she said that my father had been seized with a fit in a hackney carriage, and that as no papers were found upon him, he had not been recognized for two days.

Grown-up people are much too ready to think it is equally easy to tell lies to all children.

Now, I was a child who pondered long in my thoughts over things that were said to me, and by dint of putting a number of small facts together, I came to the conviction that I did not know the whole truth. If my father's death had occurred in the manner stated to me, why should the man-servant have asked me, one day when he took me out to walk, what had been said to me about it? And when I answered him, why did he say no more, and, being a very talkative person, why had he kept silence ever since? Why, too, did I feel the same silence all around me, in the air, sitting on every lip, hidden in every look? Why was the subject of conversation constantly changed whenever I drew near? I guessed this by many trifling signs. Why was not a single newspaper left lying about, whereas, during my father's lifetime, the three journals to which we subscribed were always to be found on a table in the salon? Above all, why did both the masters and my schoolfellows look at me so curiously, when I went back to school early in October, four months after our great misfortune? Alas! it was their curiosity which revealed the full extent of the catastrophe to me.

It was only a fortnight after the reopening of the school, when I happened to be playing one morning with two new boys; I remember their names, Rastonaix and Servoin, now, and I can see the big fat cheeks of Rastonaix and the ferret-like face of Servoin. Although we were day pupils, we were allowed a quarter of an hour's recreation at school, between the Latin and English lessons. The two boys had engaged me on the previous day for a game of ninepins, and when it was over, they came close to me, and looking at each other to keep up their courage, they put to me the following questions, point-blank:

"Is it true that the murderer of your father has been arrested?"

"And that he is to be guillotined?"

This occurred sixteen years ago, but I cannot now recall the beating of my heart at those words without horror. I must have turned frightfully pale, for the two boys, who had struck me this blow with the carelessness of their age – of our age – stood there disconcerted. A blind fury seized upon me, urging me to command them to be silent, and to hit them with my fists if they spoke again; but at the same time I felt a wild impulse of curiosity – what if this were the explanation of the silence by which I felt myself surrounded? – and also a pang of fear, the fear of the unknown. The blood rushed into my face, and I stammered out:

"I do not know."

The drum-tap, summoning us back to the schoolroom, separated us. What a day I passed, bewildered by my trouble, turning the two terrible sentences over and over again.

It would have been natural for me to question my mother; but the truth is, I felt quite unable to repeat to her what my unconscious tormentors had said. It was strange but true, that thenceforth my mother, whom nevertheless I loved with all my heart, exercised a paralyzing influence over me. She was so beautiful in her pallor, so royally beautiful and proud.

No, I should never have ventured to reveal to her that an irresistible doubt of the story she had told me was implanted in my mind merely by the two questions of my schoolfellows; but, as I could not keep silence entirely and live, I resolved to have recourse to Julie, my former nurse. She was a little woman, fifty years of age, an old maid too, with a flat, wrinkled face, like an over-ripe apple; but her eyes were full of kindness, and indeed so was her whole face, although her lips were drawn in by the loss of her front teeth, and this gave her a witch-like mouth. She had deeply mourned my father in my company, for she had been in his service before his marriage. Julie was retained specially on my account, and in addition to her the household consisted of the cook, the man-servant, and the femme de chambre. Julie put me to bed and tucked me in, heard me say my prayers, and listened to my little troubles.

"Oh! the wretches!" she exclaimed, when I opened my heart to her and repeated the words that had agitated me so terribly. "And yet it could not have been hidden from you forever." Then it was that she told me all the truth, there in my little room, speaking very low and bending over me, while I lay sobbing in my narrow bed. She suffered in the telling of that truth as much as I in the hearing of it, and the touch of her dry old hand, with fingers scarred by the needle, fell softly on my curly head as she stroked it.

That ghastly story, which bore down my youth with the weight of an impenetrable mystery, I have found written in the newspapers of the day, but not more clearly than it was narrated by my dear old Julie. Here it is, plainly set forth, as I have turned and re- turned it over and over again in my thoughts, day after day, with the vain hope of penetrating it.

My father, who was a distinguished advocate, had resigned his practice in court some years previously, and set up as a financial agent, hoping by that means to make a fortune more rapidly than by the law. His good official connection, his scrupulous probity, his extensive knowledge of the most important questions, and his great capacity for work, had speedily secured him an exceptional position. He employed ten secretaries, and the million and a half francs which my mother and I inherited formed only the beginnings of the wealth to which he aspired, partly for his own sake, much more for his son's but, above all, for his wife's – he was passionately attached to her. Notes and letters found among his papers proved that at the time of his death, he had been for a month previously in correspondence with a certain person named, or calling himself, William Henry Rochdale, who was commissioned by the firm of Crawford, in San Francisco, to obtain a railway concession in Cochin China, then recently conquered, from the French Government. It was with Rochdale that my father had the appointment of which he spoke before he left my mother, M. Termonde, and myself, after breakfast, on the last fatal morning. The Instruction had no difficulty in establishing this fact. The appointed place of meeting was the Imperial Hotel, a large building, with a long facade, in the Rue de Rivoli, not far from the Ministere de la Marine. The entire block of houses was destroyed by fire in the Commune; but during my childhood I frequently begged Julie to take me to the spot, that I might gaze, with an aching heart, upon the handsome courtyard adorned with green shrubs, the wide, carpeted staircase, and the slab of black marble, encrusted with gold, that marked the entrance to the place whither my father wended his way, while my mother was talking with M. Termonde, and I was playing in the room with them. My father had left us at a quarter-past twelve, and he must have taken a quarter of an hour to walk to the Imperial Hotel, for the concierge, having seen the corpse, recognized it, and remembered that it was just about half-past twelve when my father inquired of him what was the number of Mr. Rochdale's rooms. This gentleman, a foreigner, had arrived on the previous day, and had fixed, after some hesitation, upon an apartment situated on the second floor, and composed of a salon and a bedroom, with a small ante-room, which separated the apartment from the landing outside. From that moment he had not gone out and he dined the same evening and breakfasted the next morning in his salon. The concierge also remembered that Rochdale came down alone, at about two o'clock on the second day; but he was too much accustomed to the continual coming and going to notice whether the visitor who arrived at half- past twelve had or had not gone away again. Rochdale handed the key of his apartment to the concierge, with directions that anybody who came, wanting to see him, should be asked to wait in his salon. After this he walked away in a leisurely manner, with a business- like portfolio under his arm, smoking a cigar, and he did not reappear.

The day passed on, and towards night two housemaids entered the apartment of the foreign gentlemen to prepare his bed. They passed through the salon without observing anything unusual. The traveler's luggage, composed of a large and much-used trunk and a quite new dressing-bag, were there. His dressing-things were arranged on the top of a cabinet. The next day, towards noon, the same housemaids entered the apartment, and finding that the traveler had slept out, they merely replaced the day-covering upon the bed, and paid no attention to the salon. Precisely the same thing occurred in the evening; but on the following day, one of the women having come into the apartment early, and again finding everything intact, began to wonder what this meant. She searched about, and speedily discovered a body, lying at full length underneath the sofa, with the head wrapped in towels. She uttered a scream which brought other servants to the spot, and the corpse of my father – alas! it was he – was removed from the hiding-place in which the assassin had cunningly concealed it. It was not difficult to reconstruct the scene of the murder. A wound in the back of the neck indicated that the unfortunate man had been shot from behind, while seated at the table examining papers, by a person standing close beside him. The report had not been heard, on account of the proximity of the weapon, and also because of the constant noise in the street, and the position of the salon at the back of the ante-room. Besides, the precautions taken by the murderer rendered it reasonable to believe that he had carefully chosen a weapon which would produce but little sound. The ball had penetrated the spinal marrow and death had been instantaneous. The assassin had placed new unmarked towels in readiness, and in these he wrapped up the head and neck of his victim, so that there were no traces of blood. He had dried his hands on a similar towel, after rinsing them with water taken from the carafe; this water he had poured back into the same bottle, which was found concealed behind the drapery of the mantel-piece. Was the robbery real or pretended? My father's watch was gone, and neither his letter-case nor any paper by which his identity could be proved was found upon his body. An accidental indication led, however, to his immediate recognition. Inside the pocket of his waistcoat was a little band of tape, bearing the address of the tailor's establishment. Inquiry was made there, in the afternoon the sad discovery ensued, and after the necessary legal formalities, the body was brought home.

And the murderer? The only data on which the police could proceed were soon exhausted. The trunk left by the mysterious stranger, whose name was certainly not Rochdale, was opened. It was full of things bought haphazard, like the trunk itself, from a bric-a-brac seller who was found, but who gave a totally different description of the purchaser from that which had been obtained from the concierge of the Imperial Hotel. The latter declared that Rochdale was a dark, sunburnt man with a long thick beard; the former described him as of fair complexion and beardless. The cab on which the trunk had been placed immediately after the purchase, was traced, and the deposition of the driver coincided exactly with that of the bric-a-brac seller. The assassin had been taken in the cab, first to a shop, where he bought a dressing-bag, next to a linen-draper's where he bought the towels, thence to the Lyons railway station, and there he had deposited the trunk and the dressing-bag at the parcels office. Then the other cab which had taken him, three weeks afterwards, to the Imperial Hotel, was traced, and the description given by the second driver agreed with the deposition of the concierge. From this it was concluded that in the interval formed by these three weeks, the assassin had dyed his skin and his hair, for all the depositions were in agreement with respect to the stature, figure, bearing, and tone of voice of the individual. This hypothesis was confirmed by one Jullien, a hairdresser, who came forward of his own accord to make the following statement:

On the day in the preceding month, a man who answered to the description of Rochdale given by the first driver and the bric-a- brac seller, being fair-haired, pale, tall, and broad-shouldered, came to his shop to order a wig and a beard; these were to be so well constructed that no one could recognize him, and were intended, he said, to be worn at a fancy ball. The unknown person was accordingly furnished with a black wig and a black beard, and he provided himself with all the necessary ingredients for disguising himself as a native of South America, purchasing kohl for blackening his eyebrows, and a composition of Sienna earth and amber for coloring his complexion. He applied these so skilfully, that when he returned to the hairdresser's shop, Jullien did not recognize him. The unusualness of a fancy ball given in the middle of summer, and the perfection to which his customer carried the art of disguise, astonished the hairdresser so much that his attention was immediately attracted by the newspaper articles upon "The Mystery of the Imperial Hotel," as the affair was called. At my father's house two letters were found; both bore the signature of Rochdale, and were dated from London, but without envelopes, and were written in a reversed hand, pronounced by experts to be disguised. He would have had to forward a certain document on receipt of these letters; probably that document was in the letter- case which the assassin carried off after the crime. The firm of Crawford had a real existence at San Francisco, but had never formed the project of making a railroad in Cochin China. The authorities were confronted by one of those criminal problems which set imagination at defiance. It was probably not for the purpose of theft that the assassin had resorted to such numerous and clever devices; he would hardly have led a man of business into so skilfully laid a trap merely to rob him of a few thousand francs and a watch.

Was the murder committed for revenge?

A search into the life of my father revealed nothing whatever that could render such a theory tenable. Every suspicion, every supposition, was routed by the indisputable and inexplicable fact that Rochdale was a reality whose existence could not be contested, that he had been at the Imperial Hotel from seven o'clock in the evening of one day until two o'clock in the afternoon of the next, and that he had then vanished, like a phantom, leaving one only trace behind – ONE ONLY. This man had come there, other men had spoken to him; the manner in which he had passed the night and the morning before the crime was known. He had done his deed of murder, and then – nothing. "All Paris" was full of this affair, and when I made a collection, long afterwards, of newspapers which referred to it, I found that for six whole weeks it occupied a place in the chronicle of every day.

At length the fatal heading, "The Mystery of the Imperial Hotel," disappeared from the columns of the newspapers, as the remembrance of that ghastly enigma faded from the minds of their readers, and solicitude about it ceased to occupy the police. The tide of life, rolling that poor waif amid its waters, had swept on. Yes; but I, the son? How should I ever forget the old woman's story that had filled my childhood with tragic horror? How should I ever cease to see the pale face of the murdered man, with its fixed, open eyes? How should I not say: "I will avenge thee, thou poor ghost?" Poor ghost! When I read Hamlet for the first time, with that passionate avidity which comes from an analogy between the moral situation depicted in a work of art and some crisis of our own life, I remember that I regarded the Prince of Denmark with horror. Ah! if the ghost of my father had come to relate the drama of his death to me, with his unbreathing lips, would I have hesitated one instant? No! I protested to myself; and then? I learned all, and yet I hesitated, like him, though less than he, to dare the terrible deed. Silence! silence! Let me go back to the facts.

III

I remember little of the succeeding events. All was so trivial, so insignificant, between that first vision of horror and the vision of woe which came to me two years later, that, with one exception, I hardly recall the intervening time.

In 1864, my father died; in 1866, my mother married M. Jacques Termonde. The exceptional period of the interval was the only one during which my mother bestowed constant attention upon me. Before the fatal date my father was the only person who had cared for me; at a later period there was no one at all to do so. Our apartment in the Rue Tronchet became unbearable to us; there we could not escape from the remembrance of the terrible event, and we removed to a small hotel in the Boulevard de Latour-Maubourg. The house had belonged to a painter, and stood in a small garden which seemed larger than it was because other gardens adjoined it, and over-shadowed its boundary wall and greenery. The center of the house was a kind of hall, in the English style, which the former occupant had used as a studio; my mother made this her ordinary sitting-room.

Now, at this distance of time, I can understand my mother's character, and recognize that there was something about her, which, although it was very harmless, led her to exaggerate the outward expression of all her feelings. While she occupied herself in studying the attitudes by which her emotions were to be fittingly expressed, the sentiments themselves were fading away. For instance, she chose to condemn herself to voluntary exile and seclusion after her bereavement, receiving only a very few friends, of whom M. Jacques Termonde was one; but she very soon began to adorn herself and everything around her, with the fine and subtle tastefulness that was innate in her.

My mother was a very lovely woman; her beauty was of a refined and pensive order, her figure was tall and slender, her dark hair was very luxuriant and of remarkable length. No doubt it was to the Greek blood in her veins that she owed the classical lines of her profile, her full-lidded soft eyes, and the willowy grace of her form. Her maternal grandfather was a Greek merchant, of the name of Votronto, who had come from the Levant to Marcielles when the Ionian Islands were annexed to France.

Many times in after years I have recalled the strange contrast between her rare and refined beauty and my father's stolid sturdy form, and my own, and wondered whether the origin of many irreparable mistakes might not be traced to that contrast. But I did not reason in those days; I was under the spell of the fair being who called me, "My son." I used to look at her with a kind of idolatry when she was seated at her piano in that elegant sanctum of hers, which she had hung with draped foreign stuffs, and decorated with tall green plants and various curious things, after a fashion entirely her own. For her sake, and in spite of my natural awkwardness and untidiness, I strove to keep myself very clean and neat in the more and more elaborate costumes which she made me wear, and also more and more did the terrible image of the murdered man fade away from that home, which, nevertheless, was provided and adorned by the fortune which he had earned for us and bequeathed to us. All the ways of modern life are so opposed to the tragic in events, so far removed from the savage realities of passion and bloodshed, that when such things intrude upon the decorous life of a family, they are put out of sight with all speed, and soon come to be looked upon as a bad dream, impossible to doubt, but difficult to realize.

Yes, our life had almost resumed its normal course when my mother's second marriage was announced to me. This time I accurately remember not only the period, but also the day and hour.

I was spending my holidays with my spinster aunt, my father's sister, who lived at Compiegne, in a house situated at the far end of the town. She had three servants, one of whom was my dear old Julie, who had left us because my mother could not get on with her. My aunt Louise was a little woman of fifty, with countrified looks and manners; she had hardly ever consented to stay two whole days in Paris during my father's lifetime. Her almost invariable attire was a black silk gown made at home, with just a line of white at the neck and wrists, and she always wore a very long gold chain of ancient date, which was passed under the bodice of her gown and came out at the belt. To this chain her watch and a bunch of seals and charms were attached. Her cap, plainly trimmed with ribbon, was black like her dress, and the smooth bands of her hair, which was turning gray, framed a thoughtful brow and eyes so kind that she was pleasant to behold, although her nose was large and her mouth and chin were heavy. She had brought up my father in this same little town of Compiegne, and had given him, out of her fortune, all that she could spare from the simple needs of her frugal life, when he wished to marry Mdlle. de Slane, in order to induce my mother's family to listen to his suit.

The contrast between the portrait in my little album of my aunt and her face as I saw it now, told plainly enough how much she had suffered during the past two years. Her hair had become more white, the lines which run from the nostrils to the corners of the mouth were deepened, her eyelids had a withered look. And yet she had never been demonstrative in her grief. I was an observant little boy, and the difference between my mother's character and that of my aunt was precisely indicated to my mind by the difference in their respective sorrow. At that time it was hard for me to understand my aunt's reserve, while I could not suspect her of want of feeling. Now it is to the other sort of nature that I am unjust. My mother also had a tender heart, so tender that she did not feel able to reveal her purpose to me, and it was my Aunt Louise who undertook to do so. She had not consented to be present at the marriage, and M. Termonde, as I afterwards learned, preferred that I should not attend on the occasion, in order, no doubt, to spare the feelings of her who was to become his wife.

In spite of all her self-control, Aunt Louise had tears in her brown eyes when she led me to the far end of the garden, where my father had played when he was a child like myself. The golden tints of September had begun to touch the foliage of the trees. A vine spread its tendrils over the arbor in which we seated ourselves, and wasps were busy among the ripening grapes. My aunt took both my hands in hers, and began:

"Andre, I have to tell you a great piece of news."

I looked at her apprehensively. The shock of the dreadful event in our lives had left its mark upon my nervous system, and at the slightest surprise my heart would beat until I nearly fainted. She saw my agitation and said simply:

"Your mother is about to marry."

It was strange this sentence did not immediately produce the impression which my look at her had led my aunt to expect. I had thought from the tone of her voice, that she was going to tell me of my mother's illness or death. My sensitive imagination readily conjured up such fears. I asked calmly:

"Whom?"

"You do not guess?"

"M. Termonde?" I cried.

Even now I cannot define the reasons which sent this name to my lips so suddenly, without a moment's thought. No doubt M. Termonde had been a good deal at our house since my father's death; but had he not visited us as often, if not more frequently, before my mother's widowhood? Had he not managed every detail of our affairs for us with care and fidelity, which even then I could recognize as very rare? Why should the news of his marriage with my mother seem to me on the instant to be much worse news than if she had married no matter whom? Exactly the opposite effect ought to have been produced, surely? I had known this man for a long time; he had been very kind to me formerly – they said he spoiled me – and he was very kind to me still. My best toys were presents from him, and my prettiest books; a wonderful wooden horse which moved by clockwork, given to me when I was seven – how much my poor father was amused when I told him this horse was "a double thoroughbred" – "Don Quixote," with Dore's illustrations, this very year; in fact some new gift constantly, and yet I was never easy and light-hearted in his presence as I had formerly been. When had this restraint begun? I could not have told that, but I thought he came too often between my mother and me. I was jealous of him, I may as well confess it, with that unconscious jealousy which children feel, and which made me lavish kisses on my mother when he was by, in order to show him that she was my mother, and nothing at all to him. Had he discovered my feelings? Had they been his own also? However that might be, I now never failed to discern antipathy similar to my own in his looks, notwithstanding his flattering voice and his over-polite ways. At my then age, instinct is never deceived about such impressions.

Without any other cause than the weakness of nerves to which I had been subject ever since my father's death, I burst into tears. The same thing happened to me sometimes when I was shut up in my room alone, with the door bolted, suffering from a dread which I could not conquer, like that of a coming danger. I would forecast the worst accidents that could happen; for example, that my mother would be murdered, like my father, and then myself, and I peered under all the articles of furniture in the room. It had occurred to me, when out walking with a servant, to imagine that the harmless man might be an accomplice of the mysterious criminal, and have it in charge to take me to him, or at all events to have it in charge to take place. My too highly-wrought imagination overmastered me. I fancied myself, however, escaping from the deadly device, and in order to hide myself more effectually, making for Compiegne. Should I have enough money? Then I reflected that it might be possible to sell my watch to an old watchmaker whom I used to see, when on my way to the Lycee, at work behind the window of his little shop, with a glass fixed in his right eye. That was a sad faculty of foresight which poisoned so many of the harmless hours of my childhood! It was the same faculty that now made me break out into choking sobs when my aunt asked me what I had in my mind against M. Termonde. I related the worst of my grievances to her then, leaning my head on her shoulder, and in this one all the others were summed up. It dated from two months before. I had come back from school in a merry mood, contrary to my habit. My teacher had dismissed me with praise of my compositions and congratulations on my prizes. What good news this was to take home and how tenderly my mother would kiss me when she heard it! I put away my books, washed my hands carefully, and flew to the salon where my mother was. I entered the room without knocking at the door, and in such haste that as I sprang towards her to throw myself into her arms, she gave a little cry. She was standing beside the mantlepiece, her face was very pale, and near her stood M. Termonde. He seized me by the arm and held me back from her.

"Oh, how you frightened me!" said my mother.

"Is that the way to come into a salon?" said M. Termonde.

His voice had turned rough like his gesture. He had grasped my arm so tightly that where his fingers had fastened on it I found black marks that night when I undressed myself. But it was neither his insolent words nor the pain of his grasp which made me stand there stupidly, with a swelling heart. No, it was hearing my mother say to him:

"Don't scold Andre too much; he is so young. He will improve."

Then she drew me towards her, and rolled my curls round her fingers; but in her words, in their tone, in her glance, in her faint smile, I detected a singular timidity, almost a supplication, directed to the man before her, who frowned as he pulled his moustache with his restless fingers, as if in impatience of my presence. By what right did he, stranger, speak in the tone of a master in our house? Why had he laid his hand on me ever so lightly? Yes, by what right? Was I his son or his ward? Why did not my mother defend me against him? Even if I were in fault it was towards her only. A fit of rage seized upon me; I burned with longing to spring upon M. Termonde like a beast, to tear his face and bite him. I darted a look of fury at him and at my mother, and left the room without speaking. I was of a sullen temper, and I think this defect was due to my excessive and almost morbid sensitiveness. All my feelings were exaggerated, so that the least thing angered me, and it was misery to me to recover myself. Even my father had found it very difficult to get the better of those fits of wounded feeling, during which I strove against my own relentings with a cold and concentrated anger which both relieved and tortured me. I was well aware of this moral infirmity, and as I was not a bad child in reality, I was ashamed of it.

Therefore, my humiliation was complete when, as I went out of the room, M. Termonde said:

"Now for a week's sulk! His temper is really insufferable."

His remark had one advantage, for I made it a point of honor to give the lie to it, and did not sulk; but the scene had hurt me too deeply for me to forget it, and now my resentment was fully revived, and grew stronger and stronger while I was telling the story to my aunt. Alas! my almost unconscious second-sight, that of a too sensitive child, was not in error. That puerile but painful scene symbolized the whole history of my youth, my invincible antipathy to the man who was about to take my father's place, and the blind partiality in his favor of her who ought to have defended me from the first and always.

"He detests me!" I said through my tears; "what have I done to him?"

"Calm yourself," said the kind woman. "You are just like your poor father, making the worst of all your little troubles. And now you must try to be nice to him on account of your mother, and not to give way to this violent feeling, which frightens me. Do not make an enemy of him," she added.

It was quite natural that she should speak to me in this way, and yet her earnestness appeared strange to me from that moment out. I do not know why she also seemed surprised at my answer to her question, "What do you know?" She wanted to quiet me, and she increased the apprehension with which I regarded the usurper – so I called him ever afterwards – by the slight faltering of her voice when she spoke to him.

"You will have to write to them this evening," said she at length.

Write to them! The words sickened me. They were united; never, nevermore should I be able to think of the one without thinking of the other.

"And you?"

"I have already written."

"When are they to be married?"

"They were married yesterday," she answered, in so low a tone that I hardly heard the words.

"And where?" I asked, after a pause.

"In the country, at the house of some friends." Then she added quickly: "They preferred that you should not be there on account of the interruption of your holidays. They have gone away for three weeks; then they will go to see you in Paris before they start for Italy. You know I am not well enough to travel. I will keep you here until then. Be a good boy, and go now and write."

I had many other questions to put to her, and many more tears to weep, but I restrained myself, and a quarter of an hour later, I was seated at my dear good aunt's writing-table in her salon.

How I loved that room on the ground floor, with its glass door opening on the garden. It was filled with remembrance for me. On the wall at the side of the old-fashioned "secretary" hung the portraits, in frames of all shapes and sizes, of those whom the good and pious soul had loved and lost. This funereal little corner spoke strongly to my fancy. One of the portraits was a colored miniature, representing my great-grandmother in the costume of the Directory, with a short waist, and her hair dressed a la Proudhon. There was also a miniature of my great-uncle, her son. What an amiable, self-important visage was that of the staunch admirer of Louis Philippe and M. Thiers! Then came my paternal grandfather, with his strong parvenu physiognomy, and my father at all ages. Underneath these works of art was a bookcase, in which I found all my father's school prizes, piously preserved. What a feeling of protection I derived from the portieres in green velvet, with long bands of needlework, my aunt's masterpieces, which hung in wide folds over the doors! With what admiration I regarded the faded carpet, with its impossible flowers, which I had so often tried to gather in my babyhood! This was one of the legends of my earliest years, one of those anecdotes which are told of a beloved son, and which make him feel that the smallest details of his existence have been observed, understood, and loved. In later days I have been frozen by the ice of indifference. And my aunt, she whose life had been lived among these old-fashioned things, how I loved her, with that face in which I read nothing but supreme tenderness for me, those eyes whose gaze did me good in some mysterious part of my soul! I felt her so near to me, only through her likeness to my father, that I rose from my task four or five times to kiss her, during the time it took me to write my letter of congratulation to the worst enemy I had, to my knowledge, in the world.

And this was the second indelible date in my life.

IV

I once spoke to my aunt of the vow I had taken, the solemn promise I had made to myself that I would discover the murderer of my father, and take vengeance upon him, and she laid her hand upon my mouth. She was a pious woman, and she repeated the words of the gospel: "Vengeance is mine, saith the Lord." Then she added: "We must leave the punishment of the crime to Him; His will is hidden from us. Remember the divine precept and promise, 'Forgive and you shall be forgiven.' Never say: 'An eye for an eye, a tooth for a tooth.' Ah, no; drive this enmity out of your heart, Cornelis; yes, even this." And there were tears in her eyes.

My poor aunt! She thought me made of sterner stuff than I really was. There was no need of her advice to prevent my being consumed by the desire for vengeance which had been the fixed star of my early youth, the blood-colored beacon aflame in my night. Ah! the resolutions of boyhood, the "oaths of Hannibal" taken to ourselves, the dream of devoting all our strength to one single and unchanging aim – life sweeps all that away, together with our generous illusions, ardent enthusiasm, and noble hopes. What a difference there is – what a falling off – between the boy of fifteen, unhappy indeed, but so bold and proud in 1870, and the young man of eight years later, in 1878! And to think, only to think, that but for chance occurrences, impossible to foresee, I should still be, at this hour, the young man whose portrait hangs upon the wall above the table at which I am writing. Of a surety, the visitors to the Salon of that year (1878) who looked at this portrait among so many others, had no suspicion that it represented the son of a father who had come to so tragic an end. And I, when I look at that commonplace image of an ordinary Parisian, with eyes unlit by any fire or force of will, complexion paled by the fatigues of fashion, hair cut in the mode of the day, strictly correct dress and attitude, I am astonished to think that I could have lived as I actually did live at that period. Between the misfortunes that saddened my childhood, and those of quite recent date which have finally laid waste my life, the course of my existence was colorless, monotonous, vulgar, just like that of anybody else. I shall merely note the stages of it.

In the second half of 1870, the Franco-Prussian war takes place. The invasion finds me at Compiegne, where I am passing my holidays with my aunt. My stepfather and my mother remain in Paris during the siege. I go on with my studies under the tuition of an old priest belonging to the little town, who prepared my father for his first communion. In the autumn of 1871 I return to Versailles; in August, 1873, I take my bachelor's degree, and then I do my one year's voluntary service in the army at Angers under the easiest possible conditions. My colonel was the father of my old schoolfellow, Rocquin. In 1874 I am set free from tutelage by my stepfather's advice. This was the moment at which my task was to have been begun, the time appointed with my own soul; yet, four years afterwards, in 1878, not only was the vengeance that had been the tragic romance, and, so to speak, the religion of my childhood, unfulfilled, but I did not trouble myself about it.

I was cruelly ashamed of my indifference when I thought about it; but I am now satisfied that it was not so much the result of weakness of character as of causes apart from myself which would have acted in the same way upon any young man placed in my situation. From the first, and when I faced my task of vengeance, an insurmountable obstacle arose before me. It is equally easy and sublime to strike an attitude and exclaim: "I swear that I will never rest until I have punished the guilty one."

In reality, one never acts except in detail, and what could I do? I had to proceed in the same way as justice had proceeded, to reopen the inquiry which had been pushed to its extremity without any result.

I began with the Judge of Instruction,* who had had the carriage of the matter, and who was now a Counsellor of the Court. He was a man of fifty, very quiet and plain in his way, and he lived in the Ile de Paris, on the first floor of an ancient house, from whose windows he could see Notre Dame, primitive Paris, and the Seine, which is as narrow as a canal at that place.

* The translator renders literally those terms and phrases relating to the French criminal law and procedure which have no analogous expression in English.

M. Massol, so he was named, was quite willing to resume with me the analysis of the data which had been furnished by the Instruction. No doubt existed either as to the personality of the assassin, or the hour at which the crime was committed. My father had been killed between two and three o'clock in the day, without a struggle, by that tall, broad-shouldered personage whose extraordinary disguise indicated, according to the magistrate, "an amateur." Excess of complication is always an imprudence, for it multiplies the chances of failure. Had the assassin dyed his skin and worn a wig because my father knew him by sight?

To this M. Massol said "No; for M. Cornelis, who was very observant, and who, besides, was on his guard – this is evident from his last words when he left you – would have recognized him by his voice, his glance, and his attitude. A man cannot change his height and his figure, although he may change his face."

M. Massol's theory of this disguise was that the wearer had adopted it in order to gain time to get out of France, should the corpse be discovered on the day of the murder. Supposing that a description of a man with a very brown complexion and a black beard had been telegraphed in every direction, the assassin, having washed off his paint, laid aside his wig and beard, and put on other clothes, might have crossed the frontier without arousing the slightest suspicion. There was reason to believe that the pretended Rochdale lived abroad. He had spoke in English at the hotel, and the people there had taken him for an American; it was therefore presumable either that he was a native of the United States, or that he habitually resided there. The criminal was, then, a foreigner, American or English, or perhaps a Frenchman settled in America. As for the motive of so complicated a crime, it was difficult to admit that it could be robbery alone. "And yet," observed the Judge of Instruction, "we do not know what the notecase carried off by the assassin contained. But," he added, "the hypothesis of robbery seems to me to be utterly routed by the fact that, while Rochdale stripped the dead man of his watch, he left a ring, which was much more valuable, on his finger. From this I conclude that he took the watch merely as a precaution to throw the police off the scent. My supposition is that the man killed M. Cornelis for revenge.

Then the former Judge of Instruction gave me some singular examples of the resentment cherished against medical experts employed in legal cases, Procureurs of the Republic, and Presidents of Assize. His theory was, that in the course of his practice at the bar my father might have excited resentment of a fierce and implacable kind; for he had won many suits of importance, and no doubt had made enemies of those against whom he employed his great powers. Supposing one of those persons, being ruined by the result, had attributed that ruin to my father, there would be an explanation of all the apparatus of this deadly vengeance.

M. Massol begged me to observe that the assassin, whether he were a foreigner or not, was known in Paris. Why, if this were not so, should the man have so carefully avoided being seen in the street? He had been traced out during his first stay in Paris, when he bought the wig and the beard, and that time he put up at a small hotel in the Rue d'Aboukir under the name of Rochdale, and invariably went out in a cab. "Observe also," said the Judge, "that he kept his room on the day before the murder, and on the morning of the actual day. He breakfasted in his apartment, having breakfasted and dined there the day before. But, when he was in London, and when he lived at the hotel to which your father addressed his first letters, he came and went without any precautions."

And this was all. The addresses of three hotels – such were the meagre particulars that formed the whole of the information to which I listened with passionate eagerness; the magistrate had no more to tell me. He had small, twinkling, very light eyes, and his smooth face wore an expression of extreme keenness. His language was measured, his general demeanor was cold, obliging, and mild, he was always closely shaven, and in him one recognized at once the well-balanced and methodical mind which had given him great professional weight. He acknowledged that he had been unable to discover anything, even after a close analysis of the whole existing situation of my father, as well as his past.

"Ah, I have thought a great deal about this said he, adding that before he resigned his post as Judge of Instruction he had carefully reperused the notes of the case. He had again questioned the concierge of the Imperial Hotel and other persons. Since he had become Counsellor to the Court, he had indicated to his successor what he believed to be a clue; a robbery committed by a carefully made-up Englishman had led him to believe the thief to be identical with the pretended Rochdale. Then there was nothing more.

These steps had, however, been of use inasmuch as they barred the rule of limitation, and he laid stress on that fact. I consulted him then as to how much time still remained for me to seek out the truth on my own account. The last Act of Instruction dated from 1873, so that I had until 1883 to discover the criminal and deliver him up to public justice. What madness! Ten years had already elapsed since the crime, and I, all alone, insignificant, not possessed of the vast resources at the disposal of the police, I presumed to imagine that I should triumph, where so skillful a ferret as he had failed! Folly! Yes; it was so.

And still there was nothing, no indication whatever. Nevertheless, I tried.

I began a thorough and searching investigation of all the dead man's papers. With that unbounded tenderness of hers for my stepfather, which made me so miserable, my mother had placed all these papers in M. Termonde's keeping. Alas! Why should she have understood those niceties of feeling on my part, which rendered the fusion of her present with her past so repugnant to me, any more clearly on this point than on any other? M. Termonde had at least scrupulously respected the whole of those papers, from plans of association and prospectuses to private letters. Among the latter were several from M. Termonde himself, which bore testimony to the friendship that had formerly subsisted between my mother's first husband and her second. Had I not known this always? Why should I suffer from the knowledge?

And still there was nothing, no indication whatever to put me on the track of a suspicion.

I evoked the image of my father as he lived, just as I had seen him for the last time; I heard him replying to M. Termonde's question in the dining-room of the Rue Tronchet, and speaking of the man who awaited him to kill him: "A singular man whom I shall not be sorry to observe more closely." And then he had gone out and was walking towards his death while I was playing in the little salon, and my mother was talking to the friend who was one day to be her master and mine. What a happy home-picture, while in that hotel room – Ah! was I never to find the key of the terrible enigma? Where was I to go? What was I to do? At what door was I to knock?

At the same time that a sense of the responsibility of my task disheartened me, the novel facilities of my new way of life contributed to relax the tension of my will. During my school days, the sufferings I underwent from jealousy of my stepfather, the disappointment of my repressed affections, the meanness and penury of my surroundings, many grievous influences, had maintained the restless ardor of my feelings; but this also had undergone a change. No doubt I still continued to love my mother deeply and painfully, but I now no longer asked her for what I knew she would not give me, my unshared place, a separate shrine in her heart. I accepted her nature instead of rebelling against it.

Neither had I ceased to regard my stepfather with morose antipathy; but I no longer hated him with the old vehemence. His conduct to me after I had left school was irreproachable. Just as in my childhood, he had made it a point of honor never to raise his voice in speaking to me, so he now seemed to pique himself upon an entire absence of interference in my life as a young man. When, having passed my baccalaureate, I announced that I did not wish to adopt any profession, but without a reason – the true one was my resolution to devote myself entirely to the fulfillment of my task of justice – he had not a word to say against that strange decision; nay, more, he brought my mother to consent to it.

When my fortune was handed over to me, I found that my mother, who had acted as my guardian, and my stepfather, her co-trustee, had agreed not to touch my funds during the whole period of my education; the interest had been re-invested, and I came into possession, not of 750,000 francs, but of more than a million. Painful as I felt the obligation of gratitude towards the man whom I had for years regarded as my enemy, I was bound to acknowledge that he had acted an honorable part towards me. I was well aware that no real contradiction existed between these high-minded actions and the harshness with which he had imprisoned me at school, and, so to speak, relegated me to exile. Provided that I renounced all attempts to form a third between him and his wife, he would have no relations with me but those of perfect courtesy; but I must not not be in my mother's house. His will was to reign entirely alone over the heart and life of the woman who bore his name.

How could I have contended with him? Why, too, should I have blamed him, since I knew so well that in his place, jealous as I was, my own conduct would have been exactly similar?

I yielded, therefore, because I was powerless to contend with a love which made my mother happy; because I was weary of keeping up the daily constraint of my relations with her and him, and also because I hoped that when once I was free I should be better fitted for my task as a doer of justice. I myself asked to be permitted to leave the house, so that at nineteen I possessed absolute independence, an apartment of my own in the Avenue Montaigne, close to the round-point in the Champs Elysees, a yearly income of 50,000 francs, the entree to all the salons frequented by my mother, and the entree, too, to all the places at which one may amuse one's self. How could I have resisted the influences of such a position?

Yes, I had dreamed of being an avenger, a justiciary, and I allowed myself to be caught up almost instantly into the whirlwind of that life of pleasure whose destructive power those who see it only from the outside cannot measure. It is a futile and exacting existence which fritters away your hours as it fritters away your mind, raveling out the stuff of time thread by thread with irreparable loss, and also the more precious stuff of mental and moral strength.

With respect to that task of mine, my task as an avenger, I was incapable of immediate action – what and whom was I to attack?

And so I availed myself of all the opportunities that presented themselves of disguising my inaction by movement, and soon the days began to hurry on, and press one upon the other, amid those innumerable amusements of which the idle rich make a code of duties to be performed. What with the morning ride in the Bois, afternoon calls, dinner parties, parties to the theater and after midnight, play at the club, or the pursuit of pleasure elsewhere – how was I to find leisure for the carrying out of a project? I had horses, intrigues, an absurd duel in which I acquitted myself well, because, as I believe, the tragic ideas that were always at the bottom of my life favored me.

A woman of forty persuaded me that I was her first love; then I persuaded myself that I was in love with a Russian great lady, who was living in Paris. The latter was – indeed she still is – one of those incomparable actresses in society, who, in order to surround themselves with a sort of court, composed of admirers who are more or less rewarded, employ all the allurements of luxury, wit, and beauty, but who have not a particle of either imagination or heart, although they fascinate by a display of the most refined fancies and the most vivid emotions. I led the life of a slave to the caprices of this soulless coquette for nearly six months, and learned that women of the fashionable world and women of "the half- world" are very much alike in point of worth. The former are intolerable on account of their lies, their assumption, and their vanity; the others are equally odious by reason of their vulgarity, their stupidity, and their sordid love of lucre.

I forgot all my absurd relations with women of both orders in the excitement of play, and yet I was well aware of the meanness of that diversion, which only ceases to be insipid when it becomes odious, because it is a clever calculation upon money to be gained without working for it. There was in me something at once wildly dissipated and yet disgusted, which drove me to excess, and at the same time inspired me with bitter self-contempt. In the innermost recesses of my being the memory of my father dwelt, and poisoned my thoughts at their source. An impression of dark fatalism invaded my sick mind; it was so strange that I should live as I was living, nevertheless, I did live thus, and the visible "I" had but little likeness to the real.

Upon me, then, poor creature that I was, as upon the whole universe, a fate rested. "Let it drive me," I said, and yielded myself up to it. I went to sleep, pondering upon ideas of the most somber philosophy, and I awoke to resume an existence without worth or dignity, in which I was losing not only my power of carrying out my design of reparation towards the phantom which haunted my dreams but all self-esteem, and all conscience.

Who could have helped me reascend this fatal stream? My mother? She saw nothing but the fashionable exterior of my life, and she congratulated herself that I had "ceased to be a savage." My stepfather? But he had been, voluntarily or not, favorable to my disorderly life. Had he not made me master of my fortune at the most dangerous age? Had he not procured me admission, at the earliest moment, to the clubs to which he belonged, and in every way facilitated my entrance into society? My aunt? Ah, yes, my aunt was grieved by my mode of life; and yet, was she not glad that at any rate I had forgotten the dark resolution of hate that had always frightened her? And, besides, I hardly ever saw her now. My visits to Compiegne were few, for I was at the age when one always finds time for one's pleasures, but never has any for one's nearest duties. If, indeed, there was a voice that was constantly lifted up against the waste of my life in vulgar pleasures, it was that of the dead, who slept in the day, unavenged; that voice rose, rose, rose unceasingly, from the depths of all my musings, but I had accustomed myself to pay it no heed, to make it no answer. Was it my fault that everything, from the most important to the smallest circumstance, conspired to paralyze my will? And so I existed, in a sort of torpor which was not dispelled even by the hurly-burly of my mock passions and my mock pleasures.

The falling of a thunderbolt awoke me from this craven slumber of the will. My Aunt Louise was seized with paralysis, towards the end of the sad year 1878, in the month of December. I had come in at night, or rather in the morning, having won a large sum at play. Several letters and also a telegram awaited me. I tore open the blue envelope, while I hummed the air of a fashionable song, with a cigarette between my lips, untroubled by an idea that I was about to be apprised of an event which would become, after my father's death and my mother's second marriage, the third great date in my life. The telegram was signed by Julie, my former nurse, and it told me that my aunt had been taken ill quite suddenly, also that I must come at once, although there was a hope of her recovery.

This bad news was the more terrible to me because I had received a letter from my aunt just a week previously, and in it the dear old lady complained, as usual, that I did not come to see her. My answer to her letter was lying half-written upon my writing-table. I had not finished it; God knows for what futile reason. It needs the advent of that dread visitant, Death, to make us understand that we ought to make good haste and love WELL those whom we do love, if we would not have them pass away from us forever, before we have loved them enough.

Bitter remorse, in that I had not proved to her sufficiently how dear she was to me, increased my anxiety about my aunt's state. It was two o'clock a. m., the first train for Compiegne did not start until six; in the interval she might die. Those were very long hours of waiting, which I killed by turning over in my mind all my shortcomings towards my father's only sister, my sole kinswoman. The possibility of an irrevocable parting made me regard myself as utterly ungrateful! My mental pain grew keener when I was in the train speeding through the cold dawn of a winter's day, along the road I knew so well.

As I recognized each familiar feature of the way, I became once more the schoolboy whose heart was full of unuttered tenderness, and whose brain was laden with the weight of a terrible mission. My thoughts outstripped the engine, moving too slowly, to my impatient fancy, which summoned up that beloved face, so frank and so simple, the mouth with its thickish lips and its perfect kindliness, the eyes out of which goodness looked, with their wrinkled, tear-worn lids, the flat bands of grizzled hair. In what state should I find her? Perhaps, if on that night of repentance, wretchedness, and mental disturbance, my nerves had not been strained to the utmost – yes, perhaps I should not have experienced those wild impulses when by the side of my aunt's deathbed, which rendered me capable of disobeying the dying woman. But how can I regret my disobedience, since it was the one thing that set me on the track of the truth? No, I do not regret anything, I am better pleased to have done what I have done.

V

My good old Julie was waiting for me at the station. Her eyes had failed her of late, for she was seventy years old, nevertheless she recognized me as I stepped out of the train, and began to talk to me in her usual interminable fashion so soon as we were seated in the hired coupe, which my aunt had sent to meet me whenever I came to Complegne, from the days of my earliest childhood. How well I knew the heavy old vehicle, with its worn cushions of yellow leather, and the driver, who had been in the service of the livery stable keeper as long as I could remember. He was a little man with a merry, roguish face, and eyes twinkling with fun; but he tried to give a melancholy tone to his salutation that morning.

"It took her yesterday," said Julie, while the vehicle rumbled heavily through the streets, "but you see it had to happen. Our poor demoiselle had been changing for weeks past. She was so trustful, so gentle, so just; she scolded, she ferreted about, she suspected – there, then, her head was all astray. She talked of nothing but thieves and assassins; she thought everybody wanted to do her some harm, the tradespeople, Jean Mariette, myself – yes, I too. She went into the cellar every day to count the bottles of wine, and wrote the number down on a paper. The next day she found the same number, and she would maintain the paper was not the same, she disowned her own handwriting. I wanted to tell you this the last time you came here, but I did not venture to say anything; I was afraid it would worry you, and then I thought these were only freaks, that she was a little crazy, and it would pass off. Well, then, I came down yesterday to keep her company at her dinner, as she always liked me to do, because, you know, she was fond of me in reality, whether she was ill or well. I could not find her. Mariette, Jean, and I searched everywhere, and at last Jean bethought him of letting the dog loose; the animal brought us straight to the wood-stock, and there we found her lying at full length upon the ground. No doubt she had gone to the stack to count the logs. We lifted her up, our poor dear demoiselle! Her mouth was crooked, and one side of her could not move. She began to talk. Then we thought she was mad, for she said senseless words which we could not understand; but the doctor assures us that she is perfectly clear in her head, only that she utters one word when she means another. She gets angry if we do not obey her on the instant. Last night when I was sitting up with her she asked for some pins. I brought them and she was angry. Would you believe that it was the time of night she wanted to know? At length, by dint of questioning her, and by her yesses and noes, which she expresses with her sound hand, I have come to make out her meaning. If you only knew how troubled she was all night about you; I saw it, and when I uttered your name her eyes brightened. She repeats words, you would think she raves: she calls for you. Now look here, M. Andre, it was the ideas she had about your poor father that brought on her illness. All these last weeks she talked of nothing else. She would say: 'If only they do not kill Andre also. As for me, I am old, but he so young, so good, so gentle.' And she cried – yes, she cried incessantly. 'Who is it that you think wants to harm M. Andre?' I asked her. Then she turned away from me with a look of distrust that cut me to the heart, although I knew that her head was astray. The doctor says that she believes herself persecuted, and that it is a mania; he also says that she may recover, but will never have her speech again."

I listened to Julie's talk in silence; I made no answer. I was not surprised that my Aunt Louise had begun to be attacked by a mental malady; the trials of her life sufficiently explained this, and I could also account for several singularities that I had observed in her attitude towards me of late. She had surprised me much by asking me to bring back a book of my father's which I had never thought of taking away. "Return it to me," she said, insisting upon it so strongly, that I instituted a search for the book, and at last unearthed it from the bottom of a cupboard where it had been placed, as if on purpose, under a heap of other books. Julie's prolix narrative only enlightened me as to the sad cause of what I had taken for the oddity of a fidgety and lonely old maid.

On the other hand, I could not take the ideas of my father's death so philosophically as Julie accepted them. What were those ideas? Many a time, in the course of conversation with her, I had vaguely felt that she was not opening her heart quite freely to me. Her determined opposition to my plans of a personal inquiry might proceed from her piety, which would naturally cause her to disapprove of any thought or project of vengeance, but was there nothing else, nothing besides that piety in question? Her strange solicitude for my personal safety, which even led her to entreat me not to go out unarmed in the evening, or get into an empty compartment in a train, with other counsels of the same kind, was no doubt caused by morbid excitement; still her constant and distressing dread might possibly rest upon a less vague foundation than I imagined.

I also recalled, with a certain apprehension, that so soon as she ceased to be able completely to control her mind these strange fears took stronger possession of her than before. "What!" said I to myself, "am I becoming like her, that I let such things occur to me? Are not these fixed ideas quite natural in a person whose brain is racked by the mania of persecution, and who has lost a beloved brother under circumstances equally mysterious and tragical?"

"She is awake," said Julie, who had taken the maid's place at the foot of the bed. I approached my aunt and called her by her name. I then clearly saw her poor face distorted by paralysis.

She recognized me, and as I bent down to kiss her, she stroked my cheek with her sound hand. This caress, which was habitual with her, she repeated slowly several times. I placed her, with Julie's assistance, on her back, so that she could see me distinctly; she looked at me for a long time, and two heavy tears fell from the eyes in which I read boundless tenderness, supreme anguish, and inexpressible pity. I answered them by my own tears, which she dried with the back of her hand; then she strove to speak to me, but could only pronounce an incoherent sentence that struck me to the heart. She saw, by the expression of my face, that I had not understood her, and she made a desperate effort to find words in which to render the thought evidently precise and lucid in her mind. Once more she uttered an unintelligible phrase, and began again to make the feeble gesture of despairing helplessness which had so shocked me at her waking. She appeared, however, to take courage when I put the question to her: "What do you want of me, dear aunt?" She made a sign that Julie was to leave the room, and no sooner were we alone than her face changed. With my help she was able to slip her hand under her pillow, and withdraw her bunch of keys; then separating one key from the others she imitated the opening of a lock. I immediately remembered her groundless fears of being robbed and I asked her whether she wanted the box to which that key belonged. It was a small key of a kind that is specially made for safety locks. I saw that I had guessed aright; she was able to get out the word "yes," and her eyes brightened.

"But where is this box?" I asked. Once more she replied by a sentence of which I could make nothing; and, seeing that she was relapsing into a state of agitation, with the former heart-rending movement, I begged her to allow me to question her and to answer by gestures only. After some minutes, I succeeded in discovering that the box in question was locked up in one of the two large cupboards below stairs, and that the key of the cupboard was on the ring with the others. I went downstairs, leaving her alone, as she had desired me by signs to do. I had no difficulty in finding the casket to which the little key adapted itself; although it was carefully placed behind a bonnet-box and a case of silver forks. The casket was of sweet-scented wood, and the initials J. C. were inlaid upon the lid in gold and platinum. J. C., Justin Cornelies – so, it had belonged to my father. I tried the key in the lock, to make quite sure that I was not mistaken.

I then raised the lid, and glanced at the contents almost mechanically, supposing that I was about to find a roll of business papers, probably shares, a few trinket-cases, and rouleaux of napoleons, a small treasure in fact, hidden away from motives of fear. Instead of this, I beheld several small packets carefully wrapped in paper, each being endorsed with the words, "Justin's Letters," and the year in which they were written. My aunt had preserved these letters with the same pious care that had kept her from allowing anything whatever belonging to him in whom the deepest affection of her life had centered, to be lost, parted with, or injured.

But why had she never spoken to me of this treasure, which was more precious to me than to anyone else in the world? I asked myself that question as I closed the box; then I reflected that no doubt she desired to retain the letters to the last hour of her life; and, satisfied with this explanation, I went upstairs again.

From the doorway my eyes met hers, and I could not mistake their look of impatience and intense anxiety. I placed the little coffer on her bed and she instantly opened it, took out a packet of letters, then another, finally kept only one out, replaced those she had removed at first, locked the box, and signed to me to place it on the chest of drawers. While I was clearing away the things on the top of the drawers, to make a clear space for the box, I caught sight, in the glass opposite to me, of the sick woman. By a great effort she had turned herself partly on her side, and she was trying to throw the packet of letters which she had retained into the fireplace; it was on the right of her bed, and only about a yard away from the foot. But she could hardly raise herself at all, the movement of her hand was too weak, and the little parcel fell on the floor. I hastened to her, to replace her head on the pillows and her body in the middle of the bed, and then, with her powerless arm she again began to make that terrible gesture of despair, clutching the sheet with her thin fingers, while tears streamed from her poor eyes.

Ah! how bitterly ashamed I am of what I am going to write in this place! I will write it, however, for I have sworn to myself that I will be true, even to the avowal of that fault, even to the avowal of a worse still. I had no difficulty in understanding what was passing in my aunt's mind; the little packet – it had fallen on the carpet close to the fender – evidently contained letters which she wished to destroy, so that I should not read them. She might have burned them, dreading as she did their fatal influence upon me, long since; yet I understood why she had shrunk from doing this, year after year, I, who knew with what idolatry she worshipped the smallest objects that had belonged to my father. Had I not seen her put away the blotting-book which he used when he came to Compiegne, with the paper and envelopes that were in it at his last visit?

Yes, she had gone on waiting, still waiting, before she could bring herself to part forever with those dear and dangerous letters, and then her sudden illness came, and with it the terrible thought that these papers would come into my possession. I could also take into account that the unreasonable distrust which she had yielded to of late had prevented her from asking Jean or Julie for the little coffer. This was the secret – I understood it on the instant – of the poor thing's impatience for my arrival, the secret also of the trouble I had witnessed. And now her strength had betrayed her. She had vainly endeavored to throw the letters into the fire, that fire which she could hear crackling, without being able to raise her head so as to see the flame. All these notions which presented themselves suddenly to my thoughts took form afterwards; at the moment they melted into pity for the suffering of the helpless creature before me.

"Do not disturb yourself, dear aunt," said I, as I drew the coverlet up to her shoulders, "I am going to burn those letters."

She raised her eyes, full of eager supplication. I closed the lids with my lips and stooped to pick up the little packet. On the paper in which it was folded, I distinctly read this date: "1864 – Justin's letters." 1864! that was the last year of my father's life. I know it, I feel it, that which I did was infamous; the last wishes of the dying are sacred. I ought not, no, I ought not to have deceived her who was on the point of leaving me forever. I heard her breathing quicken at that very moment. Then came a whirlwind of thought too strong for me. If my Aunt Louise was so wildly, passionately eager that those letters should be burned, it was because they could put me on the right track of vengeance. Letters written in the last year of my father's life, and she had never spoken of them to me! I did not reason, I did not hesitate, in a lightning-flash I perceived the possibility of learning – what? I know not; but – of learning. Instead of throwing the packet of letters into the fire, I flung it to one side, under a chair, returned to the bedside and told her in a voice which I endeavored to keep steady and calm, that her directions had been obeyed, that the letters were burning. She took my hand and kissed it. Oh, what a stab that gentle caress inflicted upon me! I knelt down by her bedside, and hid my head in the sheets, so that her eyes should not meet mine. Alas! it was not for long that I had to dread her glance. At ten she fell asleep, but at noon her restlessness recurred. At two the priest came, and administered the last sacraments to her. She had a second stroke towards evening, never recovered consciousness, and died in the night.

VI

At three o'clock in the morning Julie came in to take my place, and I retired to my room, which was on the same floor as my aunt's. A boxroom divided the two. I threw myself on my bed, worn out with fatigue, and nature triumphed over my grief. I fell into that heavy sleep which follows the expenditure of nerve power, and from which one awakes able to bear life again and to carry the load that seemed unendurable. When I awoke it was day, and the wintry sky was dull and dark like that of yesterday, but it also wore a threatening aspect, from the great masses of black cloud that covered it. I went to the window and looked out for a long time at the gloomy landscape closed in by the edge of the forest. I note these small details in order that I may more faithfully recall my exact impression at the time. In turning away from the window and going towards the fire which the maid had just lighted, my eye fell upon the packet of letters stolen from my aunt. Yes, stolen – 'tis the word. It was in the place where I had put it last night, on the mantel-shelf, with my purse, rings, and cigar-case. I took up the little parcel with a beating heart. I had only to stretch out my hand and those papers would fall into the flames and my aunt's dying wish be accomplished. I sank into an easy-chair and watched the yellow flame gaining on the logs, while I weighed the packet in my hand. I thought there must be a good many letters in it. I suffered from the physical uneasiness of indecision. I am not trying to justify this second failure of my loyalty to my dear aunt, I am trying to understand it.

Those letters were not mine, I never ought to have appropriated them. I ought now to destroy them unopened; all the more that the excitement of the first moment, the sudden rush of ideas which had prevented me from obeying the agonized supplication of my poor aunt, had subsided. I asked myself once more what was the cause of her misery, while I gazed at the inscription upon the cover, in my aunt's hand: "Justin's Letters, 1864." The very room which I occupied was an evil counsellor to me in this strife between an indisputable duty and my ardent desire to know; for it had formerly been my father's room, and the furniture had not been changed since his time. The color of the hangings was faded, that was all. He had warmed himself by a fire which burned upon that self-same hearth, and he had used the same low, wide chair in which I now sat, thinking many somber thoughts. He had slept in the bed from which I had just risen, he had written at the table on which I rested my arms. No, that room deprived me of free will to act, it made my father too living. It was as though the phantom of the murdered man had come out of his grave to entreat me to keep the oft-sworn vow of vengeance. Had these letters offered me no more than one single chance, one against a thousand, of obtaining one single indication of the secrets of my father's private life, I could not have hesitated. With such sacrilegious reasoning as this did I dispel the last scruples of pious respect; but I had no need of arguments for yielding to the desire which increased with every moment.

I had there before me those letters, the last his hand had traced; those letters which would lay bare to me the recesses of his life, and I was not to read them! What an absurdity! Enough of such childish hesitation. I tore off the cover which hid the papers; the yellow sheets with their faded characters shook in my hands. I recognized the compact, square, clear writing, with spaces between the words. The dates had been omitted by my father in several instances, and then my aunt had repaired the omission by writing in the day of the month herself. My poor aunt! this pious carefulness was a fresh testimony to her constant tenderness; and yet, in my wild excitement I no longer thought of her who lay dead within a few yards of me.

Presently Julie came to consult me upon all the material details which accompany death; but I told her I was too much overwhelmed, that she must do as she thought fit, and leave me quite alone for the whole of the morning. Then I plunged so deeply into the reading of the letters, that I forgot the hour, the events taking place around me, forgot to dress myself, to eat, even to go and look upon her whom I had lost while yet I could behold her face. Traitor and ingrate that I was! I had devoured only a few lines before I understood only too well why she had been desirous to prevent me from drinking the poison which entered with each sentence into my heart, as it had entered into hers. Terrible, terrible letters! Now it was as though the phantom had spoken, and a hidden drama of which I had never dreamed unfolded itself before me.

I was quite a child when the thousand little scenes which this correspondence recorded in detail took place. I was too young then to solve the enigma of the situation; and, since, the only person who could have initiated me into that dark history was she who had concealed the existence of the too-eloquent papers from me all her life long, and on her deathbed had been more anxious for their destruction than for her eternal salvation – she, who had no doubt accused herself of having deferred the burning of them from day to day as of a crime. When at last she had brought herself to do this, it was too late.

The first letter, written in January, 1864, began with thanks to my aunt for her New Year's gift to me – a fortress with tin soldiers – with which I was delighted, said the letter, because the cavalry were in two pieces, the man detaching himself from his horse. Then, suddenly, the commonplace sentences changed into utterances of mournful tenderness. An anxious mind, a heart longing for affection, and discontent with the existing state of things, might be discerned in the tone of regret with which the brother dwelt upon his childhood, and the days when his own and his sister's life were passed together. There was a repressed repining in that first letter that immediately astonished and impressed me, for I had always believed my father and mother to have been perfectly happy with each other. Alas! that repining did but grow and also take definite form as I read on. My father wrote to his sister every Sunday, even when he had seen her in the course of the week. As it frequently happens in cases of regular and constant correspondence, the smallest events were recorded in minute detail, so that all our former daily life was resuscitated in my thoughts as I perused the lines, but accompanied by a commentary of melancholy which revealed irreparable division between those whom I had believed to be so closely united. Again I saw my father in his dressing-gown, as he greeted me in the morning at seven o'clock, on coming out of his room to breakfast with me before I started for school at eight. He would go over my lessons with me briefly, and then we would seat ourselves at the table (without a tablecloth) in the dining-room, and Julie would bring us two cups of chocolate, deliciously sweetened to my childish taste. My mother rose much later, and, after my school days, my father occupied a separate room in order to avoid waking her so early. How I enjoyed that morning meal, during which I prattled at my ease, talking of my lessons, my exercises, and my schoolmates! What a delightful recollection I retained of those happy, careless, cordial hours! In his letters my father also spoke of our early breakfasts, but in a way that showed how often he was wounded by finding out from my talk that my mother took too little care of me, according to his notions – that I filled too small a place in her dreamy, wilfully frivolous life. There were passages which the then future had since turned into prophecies. "Were I to be taken from him, what would become of him?" was one of these. At ten I came back from school; by that time my father would be occupied with his business. I had lessons to prepare, and I did not see him again until half-past eleven, at the second breakfast. Then mamma would appear in one of those tasteful morning costumes which suited her slender and supple figure so well. From afar, and beyond the cold years of my boyhood, that family table came before me like a mirage of warm homelife; how often had it become a sort of nostalgia to me when I sat between my mother and M. Termonde on my horrid half-holidays.

And now I found proof in my father's letters that a divorce of the heart already existed between the two persons who, to my filial tenderness, were but one. My father loved his wife passionately, and he felt that his wife did not love him. This was the feeling continually expressed in his letters – not in words so plain and positive, indeed; but how should I, whose boyhood had been strangely analogous with this drama of a man's life, have failed to perceive the secret signification of all he wrote? My father was taciturn, like me – even more so than I – and he allowed irreparable misunderstandings to grow up between my mother and himself. Like me afterwards, he was passionate, awkward, hopelessly timid in the presence of that proud, aristocratic woman, so different from him, the self-made man of almost peasant origin, who had risen to professional prosperity by the force of his genius. Like me – ah! not more than I – he had known the torture of false positions, which cannot be explained except by words that one will never have courage to utter. And, oh, the pity of it, that destiny should thus repeat itself; the same tendencies of the mind developing themselves in the son after they had developed themselves in the father, so that the misery of both should be identical!

My father's letters breathed sighs that my mother had never suspected – vain sighs for a complete blending of their two hearts; tender sighs for the fond dream of fully-shared happiness; despairing sighs for the ending of a moral separation, all the more complete because its origin was not to be sought in their respective faults (mutual love pardons everything), but in a complete, almost animal, contrast between the two natures. Not one of his qualities was pleasing to her; all his defects were displeasing to her. And he adored her. I had seen enough of many kinds of ill-assorted unions since I had been going about in society, to understand in full what a silent hell that one must have been, and the two figures rose up before me in perfect distinctness. I saw my mother with her gestures – a little affectation was, so to speak, natural to her – the delicacy of her hands, her fair, pale complexion, the graceful turn of her head, her studiously low-pitched voice, the something un-material that pervaded her whole person, her eyes, whose glance could be so cold, so disdainful; and, on the other hand, I saw my father with his robust, workingman's frame, his hearty laugh when he allowed himself to be merry, the professional, utilitarian, in fact, plebeian, aspect of him, in his ideas and ways, his gestures and his discourse. But the plebeian was so noble, so lofty in his generosity, in his deep feeling. He did not know how to show that feeling; therein lay his crime. On what wretched trifles, when we think of it, does absolute felicity or irremediable misfortune depend!

The name of M. Termonde occurred several times in the earlier letters, and, when I came to the eleventh, I found it mentioned in a way which brought tears to my eyes, set my hands shaking, and made my heart leap as at the sound of a cry of sharp agony. In the pages which he had written during the night – the writing showed how deeply he was moved – the husband, hitherto so self-restrained, acknowledged to his sister, his kind and faithful confidante, that he was jealous. He was jealous, and of whom? Of that very man who was destined to fill his place at our fireside, to give a new name to her who had been Madame Cornelis; of the man with cat-like ways, with pale eyes, whom my childish instinct had taught me to regard with so precocious and so fixed a hate. He was jealous of Jacques Termonde. In his sudden confession he related the growth of this jealousy, with the bitterness of tone that relieves the heart of misery too long suppressed. In that letter, the first of a series which death only was destined to interrupt, he told how far back was the date of his jealousy, and how it awoke to life with his detection of one look cast at my mother by Termonde. He told how he had at once suspected a dawning passion on the part of this man, then that Termonde had gone away on a long journey, and that he, my father, had attributed his absence to the loyalty of a sincere friend, to a noble effort to fight from the first against a criminal feeling. Termonde came back; his visits to us were soon resumed, and they became more frequent than before. There was every reason for this; my father had been his chum at the Ecole de Droit, and would have chosen him to be his best man at his marriage had not Termonde's diplomatic functions kept him out of France at the time. In this letter and the following ones my father acknowledged that he had been strongly attached to Termonde, so much so, indeed, that he had considered his own jealousy as an unworthy feeling and a sort of treachery. But it is all very well to reproach one's self for a passion; it is there in our hearts all the same, tearing and devouring them. After Termonde's return, my father's jealousy increased, with the certainty that the man's love for the wife of his friend was also growing; and yet, the unhappy husband did not think himself entitled to forbid him the house. Was not his wife the most pure and upright of women? Her very inclination to mysticism and exaggerated devotion, although he sometimes found fault with her for it, was a pledge that she would never yield to anything by which her conscience could be stained. Besides, Termonde's assiduity was accompanied by such evident, such absolute respect, that it afforded no ground for reproach. What was he to do? Have an explanation with his wife – he who could not bring himself to enter upon the slightest discussion with her? Require her to decline to receive his own friend? But, if she yielded, he would have deprived her of a real pleasure, and for that he should be unable to forgive himself. If she did not yield? So, my poor father had preferred to toss about in that Gehenna of weakness and indecision wherein dwell timid and taciturn souls. All this misery he revealed to my aunt, dwelling upon the morbid nature of his feelings, imploring advice and pity, deciding and blaming the puerility of his jealousy, but jealous all the same, unable to refrain from recurring again and again to the open wound in his heart, and incapable of the energy and decision that would have cured it.

The letters became more and more gloomy, as it always happens when one has not at once put an end to a false position; my father suffered from the consequences of his weakness, and allowed them to develop without taking action, because he could not now have checked them without painful scenes. After having tolerated the increased frequency of his friend's visits, it was torture to him to observe that his wife was sensibly influenced by this encroaching intimacy. He perceived that she took Termonde's advice on all little matters of daily life – upon a question of dress, the purchase of a present, the choice of a book. He came upon the traces of the man in the change of my mother's tastes, in music for instance. When we were alone in the evenings, he liked her to go to the piano and play to him, for hours together, at haphazard; now she would play nothing but pieces selected by Termonde, who had acquired an extensive knowledge of the German masters during his residence abroad. My father, on the contrary, having been brought up in the country with his sister, who was herself taught by a provincial music-master, retained his old-fashioned taste for Italian music.

My mother belonged, by her own family, to a totally different sphere of society from that into which her marriage with my father had introduced her. At first she did not feel any regret for her former circle, because her extreme beauty secured her a triumphant success in the new one; but it was another thing when her intimacy with Termonde, who moved in the most worldly and elegant of the Parisian "world," was perpetually reminding her of all its pleasures and habits. My father saw that she was bored and weary while doing the honors of her own salon with an absent mind. He even found the political opinions of his friend echoed by his wife, who laughed at him for what she called his Utopian liberalism. Her mockery had no malice in it; but still it was mockery, and behind it was Termonde, always Termonde.

Nevertheless, he said nothing, and the shyness, which he had always felt in my mother's presence increased with his jealousy. The more unhappy he was, the more incapable of expressing his pain he became. There are minds so constituted that suffering paralzes them into inaction. And then there was the ever-present question, what was he to do? How was he to approach an explanation, when he had no positive accusation to bring? He remained perfectly convinced of the fidelity of his wife, and he again and again affirmed this, entreating my aunt not to withdraw a particle of her esteem from his dear Marie, and imploring her never to make an allusion to the sufferings of which he was ashamed, before their innocent cause. And then he dwelt upon his own faults; he accused himself of lack of tenderness, of failing to win love, and would draw pictures of his sorrowful home, in a few words, with heart-rending humility.

Rough, commonplace minds know nothing of the scruples that rent and tortured my father's soul. They say, "I am jealous," without troubling themselves as to whether the words convey an insult or not. They forbid the house to the person to whom they object, and shut their wives mouths with, "Am I master here?" taking heed of their own feelings merely. Are they in the right? I know not; I only know that such rough methods were impossible to my poor father. He had sufficient strength to assume an icy mien towards Termonde, to address him as seldom as possible, to give him his hand with the insulting politeness that makes a gulf between two sincere friends; but Termonde affected unconsciousness of all this. My father, who did not want to have a scene with him, because the immediate consequence would have been another scene with my mother, multiplied these small affronts, and then Termonde simply changed the time of his visits, and came during my father's business hours. How vividly my father depicted his stormy rage at the idea that his wife and the man of whom he was jealous were talking together, undisturbed, in the flower-decked salon, while he was toiling to procure all the luxury that money could purchase for that wife who could never, never love him, although he believed her faithful. But, oh, that cold fidelity was not what he longed for – he who ended his letter by these words – how often have I repeated them to myself:

"It is so sad to feel that one is in the way in one's own house, that one possesses a woman by every right, that she gives one all that her duty obliges her to give, all, except her heart, which is another's unknown to herself, perhaps, unless, indeed, that – My sister, there are terrible hours in which I say to myself that I am a fool, a coward, that they laugh together at me, at my blindness, my stupid trust. Do not scold me, dear Louise. This idea is infamous, and I drive it away by taking refuge with you, to whom, at least, I am all the world."

"Unless, indeed, that – " This letter was written on the first Sunday in June, 1864; and on the following Thursday, four days later, he who had written it, and had suffered all it revealed, went out to the appointment at which he met with his mysterious death, that death by which his wife was set free to marry his felon friend. What was the idea, as dreadful, as infamous as the idea of which my father accused himself in his terrible last letter, that flashed across me now? I placed the packet of papers upon the mantelpiece, and pressed my two hands to my head, as though to still the tempest of cruel fancies which made it throb with fever.

Ah, the hideous, nameless thing! My mind got a glimpse of it only to reject it.

But, had not my aunt also been assailed by the same monstrous suspicion? A number of small facts rose up in my memory, and convinced me that my father's faithful sister had been a prey to the same idea which had just laid hold of me so strongly. How many strange things I now understood, all in a moment! On that day when she told me of my mother's second marriage, and I spontaneously uttered the accursed name of Termonde, why had she asked me, in a trembling voice: "What do you know?"

What was it she feared that I had guessed? What dreaded information did she expect to receive from my childish observation of things?

Afterwards, and when she implored me to abandon the task of avenging our beloved dead, when she quoted to me the sacred words, "Vengeance is mine, saith the Lord," who were the guilty ones whom she foresaw I must meet on my path? When she entreated me to bear with my stepfather, even to conciliate him, not to make an enemy of him, had her advice any object except the greater ease of my daily life, or did she think danger might come to me from that quarter? When she became more afraid for me, owing to the weakening of her brain by illness, and again and again enjoined upon me to beware of going out alone in the evening, was the vision of terror that came to her that of a hand which would fain strike me in the dark – the same hand that had struck my father? When she summoned up all her strength in her last moments, that she might destroy this correspondence, what was the clue which she supposed the letters would furnish? A terrific light shone upon me; what my aunt had perceived beyond the plain purport of the letters, I too perceived. Ah! I dared to entertain this idea, yet now I am ashamed to write it down. But could I have escaped from the hard logic of the situation? If my aunt had handed over those letters to the Judge of Instruction in the matter, would he not have arrived at the same conclusion that I drew from them? No, I could not. A man who has no known enemies is assassinated; it is alleged that robbery is not the motive of the murder; his wife has a lover, and shortly after the death of her husband she marries that lover. "But it is they – it is they who are guilty, they have killed the husband," the judge would say, and so would the first-comer. Why did not my aunt place those letters of my father's in the hands of justice? I understood the reason too well; she would not have me think of my mother what I was now in a fit of distraction thinking.

To conceive of this as merely possible was to be guilty of moral parricide, to commit the inexpiable sin against her who had borne me. I had always loved my mother so tenderly, so mournfully; never, never had I judged her. How many times – happening to be alone with her, and not knowing how to tell her what was weighing on my heart – how many times I had dreamed that the barrier between us would not for ever divide us. Some day I might, perhaps, become her only support, then she should see how precious she still was to me. My sufferings had not lessened my love for her; wretched as I was because she refused me a certain sort of affection, I did not condemn her for lavishing that affection upon another. As a matter of fact, until those fatal letters had done their work of disenchantment, of what was she guilty in my eyes? Of having married again? Of having chosen, being left a widow at thirty, to construct a new life for herself? What could be more legitimate? Of having failed to understand the relations of the child who remained to her with the man whom she had chosen? What was more natural? She was more wife than mother, and besides, fanciful and fragile beings such as she was recoil from daily contests; they shrink from facing realities which would demand sustained courage and energy on their part. I had admitted all these explanations of my mother's attitude towards me, at first from instinct and afterwards on reflection. But now, the inexhaustible spring of indulgence for those who really hold our heart-strings was dried up in a moment, and a flood of odious, abominable suspicion overwhelmed me instead.

This sudden invasion of a horrible, torturing idea was not lasting. I could not have borne it. Had it implanted itself in me then and there, definite, overwhelming in evidence, impossible of rejection, I must have taken a pistol and shot myself, to escape from agony such as I endured in the few minutes which followed my reading of the letters. But the tension was relaxed, I reflected, and my love for my mother began to strive against the horrible suggestion. To the onslaught of these execrable fancies I opposed the facts, in their certainty and completeness. I recalled the smallest particulars of that last occasion on which I saw my father and mother in each other's presence. It was at the table from which he rose to go forth and meet his murderer. But was not my mother cheerful and smiling that morning, as usual? Was not Jacques Termonde with us at breakfast, and did he not stay on, after my father had gone out, talking with my mother while I played with my toys in the room? It was at that very time, between one and two o'clock, that the mysterious Rochdale committed the crime.

Termonde could not be, at one and the same moment, in our salon and at the Imperial Hotel, any more than my mother, impressionable and emotional as I knew her to be, could have gone on talking quietly and happily, if she had known that her husband was being murdered at that very hour. Why, I must have been mad to allow such a notion to present its monstrous image before my eyes for a single moment, and it was infamous of me to have gone so far beyond the most insulting of my father's suspicions.

Already, and without any proof except the expression of jealousy acknowledged by himself to be unreasonable, I had reached a point to which the unhappy but still loving man had not dared to go, even to the extreme outrage against my mother. What if, during the lifetime of her first husband, she had inspired him whom she was one day to marry with too strong a sentiment, did this prove that she had shared it? If she had shared it, would that have proved her to be a fallen woman? Why should she not have entertained an affection for Termonde, which, while it in no wise interfered with her fidelity to her wifely duties, made my father not unnaturally jealous?

Thus did I justify her, not only from any participation in the crime, but from any failure in her duty. And then again my ideas changed; I remembered the cry that she had uttered in presence of my father's dead body: "I am punished by God!" I was not sufficiently charitable to her to admit that those words might be merely the utterance of a refined and scrupulous mind which reproached itself even with its thoughts. I also recalled the gleaming eyes and shaking hands of Termonde, when he was talking with my mother about my father's mysterious disappearance. If they were accomplices, this was a piece of acting performed before me, an innocent witness, so that they might invoke my childish testimony on occasion. These recollections once more drove me upon my fated way. The idea of a guilty tie between her and him now took possession of me, and then came swiftly the thought that they had profited by the murder, that they alone had an engrossing interest in it. So violent was the assault of suspicion that it overthrew all the barriers I had raised against it. I accumulated all the objections founded upon a physical alibi and a moral improbability, and thence I forced myself to say it was, strictly speaking, impossible they could have anything to do with the murder; impossible, impossible! I repeated this frantically; but even as it passed my lips, the hallucination returned, and struck me down. There are moments when the disordered mind is unable to quell visions which it knows to be false, when the imaginary and the real mingle in a nightmare-panic, and the judgment is powerless to distinguish between them. Who is there that, having been jealous, does not know this condition of mind? What did I not suffer from it during the day after I had read those letters! I wandered about the house, incapable of attending to any duty, struck stupid by emotions which all around me attributed to grief for my aunt's death. Several times I tried to sit for a while beside her bed; but the sight of her pale face, with its pinched nostrils, and its deepening expression of sadness, was unbearable to me. It renewed my miserable doubts.

At four o'clock I received a telegram. It was from my mother, and announced her arrival by evening train. When the slip of blue paper was in my hand my wretchedness was for a moment relieved. She was coming. She had thought of my trouble; she was coming. That assurance [error in text – line missing] criminal thoughts in my face?

But those absurd and infamous notions took possession of me once more. Perhaps she thinks, so ran my thoughts, that the correspondence between my father and my aunt had not been destroyed, and she is coming in order to get hold of those letters before I see them, and to find out what my aunt said to me when she was dying. If she and Termonde are guilty, they must have lived in constant dread of the old maid's penetration. Ah! I had been very unhappy in my childhood, but how gladly would I have gone back to be the school-boy, meditating during the dull and interminable evening hours of study, and not the young man who walked to and fro that night in the station at Compiegne, awaiting the arrival of a mother, suspected as mine was. Just God! Did not I expiate everything in anticipation by that one hour?

VII

The train from Paris approached, and stopped. The railway officials called out the name of the station, as they opened the doors of the carriages one after another, very slowly as it seemed to me. I went from carriage to carriage seeking my mother. Had she at the last moment decided not to come! What a trial to me if it were so! What a night I should have to pass in all the torment of suspicions which, I knew too well, her mere presence would dispel.

A voice called me. It was hers. Then I saw her, dressed in black, and never in my life did I clasp her in my arms as I did then, utterly forgetting that we were in a public place, and why she had come, in the joy of feeling my horrible imaginations vanish, melt away at the mere touch of the being whom I loved so profoundly, the only one who was dear to me, notwithstanding our differences, in the very depths of my heart, now that I had lost my Aunt Louise.

After that first movement, which resembled the grasp in which a drowning man seizes the swimmer who dives for him, I looked at my mother without speaking, holding both her hands. She had thrown back her veil, and in the flickering light of the station I saw that she was very pale and had been weeping. I had only to meet her eyes, which were still wet with tears, to know that I had been mad. I felt this, with the first words she uttered, telling me so tenderly of her grief, and that she had resolved to come at once, although my stepfather was ill. M. Termonde had suffered of late from frequent attacks of liver-complaint.

But neither her grief nor her anxiety about her husband had prevented my poor mother from providing herself, for this little excursion of a few hours, with all her customary appliances of comfort and elegance. Her maid stood behind her, accompanied by a porter, and both were laden with three or four bags of different sizes, of the best English make, carefully buttoned up in their waterproof covers; a dressing-case, a writing-case, an elegant wallet to hold the traveler's purse, handkerchief, book, and second veil; a hot-water bottle for her feet, two cushions for her head, and a little clock suspended from a swinging disc.

"You see," said she, while I was pointing out the carriage to the maid, so that she might get rid of her impedimenta, "I shall not have my right mourning until to-morrow" - and now I perceived that her gown was dark brown and only braided with black – "they could not have the things ready in time, but will send them as early as possible." Then, as I placed her in the carriage, she added: "There is still a trunk and a bonnet-box." She half smiled in saying this, to make me smile too, for the mass of luggage and the number of small parcels with which she encumbered herself had been of old a subject of mild quarrel between us.

In any other state of mind I should have been pained to find the unfailing evidence of her frivolity side by side with the mark of affection she had given me by coming. Was not this one of the small causes of my great misery? True, but her frivolity was delightful to me at that moment. This then was the woman whom I had been picturing to myself as coming to the house of death, with the sinister purpose of searching my dead aunt's papers and stealing or destroying any accusing pages which she might find among them! This was the woman whom I had represented to myself, that morning, as a criminal steeped in the guilt of a cowardly murder! Yes! I had been mad! had been like a runaway horse galloping after its own shadow. But what a relief to make sure that it was madness, what a blessed relief! It almost made me forget the dear dead woman.

I was very sad at heart in reality, and yet I was happy, while we were rattling through the town in the old coupe, past the long lines of lighted windows. I held my mother's hand; I longed to beg her pardon, to kiss the hem of her dress, to tell her again and again that I loved and revered her. She perceived my emotion very plainly; but she attributed it to the affliction that had just befallen me, and she condoled with me. She said, "My Andre," several times. How rare it was for me to have her thus, all my own, and just in that mood of feeling for which my sick heart pined!

I had had the room on the ground floor, next to the salon, prepared for my mother. I remembered that she had occupied it, when she came to Compiegne with my father, a few days after her marriage, and I felt sure that the impression which would be produced upon her by the sight of the house in the first instance, and then by the sight of the room, would help me to get rid of my dreadful suspicions. I was determined to note minutely the slightest signs of agitation which she might betray at the contact of a resuscitated past, rendered more striking by the aspect of things that do not change so quickly as the heart of a woman. And now, I blushed for that idea, worthy of a detective; for I felt it a shameful thing to judge one's mother: one ought to make an Act of Faith in her which would resist any evidence. I felt this, alas! all the more, because the innocent woman was quite off her guard, as was perfectly natural.

She entered the room with a thoughtful look, seated herself before the fire, and held her slender feet towards the flames, which touched her pale cheeks with red; and, with her jet black hair, her elegant figure, which still retained its youthful grace, she shed upon the dim twilight of the old-fashioned room that refined and aristocratic charm of which my father spoke in his letters. She looked slowly all around her, recognizing most of the things which my aunt's pious care had preserved in their former place, and said, sorrowfully: "What recollections!" But there was no bitterness in the emotion depicted on her face. Ah! no; a woman who is brought, after twenty years, into the room which she had occupied, as a bride, with the husband whose murder she had contrived after having betrayed him, has not such eyes, such a brow, such a mouth as hers.

VIII

There was but one remedy to be applied to my unbearable malady – that remedy which had already been successful in the case of my suspicions of my mother. I must at once proceed to place the real in opposition to the suggestions of imagination. I must seek the presence of the man whom I suspected, look him straight in the face, and see him as he was, not as my fancy, growing more feverish day by day, represented him. Then I should discern whether I had or had not been the sport of a delusion; and the sooner I resorted to this test the better, for my sufferings were terribly increased by solitude.

My head became confused; at last I ceased even to doubt. That which ought to have been only a faint indication, assumed to my mind the importance of an overwhelming proof. In the interest of my inquiry itself it was full time to resist this, if I were ever to pursue my inquiry farther, or else I should fall into the nervous state which I knew so well, and which rendered any kind of action in cold blood impossible to me.

I made up my mind to leave Compiegne, see my stepfather, and form my judgment of whether there was or was not anything in my suspicions upon the first effect produced on him by my sudden and unexpected appearance before him. I founded this hope on an argument which I had already used in the case of my mother, namely, that if M. Termonde had really been concerned in the assassination of my father, he had dreaded my aunt's penetration beyond all things. Their relations had been formal, with an undercurrent of enmity on her part which had assuredly not escaped a man so astute as he. If he were guilty, would he not have feared that my aunt would have confided her thoughts to me on her death-bed? The attitude that he should assume towards me, at and after our first interview, would be a proof, complete in proportion to its suddenness, and he must have no time for preparation.

I returned to Paris, therefore, without having informed even my valet of my intention, and proceeded almost immediately to my mother's hotel.

I rang the bell.

The door was opened, and the narrow court, the glass porch, the red carpet of the staircase, were before me. The concierge, who saluted me, was not he by whom I had fancied myself slighted in my childhood; but the old valet de chambre who opened the door to me was the same. His close-shaven face wore its former impassive expression, the look that used to convey to me such an impression of insult and insolence when I came home from school. What childish absurdity!

To my question the man replied that my mother was in, also H. Termonde, and Madame Bernard, a friend of theirs. The latter name brought me back at once to the reality of the situation. Madame Bernard was a prettyish woman, very slight and very dark, with a "tip-tilted" nose, frizzy hair worn low upon her forehead, very white teeth which were continually shown by a constant smile, a short upper lip, and all the manners and ways of a woman of society well up to its latest gossip. I fell at once from my fancied height as an imaginary Grand Judiciary into the shallows of Parisian frivolity. I felt about to hear chatter upon the last new play, the latest suit for separation, the latest love affairs, and the newest bonnet. It was for this that I had eaten my heart out all these days!

The servant preceded me to the hall I knew so well, with its Oriental divan, its green plants, its strange furniture, its slightly faded carpet, its Meissonier on a draped easel, in the place formerly occupied by my father's portrait, its crowd of ornamental trifles, and the wide-spreading Japanese parasol open in the middle of the ceiling. The walls were hung with large pieces of Chinese stuff embroidered in black and white silk. My mother was half-reclining in an American rocking-chair, and shading her face from the fire with a hand-screen; Madame Bernard, who sat opposite to her, was holding her muff with one hand and gesticulating with the other; M. Termonde, in walking-dress, was standing with his back to the chimney, smoking a cigar, and warming the sole of one of his boots.

On my appearance, my mother uttered a little cry of glad surprise, and rose to welcome me. Madame Bernard instantly assumed the air with which a well-bred woman prepares to condole with a person of her acquaintance upon a bereavement. All these little details I perceived in a moment, and also the shrug of M. Termonde's shoulders, the quick flutter of his eyelids, the rapidly-dismissed expression of disagreeable surprise which my sudden appearance called forth. But what then? Was it not the same with myself? I could have sworn that at the same moment he experienced sensations exactly similar to those which were catching me at the chest and by the throat. What did this prove but that a current of antipathy existed between him and me? Was it a reason for the man's being a murderer? He was simply my stepfather, and a stepfather who did not like his stepson.

Matters had stood thus for years, and yet, after the week of miserable suspicion I had lived through, the quick look and shrug struck me strangely, even while I took his hand after I had kissed my mother and saluted Madame Bernard. His hand? No, only his finger tips as usual, and they trembled a little as I touched them. How often had my own hand shrunk with unconquerable repugnance from that contact! I listened while he repeated the same phrases of sympathy with my sorrow which he had already written to me while I was at Compiegne. I listened while Madame Bernard uttered other phrases to the same effect; and then the conversation resumed its course, and, during the half-hour that ensued, I looked on, speaking hardly at all, but mentally comparing the physiognomy of my stepfather with that of the visitor, and that of my mother. The contemplation of those three faces produced a curious impression upon me; it was that of their difference, not only of age, but of intensity, of depth. There was no mystery in my mother's face, it was as easy to read as a page in dear handwriting! The mind of Madame Bernard, a worldly, trumpery, poor mind, but harmless enough, was readily to be discerned in her features which were at once refined and commonplace. How little there was of reflection, of decision, of exercise of will, in short of individuality, behind the poetic grace of the one and the pretty affectations of the other! What a face, on the contrary, was that of my stepfather, with its strong individuality, and its vivid expression! In this man of the world, as he stood there talking with two women of the world, in his blue, furtive eyes, too wide apart, and always seeming to shun observation, in his prematurely gray hair, his mouth set round with deep wrinkles, in his dark, blotched, bilious complexion, there seemed to be a creature of another race. What passions had worn those furrows? what vigils had hollowed those eyeballs? Was this the face of a happy man, with whom everything had succeeded, who, having been born to wealth and of an excellent family, had married the woman he loved; who had known neither the wearing cares of ambition, the toil of money-getting, nor the stings of wounded self-love? It is true, he suffered from liver complaint; but why was it that, although I had hitherto been satisfied with this answer, it now appeared to me childish and even foolish? Why did all these marks of trouble and exhaustion suddenly strike me as effects of a secret cause, and why was I astonished that I had not sooner sought for it? Why was it that in his presence, contrary to my expectations, contrary to what had happened about my mother, I was plunged more deeply into the gulf of suspicion from which I had hoped to emerge with a free mind? Why, when our eyes met for just one second, was I afraid that he might read my thoughts in my glance, and why did I shift them with a pang of shame and terror? Ah! coward that I was, triple coward! Either I was wrong to think thus, and at any price I must know that I was wrong; or, I was right and I must know that too. The sole resource henceforth remaining to me for the preservation of my self-respect was ardent and ceaseless search after certainty.

That such a search was beset with difficulty I was well aware. How was I to get at facts? The very position of the problem which I had before me forbade all hope of discovering anything whatsoever by a formal inquiry. What, in fact, was the matter in question? It was to make myself certain whether M. Termonde was or was not the accomplice of the man who had led my father into the trap in which he had lost his life. But I did not know that man himself; I had no data to go upon except the particulars of his disguise and the vague speculations of a Judge of Instruction. If I could only have consulted that Judge, and availed myself of his experience? How often since have I taken out the packet containing the denunciatory letters, with the intention of showing them to him and imploring advice, support, suggestions, from him. But I have always stopped short before the door of his house; the thought of my mother barred its entrance against me. What if he, the Judge of Instruction in the case, were to suspect her as my aunt had done? Then I would go back to my own abode, and shut myself up for hours, lying on the divan in my smoking-room and drugging my senses with tobacco. During that time I read and re-read the fatal letters, although I knew them by heart, in order to verify my first impression with the hope of dispelling it. It was, on the contrary, deepened. The only gain I obtained from my repeated perusals was the knowledge that this certainty, of which I had made a point of honor to myself, could only be psychological. In short, all my fancies started from the moral data of the crime, apart from physical data which I could not obtain. I was therefore obliged to rely entirely, absolutely, upon those moral data, and I began again to reason as I had done at Compiegne. "Supposing," said I to myself, "that M. Termonde is guilty, what state of mind must he be in? This state of mind being once ascertained, how can I act so as to wrest some sign of his guilt from him?" As to his state of mind I had no doubt. Ill and depressed as I knew him to be, his mind troubled to the point of torment, if that suffering, that gloom, that misery were accompanied by the recollection of a murder committed in the past, the man was the victim of secret remorse. The point was then to invent a plan which should give, as it were, a form to his remorse, to raise the specter of the deed he had done roughly and suddenly before him. If guilty, it was impossible but that he would tremble; if innocent, he would not even be aware of the experiment. But how was this sudden summoning-up of his crime before the man whom I suspected to be accomplished? On the stage and in novels one confronts an assassin with the spectacle of his crime, and keeps watch upon his face for the one second during which he loses his self-possession; but in reality there is no instrument except unwieldy, unmanageable speech wherewith to probe a human conscience. I could not, however, go straight to M. Termonde and say to his face: "You had my father killed!" Innocent or guilty, he would have had me turned from the door as a madman!

After several hours of reflection, I came to the conclusion that only one plan was reasonable, and available: this was to have a private talk with my stepfather at a moment when he would least expect it, an interview in which all should be hints, shades, double meanings, in which each word should be like the laying of a finger upon the sorest spots in his breast, if indeed his reflections were those of a murderer.

Every sentence of mine must be so contrived as to force him to ask himself: "Why does he say this to me if he knows nothing? He does know something. How much does he know?"

So well acquainted was I with every physical trait of his, the slightest variations of his countenance, his simplest gestures, that no sign of disturbance on his part, however slight, could escape me. If I did not succeed in discovering the seat of the malady by this process, I should be convinced of the baselessness of those suspicions which were constantly springing up afresh in my mind since the death of my aunt. I would then admit the simple and probable explanation – nothing in my father's letters discredited it – that M. Termonde had loved my mother without hope in the lifetime of her first husband, and had then profited by her widowhood, of which he had not even ventured to think.

If, on the contrary, I observed during our interview that he was alive to my suspicions, that he divined them, and anxiously followed my words; if I surprised that swift gleam in his eye which reveals the instinctive terror of an animal, attacked at the moment of its fancied security, if the experiment succeeded, then – then – I dared not think of what then?

The mere possibility was too overwhelming.

But should I have the strength to carry on such a conversation? At the mere thought of it my heart-beats were quickened, and my nerves thrilled. What! this was the first opportunity that had been offered to me of action, of devoting myself to the task of vengeance, so coveted, so fully accepted during all my early years, and I could hesitate?

Happily, or unhappily, I had near me a counsellor stronger than my doubts, my father's portrait, which was hung in my smoking-room. When I awoke in the night and plunged into those thoughts, I would light my candle and go to look at the picture. How like we were to each other, my father and I, although I was more slightly built! How exactly the same we were! How near to me I felt him, and how dearly I loved him! With what emotion I studied those features, the lofty forehead, the brown eyes, the rather large mouth, the rather long chin, the mouth especially half-hidden by a black moustache cut like my own; it had no need to open, and cry out: "Andre, Andre, remember me!" Ah, no, my dear dead father, I could not leave you thus, without having done my utmost to avenge you, and it was only an interview to be faced, only an interview!

My nervousness gave way to determination at once feverish and fixed – yes, it was both – and it was in a mood of perfect self-mastery, that, after a long period of mental conflict, I repaired to the hotel on the boulevard, with the plan of my discourse clearly laid out. I felt almost sure of finding my stepfather alone; for my mother was to breakfast on that day with Madame Bernard. M. Termonde was at home, and, as I expected, alone in his study.

When I entered the room, he was sitting in a low chair, close to the fire, looking chilly, and smoking. Like myself in my dark hours, he drugged himself with tobacco. The room was a large one, and both luxurious and ordinary. A handsome bookcase lined one of the walls. Its contents were various, ranging from grave works on history and political economy, to the lightest novels of the day. A large, flat writing-table, on which every kind of writing- material was carefully arranged, occupied the middle of the room, and was adorned with photographs in plain leather cases. These were portraits of my mother and M. Termonde's father and mother. At least one prominent trait of its owner's character, his scrupulous attention to order and correctness of detail, was revealed by the aspect of my stepfather's study; but this quality, which is common to so many persons of his position in the world, may belong to the most commonplace character as well as to the most refined hypocrite. It was not only in the external order and bearing of his life that my stepfather was impenetrable, none could tell whether profound thoughts were or were not hidden behind his politeness and elegance of manner. I had often reflected on this, at a period when as yet I had no stronger motive for examining into the recesses of the man's character than curiosity, and the impression came to me with extreme intensity at the moment when I entered his presence with a firm resolve to read in the book of his past life.

We shook hands, I took a seat opposite to his on the other side of the hearth, lighted a cigar, and said, as if to explain my unaccustomed presence:

"Mamma is not here?"

"Did she not tell you, the other day, that she was to breakfast with Madame Bernard? There's an expedition to Lozano's studio" (Lozano was a Spanish painter much in vogue just then), "to see a portrait he is painting of Madame Bernard. Is there anything you want to have told to your mother?" he added, simply.

These few words were sufficient to show me that he had remarked the singularity of my visit. Ought I to regret or to rejoice at this? He was, then, already aware that I had some particular motive for coming; but this very fact would give all their intended weight to my words. I began by turning the conversation on an indifferent matter, talking of the painter Lozano and a good picture of his which I knew, "A Gipsy-dance in a Tavern-yard at Grenada." I described the bold attitudes, the pale complexions, the Moorish faces of the "gitanas," and the red carnations stuck into the heavy braids of their black hair, and I questioned him about Spain.

He answered me, but evidently out of mere politeness.

While continuing to smoke his cigar, he raked the fire with the tongs, taking up one small piece of charred wood after another between their points. By the quivering of his fingers, the only sign of his nervous sensitiveness which he was unable entirely to keep down, I could observe that my presence was then, as it always was, disagreeable to him. Nevertheless he talked on with his habitual courtesy, in his low voice, almost without tone or accent, as though he had trained himself to talk thus. His eyes were fixed on the flame, and his face, which I saw in profile, wore the expression of infinite weariness that I knew well, in indescribable stillness and sadness, with long deep lines, and the mouth was contracted as though by some bitter thought ever present. Suddenly, I looked straight at that detested profile, concentrating all the attention I had in me upon it, and, passing from one subject to another without transition, I said:

"I paid a very interesting visit this morning."

"In that you are agreeably distinguished from me," was his reply, made in a tone of utter indifference, "for I wasted my morning in putting my correspondence in order."

"Yes," I continued, "very interesting. I passed two hours with M. Massol."

I had reckoned a good deal on the effect of this name, which must have instantly recalled the inquiry into the mystery of the Imperial Hotel to his memory. The muscles of his face did not move. He laid down the tongs, leaned back in his chair, and said in an absent manner:

"The former Judge of Instruction? What is he doing now?"

Was it possible that he really did not know where the man, whom, if he were guilty, he ought to have dreaded most of all men, was then living? How was I to know whether this indifference was feigned? The trap I had set appeared to me all at once a childish notion. Admitting that my stepfather's pulses were even now throbbing with fever, and that he was saying to himself with dread: "What is he coming to? What does he mean?" why, this was a reason why he should conceal his emotion all the more carefully. No matter. I had begun; I was bound to go on, and to hit hard.

"M. Massol is Counsellor to the Court," I replied, and I added – although this was not true – "I see him often. We were talking this morning of criminals who have escaped punishment. Only fancy his being convinced that Troppman had an accomplice. He founds his belief on the details of the crime, which presuppose two men, he says. If this be true it must be admitted that 'Messieurs les assassins' have a kind of honor of their own, however odd that may appear, since the child-killing monster let his own head be cut off without denouncing the other. Nevertheless, the accomplice must have put some bad time over him, after the discovery of the bodies and the arrest of his comrade. I, for my part, would not trust to that honor, and if the humor took me to commit a crime, I should do it by myself. Would you?" I asked jestingly.

These two little words meant nothing, were merely an insignificant jest, if the man to whom I put my odd question was innocent. But, if he were guilty, those two little words were enough to freeze the marrow in his bones. He surrounded himself with smoke while listening to me, his eye-lids half veiled his eyes; I could no longer see his left hand, which hung over the far side of his chair, and he had put the right into the pocket of his morning-coat. There was a short pause before he answered me – very short – but the interval, perhaps a minute, that divided his reply from my question, was a burning one for me. But what of this? It was not his way to speak in a hurry; and besides, my question had nothing interesting in it if he were not guilty, and if he were, would he not have to calculate the bearing of the phrase which he was about to utter with the quickness of thought? He closed his eyes completely – his constant habit – and said, in the unconcerned tone of a man who is talking generalities:

"It is a fact that scraps of conscience do remain intact in very depraved individuals. One sees instances of this especially in countries where habits and morals are more genuine and true to nature than ours. There's Spain, for instance, the country that interests you so much; when I lived in Spain, it was still infested by brigands. One had to make treaties with them in order to cross the Sierras in safety; there was no case known in which they broke the contract. The history of celebrated criminal cases swarms with scoundrels who have been excellent friends, devoted sons, and constant lovers. But I am of your opinion, and I think it is best not to count too much upon them."

He smiled as he uttered the last words, and now he looked full at me with those light blue eyes which were so mysterious and impossible. No, I was not of stature to cope with him, to read his heart by force. It needed capacity of another kind than mine to play in the case of this personage the part of the magnate of police who magnetizes a criminal. And yet, why did my suspicions gather force as I felt the masked, dissimulating, guarded nature of the man in all its strength? Are there not natures so constituted that they shut themselves up without cause, just as others reveal themselves; are there not souls that love darkness as others love daylight? Courage, then, let me strike again.

"M. Massol and I," I resumed, "have been talking about what kind of life Troppmann's accomplice must be leading; and also Rochdale's; for neither of us has relinquished the intention of finding him. Before M. Massol's retirement he took the precaution to bar the limitation by a formal notice, and we have several years before us in which to search for the man. Do these criminals sleep in peace? Are they punished by remorse, or by the apprehension of danger, even in their momentary security? It would be strange if they were both at this moment good, quiet citizens, smoking their cigars like you and me, loved and loving. Do you believe in remorse?"

"Yes, I do believe in remorse," he answered.

Was it the contrast between the affected levity of my speech, and the seriousness with which he had spoken, that caused his voice to sound grave and deep to my ears? No, no; I was deceiving myself, for without a thrill he had heard the news that the limitation had been barred, that the case might be reopened any day – terrible news for him if he were mixed up with the murder – and he added, calmly, referring to the philosophic side of my question only:

"And does M. Massol believe in remorse?"

"M. Massol," said I, "is a cynic. He has seen too much wickedness, known too many terrible stories. He says that remorse is a question of stomach and religious education, and that a man with a sound digestion, who had never heard anything about hell in his childhood, might rob and kill from morning to night without feeling any other remorse than fear of the police. He also maintains, being a sceptic, that we do not know what part that question of the other life plays in solitude; and I think he is right, for I often begin to think of death, at night, and I am afraid; – yes, I, who don't believe in anything very much, am afraid. And you," I continued, "do you believe in another world?"

"Yes." This time I was sure that there was an alteration in his voice.

"And in the justice of God?"

"In His justice and His mercy," he answered, in a strange tone.

"Singular justice," I said vehemently, "which is able to do everything, and yet delays to punish! My poor aunt used always to say to me when I talked to her about avenging my father: 'I leave it to God to punish,' but, for my part, if I had got hold of the murderer, and he was there before me – if I were sure – no, I would not wait for the hour of that tardy justice of God."

I had risen while uttering these words, carried away by involuntary excitement which I knew to be unwise. M. Termonde had bent over the fire again, and once more taken up the tongs. He made no answer to my outburst. Had he really felt some slight disturbance, as I believed for an instant, at hearing me speak of that inevitable and dreadful morrow of the grave which fills myself with such fear now that there is blood upon my hands?

I could not tell. His profile was, as usual, calm and sad.

The restlessness of his hands – recalling to my mind the gesture with which he turned and returned his cane while my mother was telling him of the disappearance of my father – yes, the restlessness of his hands was extreme; but he had been working at the fire with the same feverish eagerness just before. Silence had fallen between us suddenly; but how often had the same thing happened? Did it ever fail to happen when he and I were in each other's company? And then, what could he have to say against the outburst of my grief and wrath, orphan that I was? Guilty or innocent, it was for him to be silent, and he held his peace. My heart sank; but, at the same time, a senseless rage seized upon me. At that moment I would have given my remaining life for the power of forcing their secret from those shut lips, by any mode of torture.

My stepfather looked at the clock – he, too, had risen now – and said: "Shall I put you down anywhere? I have ordered the carriage for three o'clock, as I have to be at the club at half-past. There's a ballot coming off tomorrow." Instead of the downstricken criminal I had dreamed of, there stood before me a man of society thinking about the affairs of his club. He came with me so far as the hall, and took leave of me with a smile.

Why, then, a quarter of an hour afterwards, when we passed each other on the quay, I going homeward on foot, he in his coupe – yes – why was his face so transformed, so dark and tragic? He did not see me. He was sitting back in the corner, and his clay-colored face was thrown out by the green leather behind his head. His eyes were looking – where, and at what? The vision of distress that passed before me was so different from the smiling countenance of a while ago that it shook me from head to foot with an extraordinary emotion, and forced me to exclaim, as though frightened at my own success:

"Have I struck home?"

IX

This impression of dread kept hold of me during the whole of that evening, and for several days afterwards. There is an infinite distance between our fancies, however precise they may be, and the least bit of reality.

My father's letters had stirred my being to its utmost depths, had summoned up tragic pictures before my eyes; but the simple fact of my having seen the agonized look in my stepfather's face, after my interview with him, gave me a shock of an entirely different kind.

Even after I had read the letters repeatedly, I had cherished a secret hope that I was mistaken, that some slight proof would arise and dispel suspicions which I denounced as senseless, perhaps because I had a foreknowledge of the dreadful duty that would devolve upon me when the hour of certainty had come. Then I should be obliged to act on a resolution, and I dared not look the necessity in the face. No, I had not so regarded it, previous to my meeting with my enemy, when I saw him cowering in anguish upon the cushions of his carriage. Now I would force myself to contemplate it. What should my course be, if he were guilty? I put this question to myself plainly, and I perceived all the horror of the situation. On whatever side I turned I was confronted with intolerable misery.

That things should remain as they were I could not endure. I saw my mother approach M. Termonde, as she often did, and touch his forehead caressingly with her hand or her lips. That she should do this to the murderer of my father! My very bones burned at the mere thought of it, and I felt as though an arrow pierced my breast. So be it! I would act; I would find strength to go to my mother and say: "This man is an assassin," and prove it to her – and lo! I was already shrinking from the pain that my words must inflict on her. It seemed to me that while I was speaking I should see her eyes open wide, and, through the distended pupils, discern the rending asunder of her being, even to her heart, and that she would go mad or fall down dead on the spot, before my eyes. No, I would speak to her myself. If I held the convincing proof in my hands I would appeal to justice.

But then a new scene arose before me. I pictured my mother at the moment of her husband's arrest. She would be there, in the room, close to him. "Of what crime is he accused?" she would ask, and she would have to hear the inevitable answer. And I should be the voluntary cause of this, I, who, since my childhood, and to spare her a pang, had stifled all my complaints at the time when my heart was laden with so many sighs, so many tears, so much sorrow, that it would have been a supreme relief to have poured them out to her. I had not done so then, because I knew that she was happy in her life, and that it was her happiness only that blinded her to my pain. I preferred that she should be blind and happy. And now? Ah! how could I strike her such a cruel blow, dear and fragile being that she was?

The first glimpse of the double prospect of misery which my future offered if my suspicions proved just was too terrible for endurance, and I summoned all my strength of will to shut out a vision which must bring about such consequences. Contrary to my habit, I persuaded myself into a happy solution. My stepfather looked sad when he passed me in his coupé; true, but what did this prove? Had he not many causes of care and trouble, beginning with his health, which was failing from day to day?

One fact only would have furnished me with absolute, indisputable proof; if he had been shaken by a nervous convulsion while we were talking, if I had seen him (as Hamlet, my brother in anguish, saw his uncle) start up with distorted face, before the suddenly-evoked specter of his crime. Not a muscle of his face had moved, not an eyelash had quivered; – why, then, should I set down this untroubled calm to amazing hypocrisy, and take the discomposure of his countenance half an hour later for a revelation of the truth? This was just reasoning, or at least it appears so to me, now that I am writing down my recollections in cold blood. They did not prevail against the sort of fatal instinct which forced me to follow this trail. Yes, it was absurd, it was mad, gratuitously to imagine that M. Termonde had employed another person to murder my father; yet I could not prevent myself constantly admitting that this most unlikely suggestion of my fancy was possible, and sometimes that it was certain.

When a man has given place in his mind to ideas of this kind he is no longer his own master; either he is a coward, or the thing must be fought out. It was due to my father, my mother, and myself that I should KNOW.

I walked about my rooms for hours, revolving these thoughts, and more than once I took up a pistol, saying to myself: "Just a touch, a slight movement like this" – I made the gesture – "and I am cured forever of my mortal pain." But the very handling of the weapon, the touch of the smooth barrel, reminded me of the mysterious scene of my father's death. It called up before me the sitting-room in the Imperial Hotel, the disguised man waiting, my father coming in, taking a seat at the table, turning over the papers laid before him, while a pistol, like this one in my hand, was levelled at him, close to the back of his neck; and then the fatal crack of the weapon, the head dropping down upon the table, the murderer wrapping the bleeding neck in towels and washing his hands, coolly, leisurely, as though he had just completed some ordinary task. The picture roused in me a raging thirst for vengeance. I approached the portrait of the dead man, which looked at me with its motionless eyes. What! I had my suspicions of the instigator of this murder, and I would leave them unverified because I was afraid of what I should have to do afterwards! No, no; at any price, I must in the first place know!

Three days elapsed. I was suffering tortures of irresolution, mingled with incoherent projects no sooner formed than they were rejected as impracticable. To know? – this was easily said, but I, who was so eager, nervous, and excitable, so little able to restrain my quickly-varying emotions, would never be able to extort his secret from so resolute a man, one so completely master of himself as my stepfather. My consciousness of his strength and my weakness made me dread his presence as much as I desired it. I was like a novice in arms who was about to fight a duel with a very skillful adversary; he desires to defend himself and to be victorious, but he is doubtful of his own coolness. What was I to do now, when I had struck a first blow and it had not been decisive? If our interview had really told upon his conscience, how was I to proceed to the redoubling of the first effect, to the final reduction of that proud spirit?

My reflections had arrived and stopped at this point, I was forming and re-forming plans only to abandon them, when a note reached me from my mother, complaining that I had not gone to her house since the day on which I had missed seeing her, and telling me that my stepfather had been very ill indeed two days previously with his customary liver complaint.

Two days previously, that was on the day after my conversation with him.

Here again it might be said that fate was making sport of me, redoubling the ambiguity of the signs, the chief cause of my despair. Was the imminence of this attack explanatory of the agonized expression on my stepfather's face when he passed me in his carriage? Was it a cause, or merely the effect of the terror by which he had been assailed, if he was guilty, under his mask of indifference, while I flung my menacing words in his face? Oh, how intolerable was this uncertainty, and my mother increased it, when I went to her, by her first words.

"This," she said, "is the second attack he has had in two months; they have never come so near together until now. What alarms me most is the strength of the doses of morphine he takes to lull the pain. He has never been a sound sleeper, and for some years he has not slept one single night without having recourse to narcotics; but he used to be moderate – whereas, now – "

She shook her head dejectedly, poor woman, and I, instead of compassionating her sorrow, was conjecturing whether this, too, was not a sign, whether the man's sleeplessness did not arise from terrible, invincible remorse, or whether it also could be merely the result of illness.

"Would you like to see him?" asked my mother, almost timidly, and as I hesitated she added, under the impression that I was afraid of fatiguing him, whereas I was much surprised by the proposal, "he asked to see you himself; he wants to hear the news from you about yesterday's ballot at the club." Was this the real motive of a desire to see me, which I could not but regard as singular, or did he want to prove that our interview had left him wholly unmoved? Was I to interpret the message which he had sent me by my mother as an additional sign of the extreme importance that he attached to the details of "society" life, or was he, apprehending my suspicions, forestalling them? Or, yet again, was he, too, tortured by the desire TO KNOW, by the urgent need of satisfying his curiosity by the sight of my face, whereon he might decipher my thoughts?

I entered the room – it was the same that had been mine when I was a child, but I had not been inside its door for years – in a state of mind similar to that in which I had gone to my former interview with him. I had, however, no hope now that M. Termonde would be brought to his knees by my direct allusion to the hideous crime of which I imagined him to be guilty. My stepfather occupied the room as a sleeping-apartment when he was ill, ordinarily he only dressed there. The walls, hung with dark green damask, ill-lighted by one lamp, with a pink shade, placed upon a pedestal at some distance from the bed, to avoid fatigue to the sick man's eyes, had for their only ornament a likeness of my mother by Bonnat, one of his first female portraits. The picture was hung between the two windows, facing the bed, so that M. Termonde, when he slept in that room, might turn his last look at night and his first look in the morning upon the face whose long-descended beauty the painter had very finely rendered. No less finely had he conveyed the something half-theatrical which characterized that face, the slightly affected set of the mouth, the far-off look in the eyes, the elaborate arrangement of the hair.

First, I looked at this portrait; it confronted me on entering the room; then my glance fell on my stepfather in the bed. His head, with its white hair, and his thin yellow face were supported by the large pillows, round his neck was tied a handkerchief of pale blue silk which I recognized, for I had seen it on my mother's neck, and I also recognized the red woollen coverlet that she had knitted for him; it was exactly the same as one she had made for me; a pretty bit of woman's work on which I had seen her occupied for hours, ornamented with ribbons and lined with silk. Ever and always the smallest details were destined to renew that impression of a shared interest in my mother's life from which I suffered so much, and more cruelly than ever now, by reason of my suspicion.

I felt that my looks must needs betray the tumult of such feelings, and, while I seated myself by the side of the bed, and asked my stepfather how he was, in a voice that sounded to me like that of another person, I avoided meeting his eyes.

My mother had gone out immediately after announcing me, to attend to some small matters relative to the well-being of her dear invalid. My stepfather questioned me upon the ballot at the club which he had assigned as a pretext for his wish to see me. I sat with my elbow on the marble top of the table and my forehead resting in my hand; although I did not catch his eye I felt that he was studying my face, and I persisted in looking fixedly into the half-open drawer where a small pocket-pistol, of English make, lay side by side with his watch, and a brown silk purse, also made for him by my mother. What were the dark misgivings revealed by the presence of this weapon placed within reach of his hand and probably habitually placed there? Did he interpret my thoughts from my steady observation? Or had he, too, let his glance fall by chance upon the pistol, and was he pursuing the ideas that it suggested in order to keep up the talk it was always so difficult to maintain between us? The fact is that he said, as though replying to the question in my mind: "You are looking at that pistol, it is a pretty thing, is it not?" He took it up, turned in about in his hand, and then replaced it in the drawer, which he closed. "I have a strange fancy, quite a mania; I could not sleep unless I had a loaded pistol there, quite close to me. After all, it is a habit which does no harm to anyone, and might have its advantages. If your poor father had carried a weapon like that upon him when he went to the Imperial Hotel, things would not have gone so easily with the assassin."

This time I could not refrain from raising my eyes and seeking his. How, if he were guilty, did he dare to recall this remembrance? Why, if he were not, did his glance sink before mine? Was it merely in following out an association of ideas that he referred thus to the death of my father; was it for the purpose of displaying his entire unconcern respecting the subject-matter of our last interview; or was he using a probe to discover the depth of my suspicion? After this allusion to the mysterious murder which had made me fatherless, he went on to say:

"And, by-the-bye, have you seen M. Massol again?"

"No," said I, "not since the other day."

"He is a very intelligent man. At the time of that terrible affair, I had a great deal of talk with him, in my capacity as the intimate friend of both your father and mother. If I had known that you were in the habit of seeing him latterly, I should have asked you to convey my kind regards."

"He has not forgotten you," I answered. In this I lied; for M. Massol had never spoken of my stepfather to me; but that frenzy which had made me attack him almost madly in the conversation of the other evening had seized upon me again. Should I never find the vulnerable spot in that dark soul for which I was always looking? This time his eyes did not falter, and whatever there was of the enigmatical in what I had said, did not lead him to question me farther. On the contrary, he put his finger on his lips. Used as he was to all the sounds of the house, he had heard a step approaching, and knew it was my mother's.

Did I deceive myself, or was there an entreaty that I would respect the unsuspecting security of an innocent woman in the gesture by which he enjoined silence?

Was I to translate the look that accompanied the sign into: "Do not awaken suspicion in your mother's mind, she would suffer too much;" and was his motive merely the solicitude of a man who desires to save his wife from the revival of a sad remembrance.

She came in; with the same glance she saw us both, lighted by the same ray from the lamp, and she gave us a smile, meant for both of us in common, and fraught with the same tenderness for each. It had been the dream of her life that we should be together thus, and both of us with her, and, as she had told me at Compiegne, she imputed the obstacles which had hindered the realization of her dream to my moody disposition. She came towards us, smiling, and carrying a silver tray with a glass of Vichy water upon it; this she held out to my stepfather, who drank the water eagerly, and, returning the glass to her, kissed her hand.

"Let us leave him to rest," she said, "his head is burning." Indeed, in merely touching the tips of his fingers, which he placed in mine, I could feel that he was highly feverish; but how was I to interpret this symptom, which was ambiguous like all the others, and might, like them, signify either moral or physical distress? I had sworn to myself that I would KNOW; but how? how?

I had been surprised by my stepfather's having expressed a wish to see me during his illness; but I was far more surprised when, a fortnight later, my servant announced M. Termonde in person, at my abode. I was in my study, and occupied in arranging some papers of my father's which I had brought up from Compiegne. I had passed these two weeks at my poor aunt's house, making a pretext of a final settlement of affairs, but in reality because I needed to reflect at leisure upon the course to be taken with respect to M. Termonde, and my reflections had increased my doubts. At my request, my mother had written to me three times, giving me news of the patient, so that I was aware he was now better and able to go out. On my return, the day before, I had selected a time at which I was almost sure not to see anyone for my visit to my mother's home. And now, here was my stepfather, who had not been inside my door ten times since I had been installed in an apartment of my own, paying me a visit without the loss of an hour. My mother, he said, had sent him with a message to me. She had lent me two numbers of a review, and she now wanted them back as she was sending the yearly volume to be bound; so, as he was passing the door, he had stepped in to ask me for them. I examined him closely while he was giving this simple explanation of his visit, without being able to decide whether the pretext did or did not conceal his real motive. His complexion was more sallow than usual, the look in his eyes was more glittering, he handled his hat nervously.

"The reviews are not here," I answered; "we shall probably find them in the smoking-room."

It was not true that the two numbers were not there; I knew their exact place on the table in my study; but my father's portrait hung in the smoking-room, and the notion of bringing M. Termonde face to face with the picture, to see how he would bear the confrontation, had occurred to me. At first he did not observe the portrait at all; but I went to the side of the room on which the easel supporting it stood, and his eyes, following all my movements, encountered it. His eyelids opened and closed rapidly, and a sort of dark thrill passed over his face; then he turned his eyes carelessly upon another little picture hanging upon the wall. I did not give him time to recover from the shock; but, in pursuance of the almost brutal method from which I had hitherto gained so little, I persisted:

"Do you not think," said I, "that my father's portrait is strikingly like me? A friend of mine was saying the other day that, if I had my hair cut in the same way, my head would be exactly like – "

He looked first at me, and then at the picture, in the most leisurely way, like an expert in painting examining a work of art, without any other motive than that of establishing its authenticity. If this man had procured the death of him whose portrait he studied thus, his power over himself was indeed wonderful. But – was not the experiment a crucial one for him? To betray his trouble would be to avow all? How ardently I longed to place my hand upon his heart at that moment and to count its beats.

"You do resemble him," he said at length, "but not to that degree. The lower part of the chin especially, the nose and the mouth, are alike, but you have not the same look in the eyes, and the brows, forehead, and cheeks are not the same shape."

"Do you think," said I, "that the resemblance is strong enough for me to startle the murderer if he were to meet me suddenly here, and thus?" – I advanced upon him, looking into the depths of his eyes as though I were imitating a dramatic scene. "Yes," I continued, "would the likeness of feature enable me to produce the effect of a specter, on saying to the man, 'Do you recognize the son of him whom you killed?'"

"Now we are returning to our former discussion," he replied, without any farther alteration of his countenance; "that would depend upon the man's remorse, if he had any, and on his nervous system."

Again we were silent. His pale and sickly but motionless face exasperated me by its complete absence of expression. In those minutes – and how many such scenes have we not acted together since my suspicion was first conceived – I felt myself as bold and resolute as I was the reverse when alone with my own thoughts. His impassive manner drove me wild again; I did not limit myself to this second experiment, but immediately devised a third, which ought to make him suffer as much as the two others, if he were guilty. I was like a man who strikes his enemy with a broken-handled knife, holding it by the blade in his shut hand; the blow draws his own blood also. But no, no; I was not exactly that man; I could not doubt or deny the harm that I was doing to myself by these cruel experiments, while he, my adversary, hid his wound so well that I saw it not. No matter, the mad desire TO KNOW overcame my pain.

"How strange those resemblances are," I said. "My father's handwriting and mine are exactly the same. Look here."

I opened an iron safe built into the wall, in which I kept papers which I especially valued, and took out first the letters from my father to my aunt which I had selected and placed on top of the packet. These were the latest in date, and I held them out to him, just as I had arranged them in their envelopes. The letters were addressed to "Mademoiselle Louise Cornelis, Compiegne;" they bore the postmark and the quite legible stamp of the days on which they were posted in the April and May of 1864. It was the former process over again. If M. Termonde were guilty, he would be conscious that the sudden change of my attitude towards himself, the boldness of my allusions, the vigor of my attacks were all explained by these letters, and also that I had found the documents among my dead aunt's papers. It was impossible that he should not seek with intense anxiety to ascertain what was contained in those letters that had aroused such suspicions in me. When he had the envelopes in his hands I saw him bend his brows, and I had a momentary hope that I had shattered the mask that hid his true face, that face in which the inner workings of the soul are reflected. The bent brow was, however, merely a contraction of the muscles of the eye, caused by regarding an object closely, and it cleared immediately. He handed me back the letters without any question as to their contents.

"This time," said he simply, "there really is an astonishing resemblance." Then, returning to the ostensible object of his visit – "And the reviews?" he asked.

I could have shed tears of rage. Once more I was conscious that I was a nervous youth engaged in a struggle with a resolutely self- possessed man. I locked up the letters in the safe, and I now rummaged the small bookcase in the smoking-room, then the large one in my study, and finally pretended to be greatly astonished at finding the two reviews under a heap of newspapers on my table. What a silly farce! Was my stepfather taken in by it? When I had handed him the two numbers, he rose from the chair that he had sat in during my pretended search in the chimney-corner of the smoking- room, with his back to my father's portrait. But, again, what did this attitude prove? Why should he care to contemplate an image which could not be anything but painful to him, even if he were innocent?

"I am going to take advantage of the sunshine to have a turn in the Bois," said he. "I have my coupe; will you come with me?"

Was he sincere in proposing this tete-a-tete drive which was so contrary to our habits? What was his motive: the wish to show me that he had not even understood my attack, or the yearning of the sick man who dreads to be alone?

I accepted the offer at all hazards, in order to continue my observation of him, and a quarter of an hour afterwards we were speeding towards the Arc de Triomphe in that same carriage in which I had seen him pass by me, beaten, broken, almost killed, after our first interview.

This time, he looked like another man. Warmly wrapped in an overcoat lined with seal fur, smoking a cigar, waving his hand to this person or that through the open window, he talked on and on, telling me anecdotes of all sorts, which I had either heard or not heard previously, about people whose carriages crossed ours. He seemed to be talking before me and not with me, so little heed did he take of whether he was telling what I might know, or apprising me of what I did not know. I concluded from this – for, in certain states of mind, every mood is significant – that he was talking thus in order to ward off some fresh attempt on my part. But I had not the courage to recommence my efforts to open the wound in his heart and set it bleeding afresh so soon. I merely listened to him, and once again I remarked the strange contrast between his private thoughts and the rigid doctrines which he generally professed. One would have said that in his eyes the high society, whose principles he habitually defended, was a brigand's cave. It was the hour at which women of fashion go out for their shopping and their calls, and he related all the scandals of their conduct, false or true. He dwelt on all these stories and calumnies with a horrid pleasure, as though he rejoiced in the vileness of humanity. Did this mean the facile misanthropy of a profligate, accustomed to such conversations at the club, or in sporting circles, during which each man lays bare his brutal egotism, and voluntarily exaggerates the depth of his own disenchantment that he may boast more largely of his experience? Was this the cynicism of a villain, guilty of the most hideous of crimes, and glad to demonstrate that others were less worthy than he? To hear him laugh and talk thus threw me into a singular state of dejection.

We had passed the last houses in the Avenue de Bois, and were driving along an alley on the right in which there were but few carriages. On the bare hedgerows a beautiful light shone, coming from that lofty, pale blue sky which is seen only over Paris.

He continued to sneer and chuckle, and I reflected that perhaps he was right, that the seamy side of the world was what he depicted it. Why not? Was not I there, in the same carriage with this man, and I suspected him of having had my father murdered! All the bitterness of life filled my heart with a rush. Did my stepfather perceive, by my silence and my face, that his gay talk was torturing me? Was he weary of his own effort?

He suddenly left off talking, and as we had reached a forsaken corner of the Bois, we got out of the carriage to walk a little. How strongly present to my mind is that by-path, a gray line between the poor spare grass and the bare trees, the cold winter sky, the wide road at a little distance with the carriage advancing slowly, drawn by the bay horse, shaking its head and its bit, and driven by a wooden-faced coachman – then, the man. He walked by my side, a tall figure in a long overcoat. The collar of dark brown fur brought out the premature whiteness of his hair. He held a cane in his gloved hand, and struck away the pebbles with it impatiently. Why does his image return to me at this hour with an unendurable exactness? It is because, as I observed him walking along the wintry road, with his head bent forward, I was struck as I had never been before with the sense of his absolute unremitting wretchedness. Was this due to the influence of our conversation of that afternoon, to the dejection which his sneering, sniggering talk had produced in me, or to the death of nature all around us? For the first time since I knew him, a pang of pity mingled with my hatred of him, while he walked by my side, trying to warm himself in the pale sunshine, a shrunken, weary, lamentable creature. Suddenly he turned his face, which was contracted with pain, to me, and said:

"I do not feel well. Let us go home." When we were in the carriage, he said, putting his sudden seizure upon the pretext of his health:

"I have not long to live, and I suffer so much that I should have made an end of it all years ago, had it not been for your mother." Then he went on talking of her with the blindness that I had already remarked in him. Never, in my most hostile hours, had I doubted that his worship of his wife was perfectly sincere, and once again I listened to him, as we drove rapidly into Paris in the gathering twilight, and all that he said proved how much he loved her. Alas! his passion rated her more highly than my tenderness. He praised the exquisite tact with which my mother discerned the things of the heart, to me, who knew so well her want of feeling! He lauded the keenness of her intelligence to me, whom she had so little understood! And he added, he who had so largely contributed to our separation:

"Love her dearly; you will soon be the only one to love her."

If he were the criminal I believed him to be, he was certainly aware that in thus placing my mother between himself and me he was putting in my way the only barrier which I could never, never break down, and I on my side understood clearly, and with bitterness of soul, that the obstacles so placed would be stronger than even the most fatal certainty. What, then, was the good of seeking any further? Why not renounce my useless quest at once? But it was already too late.

X

At the beginning of the summer, six months after my aunt's death, I was in exactly the same position with respect to my stepfather as on that already distant day when, maddened with suspicion by my father's letters, I entered his study, to play the part of the physician who examines a man's body, searching with his finger for the tender spot that is probably a symptom of a hidden abscess.

I was full of intuitions now, just as I was at the moment when he passed me in his carriage with his terrible face, but I did not grasp a single certainty. Would I have persisted in a struggle in which I felt beforehand that I must be beaten?

I cannot tell; for, when I no longer expected any solution to the problem set before me for my grief, a grief, too, that was both sterile and mortal, a day came on which I had a conversation with my mother so startling and appalling that to this hour my heart stands still when I think of it. I have spoken of dates; among them is the 25th of May, 1879.

My stepfather, who was on the eve of his departure for Vichy, had just had a severe attack of liver-complaint, the first since his illness after our terrible conversation in the month of January. I know that I counted for nothing – at least in any direct or positive way – in this acute revival of his malady. The fight between us, which went on without the utterance of a word on either side, and with no witnesses except ourselves, had not been marked by any fresh episode; I therefore attributed this complication to the natural development of the disease under which he labored.

I can exactly recall what I was thinking of on the 25th of May, at five o'clock in the evening, as I walked up the stairs in the hotel on the Boulevard de Latour-Marbourg. I hoped to learn that my stepfather was better, because I had been witnessing my mother's distress for a whole week, and also – I must tell all – because to know he was going to the watering-place was a great relief to me, on account of the separation it would bring about. I was so tired of my unprofitable pain! My wretched nerves were in such a state of tension that the slightest disagreeable impression became a torment. I could not sleep without the aid of narcotics, and such sleep as these procured was full of cruel dreams in which I walked by my father's side, while knowing and feeling that he was dead.

One particular nightmare used to recur so regularly that it rendered my dread of the night almost unbearable. I stood in a street crowded with people and was looking into a shop window; on a sudden I heard a man's step approaching, that of M. Termonde. I did not see him, and yet I was certain it was he. I tried to move on, but my feet were leaden; to turn my head, but my neck was immovable. The step drew nearer, my enemy was behind me, I heard his breathing, and knew that he was about to strike me. He passed his arm over my shoulder. I saw his hand, it grasped a knife, and sought for the spot where my heart lay; then it drove the blade in, slowly, slowly, and I awoke in unspeakable agony.

So often had this nightmare recurred within a few weeks, that I had taken to counting the days until my stepfather's departure, which had been at first fixed for the 21st, and then put off until he should be stronger. I hoped that when he was absent I should be at rest at least for a time. I had not the courage to go away myself, attracted as I was every day by that presence which I hated, and yet sought with feverish eagerness; but I secretly rejoiced that the obstacle was of his raising, that his absence gave me breathing-time, without my being obliged to reproach myself with weakness.

Such were my reflections as I mounted the wooden staircase, covered with a red carpet, and lighted by stained-glass windows, that led to my mother's favorite hall. The servant who opened the door informed me in answer to my question that my stepfather was better, and I entered the room with which my saddest recollections were connected, more cheerfully than usual. Little did I think that the dial hung upon one of the walls was ticking off in minutes one of the most solemn hours of my life!

My mother was seated before a small writing-table, placed in a corner of the deep glazed projection which formed the garden-end of the hall. Her left hand supported her head, and in the right, instead of going on with the letter she had begun to write, she held her idle pen, in a golden holder with a fine pearl set in the top of it (the latter small detail was itself a revelation of her luxurious habits). She was so lost in reverie that she did not hear me enter the room, and I looked at her for some time without moving, startled by the expression of misery in her refined and lovely face. What dark thought was it that closed her mouth, furrowed her brow, and transformed her features? The alteration in her looks and the evident absorption of her mind contrasted so strongly with the habitual serenity of her countenance that it at once alarmed me. But, what was the matter? Her husband was better; why, then, should the anxiety of the last few days have developed into this acute trouble? Did she suspect what had been going on close to her, in her own house, for months past? Had M. Termonde made up his mind to complain to her, in order to procure the cessation of the torture inflicted upon him by my assiduity? No. If he had divined my meaning from the very first day, as I thought he had, unless he were sure he could not have said to her: "Andre suspects me of having had his father killed." Or had the doctor discerned dangerous symptoms behind this seeming improvement in the invalid?

Was my stepfather in danger of death?

At the idea, my first feeling was joy, my second was rage – joy that he should disappear from my life, and for ever; rage that, being guilty, he should die without having felt my full vengeance. Beneath all my hesitation, my scruples, my doubts, there lurked that savage appetite for revenge which I had allowed to grow up in me, revenge that is not satisfied with the death of the hated object unless it be caused by one's self. I thirsted for revenge as a dog thirsts for water after running in the sun on a summer day. I wanted to roll myself in it, as the dog in question rolls himself in the water when he comes to it, were it the sludge of a swamp. I continued to gaze at my mother without moving. Presently she heaved a deep sigh and said aloud: "Oh, me, oh, me! what misery it is!" Then lifting up her tear-stained face, she saw me, and uttered a cry of surprise. I hastened towards her.

"You are in trouble, mother," I said. "What ails you?"

Dread of her answer made my voice falter; I knelt down before her as I used to do when a child, and, taking both her hands, I covered them with kisses. Again, at this solemn hour, my lips were met by that golden wedding-ring which I hated like a living person; yet the feeling did not hinder me from speaking to her almost childishly. "Ah," I said, "you have troubles, and to whom should you tell them if not to me? Where will you find anyone to love you more? Be good to me," I went on; "do you not feel how dear you are to me?"

She bent her head twice, made a sign that she could not speak, and burst into painful sobs.

"Has your trouble anything to do with me?" I asked.

She shook her head as an emphatic negative, and then said in a half-stifled voice, while she smoothed my hair with her hands, as she used to do in the old times:

"You are very nice to me, my Andre."

How simple those few words were, and yet they caught my heart and gripped it as a hand might do. How had I longed for some of those little words which she had never uttered, some of those gracious phrases which are like the gestures of the mind, some of her involuntary tender caresses. Now I had what I had so earnestly desired, but at what a moment and by what means! It was, nevertheless, very sweet to feel that she loved me. I told her so, employing words which scorched my lips, so that I might be kind to her.

"Is our dear invalid worse?"

"No, he is better. He is resting now," she answered, pointing in the direction of my stepfather's room.

"Mother, speak to me," I urged, "trust yourself to me; let me grieve with you, perhaps I may help you. It is so cruel for me that I must take you by surprise in order to see your tears."

I went on, pressing her by my questions and my complaining. What, then, did I hope to tear from those lips which quivered but yet kept silence? At any price I WOULD know; I was in no state to endure fresh mysteries, and I was certain that my stepfather was somehow concerned in this inexplicable trouble, for it was only he and I who so deeply moved that woman's heart of hers. She was not thus troubled on account of me, she had just told me so; the cause of her grief must have reference to him, and it was not his health. Had she, too, made any discovery? Had the terrible suspicion crossed her mind also? At the mere idea a burning fever seized upon me; I insisted and insisted again. I felt that she was yielding, if it were only by the leaning of her head towards me, the passing of her trembling hand over my hair, and the quickening of her breath.

"If I were sure," said she at length, "that this secret would die with you and me."

"Oh, mother!" I exclaimed, in so reproachful a tone that the blood flew to her cheeks. Perhaps this little betrayal of shame decided her; she pressed a lingering kiss on my forehead, as though she would have effaced the frown which her unjust distrust had set there.

"Forgive me, my Andre," she said, "I was wrong. In whom should I trust, to whom confide this thing, except to you? From whom ask counsel?" And then she went on as though she were speaking to herself, "If he were ever to apply to him?"

"He! Whom?"

"Andre, will you swear to me by your love for me, that you will never, you understand me, never, make the least illusion to what I am going to tell you?"

"Mother!" I replied, in the same tone of reproach, and then added at once, to draw her on, "I give you my word of honor!"

"Nor – " she did not pronounce a name, but she pointed anew to the door of the sick man's room.

"Never."

"You have heard of Edmond Termonde, his brother?" Her voice was lowered, as though she were afraid of the words she uttered, and now her eyes only were turned towards the closed door, indicating that she meant the brother of her husband. I had a vague knowledge of the story; it was of this brother I had thought when I was reviewing the mental history of my stepfather's family. I knew that Edmond Termonde had dissipated his share of the family fortune, no less than 1,200,000 francs, in a few years; that he had been enlisted, that he had gone on leading a debauched life in his regiment; that, having no money to come into from any quarter, and after a heavy loss at cards, he had been tempted into committing both theft and forgery. Then, finding himself on the brink of being detected, he had deserted. The end was that he did justice on himself by drowning himself in the Seine, after he had implored his brother's forgiveness in terms which proved that some sense of moral decency still lingered in him. The stolen money was made good by my stepfather; the scandal was hushed up, thanks to the scoundrel's disappearance. I had reconstructed the whole story in my mind from the gossip of my good old nurse, and also from certain traces of it which I had found in some passages of my father's correspondence. Thus, when my mother put her question to me in so agitated a way, I supposed she was about to tell me of family grievances on the part of her husband which were totally indifferent to me, and it was with a feeling of disappointment that I asked her:

"Edmond Termonde? The man who killed himself?"

She bent her head to answer, yes, to the first part of my question; then, in a still lower voice, she said:

"He did not kill himself, he is still alive."

"He is still alive," I repeated mechanically, and without a notion of what could be the relation between the existence of this brother and the tears which I had seen her shed.

"Now you know the secret of my sorrow," she resumed, in a firmer, almost a relieved tone. "This infamous brother is a tormentor of my Jacques; he puts him to death daily by the agonies which he inflicts upon him. No; the suicide never took place. Such men as he have not the courage to kill themselves. Jacques dictated that letter to save him from penal servitude after he had arranged everything for his flight, and given him the wherewithal to lead a new life, if he would have done so. My poor love, he hoped at least to save the integrity of his name out of all the terrible wreck. Edmond had, of course, to renounce the name of Termonde, to escape pursuit, and he went to America. There he lived – as he had lived here. The money he took with him was soon exhausted, and again he had recourse to his brother. Ah! the wretch knew well that Jacques had made all these sacrifices to the honor of his name, and when my husband refused him the money he demanded, he made use of the weapon which he knew would avail.

"Then began the vilest persecution, the most atrocious levying of black-mail. Edmond threatened to return to France; between going to the galleys here or starving in America, he said, he preferred the galleys here and Jacques yielded the first time – he loved him; after all, he was his only brother. You know when you have once shown weakness in dealing with people of this sort you are lost. The threat to return had succeeded, and the other has since used it to extort sums of which you have no idea.

"This abominable persecution has been going on for years, but I have only been aware of it since the war. I saw that my husband was utterly miserable about something; I knew that a hidden trouble was preying on him, and then, one day, he told me all. Would you believe it? It was for me that he was afraid. 'What can he possibly do to me?' I asked my Jacques. 'Ah,' he said, 'he is capable of anything for the sake of revenge. And then he saw me so overwhelmed by distress at his fits of melancholy, and I so earnestly entreated him, that at length he made a stand. He positively refused to give any more money. We have not heard of the wretch for some time – he has kept his word – Andre he is in Paris!"

I had listened to my mother with growing attention. At any period of my life, I, who had not the same notions of my stepfather's sensitiveness of feeling which my dear mother entertained, would have been astonished at the influence exercised by this disgraced brother. There are similar pests in so many families, that it is plainly to the interest of society to separate the various representatives of the same name from each other. At any time I should have doubted whether M. Termonde, a bold and violent man as I knew him to be, had yielded under the menace of a scandal whose real importance he would have estimated quite correctly. Then I would have explained this weakness by the recollections of his childhood, by a promise made to his dying parents; but now, in the actual state of my mind, full as I was of the suspicions which had been occupying my thoughts for weeks, it was inevitable that another idea should occur to me. And that idea grew, and grew, taking form as my mother went on speaking. No doubt my face betrayed the dread with which the notion inspired me, for she interrupted her narrative to ask me:

"Are you feeling ill, Andre?"

I found strength to answer, "No; I am upset by having found you in tears. It is nothing."

She believed me; she had just seen me overcome by her emotion; she kissed me tenderly, and I begged her to continue. She then told me that one day in the previous week a stranger, coming ostensibly from one of their friends in London, had asked to see my stepfather. He was ushered into the hall, and into her presence, and she guessed at once by the extraordinary agitation which M. Termonde displayed that the man was Edmond. The two brothers went into my stepfather's private room, while my mother remained in the hall, half dead with anxiety and suspense, every now and then hearing the angry tones of their voices, but unable to distinguish any words. At length the brother came out, through the hall, and looked at her as he passed by with eyes that transfixed her with fear.

"And the same evening," she went on, "Jacques took to his bed. Now, do you understand my despair? Ah, it is not our name that I care for. I wear myself out with repeating, 'What has this to do with us? How can we be spattered by this mud?' It is his health, his precious health! The doctor says that every violent emotion is a dose of poison to him. Ah!" she cried, with a gesture of despair, "this man will kill him."

To hear that cry, which once again revealed to me the depth of her passion for my stepfather, to hear it at this moment, and to think what I was thinking!

"You saw him?" I asked, hardly knowing what I said. "Have I not told you that he passed by me, there?" and with terror depicted in her face, she showed me the place on the carpet.

"And you are sure that the man was his brother?"

"Jacques told me so in the evening; but I did not require that;

I should have recognized him by the eyes. How strange it is! Those two brothers, so different; Jacques so refined, so distinguished, so noble-minded, and the other, a big, heavy, vulgar lout, common- looking, and a rascal – well, they have the same look in their eyes."

"And under what name is he in Paris?"

"I do not know. I dare not speak of him any more. If he knew that I have told you this, with his ideas! But then, dear, you would have heard it at some time or other; and besides," she added with firmness, "I would have told you long ago about this wretched secret if I had dared! You are a man now, and you are not bound by this excessively scrupulous fraternal affection. Advise me, Andre; what is to be done?"

"I do not understand you."

"Yes, yes. There must be some means of informing the police and having this man arrested without its being talked of in the newspapers or elsewhere. Jacques would not do this, because the man is his brother; but if we were to act, you and I, on our own side? I have heard you say that you visit M. Massol, whom we knew at the time of our great misfortune; suppose I were to go to him and ask his advice? Ah! I must keep my husband alive – he must be saved! I love him too much!"

Why was I seized with a panic at the idea that she might carry out this project, and apply to the former Judge of Instruction – I, who had not ventured to go to his house since my aunt's death for fear he should divine my suspicions merely by looking at me? What was it that I saw so clearly, that made me implore her to abandon her idea in the very name of the love she bore her husband?

"You will not do this," I said; "you have no right to do it. He would never forgive you, and he would have just cause; it would be betraying him."

"Betraying him! It would be saving him!"

"And if his brother's arrest were to strike him a fresh blow? If you were to see him ill, more ill than ever, on account of what you had done?"

I had used the only argument that could have convinced her. Strange irony of fate! I calmed her, I persuaded her not to act – I, who had suddenly conceived the monstrous notion that the doer of the murderous deed, the docile instrument in my stepfather's hands, was this infamous brother – that Edmond Termonde and Rochdale were one and the same man!

XI

The night which followed that conversation with my mother remains in my memory as the most wretched I had hitherto endured; and yet how many sleepless nights had I passed, while all the world around me slept, in bitter conflict with a thought which held mine eyes waking and devoured my heart! I was like a prisoner who has sounded every inch of his dungeon – the walls, the floor, the ceiling – and who, on shaking the bars of his window for the hundredth time, feels one of the iron rods loosen under the pressure. He hardly dares to believe in his good fortune, and he sits down upon the ground almost dazed by the vision of deliverance that has dawned upon him. "I must be cool-headed now," said I to myself, as I walked to and fro in the smoking-room, whither I had retired without tasting the meal that was served on my return. Evening came, then the black night; the dawn followed, and once more the full day. Still I was there, striving to see clearly amid the cloud of suppositions in which an event, simple in itself (only that in my state of mind no event would have seemed simple), had wrapped me.

I was too well used to these mental tempests not to know that the only safety consisted in clinging to the positive facts, as though to immovable rocks.

In the present instance, the positive facts reduced themselves to two: first, I had just learned that a brother of M. Termonde, who passed for dead, and of whom my stepfather never spoke, existed; secondly, that this man, disgraced, proscribed, ruined, an outlaw in fact, exercised a dictatorship of terror over his rich, honored, and irreproachable brother. The first of these two facts explained itself. It was quite natural that Jacques Termonde should not dispel the legend of the suicide, which was of his own invention, and had saved the other from the galleys. It is never pleasant to have to own a thief, a forger, or a deserter, for one's nearest relation; but this, after all, is only an excessively disagreeable matter.

The second fact was of a different kind. The disproportion between the cause assigned by my stepfather and its result in the terror from which he was suffering was too great. The dominion which Edmond Termonde exercised over his brother was not to be justified by the threat of his return, if that return were not to have any other consequence than a transient scandal. My mother, who regarded her husband as a noble-minded, high-souled, great-hearted man, might be satisfied with the alleged reason; but not I. It occurred to me to consult the Code of Military Justice, and I ascertained, by the 184th clause, that a deserter cannot claim immunity from punishment until after he has attained his forty-seventh year, so that it was most likely Edmond Termonde was still within the reach of the law.

Was it possible that his desire to shield his brother from the punishment of the offense of desertion should throw my stepfather into such a state of illness and agitation? I discerned another reason for this dominion – some dark and terrible bond of complicity between the two men. What if Jacques Termonde had employed his brother to kill my father, and proof of the transaction was still in the murderer's possession? No doubt his hands would be tied so far as the magistrates were concerned; he had it in his power to enlighten my mother, and the mere threat of doing this would suffice to make a loving husband tremble, and tame his fierce pride.

"I must be cool," I repeated, "I must be cool;" and I put all my strength to recalling the physical and moral particulars respecting the crime which were in my possession. It was my business now to try whether one single point remained obscure when tested by the theory of the identity of Rochdale with Edmond Termonde. The witnesses were agreed in representing Rochdale as tall and stout, my mother had described Edmond Termonde as a big, heavy man. Fifteen years lay between the assassin of 1864, and the elderly rake of 1879; but nothing prevented the two from being identical. My mother had dwelt upon the color of Edmond Termonde's eyes, pale blue like those of his brother; the concierge of the Imperial Hotel had mentioned the pale blue color and the brightness of Rochdale's eyes in his deposition, which I knew by heart. He had noticed this peculiarity on account of the contrast of the eyes with the man's bronzed complexion. Edmond Termonde had taken refuge in America after his alleged suicide, and what had M. Massol said? I could hear him repeat, with his well-modulated voice, and methodical movement of the hand: "A foreigner, American or English, or, perhaps, a Frenchman settled in America." Physical impossibility there existed none.

And moral impossibility? That was equally absent. In order to convince myself more fully of this, I took up the history of the crime from the moment at which my father's correspondence concerning Jacques Termonde became explicit, that is to say, in January, 1864.

So as to rid my judgment of every trace of personal enmity, I suppressed the names in my thoughts, reducing the dreadful occurrence by which I had suffered to the bareness of an abstract narrative. A man is desperately in love with the wife of one of his intimate friends, a woman whom he knows to be absolutely, spotlessly virtuous; he knows, he feels, that if she were free she would love him; but that, not being free, she will never, never be his. This man is of the temperament which makes criminals, his passions are violent in the extreme, he has no scruples and a despotic will; he is accustomed to see everything give way to his desires. He perceives that his friend is growing jealous; a little later and the house will no longer be open to him.

Would not the thought come to him – if the husband could be got rid of? And yet – ?

This dream of the death of him, who forms the sole obstacle to his happiness, troubles the man's head, it recurs once, twice, many times, and he turns the fatal idea over and over again in his brain until he becomes used to it. He arrives at the "If I dared," which is the starting point of the blackest villainies. The idea takes a precise form; he conceives that he might have the man whom he now hates, and by whom he feels that he is hated, killed. Has he not, far away, a wretch of a brother, whose actual existence, to say nothing of his present abode, is absolutely unknown? What an admirable instrument of murder he should find in this infamous, depraved, and needy brother, whom he holds at his beck and call by the aid in money that he sends him! And the temptation grows and grows. An hour comes when it is stronger than all besides, and the man, resolved to play this desperate game, summons his brother to Paris. How? By one or two letters in which he excites the rascal's hopes of a large sum of money to be gained, at the same time that he imposes the condition of absolute secrecy as to his voyage. The other accepts; he is a social failure, a bankrupt in life, he has neither relations nor ties, he has been leading an anonymous and haphazard existence for years. The two brothers are face to face. Up to that point all is logical, all is in conformity with the possible stages of a project of this order.

I arrived at the execution of it; and I continued to reason in the same way, impersonally. The rich brother proposes the blood-bargain to the poor brother. He offers him money; a hundred thousand francs, two hundred thousand, three hundred thousand.

From what motive should the scoundrel hesitate to accept the offer?

Moral ideas? What is the morality of a rake who has gone from libertinism to theft? Under the influence of my vengeful thoughts I had read the criminal news of the day in the journals, and the reports of criminal trials, too assiduously for years past, not to know how a man becomes a murderer. How many cases of stabbing, shooting, and poisoning have there not been, in which the gain was entirely uncertain, and the conditions of danger extreme, merely to enable the perpetrators to go, presently, and expend the murder- money in some low haunt of depravity?

Fear of the scaffold? Then nobody would kill. Besides, debauchees, whether they stop short at vice or roll down the descent into crime, have no foresight of the future. Present sensation is too strong for them; its image abolishes all other images, and absorbs all the vital forces of the temperament and the soul. An old dying mother, children perishing of hunger, a despairing wife; have these pictures of their deeds ever arrested drunkards, gamblers, or profligates? No more have the tragic phantoms of the tribunal, the prison, and the guillotine, when, thirsting for gold, they kill to procure it. The scaffold is far off, the brothel is at the street corner, and the being sunk in vice kills a man, just as a butcher would kill a beast, that he may go thither, or to the tavern, or to the low gaming-house, with a pocket full of money. This is the daily mode of procedure in crime.

Why should not the desire of a more elevated kind of debauch possess the same wicked attraction for men who are indeed more refined, but are quite as incapable of moral goodness as the rascally frequenters of the lowest dens of iniquity?

Ah! the thought that my father's blood might have paid for suppers in a New York night-house was too cruel and unendurable. I lost courage to pursue my cold, calm, reasonable deductions, a kind of hallucination came upon me – a mental picture of the hideous scene – and I felt my reason reel. With a great effort I turned to the portrait of my father, gazed at it long, and spoke to him as if he could have heard me, aloud, in abject entreaty. "Help me, help me!"

And then, I once more became strong enough to resume the dreadful hypothesis, and to criticise it point by point. Against it was its utter unlikelihood; it resembled nothing but the nightmare of a diseased imagination. A brother who employs his brother as the assassin of a man whose wife he wants to marry! Still, although the conception of such a devilish plot belonged to the domain of the wildest fantasies, I said to myself: "This may be so, but in the way of crime, there is no such thing as unlikelihood. The assassin ceases to move in the habitual grooves of social life by the mere fact that he makes up his mind to murder." And then a score of examples of crimes committed under circumstances as strange and exceptional as those whose greater or less probability

I was then discussing with myself recurred to my memory.

One objection arose at once. Admitting this complicated crime to be possible only, how came I to be the first to form a suspicion of it? Why had not the keen, subtle, experienced old magistrate, M. Massol, looked in that direction for an explanation of the mystery in whose presence he confessed himself powerless? The answer came ready. M. Massol did not think of it, that was all. The important thing is to know, not whether the Judge of Instruction suspected the fact, or did not suspect it; but whether the fact itself is, or is not, real.

Again, what indications had reached M. Massol to put him on this scent? If he had thoroughly studied my father's home and his domestic life, he had acquired the certainty that my mother was a faithful wife and a good woman. He had witnessed her sincere grief, and he had not seen, as I had, letters written by my father in which he acknowledged his jealousy, and revealed the passion of his false friend.

But, even supposing the judge had from the first suspected the villainy of my future stepfather, the discovery of his accomplices would have been the first thing to be done, since, in any case, the presence of M. Termonde in our house at the time of the murder was an ascertained fact.

Supposing M. Massol had been led to think of the brother who had disappeared, what then? Where were the traces of that brother to be found? Where and how? If Edmond and Jacques had been accomplices in the crime, would not their chief care be to contrive a means of correspondence which should defy the vigilance of the police? Did they not cease for a time to communicate with each other by letters? What had they to communicate, indeed? Edmond was in possession of the price of the murder, and Jacques was occupied in completing his conquest of my mother's heart.

I resumed my argument; all this granted again, but, although M. Massol was ignorant of the essential factor in the case, although he was unaware of Jacques Termonde's passion for the wife of the murdered man, my aunt knew it well, she had in her hands indisputable proofs of my father's suspicions; how came she not to have thought as I was now thinking. And how did I know that she had NOT thought just as I was thinking? She had been tormented by suspicions, even she, too; she had lived and died haunted by them. The only difference was that she had included my mother in them, being incapable of forgiving her the sufferings of the brother whom she loved so deeply. To act against my mother was to act against me, so she had forsworn that idea forever. But if she would have acted against my mother, how could she have gone beyond the domain of vague inductions, since she, no more than I, could have divined my stepfather's alibi, or known of the actual existence of Edmond Termonde? No; that I should be the first to explain the murder of my father as I did, proved only that I had come into possession of additional information respecting the surroundings of the crime, and not that the conjectures drawn from it were baseless.

Other objections presented themselves. If my stepfather had employed his brother to commit the murder, how came he to reveal the existence of that brother to his wife? An answer to this question was not far to seek. If the crime had been committed under conditions of complicity, only one proof of the fact could remain, namely, the letters written by Jacques Termonde to Edmond, in which the former recalled the latter to Europe and gave him instructions for his journey; these letters Edmond had of course preserved, and it was through them, and by the threat of showing them to my mother, that he kept a hold over his brother. To tell his wife so much as he had told her was to forestall and neutralize this threat, at least to a certain extent; for, if the doer of the deed should ever resolve on revealing the common secret to the victim's widow, now the wife of him who had inspired it, the latter would be able to deny the authenticity of the letters, to plead the former confidence reposed in her respecting his brother, and to point out that the denunciation was an atrocious act of revenge achieved by a forgery. And, besides, if indeed the crime had been committed in the manner that I imagined, was not that revelation to my mother justified by another reason?

The remorseful moods by which I believed my stepfather to

be tortured were not likely to escape the observant affection of his wife; she could not fail to know that there was a dark shadow on his life which even her love could not dispel. Who knows but she had suffered from the worst of all jealousy, that which is inspired by a constant thought not imparted, a strange emotion hidden from one? And he had revealed a portion of the truth to her so as to spare her uneasiness of that kind, and to protect himself from questions which his conscience rendered intolerable to him. There was then no contradiction between this half-revelation made to my mother, and my own theory of the complicity of the two brothers. It was also clear to me that in making that revelation he had been unable to go beyond a certain point in urging upon her the necessity of silence towards me – silence which would never have been broken but for her unforeseen emotion, but for my affectionate entreaties, but for the sudden arrival of Edmond Termonde, which had literally bewildered the poor woman. But how was my stepfather's imprudence in refusing money to this brother, who was at bay and ready to dare any and every thing, to be explained? This, too, I succeeded in explaining to myself. It had happened before my aunt's death, at a period when my stepfather believed himself to be guaranteed from all risk on my side. He believed himself to be sheltered from justice by the statute of limitations. He was ill. What, then, was more natural than that he should wish to recover those papers which might become a means of levying blackmail upon his widow after his death, and dishonoring his memory in the heart of that woman whom he had loved – even to crime – at any price? Such a negotiation could only be conducted in person. My stepfather would have reflected that his brother would not fulfil his threat without making a last attempt; he would come to Paris, and the accomplices would again be face to face after all these years. A fresh but final offer of money would have to be made to Edmond, the price of the relinquishment of the sole proof whereby the mystery of the Imperial Hotel could be cleared up. In this calculation my stepfather had omitted to forecast the chance that his brother might come to the hotel on the Boulevard de Latour-Maubourg, that he would be ushered into my mother's presence, and that the result of the shock to himself – his health being already undermined by his prolonged mental anguish – would be a fresh attack of his malady. In events, there is always the unexpected to put to rout the skillful calculations of the most astute and the most prudent, and when I reflected that so much cunning, such continual watchfulness over himself and others had all come to this – unless indeed these surmises of mine were but fallacies of a brain disturbed by fever and the consuming desire for vengeance – I once more felt the passage of the wind of destiny over us all.

However, whether reality or fancy, there they were, and I could not remain in ignorance or in doubt. At the end of all my various arguments for and against the probability of my new explanation of the mystery, I arrived at a positive fact: rightly or wrongly I had conceived the possibility of a plot in which Edmond Termonde had served as the instrument of murder in his brother's hand. Were there only one single chance, one against a thousand, that my father had been killed in this way, I was bound to follow up the clew to the end, on pain of having to despise myself as the veriest coward that lived. The time of sorrowful dreaming was over; it was now necessary to act, and to act was to know.

Morning dawned upon these thoughts of mine. I opened my window, I saw the faces of the lofty houses livid in the first light of day, and I swore solemnly to myself, in the presence of reawakening life, that this day should see me begin to do what I ought, and the morrow should see me continue, and the following days should see the same, until I could say to myself: "I am certain."

I resolutely repressed the wild feelings which had taken hold of me during the night, and I fixed my mind upon the problem: "Does there exist any means of making sure whether Edmond Termonde is, or is not, identical with the man who in 1864 called himself Rochdale?"

For the answer to this question I had only myself, the resources of my own intelligence, and my personal will to rely upon. I must do myself the justice to state that not for one minute, during all those cruel hours, was I tempted to rid myself once for all of the difficulties of my tragic task by appealing to justice, as I should have done had I not taken my mother's sufferings into account. I had resolved that the terrible blow of learning that for fifteen years she had been the wife of an assassin should never be dealt to her by me. In order that she might always remain in ignorance of this story of crime, it was necessary for the struggle to be strictly confined to my stepfather and myself.

And yet, I thought, what if I find that he is guilty?

At this idea, no longer vague and distant, but liable today, to- morrow, at any time, to become an indisputable truth, a terrible project presented itself to my mind. But I would not look in that direction, I made answer to myself: "I will think of this later on," and I forced myself to concentrate all my reflections upon the actual day and its problem: How to verify the identity of Edmond Termonde with the false Rochdale?

To tear the secret from my stepfather was impossible. I had vainly endeavored for months to find the flaw in his armor of dissimulation; I had but broken not one dagger, but twenty against the plates of that cuirass. If I had had all the tormentors of the Middle Ages at my service, I could not have forced his fast-shut lips to open, or extorted an admission from his woebegone and yet impenetrable face.

There remained the other; but in order to attack him, I must first discover under what name he was hiding in Paris, and where. No great effort of imagination was required to hit upon a certain means of discovering these particulars. I had only to recall the circumstances under which I had learned the fact of Edmond Termonde's arrival in Paris. For some reason or other – remembrance of a guilty complicity or fear of a scandal – my stepfather trembled with fear at the mere idea of his brother's return. His brother had returned, and my stepfather would undoubtedly make every effort to induce him to go away again. He would see him, but not at the house on the Boulevard de Latour-Maubourg, on account of my mother and the servants. I had, therefore, a sure means of finding out where Edmond Termonde was living; I would have his brother followed.

There were two alternatives: either he would arrange a meeting in some lonely place, or he would go himself to Edmond Termonde's abode. In the latter case, I should have the information I wanted at once; in the former, it would be sufficient to give the description of Edmond Termonde just as I had received it from my mother, and to have him also followed on his return from the place of meeting. The spy-system has always seemed to me to be infamous, and even at that moment I felt all the ignominy of setting this trap for my stepfather; but when one is fighting, one must use the weapons that will avail. To attain my end, I would have trodden everything under foot except my mother's grief.

And then? Supposing myself in possession of the false name of Edmond Termonde and his address, WHAT WAS I TO DO? I could not, in imitation of the police, lay my hand upon him and his papers, and get off with profuse excuses for the action when the search was finished. I remember to have turned over twenty plans in my mind, all more or less ingenious, and rejected them all in succession, concluding by again fixing my mind on the bare facts.

Supposing the man really had killed my father, it was impossible that the scene of the murder should not be indelibly impressed upon his memory. In his dark hours the face of the dead man, whom I resembled so closely, must have been visible to his mind's eye.

Once more I studied the portrait at which my stepfather had hardly dared to glance, and recalled my own words: "Do you think the likeness is sufficiently strong for me to have the effect of a specter upon the criminal?"

Why not utilize this resemblance? I had only to present myself suddenly before Edmond Termonde, and call him by the name – Rochdale – to his ears its syllables would have the sound of a funeral bell. Yes! that was the way to do it; to go into the room he now occupied, just as my father had gone into the room at the Imperial Hotel, and to ask for him by the name under which my father had asked for him, showing him the very face of his victim. If he was not guilty, I should merely have to apologize for having knocked at his door by mistake; if he was guilty, he would be so terrified for some minutes that his fear would amount to an avowal. It would then be for me to avail myself of that terror to wring the whole of his secret from him.

What motives would inspire him? Two, manifestly – the fear of punishment, and the love of money. It would then be necessary for me to be provided with a large sum when taking him unawares, and to let him choose between two alternatives, either that he should sell me the letters which had enabled him to blackmail his brother for years past, or that I should shoot him on the spot.

And what if he refused to give up the letters to me? Is it likely that a ruffian of his kind would hesitate?

Well, then, he would accept the bargain, hand me over the papers by which my stepfather is convicted of murder, and take himself off; and I must let him go away just as he had gone away from the Imperial Hotel, smoking a cigar, and paid for his treachery to his brother, even as he had been paid for his treachery to my father! Yes, I must let him go away thus, because to kill him with my own hand would be to place myself under the necessity of revealing the whole of the crime, which I am bound to conceal at all hazards.

"Ah, mother! what will you not cost me!" I murmured with tears.

Fixing my eyes again upon the portrait of the dead man, it seemed to me that I read in its eyes and mouth an injunction never to wound the heart of the woman he had so dearly loved – even for the sake of avenging him. "I will obey you," I made answer to my father, and bade adieu to that part of my vengeance.

It was very hard, very cruel to myself; nevertheless, it was possible; for, after all, did I hate the wretch himself? He had struck the blow, it is true, but only as a servile tool in the hand of another.

Ah! that other, I would not let HIM escape, when he should

be in my grip; he who had conceived, meditated, arranged, and paid for the deed; he who had stolen all from me, all, all, from my father's life even to my mother's love; he, the real, the only culprit. Yes, I would lay hold of him, and contrive and execute my vengeance, while my mother should never suspect the existence of that duel out of which I should come triumphant. I was intoxicated beforehand with the idea of the punishment which I would find means to inflict upon the man whom I execrated. It warmed my heart only to think of how this would repay my long, cruel martyrdom.

"To work! to work!" I cried aloud.

I trembled lest this should be nothing but a delusion, lest Edmond Termonde should have already left the country, my stepfather having previously purchased his silence.

At nine o'clock I was in an abominable Private Inquiry Office – merely to have passed its threshold would have seemed to me a shameful action, only a few hours before. At ten I was with my broker, giving him instructions to sell out 100,000 francs' worth of shares for me. That day passed, and then a second. How I bore the succession of the hours, I know not. I do know that I had not courage to go to my mother's house, or to see her again. I feared she might detect my wild hope in my eyes, and unconsciously forewarn my stepfather by a sentence or a word, as she had unconsciously informed me.

Towards noon, on the third day, I learned that my stepfather had gone out that morning. It was a Wednesday, and on that day my mother always attended a meeting for some charitable purpose in the Grenelle quarter. M. Termonde had changed his cab twice, and had alighted from the second vehicle at the Grand Hotel. There he had paid a visit to a traveler who occupied a room on the second floor (No. 353); this person's name was entered in the list of arrivals as Stanbury. At noon I was in possession of these particulars, and at two o'clock I ascended the staircase of the Grand Hotel, with a loaded revolver and a note-case containing one hundred banknotes, wherewith to purchase the letters, in my pocket.

Was I about to enter on a formidable scene in the drama of my life, or was I about to be convinced that I had been once more made the dupe of my own imagination?

At all events, I should have done my duty.

XII

I had reached the second floor. At one corner of the long corridor there was a notification that the numbers ran from 300 to 360. A waiter passed me, whistling; two girls were chattering and laughing in a kind of office at the stair-head; the various noises of the courtyard came up through the open windows.

The moment was opportune for the execution of my project. With these people about the man could not hope to escape from the house. 345, 350, 351, 353 – I stood before the door of Edmond Termonde's room; the key was in the lock; chance had served my purpose better than I had ventured to hope. This trifling particular bore witness to the security in which the man whom I was about to surprise was living. Was he even aware that I existed?

I paused a moment before the closed door. I wore a short coat, so as to have my revolver within easy reach in the pocket, and I put my right hand upon it, opened the door with my left, and entered without knocking.

"Who is there?" said a man who was lying rather than sitting in an arm-chair, with his feet on a table; he was reading a newspaper and smoking, and his back was turned to the door. He did not trouble himself to rise and see whose hand had opened the door, thinking, no doubt, that a servant had come in; he merely turned his head slightly, and I did not give him time to look completely round.

"M. Rochdale?" I asked.

He started to his feet, pushed away the chair, and rushed to the other side of the table, staring at me with a terrified countenance; his light blue eyes were unnaturally distended, his face was livid, his mouth was half open, his legs bent under him. His tall, robust frame had sustained one of those shocks of excessive terror which almost paralyze the forces of life. He uttered but one word – "Cornelis!"

At last I held in my victorious hand the proof that I had been seeking for months, and in that moment I was master of all the resources of my being. Yes, I was as calm, as clear of purpose, as my adversary was the reverse. He was not accustomed to live, like his accomplice, in the daily habits of studied dissimulation. The name, "Rochdale," the terrifying likeness, the unlooked-for arrival! I had not been mistaken in my calculation. With the amazing rapidity of thought that accompanies action I perceived the necessity of following up this first shock of moral terror by a shock of physical terror. Otherwise, the man would hurl himself upon me, in the moment of reaction, thrust me aside and rush away like a madman, at the risk of being stopped on the stairs by the servants, and then? But I had already taken out my revolver, and I now covered the wretch with it, calling him by his real name, to prove that I knew all about him.

"M. Edmond Termonde," I said, "if you make one step towards me, I will kill you, like the assassin that you are, as you killed my father."

Pointing to a chair at the corner of the half-open window, I added:

"Sit down!"

He obeyed mechanically. At that instant I exercised absolute control over him; but I felt sure this would cease so soon as he recovered his presence of mind. But even though the rest of the interview were now to go against me, that could not alter the certainty which I had acquired. I had wanted to know whether Edmond Termonde was the man who had called himself Rochdale, and I had secured undeniable proof of the fact. Nevertheless, it was due to myself that I should extract from my enemy the proof of the truth of all my conjectures, that proof which would place my stepfather at my mercy. This was a fresh phase of the struggle.

I glanced round the room in which I was shut up with the

assassin. On the bed, placed on my left, lay a loaded cane, a hat and an overcoat; on a small table were a steel "knuckle-duster" and a revolver. Among the articles laid out on a chest of drawers on my right a bowie-knife was conspicuous, a valise was placed against an unused door, a wardrobe with a looking-glass stood before another unused door, then came the toilet-stand, and the man, crouching under the aim of my revolver, between the table and the window. He could neither escape, nor reach to any means of defense without a personal struggle with me; but he would have to stand my fire first, and besides, if he was tall and robust, I was neither short or feeble. I was twenty-five, he was fifty. All the moral forces were for me, I must win.

"Now," said I, as I took a seat, but without releasing him from the covering barrel of my pistol, "let us talk."

"What do you want of me?" he asked roughly. His voice was both hoarse and muffled; the blood had gone back into his cheeks, his eyes, those eyes so exactly like his brother's, sparkled. The brute-nature was reviving in him after having sustained a fearful shock, as though astonished that it still lived.

"Come, then," he added, clenching his fists, "I am caught. Fire on me, and let this end."

Then, as I made him no answer, but continued to threaten him with my pistol, he exclaimed:

"Ah! I understand; it is that blackguard Jacques who has sold me to you in order to get rid of me himself. There's the statute of limitations – he thinks he is safe! But has he told you that he was in it himself, good, honest man, and that I have the proof of this? Ah! he thinks I am going to let you kill me, like that, without speaking? No, I shall call out, we shall be arrested, and all will be known."

Fury had seized upon him; he was about to shout "Help!" and the worst of it was that rage was rising in me also. It was he, with that same hand which I saw creeping along the table, strong, hairy, seeking something to throw at me – yes – it was he who had killed my father.

One impulse more of anger and I was lost; a bullet was lodged in his body, and I saw his blood flow. Oh, what good it would have done me to see that sight!

But no, I soon made the sacrifice of this particular vengeance. In a second, I beheld myself arrested, obliged to explain everything, and my mother exposed to all the misery of it.

Happily for me, he also had an interval of reflection. The first idea that must have occurred to him was that his brother had betrayed him, by telling me one-half of the truth, so as to deliver him up to my vengeance. The second, no doubt, was that, for a son who came to avenge his dead father, I was making a good deal of delay about it. There was a momentary silence between us. This allowed me to regain my coolness, and to say: "You are mistaken," so quietly that his amazement was visible in his face. He looked at me, then closed his eyes, and knitted his brow. I felt that he could not endure my resemblance to my father.

"Yes, you are mistaken," I continued deliberately, giving the tone of a business conversation to this terrible interview. "I have not come here either to have you arrested or to kill you. Unless," I added, "you oblige me to do so yourself, as I feared just now you would oblige me. I have come to propose a bargain to you, but it is on the condition that you listen, as I shall speak, with coolness."

Once more we were both silent. In the corridor, almost at the door of the room, there were sounds of feet, voices, and peals of laughter. This was enough to recall me to the necessity of controlling myself, and him to the consciousness that he was playing a dangerous game. A shot, a cry, and someone would enter the room, for it opened upon the corridor. Edmond Termonde had heard me with extreme attention; a gleam of hope, succeeded by a singular look of suspicion, had passed over his face.

"Make your conditions," said he.

"If I had intended to kill you," I resumed, so as to convince him of my sincerity by the evidence of his senses, "you would be dead already." I raised the revolver. "If I had intended to have you arrested, I would not have taken the trouble to come here myself; two policemen would have been sufficient, for you don't forget that you are a deserter, and still amenable to the law."

"True," he replied simply, and then added, following out a mental argument which was of vital importance to the issue of our interview:

"If it is not Jacques, then who is it that has sold me?"

"I held you at my disposal," I continued, without noticing what he had said, "and I have not availed myself of that. Therefore I had a strong reason for sparing you yesterday, ere yesterday, this morning, a little while ago, at the present moment; and it depends upon yourself whether I spare you altogether."

"And you want me to believe you," he answered, pointing to my revolver which I still continued to hold in my hand, but no longer covering him with it. "No, no," and he added, with an expression which smacked of the barrack-room, "I don't tumble to that sort of thing."

"Listen to me," said I, now assuming a tone of extreme contempt. "The powerful motive which I have for not shooting you like a mad dog, you shall learn. I do not choose that my mother should ever know what a man she married in your brother. Do you now understand why I resolved to let you go? Provided you are of the same mind, however; for even the idea of my mother would not stop me, if you pushed me too far. I will add, for your guidance, that the limitation by which you supposed yourself to be safe from pursuit for the murder in 1864 has been traversed; you are therefore staking your head at this moment. For ten years past you have been successfully levying blackmail on your brother. I do not suppose you have merely played upon the chord of fraternal love. When you came from America to assume the personality of Rochdale, it was clearly necessary that he should send you some instructions. You have kept those letters. I offer you one hundred thousand francs for them."

"Sir," he replied slowly, and his tone showed me that for the moment he had recovered his self-control, "how can you imagine that I should take such a proposal seriously? Admitting that any such letters were ever written, and that I had kept them, why should I give up a document of this kind to you? What security should I have that you would not have me laid by the heels the moment after! Ah!" he cried, looking me straight in the face, "you know nothing! That name! That likeness! Idiot that I am, you have tricked me."

His face turned crimson with rage, and he uttered an oath.

"You shall pay for this!" he cried; and at the same instant, when he was no longer covered by my pistol, he pushed the table upon me so violently, that if I had not sprung backwards I must have been thrown down; but he already had time to fling himself upon me and seize me round the body. Happily for me the violence of the attack had knocked the pistol out of my hands, so that I could not be tempted to use it, and a struggle began between us in which not one word was spoken by either.

With his first rush he had flung me to the ground; but I was strong, and the strange premonitions of danger, from which I suffered in my youth, had led me to develop all my physical energy and adroitness.

I felt his breath on my face, his skin upon my skin, his muscles striving against mine, and at the same time the dread that our conflict might be overheard gave me the coolness which he had lost. After a few minutes of this tussle, and just as his strength was failing, he fastened his teeth in my shoulder so savagely that the pain of the bite maddened me. I wrenched one of my arms from his grasp and seized him by the throat at the risk of choking him. I held him under me now, and I struck his bead against the floor as though I meant to smash it. He remained motionless for a minute, and I thought I had killed him. I first picked up my pistol, which had rolled away to the door, and then bathed his forehead with water in order to revive him.

When I caught sight of myself in the glass, with my coat-collar torn, my face bruised, my cravat in rags, I shuddered as if I had seen the specter of another Andre Cornelis. The ignoble nature of this adventure filled me with disgust; but it was not a question of fine-gentleman fastidiousness. My enemy was coming to himself, I must end this. I knew in my conscience I had done all that was possible to fulfill my vow in regard to my mother. The blame must fall upon destiny. the wretch had half-raised himself, and was looking at me; I bent over him, and put the barrel of my revolver within a hair's breadth of his temple.

"There is still time," I said. "I give you five minutes to decide upon the bargain which I proposed to you just now; the letters, and one hundred thousand francs, with your liberty; if not, a bullet in your head. Choose. I wished to spare you on account of my mother; but I will not lose my vengeance both ways. I shall be arrested, your papers will be searched, the letters will be found, it will be known that I had a right to shoot you. My mother will go mad with grief; but I shall be avenged. I have spoken. You have five minutes, not one more."

No doubt my face expressed invincible resolution. The assassin looked at that face, then at the clock. He tried to make a movement, but saw that my finger was about to press the trigger.

"I yield," he said.

I ordered him to rise, and he obeyed me.

"Where are the letters?"

"When you have them," he implored, with the terror of a trapped beast in his abject face, "you will let me go away?"

"I swear it," I answered; and, as I saw doubt and dread in his quailing eyes, I added, "by the memory of my father. Where are the letters?"

"There."

He pointed to a valise in a corner of the room.

"Here is the money."

I flung him the note-case which contained it. Is there a sort of moral magnetism in the tone of certain words and in certain expressions of countenance? Was it the nature of the oath which I had just taken, so deeply impressive at that moment, or had this man sufficient strength of mind to say to himself that his single chance of safety resided in belief in my good faith? However that may be, he did not hesitate for a moment; he opened the iron-bound valise, took out a yellow-leather box with a patent lock, and, having opened it, flung its contents – a large sealed envelope-to me, exactly as I had flung the banknotes to him. I, too, for my part, had not a moment's fear that he would produce a weapon from the valise and attack me while I was verifying the contents of the envelope. These consisted of three letters only; the two first bore the double stamp of Paris and New York, the third those of New York and Liverpool, and all three bore the January or February post-marks of the year 1864.

"Is that all?" he asked.

"Not yet," I answered; "you must undertake to leave Paris this evening by the first train, without having seen your brother or written to him."

"I promise; and then?"

"When was he to come back here to see you?"

"On Saturday," he answered, with a shrug of his shoulders. "The bargain was concluded. He was determined to wait until the day came for me to set out for Havre before paying me the money, so that he might make quite sure I should not stay on in Paris. – The game is up," he added, "and now I wash my hands of it."

"Edmond Termonde," said I, rising, but not loosing him from the hold of my eye, "remember that I have spared you; but you must not tempt me a second time by putting yourself in my way, or crossing the path of any whom I love."

Then, with a threatening gesture, I quitted the room, leaving him seated at the table near the window. I had hardly reached the corridor when my nerves, which had been so strangely under my control during the struggle, failed me. My legs bent under me, and I feared I was about to fall. How was I to account for the disorder of my clothes? I made a great effort, concealed the torn ends of my cravat, turned up the collar of my coat to hide the condition of my shirt, and did my best to repair the damage that had been done to my hat. I then wiped my face with my handkerchief, and went downstairs with a slow and careless step. The inspector of the first floor was, doubtless, occupied at the other end of the corridor; but two of the waiters saw me and were evidently surprised at my aspect. They were, however, too busy, luckily for me, to stop me and inquire into the cause of my discomposure. At last I reached the courtyard. If anybody who knew me had been there? I got into the first cab and gave my address. I had kept my word. I had conquered.

I am afraid to kill; but had I been born in Italy, in the fifteenth century, would I have hesitated to poison my father's murderer? Would I have hesitated to shoot him, had I been born in Corsica fifty years ago? Am I then nothing but a civilized person, a wretched and impotent dreamer, who would fain act, but shrinks from soiling his hands in the action? I forced myself to contemplate the dilemma in which I stood, in its absolute, imperative, inevitable distinctness. I must either avenge my father by handing over his murderer to be dealt with by the law, since M. Massol had prudently fulfilled all the formalities necessary to bar the limitation, or I must be my own minister of justice. There was a third alternative; that I should spare the murderous wretch, allow him to live on in occupation of his victim's place in my mother's home, from which he had driven me; but at the thought of this my rage revived. The scruples of the civilized man did indeed give him pause; but that hesitation did not hinder the savage, who slumbers in us all, from feeling the appetite for retaliation which stirs the animal nature of man – all his flesh, and all his blood – as hunger and thirst stir it. "Well, then," said I to myself, "I will assassinate my stepfather, since that is the right word. Was he afraid to assassinate my father? He killed; he shall be killed. An eye for an eye, a tooth for a tooth; that is the primitive law, and all the rest is a lie."

Evening had come while this strife was raging in my soul. I was laboring under excitement which contrasted strangely with the calmness I had felt a few hours previously, when ascending the stairs in the Grand Hotel. The situation also had undergone a change; then I was preparing for a struggle, a kind of duel; I was about to confront a man whom I had to conquer, to attack him face to face without any treachery, and I had not flinched. It was the mean hypocrisy of clandestine murder that had made me shrink from the idea of killing my stepfather, by luring him into a snare. I had controlled this trembling the first time; but I was afraid of its coming again, and that I should have a sleepless night, and be unfit to act next day with the cool calmness I desired.

I felt that I could not bear suspense; on the morrow I must act. The plan on which I should decide, be it what it might, must be executed within the twenty-four hours.

The best means of calming my nerves was by making a beginning now, at once; by doing something beforehand to guard against suspicion. I determined upon letting myself be seen by persons who could bear witness, if necessary, that they had seen me, careless, easy, almost gay. I dressed and went out, intending to dine at a place where I was known, and to pass the most of the night at the club.

When I was in the Avenue des Champs-Elysees, crowded with carriages and people on foot – the May evening was delicious – I shared the physical sensation of the joy of living, which was abroad in the air. The sky quivered with the innumerable throbs of the stars, and the young leaves shook at the touch of a slow and gentle breeze. Garlands of light illumined the various pleasure-gardens. I passed in front of a restaurant where the tables extended to the edge of the footpath, and young men and women were finishing their dinner gaily.

The contrast between the spring-festival aspect of Paris and the tragedy of my own destiny came home to me too strongly. What had I done to Fate to deserve that I should be the one only person, amid all this crowd, condemned to such an experience? Why had my path been crossed by a man capable of pushing passion to the point of crime, in a society in which passion is ordinarily so mild, so harmless, and so lukewarm? Probably there did not exist in all the "good" society of Paris four persons with daring enough to conceive such a plan as that which Jacques

Termonde had executed with such cool deliberation under the influence of his passion. And this villain, who could love so intensely, was my stepfather!

Once more the breath of fatality, which had already thrilled me with a kind of mysterious horror, passed over me, and I felt that I could no longer bear the sight of the human face. Turning my back upon the lit-up, noisy quarter of the Champs Elysees, I walked on towards the Arc de Triomphe. Without thinking about it I took the road to the Bois, bore to the right to avoid the vehicles, and turned into one of the loneliest paths. Had I unconsciously obeyed one of those almost animal impulses of memory, which bring us back to ways that we have already trodden? By the soft, bluish light of the spring moon I recognized the place where I had walked with my stepfather in the winter, on the occasion of our first drive to the Bois. It was on that day I obliged him to look the portrait of his victim in the face, on that day he came to me on the pretext of asking for the Review which my mother had lent me. In my thoughts I beheld him, as he then was, and recalled the strange pity which had stirred my heart at the sight of him, so sad, broken-down, and, so to speak, conquered. He stood before me, in the light of that remembrance, as living and real as if he had been there, close beside me, and the acute sensation of his existence made me feel at the same time all the signification of those fearful and mysterious words: to kill. To kill? I was going to kill him, in a few hours it might be, at the latest in a few days.

I heard voices, and I withdrew into the shade. Two forms passed me, a young man and a girl, lovers, who did not see me. The moonlight fell upon them, as they went on their way, hand in hand. I burst into tears, and wept long, unrestrainedly; for I too was young; in my heart there was a flood of pent-up tenderness, and here I was, on this perfumed, moonlit, starlit night, crouching in a dark corner, meditating murder!

No, not murder, an execution. Has my stepfather deserved death? Yes. Is the executioner who lets down the knife on the neck of the condemned criminal to be called an assassin? No! Well, then I shall be the executioner and nothing else. I rose from the bench where I had shed my last tears of resolution and cowardice – for thus I regarded those hot tears to which I now appeal, as a last proof that I was not born for what I have done.

While walking back to Paris, I multiplied and reiterated my arguments. Sometimes I succeeded in silencing a voice within me, stronger than my reasoning and my longing for vengeance, a voice which pronounced the words formerly uttered by my aunt: "Vengeance is mine, saith the Lord God." And if there be no God? And if there be, is not the fault His, for He has let this thing be? Yes, such were my wild words and thoughts; and then all these scruples of my conscience appeared to me mere vain, futile quibbles, fitting for philosophers and confessors.

There remained one indisputable, absolute fact; I could not endure that the murderer of my father should continue to be the husband of my mother.

There was a second no less evident fact; I could not place this man in the hands of justice without, probably, killing my mother on the spot, or, quite certainly, laying her whole life waste. Therefore I would have to be my own tribunal, judge, and executioner in my own cause. What mattered to me the arguments for or against? I was bound to give heed first to my final instinct, and it cried out to me "Kill!"

I walked fast, keeping my mind fixed on this idea with a kind of tragic pleasure, for I felt that my irresolution was gone, and that I should act. All of a sudden, as I came close to the Arc de Triomphe, I remembered how, on that very spot, I had met one of my club companions for the last time. He shot himself the next day. Why did this remembrance suddenly suggest to me a series of new thoughts?

I stopped short with a beating heart. I had caught a glimpse of the way of safety. Fool that I had been, led away as usual by an undisciplined imagination! My stepfather should die. I had sentenced him in the name of my inalienable right as an avenging son; but could I not condemn him to die by his own hand? Had I not that in my possession which would drive him to suicide? If I went to him without any more reserves or circumlocution, and if

I said to him, "I hold the proof that you are the murderer of my father. I give you the choice – either you will kill yourself, or I denounce you to my mother," what would his answer be? He, who loved his wife with that reciprocated devotion by which I had suffered so much, would he consent that she should know the truth, that she should regard him as a base, cowardly assassin? No, never; he would rather die.

My heart, weary and worn with pain, rushed towards this door of hope, so suddenly opened. "I shall have done my duty," I thought, "and I shall have no blood on my hands. My conscience will not be stained." I experienced an immense relief from the weight of foreseen remorse that had caused me such agony, and I went on drawing a picture of the future, freed at last from one dark image which had veiled the sunshine of my youth. "He will kill himself; my mother will weep for him; but I shall be able to dry her tears. Her heart will bleed, but I will heal the wound with the balm of my tenderness. When the assassin is no longer there, she and I will live over again all the dear time that he stole from us, and then I shall be able to show her how I love her. The caresses which I did not give her when I was a child, because the other froze me by his mere presence, I will give her then; the words which I did not speak, the tender words that were stopped upon my lips, she shall hear then. We will leave Paris, and get rid of these sad remembrances. We will retire to some quiet spot, far, far away, where she will have none but me, I none but her, and I will devote myself to her old age. What do I want with any other love, with any other tie? Suffering softens the heart; her grief will make her love me more. Ah! how happy we shall be." But once more the voice within resumed: "What if the wretch refuse to kill himself? What if he were not to believe me when I threaten to denounce him?" Had I not been acting for months as his accomplice in maintaining the deceit practiced upon my mother? Did he not know how much I loved her, he who had been jealous of me as her son, as I had been jealous of him as her husband? Would he not answer: "Denounce me!" being well assured that I would not deal such a blow at the poor woman? To these objections I replied, that, whereas I had suspected previously, now I knew. No, he will not be entirely convinced that the evidence I hold will make me dare everything. Well then, if he refuse, I shall have attempted the impossible to avoid murder – let destiny be accomplished!

XIII

It was four o'clock in the afternoon on the following day, when I presented myself at the hotel on the Boulevard de Latour-Maubourg. I knew that my mother would most probably be out. I also thought it likely my stepfather would he feeling none the better of his early excursion to the Grand Hotel on the previous day, and I therefore hoped to find him at home, perhaps in his bed. I was right; my mother was out, and he had remained at home. He was in his study, the room in which our first explanation had taken place. That upon which I was now bent was of far greater importance, and yet I was less agitated than on the former occasion. At last I was completely certain of the facts, and with that certainty a strange calmness had come to me. I can recall my having talked for a few moments with the servant who announced me, about a child of his who was ill. I also remember to have observed for the first time that the smoky chimney of some manufacturing works at the back of the garden, built, no doubt, during the last winter, was visible through the window of the staircase.

I record these things because I am bound to recognize that my mind was quite clear and free – for I will be sincere to the end – when I entered the spacious room.

My stepfather was reclining in a deep armchair at the far side of the fireplace, and occupied in cutting the pages of a new book with a dagger. The blade of this weapon was broad, short, and strong. He had brought the knife back from Spain, with several other kinds of arms, which lay about in the rooms he habitually occupied. I now understood the order of ideas which this singular taste indicated. He was dressed for walking; but his altered looks bore witness to the intensity of the crisis through which he had passed. It had affected his whole being.

Very likely my face was expressive of an extraordinary resolution, for I saw by his eyes, as our looks met, that he had read the depths of my thoughts at a glance. Nevertheless, he said: "Ah, is it you, Andre? It is very kind of you to come," thus exhibiting once more the power of his self-control, and he put out his hand. I did not take it, and my refusal, contrasting with his gesture of welcome, the silence which I kept for some minutes, the contraction of my features, and, no doubt, the menace in my eyes, entirely enlightened him as to the mood in which I came to him. Very quietly, he laid down his book and the Spanish knife he had been using, on a large table within his reach, and then he rose from his chair, leaned his back against the mantelpiece, and crossing his arms, looked at me with the haughty stare I knew so well, and which had so often humiliated me in my boyhood. I was the first to break the silence; replying to his polite greeting in a harsh tone, and looking him straight in the face, I said:

"The time of lies is past. You have guessed that I know all?"

He bent his brows into the stern frown he always assumed when he felt anger he was bound to suppress, his eyes met mine with indomitable pride, and he merely replied:

"I do not understand you."

"You do not understand me? Very well, I am about to enlighten you." My voice shook in uttering these words; my coolness was forsaking me. The day before, and in my conversation with the brother, I had come in contact with the vile infamy of a knave and a coward; but the enemy whom I was now facing, although a greater scoundrel than the other, found means to preserve a sort of moral superiority, even in that terrible hour when he knew well he was face to face with his crime.

Yes, this man was a criminal, but of a grand kind, and there was no cowardice in him. Pride sat upon that brow so laden with dark thoughts, but fear set no mark upon it, any more than did repentance. In his eyes – exactly like those of his brother – a fierce resolution shone; I felt that he would defend himself to the end. He would yield to evidence only, and such strength of mind displayed at such a moment had the effect of exasperating me. The blood flew to my head, and my heart beat rapidly, as I went on:

"Allow me to take up the matter a little farther back. In 1864, there was in Paris a man who loved the wife of his most intimate friend. Although that friend was very trusting, very noble, very easily duped, he became aware of this love, and he began to suffer from it. He grew jealous – although he never doubted his wife's purity of heart – jealous as everyone is who loves too well.

"The man who was the object of his jealousy perceived it, understood that he was about to be forbidden the house, knew that the woman whom he loved would never degrade herself by listening to a lover, and this is the plan which be conceived:

"He had a brother somewhere in a distant land, an infamous scoundrel who was supposed to be dead, a creature sunk in shame, a thief, a forger, a deserter, and he bethought him of this brother as an instrument ready to his hand wherewith to rid himself of the friend who stood in the way of his passion. He sent for the fellow secretly, he appointed to meet him in one of the loneliest corners of Paris – in a street adjoining the Jardin des Plantes, and at night – you see I am well informed. It is easy to imagine how he persuaded the former thief to play the part of bravo. A few months after, the husband was assassinated by this brother, who eluded justice. The felon-friend married almost immediately the woman whom he loved; he is now a man in society, wealthy and respected, and his pure and pious wife loves, admires, nay, worships him. Do you now begin to understand?"

"No more than before," he answered, with the same impassive face. He did well not to flinch. What I had said might be only an attempt to wrest his secret from him by feigning to know all. Nevertheless, the detail concerning the place where he had appointed to meet his brother had made him start. That was the spot to hit, and quickly.

"The cowardly assassin," I continued, "yes, the coward, because he dared not commit the crime himself, had carefully calculated all the circumstances of the murder; but he had reckoned without certain little accidents, for instance, that his brother would keep the three letters he had received, the first two at New York, the last at Liverpool, and which contained instructions relating to the stages of this clandestine journey. Neither had he taken into account that the son of his victim would grow up, would become a man, would conceive certain suspicions of the true cause of his father's death, and would succeed in procuring overwhelming proof of the dark conspiracy. Come, then," I added fiercely, "off with the mask! M. Jacques Termonde, it is you who had my unhappy father killed by your brother Edmond. I have in my possession the letters you wrote him in January, 1864, to induce him to come to Europe, first under the false name of Rochester and afterwards under that of Rochdale. It is not worth your while to play the indignant or the astonished with me – the game is up."

He had turned frightfully pale; but his arms still remained crossed, and his bold eyes did not droop. He made one last attempt to parry the straight blow I had aimed at him, and he had the hardihood to say:

"How much did that wretch Edmond ask as the price of the forgery which he fabricated in revenge for my refusal to give him money?"

"Be silent, you – " said I still more fiercely. "Is it to me that you dare to speak thus – to me? Did I need those letters in order to learn all? Have we not known for weeks past, I, that you had committed the crime, and you, that I had divined your guilt? What I still needed was the written, indisputable, undeniable proof, that which can be laid before a magistrate. You refused him money? You were about to give him money, only that you mistrusted him, and chose to wait until the day of his departure. You did not suspect that I was upon your track. Shall I tell you when it was you saw him for the last time? Yesterday, at ten o'clock in the morning, you went out, you changed your cab first at the Place de la Concorde, and a second time at the Palais Royal. You went to the Grand Hotel, and you asked whether Mr. Stanbury was in his room. A few hours later I, myself, was in that same room. Ah! how much did Edmond Termonde ask from me for the letters? Why, I tore them from him, pistol in hand, after a struggle in which I was nearly killed. You see now that you can deceive me no more, and that it is no longer worth your while to deny."

I thought he was about to drop dead before me. His face changed, until it was hardly human, as I went on, on, on, piling up the exact facts, tracking his falsehood, as one tracks a wild beast, and proving to him that his brother had defended himself after his fashion, even as he had done. He clasped his hands about his head, when I ceased to speak, as though to compress the maddening thoughts which rushed upon him; then, once more looking me in the face, but this time with infinite despair in his eyes, he uttered exactly the same sentence as his brother had spoken, but with quite another expression and tone:

"This hour too was bound to come. What do you want from me now?"

"That you should do justice on yourself," I answered. "You have twenty-four hours before you. If, to-morrow at this hour, you are still living, I place the letters in my mother's hands."

Every sort of feeling was depicted upon his livid face while I placed this ultimatum before him, in a firm voice which admitted of no farther discussion. I was standing up, and I leaned against the large table; he came towards me, with a sort of delirium in his eyes as they strove to meet mine.

"No," he cried, "no, Andre, not yet! Pity me, Andre, pity me! See now, I am a condemned man, I have not six months to live. Your revenge! Ah! you had no need to undertake it. What! If I have done a terrible deed, do you think I have not been punished for it? Look at me, only look at me; I am dying of this frightful secret. It is all over; my days are numbered. The few that remain, leave, oh, leave them to me! Understand this, I am not afraid to die; but to kill myself, to go away, leaving this grief to her whom you love as I do! It is true that, to win her, I have done an atrocious deed; but say, answer, has there ever been an hour, a minute since, in which her happiness was not my only aim? And you would have me leave her thus, inflict upon her the torment of thinking that while I might have grown old by her side, I preferred to go away, to forsake her before the time? No, Andre – this last year, leave it to me! Ah, leave it to me, leave it to us, for I assure you that I am hopelessly ill, that I know it, that the doctors have not hidden it from me. In a few months – fix a date – if the disease has not carried me off, you can come back. But I shall be dead. She will weep for me, without the horror of that idea that I have forestalled my hour, she who is so pious! You only will be there to console her, to love her. Have pity upon her, if not upon me. See, I have no more pride towards you, I entreat you in her name, in the name of her dear heart, for well you know its tenderness. You love her, I know that; I have guessed truly that you hid your suspicions to spare her pain. I tell you once again, my life is a hell, and I would joyfully give it to you in expiation of what I have done; but she, Andre, she, your mother, who has never, never cherished a thought that was not pure and noble, no, do not inflict this torture upon her."

"Words, words!" I answered, moved to the bottom of my soul in spite of myself, by the outburst of an anguish in which I was forced to recognize sincerity. "It is because my mother is noble and pure that I will not have her remain the wife of a vile murderer for a day longer. You shall kill yourself, or she shall know all."

"Do it then if you dare," he replied, with a return to the natural pride of his character, at the ferocity of my answer. "Do it if you dare! Yes, she is my wife, yes, she loves me; go and tell her, and kill her yourself with the words. Ha, you see! You turn pale at the mere thought. I have allowed you to live, yes, I, on account of her, and do you suppose I do not hate you as much as you hate me? Nevertheless, I have respected you because you were dear to her, and you will have to do the same with me. Yes, do you hear, it must be so – "

It was he who was giving orders now, he who was threatening. How plainly had he read my mind, to stand up before me in such an attitude! Furious passion broke loose in me; I took in the facts of the situation. This man had loved my mother madly enough to purchase her at the cost of the murder of his most intimate friend, and he loved her after all those years passionately enough to desire that not one of the days he had still to pass with her might be lost to him. And it was also true that never, never should I have the courage to reveal the terrific truth to the poor woman.

I was suddenly carried away by rage to the point of losing all control over my frenzy. "Ah!" I cried, "since you will not do justice on yourself, die then, at once!" I stretched out my hand and seized the dagger which he had recently placed upon the table. He looked at me without flinching, or recoiling; indeed presenting his breast to me, as though to brave my childish rage. I was on his left bending down, and ready to spring. I saw his smile of contempt, and then with all my strength I struck him with the knife in the direction of the heart.

The blade entered his body to the hilt.

No sooner had I done this thing than I recoiled, wild with terror at the deed. He uttered a cry. His face was distorted with terrible agony, and he moved his right hand towards the wound, as though he would draw out the dagger. He looked at me, convulsed; I saw that he wanted to speak; his lips moved, but no sound issued from his mouth. The expression of a supreme effort passed into his eyes, he turned to the table, took a pen, dipped it into the inkstand, and traced two lines on a sheet of paper within his reach. He looked at me again, his lips moved once more, then he fell down like a log.

I remember – I saw the body stretched upon the carpet, between the table and the tall mantelpiece, within two feet of me. I approached him, I bent over his face. His eyes seemed to follow me even after death.

Yes, he was dead.

The doctor who certified the death explained afterwards that the knife had passed through the cardiac muscle without completely penetrating the left cavity of the heart, and that, the blood not being shed all at once, death had not been instantaneous.

I cannot tell how long he lived after I struck him, nor do I know how long I remained in the same place, overwhelmed by the thought: "Someone will come, and I am lost." It was not for myself that I trembled. What could be done to a son who had but avenged his murdered father? But, my mother? This was what all my resolutions to spare her at any cost, my daily solicitude for her welfare, my unseen tears, my tender silence, had come to in the end! I must now, inevitably, either explain myself, or leave her to think I was a mere murderer. I was lost. But if I called, if I cried out suddenly that my stepfather had just killed himself in my presence, should I be believed? And, besides, had he not written what would convict me of murder, on that sheet of paper lying on the table? Was I going to destroy it, as a practiced criminal destroys every vestige of his presence before he leaves the scene of his crime?

I seized the sheet of paper; the lines were written upon it in characters rather larger than usual. How it shook in my hand while I read these words: "Forgive me, Marie. I was suffering too much. I wanted to be done with it." And he had had the strength to affix his signature!

So then, his last thought had been for her. In the brief moments that had elapsed between my blow with the knife, and his death, he had perceived the dreadful truth, that I should be arrested, that I would speak to explain my deed, that my mother would then learn his crime – and he had saved me by compelling me to silence.

But was I going to profit by this means of safety? Was I going to accept the terrible generosity by which the man, whom I had so profoundly detested, would stand acquitted towards me for evermore? I must render so much justice to my honor; my first impulse was to destroy that paper, to annihilate with it even the memory of the debt imposed upon my hatred by the atrocious but sublime action of the murderer of my father.

At that moment I caught sight of a portrait of my mother, on the table, close to where he had been sitting. It was a photograph, taken in her youth; she was represented in brilliant evening attire, her bare arms shaded with lace, pearls in her hair, gay, ay, better than gay, happy, with an ineffably pure expression overspreading her face. My stepfather had sacrificed all to save her from despair on learning the truth, and was she to receive the fatal blow from me, to learn at the same moment that the man she loved had killed her first husband, and that he had been killed by her son?

I desire to believe, so that I may continue to hold myself in some esteem, that only the vision of her grief led me to my decision. I replaced the sheet of paper on the table, and turned away from the corpse lying on the carpet, without casting a glance at it. The remembrance of my flight from the Grand Hotel, on the previous day, gave me courage; I must try a second time to get away without betraying discomposure.

I found my hat, left the room, and closed the door carelessly. I crossed the hall and went down the staircase, passing by the footman who stood up mechanically, and then the concierge who saluted me. The two servants had not even put me out of countenance.

I returned to my room as I had done the day before, but in a far more tragic state of suspense. Was I saved? Was I lost? All depended on the moment at which somebody might go into my stepfather's room. If my mother were to return within a few minutes of my departure; if the footman were to go upstairs with some letter, I should instantly be suspected, in spite of the declaration written by M. Termonde. I felt that my courage was exhausted. I knew that, if accused, I should not have moral strength to defend myself, for my weariness was so overwhelming that I did not suffer any longer. The only thing I had strength to do was to watch the swing of the pendulum of the timepiece on the mantelshelf, and to mark the movement of the hands. A quarter of an hour elapsed, half an hour, a whole hour.

It was an hour and a half after I had left the fatal room, when the bell at the door was rung. I heard it through the walls. A servant brought me a laconic note from my mother scribbled in pencil and hardly legible. It informed me that my stepfather had destroyed himself in an attack of severe pain. The poor woman implored me to go to her immediately. Ah, she would now never know the truth!

XIV

The confession that I wished to write is written. To what end could I add fresh facts to it now? I hoped to ease my heart by passing in review all the details of this dark story, but I have only revived the dread memory of the scenes in which I have been an actor; from the first – when I saw my father stretched dead upon his bed, and my mother weeping by his side, to the last – when I noiselessly entered a room in which the unhappy woman was again kneeling and weeping. Again upon the bed there lay a corpse, and she rose as she had done before, and uttered the same despairing cry: "My Andre – my son." And I had to answer her questions; I had to invent for her a false conversation with my stepfather, to tell her that I left him rather depressed, but with nothing in his appearance or manner to indicate a fatal resolution. I had to take the necessary steps to prevent this alleged suicide from getting known, to see the commissary of police and the "doctor of the dead." I had to preside at the funeral ceremonies, to receive the guests and act as chief mourner. And always, always, he was present to me, with the dagger in his breast, writing the lines that had saved me, and looking at me, while his lips moved.

Ah, begone, begone, abhorred phantom! Yes! I have done it; yes! I have killed you; yes! it was just. You know well that it was just. Why are you still here now? Ah! I WILL live; I WILL forget. If I could only cease to think of you for one day, only one day, just to breathe, and walk, and see the sky, without your image returning to haunt my poor head which is racked by this hallucination, and troubled? My God! have pity on me. I did not ask for this dreadful fate; it is Thou that hast sent it to me. Why dost Thou punish me? Oh, my God, have pity on me! Miserere mei, Domine.

Vain prayers! Is there any God, any justice, is there either good or evil? None, none, none, none! There is nothing but a pitiless destiny which broods over the human race, iniquitous and blind, distributing joy and grief at haphazard. A God who says, "Thou shalt not kill," to him whose father has been killed? No, I don't believe it. No, if hell were there before me, gaping open, I would make answer: "I have done well," and I would not repent. I do not repent. My remorse is not for having seized the weapon and struck the blow, it is that I owe to him – to him – that infamous good service which he did me – that I cannot to the present hour shake from me the horrible gift I have received from that man. If I had destroyed the paper, if I had gone and given myself up, if I had appeared before a jury, revealing, proclaiming my deed, I should not be ashamed; I could still hold up my head. What relief, what joy it would be if I might cry aloud to all men that I killed him, that he lied, and I lied, that it was I, I, who took the weapon and plunged it into him! And yet, I ought not to suffer from having accepted – no – endured the odious immunity. Was it from any motive of cowardice that I acted thus? What was I afraid of? Of torturing my mother, nothing more. Why, then, do I suffer this unendurable anguish? Ah, it is she, it is my mother who, without intending it, makes the dead so living to me, by her own despair. She lives, shut up in the rooms where they lived together for sixteen years; she has not allowed a single article of furniture to be touched; she surrounds the man's accursed memory with the same pious reverence that my aunt formerly lavished on my unhappy father. I recognize the invincible influence of the dead in the pallor of her cheeks, the wrinkles in her eyelids, the white streaks in her hair. He disputes her with me from the darkness of his coffin; he takes her from me, hour by hour, and I am powerless against that love. If I were to tell her, as I would like to tell her, all the truth, from the hideous crime which he committed, down to the execution carried out by me, it is I whom she would hate, for having killed him. She will grow old thus and I shall see her weep, always, always – What good is it to have done what I did, since I have not killed him in her heart?

Anonymous

The Last of the Costellos

After several years' service on the staff of a great daily newspaper in San Francisco, Gerald Ffrench returned to his home in Ireland to enjoy a three months' vacation. A brief visit, when the time consumed in traveling was deducted, and the young journalist, on this January afternoon, realized that it was nearly over, and that his further stay in the country of his birth was now to be reckoned by days.

He had been spending an hour with his old friend, Dr. Lynn, and the clergyman accompanied him to the foot of the rectory lawn, and thence, through a wicket gate that opened upon the churchyard, along the narrow path among the graves. It was an obscure little country burying-ground, and very ancient. The grass sprang luxuriant from the mouldering dust of three hundred years; for so long at least had these few acres been consecrated to their present purpose.

"Well, I won't go any further," says Dr. Lynn, halting at the boundary wall, spanned by a ladder-like flight of wooden steps which connected the churchyard with the little bye-road. "I'll say good evening, Gerald, and assure you I appreciate your kindness in coming over to see a stupid old man."

"I would not hear thine enemy say that," quoted Gerald with a light laugh. "I hope to spend another day as pleasantly before I turn my back on old Ireland." He ran up the steps as he spoke and stood on the top of the wall, looking back to wave a last greeting before he descended. Suddenly he stopped.

"What's that?" he asked, pointing down among the graves.

The rector turned, but the tall grass and taller nettles concealed from his view the object, whatever it might be, which Gerald had seen from his temporary elevation.

"It looks like a coffin," and coming rapidly down again the young man pushed his way through the rank growth. The clergyman followed.

In a little depression between the mounds of two graves lay a plain coffin of stained wood. It was closed, but an attempt to move it showed that it was not empty. A nearer inspection revealed that the lid was not screwed down in the usual manner, but hastily fastened with nails. Dr. Lynn and Gerald looked at each other. There was something mysterious in the presence of this coffin above ground.

"Has there been a funeral – interrupted – or anything of that kind?" asked Gerald.

"Nothing of the sort. I wish Bolan were here. He might have something to say about it."

Bolan was the sexton. Gerald knew where he lived, within a stone's throw of the spot, and volunteered to fetch him. Dr. Lynn looked all over the sinister black box, but no plate or mark of any kind rewarded his search. Meanwhile, young Ffrench sped along the lower road to Bolan's house.

The sexton was in, just preparing for a smoke in company with the local blacksmith, when Gerald entered with the news of the uncanny discovery in the churchyard. Eleven young Bolans, grouped around the turf fire, drank in the intelligence and instantly scattered to spread the report in eleven different directions. A tale confided to the Bolan household was confided to rumor.

Blacksmith and sexton rose together and accompanied Gerald to the spot where he had left Dr. Lynn, but Dr. Lynn was no longer alone. The rector had heard steps in the road; it was a constabulary patrol on its round, and the old gentleman's hail had brought two policemen to his side. There they stood, profoundly puzzled and completely in the dark, except for the light given by their bull's- eye lanterns. But the glare of these lanterns had been seen from the road. Some people shunned them, as lights in a graveyard should always be shunned; but others, hearing voices, had suffered their curiosity to overcome their misgivings, and were gathered around, silent, open-mouthed, wondering. So stood the group when Gerald and his companions joined it.

In reply to general questions Bolan was dumb. In reply to particular interrogations he did not hesitate to admit that he was "clane bate." Gerald, seeing that no one had ventured to touch the grim casket, hinted that it would be well to open it. There was a dubious murmur from the crowd and a glance at the constables as the visible representatives of the powers that be. The officers tightened their belts and seemed undecided, and Dr. Lynn took the lead with a clear, distinct order, "Take off the lid, Andy," he said.

"An' why not? Isn't his riverince a magistrate? Go in, Andy, yer sowl ye, and off wid it." Thus the crowd.

So encouraged, the blacksmith stepped forward. Without much difficulty he burst the insecure fastenings and removed the lid. The constables turned their bull's-eyes on the inside of the coffin. The crowd pressed forward, Gerald in the front rank.

There was an occupant. A young girl, white with the pallor of death, lay under the light of the lanterns. The face was as placid and composed as if she had just fallen asleep, and it was a handsome face with regular features and strongly defined black eyebrows. The form was fully dressed, and the clothes seemed expensive and fashionable. A few raven locks straggled out from beneath a lace scarf which was tied around the head. The hands, crossed below the breast, were neatly gloved. There she lay, a mystery, for not one of those present had ever seen her face before.

Murmurs of wonder and sympathy went up from the bystanders. "Ah, the poor thing!" "Isn't she purty?" "So young, too!" "Musha, it's the beautiful angel she is be this time."

"Does anyone know her?" asked the rector; and then, as there was no reply, he put a question that was destined for many a day to agitate the neighborhood of Drim, and ring through the length and breadth of Ireland – "How did she come here?"

The investigation made at the moment was unsatisfactory. The grass on all sides had been trampled and pressed down by the curious throng, and such tracks as the coffin-bearers had made were completely obliterated. It was clearly a case for the coroner, and when that official arrived and took charge the crowd slowly dispersed.

The inquest furnished no new light. Medical testimony swept away the theory of murder, for death was proved to have resulted from organic disease of the heart. The coffin might have been placed where it was found at any time within thirty-six hours, for it could not be shown that anyone had crossed the churchyard path since the morning previous, and indeed a dozen might have passed that way without noticing that which Gerald only discovered through the accident of having looked back at the moment that he mounted the wall. Still, it did not seem likely that an object of such size could have lain long unnoticed, and the doctors were of opinion that the woman had been alive twenty-four hours before her body was found.

In the absence of suspicion of any crime – and the medical examination furnished none – interest centered in the question of identity; and this was sufficiently puzzling.

The story got into the newspapers – into the Dublin papers; afterwards into the great London journals, and was widely discussed under the title of "The Drim Churchyard Mystery," but all this publicity and a thorough investigation of the few available clues led to nothing. No one was missing; widely distributed photographs of the deceased found no recognition; and the quest was finally abandoned even in the immediate neighborhood. The unknown dead slept beneath the very sod on which they had found her.

Gerald Ffrench, who, like most good journalists, had a strongly developed detective instinct, alone kept the mystery in mind and worked at it incessantly. He devoted the few remaining days of his stay in Ireland to a patient, systematic inquiry, starting from the clues that had developed at the inquest. He had provided himself with a good photograph of the dead girl, and a minute, carefully written description of her apparel, from the lace scarf which had been wound round her head to the dainty little French boots on her feet. The first examination had produced no result. Railway officials and hotel-keepers, supplied with the photographs, could not say that they had ever seen the original in life. Even the coffin, a cheap, ready-made affair, could be traced to no local dealer in such wares. A chatelaine bag, slung round the waist of the dead girl, had evidently been marked with initials, for the leather showed the holes in which the letters had been fastened, and the traces of the knife employed in their hurried removal. But the pretty feminine trifle was empty, and in its present condition had nothing to suggest save that a determined effort had been made to hide the identity of the dead. The linen on the corpse was new and of good material, but utterly without mark. Only a handkerchief which was found in the pocket bore a coat of arms exquisitely embroidered on the corner.

The shield showed the head and shoulders of a knight with visor closed, party per fess on counter-vair. Gerald, whose smattering of heraldry told him so much, could not be sure that the lines of the embroidery properly indicated the colors of the shield; but he was sanguine that a device so unusual would be recognized by the learned in such matters, and, having carefully sketched it, he sent a copy to the Heralds' College, preserving the original drawing for his own use. The handkerchief itself, with the other things found on the body, was of course beyond his reach.

The answer from the Heralds' College arrived a day or two before the approaching close of his vacation forced Gerald to leave Ireland, but the information furnished served only to make the mystery deeper.

The arms had been readily recognized from his sketch, and the college, in return for his fee, had furnished him with an illuminated drawing, showing that the embroidery had been accurate. The shield was party per fess, argent above, azure below, and from this Gerald concluded that the handkerchief had been marked by someone accustomed to blazonries; he thought it likely that the work had been done in a French convent. The motto, Nemo me impune lacessit, appeared below. The bearings and cognizance were those of the noble family of Costello, which had left Ireland about the middle of the seventeenth century and had settled in Spain. The last representative had fallen some sixty years ago at the battle of Vittoria, in the Peninsular war, and the name was now extinct. So pronounced the unimpeachable authority of the Heralds' College.

And yet Gerald had seen those very arms embroidered on a handkerchief which had been found in the pocket of a nameless girl, whose corpse he himself had been the first to discover some two weeks before, in the lonely little burying-ground at Drim. What was he to think? Through what strange, undreamed-of ramifications was this affair to be pursued?

The day before his departure, Ffrench walked over to the rectory to say good-bye to Dr. Lynn. Gerald knew that the rector was an authority in county history, and thought it possible that the old gentleman could tell him something about the Costellos, a name linked with many a Westmeath tradition. He was not disappointed, and the mystery he was investigating took on a new interest from what he heard. The Costellos had been one of the midland chieftains in Cromwell's time; the clan had offered the most determined resistance, and it had been extirpated root and branch by the Protector. The Ffrench estate of Ballyvore had once formed portion of the Costello property, and had been purchased by Gerald's ancestor from the Cromwellian Puritan to whom it had been granted on confiscation.

The young man was now deeply interested in the inquiry, and to it he devoted every movement of the time he could still call his own.

But the last day of Gerald's visit slipped away without result, and one fine morning Larry, his brother's servant, drove him into Athlone to take the train for Queenstown.

"Ye'll not be lettin' another six years go by without comin' home agen, will ye, sir?" said the groom, who was really concerned at Gerald's departure.

"I don't know," answered Gerald; "it all depends. Say, Larry!"

"Sir."

"Keep an eye out, and if anything turns up about that dead girl, let me know, won't you?" Ffrench had already made a similar request of his brother, but he was determined to leave no chance untried.

"An' are ye thinkin' of that yet, an' you goin' to America?" said Larry with admiring wonder.

"Of course I'm thinking of it. I can't get it out of my head," replied Gerald impatiently.

"Well, well d'ye mind that now?" said the groom meditatively. "Well, sir, if anything does turn up, I'll let ye know, never fear; but sure she's underground now, an' if we'd been goin' to larn anything about the matter, we'd ha' had it long ago."

Gerald shook hands with the faithful Larry at parting, and left a sovereign in his palm.

The groom watched the train moving slowly out of the station.

"It's a mortal pity to see a fine young jintleman like that so far gone in love with a dead girl."

This was Larry's comment on his young master's detective tastes.

At Queenstown Ffrench bought a paper and looked over it while the tender was carrying him, in company with many a weeping emigrant, to the great steamer out in the bay. From time to time the journals still contained references to the subject which was uppermost in Gerald's thoughts. The familiar words, "The Drim Churchyard Mystery," caught his eye, and he read a brief paragraph, which had nothing to say except that all investigations had failed to throw any light on the strange business.

"Ay, and will fail," he mused, as the tender came alongside the steamer; "at any rate, if anything is found out it won't be by me, for I shall be in California, and I can scarcely run across any clues there."

And yet, as Gerald paced the deck, and watched the bleak

shores of Cork fading in the distance, his thoughts were full of the banished Costellos, and he wondered with what eyes those exiles had looked their last on the Old Head of Kinsale a quarter of a millennium ago. Those fierce old chieftains, to whom the Ffrenches – proud county family as they esteemed themselves – were but as mushrooms; what lives had they lived, what deaths had they died, and how came their haughty cognizance, so well expressing its defiant motto, on the handkerchief of the nameless stranger who slept in Drim churchyard – Drim, the old, old graveyard; Drim, that had been fenced in as God's acre in the days of the Costellos themselves? Was it mere chance that had selected this spot as the last resting-place of one who bore the arms of the race? Was it possible the girl had shared the Costello blood?

Gerald glanced over his letter from the Heralds' College and shook his head. The family had been extinct for more than sixty years.

About two months after Gerald's return to California a despatch was received from the Evening Mail's regular correspondent in Marysville, relating the particulars of an encounter between the Mexican holders of a large ranch in Yuba County and certain American land-grabbers who had set up a claim to a portion of the estate. The matter was in course of adjudication in the Marysville courts, but the claimants, impatient at the slow process of the law, had endeavored to seize the disputed land by force. Shots had been fired, blood had been spilled, and the whole affair added nothing to Yuba County's reputation for law and order. The matter created some talk in San Francisco, and the Evening Mail, among other papers, expressed its opinion in one of those trenchant personal articles which are the spice of Western journalism. Two or three days later, when the incident had been almost forgotten in the office, the city editor sent for Gerald Ffrench.

"Ffrench," said that gentleman, as the young man approached his desk, "I've just received a letter from Don Miguel y – y – something or other. I can't read his whole name, and it don't matter much. It's Vincenza, you know, the owner of that ranch where they had the shooting scrape the other day. He is anxious to make a statement of the matter for publication, and has come down to the Bay on purpose. Suppose you go and see what he has to say? He's staying at the Lick."

The same morning Gerald sent up his card and was ushered into the apartment of Don Miguel Vincenza at the Lick House.

The senor was a young man, not much older than Gerald himself. He had the appearance and manners of a gentleman, as Ffrench quickly discovered, and he spoke fluent, well-chosen English with scarcely a trace of accent, a circumstance for which the interviewer felt he could not be sufficiently grateful.

"Ah, you are from the Evening Mail," said the young Spaniard, rising as Gerald entered; "most kind of you to come, and to come so promptly. Won't you be seated? Try a cigar. No? You'll excuse me if I light a cigarette. I want to make myself clear, and I'm always clearest when I'm in a cloud." He gave a little laugh, and with one twirl of his slender fingers he converted a morsel of tissue paper and a pinch of tobacco into a compact roll, which he lighted, and exhausted in half-a-dozen puffs as he spoke.

"This man, this Jenkinson's claim is perfectly preposterous," he began, "but I won't go into that. The matter is before the courts. What I want to give you is a true statement of that unfortunate affair at the ranch, with which, I beg you to believe, I had nothing whatever to do."

Senor Vincenza's tale might have had the merit of truth; it certainly lacked that of brevity. He talked on, rolling a fresh cigarette at every second sentence, and Gerald made notes of such points as he considered important, but at the conclusion of the Spaniard's statement the journalist could not see that it had differed much from the published accounts, and he told the other as much.

"Well, you see," said Vincenza, "I am in a delicate position. It is not as if I were acting for myself. I am only my sister's agent – my half-sister's, I should say – poor little Catalina;" and the speaker broke off with a sigh and rolled a fresh cigarette before he resumed.

"It's her property, all of it, and I cannot bear to have her misrepresented in any way."

"I understand," said Gerald, making a note of the fact. "The property, I suppose, passed to your sister from – "

"From her father. I was in the land of the living some years before he met and wooed and won my widowed mother. They are both dead now, and Catalina has none but myself to look out for her, except distant relatives on the father's side, who will inherit the property if she dies unmarried, and whom she cordially detests."

Gerald was not particularly romantic, but the idea of this fair young Spaniard, owner of one of the finest ranches in Yuba County, unmarried, and handsome too, if she were anything like her mother, inflamed his imagination a little. He shook hands cordially with the young man as he rose to go, and could not help wishing they were better acquainted.

"You may be sure I will publish your statement exactly as you have given it to me, and as fully as possible," said Gerald. Before the young heiress had been mentioned, the journalist had scarcely seen material enough in the interview for a paragraph.

It is fair to presume that Senor Vincenza was satisfied with the treatment he received in the Evening Mail, for a polite note conveyed to Ffrench the expression of his thanks. So that incident passed into the limbo of forgetfulness, though Gerald afterwards took more interest in the newspaper paragraphs, often scant enough, which told of the progress of the great land case in the Marysville courts.

A curt despatch, worded with that exasperating brevity which is a peculiarity of all but the most important telegrams, wound up the matter with an announcement that a decision had been reached in favor of the defendant, and that Mr. Isaac Hall, of the law firm of Hall and McGowan, had returned to San Francisco, having conducted the case to a successful issue. Gerald was pleased to hear that the young lady had been sustained in her rights, and determined to interview Mr. Hall, with whom he was well acquainted. Accordingly, after two or three unsuccessful attempts, he managed to catch the busy lawyer with half an hour's spare time on his hands, and well enough disposed to welcome his young friend.

"Mr. Hall," said Gerald, dropping into the spare chair in the attorney's private room, "I want to ask you a few questions about that Marysville land case."

"Fire ahead, my boy; I can give you twenty minutes," answered the lawyer, who was disposed to make a great deal more of the victory he had won than the newspapers had hitherto done, and who was consequently by no means averse from an interview. "What do you want to know?"

"Hard fight, wasn't it?" asked the journalist.

"Yes," replied Mr. Hall, "tough in a way; but we had right on our side as well as possession. A good lawyer ought always to win when he has those; to beat law and facts and everything else is harder scratching; though I've done that too," and the old gentleman chuckled as if well satisfied with himself.

"That's what your opponents had to do here, I suppose?" remarked Gerald, echoing the other's laugh.

"Pretty much, only they didn't do it," said the lawyer.

"I met Vincenza when he was down last month," pursued Gerald. "He seems a decentish sort of a fellow for a greaser."

"He's no greaser; he's a pure-blooded Castilian, and very much of the gentleman," answered Hall.

"So I found him," said Gerald. "I only used the 'greaser' as a generic term. He talks English as well as I do."

"That's a great compliment from an Irishman," remarked Mr. Hall with another chuckle.

"I suppose the sister's just as nice in her own way," went on Gerald, seeing an opportunity to satisfy a certain curiosity he had felt about the heiress since he first heard of her existence. "Did she make a good witness?"

"Who? What sister? What the deuce are you talking about?" asked the lawyer.

"Why, Vincenza's sister, half-sister, whatever she is. I understood from him that she was the real owner of the property."

"Oh, ay, to be sure," said Mr. Hall slowly; "these details escape one. Vincenza was my client; he acts for the girl under power of attorney, and really her name has hardly come up since the very beginning of the case."

"You didn't see her, then?" said Gerald, conscious of a vague sense of disappointment.

"See her?" repeated the lawyer. "No; how could I? She's in Europe for educational advantages – at a convent somewhere, I believe."

"Oh," said Gerald, "a child, is she? I had fancied, I don't know why, that she was a grown-up young lady."

"I couldn't tell you what her age is, but it must be over twenty- one or she couldn't have executed the power of attorney, and that was looked into at the start and found quite regular."

"I see," replied Gerald slowly; but the topic had started Mr. Hall on a fresh trail, and he broke in –

"And it was the only thing in order in the whole business. Do you know we came within an ace of losing, all through their confounded careless way of keeping their papers?"

"How did they keep them?" inquired Gerald listlessly. The suit appeared to be a commonplace one, and the young man's interest began to wane.

"They didn't keep them at all," exclaimed Mr. Hall indignantly. "Fancy, the original deed – the old Spanish grant – the very keystone of our case, was not to be found till the last moment, and then only by the merest accident, and where do you suppose it was?"

"I haven't an idea," answered Gerald, stifling a yawn.

"At the back of an old print of the Madonna. It had been framed and hung up as an ornament, I suppose, Heaven knows when; and by- and-by some smart Aleck came along and thought the mother and child superior as a work of art and slapped it into the frame over the deed, and there it has hung for ten years anyhow."

"That's really very curious," said Gerald, whose attention began to revive as he saw a possible column to be compiled on the details of the case that had seemed so uninteresting to his contemporaries.

"Curious! I call it sinful – positively wicked," said the old gentleman wrathfully. "Just fancy two hundred thousand dollars hanging on the accident of finding a parchment in such a place as that."

"How did you happen to find it?" asked Gerald. "I should never have thought of looking for it there."

"No; nor any other sane man," sputtered the lawyer, irritated, as he recalled the anxiety the missing deed had caused him. "It was found by accident, I tell you. Some blundering, awkward, heaven- guided servant knocked the picture down and broke the frame. The Madonna was removed, and the missing paper came to light."

"And that was the turning-point of the case. Very interesting indeed," said Gerald, who saw in the working out of this legal romance a bit of detective writing such as his soul loved. "I suppose they'll have sense enough to put it in a safer place next time?"

"I will, you may bet your life. I've taken charge of all the family documents; and if they get away from me, they'll do something that nothing's ever done before;" and the old lawyer chuckled with renewed satisfaction as he pointed to the massive safe in a corner of the office.

"So the deed is there, is it?" asked Gerald, following Mr.

Hall's eyes.

"Yes, it's there. A curious old document too; one of the oldest grants I have ever come across. Would you like to see it?" and the lawyer rose and opened the safe.

It was a curious old document drawn up in curious old Spanish, on an old discolored piece of parchment. The body of the instrument was unintelligible to Ffrench, but down in one corner was something that riveted his attention in a moment and seemed to make his heart stand still.

There was a signature in old-fashioned angular handwriting, Rodriguez Costello y Ugarte, and opposite to it a large, spreading seal. The impression showed a knight's head and shoulders in full armor, below it the motto, Nemo me impune lacessit, and a shield of arms, party per fess, azure below, argent above, counter-vair on the argent. Point for point the identical blazonry which Ffrench had received from the Heralds' College in England – the shield that he had first seen embroidered on the dead girl's handkerchief at Drim.

"What's the matter with you? Didn't you ever see an old Spanish deed before, or has it any of the properties of Medusa's head?" inquired Mr. Hall, noticing Gerald's start of amazement and intent scrutiny of the seal.

"I've seen these arms before," said the young man slowly. "But the name – " He placed his finger on the signature. "Of course, I knew Vincenza's name must be different from his half-sister's; but is that hers?"

"Ugarte? Yes," said the lawyer, glancing at the parchment.

"I mean the whole name," and Gerald pointed again.

"Costello!" Mr. Hall gave the word its Spanish pronunciation, "Costelyo," and it sounded strange and foreign in the young man's ears. "Costello, yes, I suppose so; but I don't try to keep track of more of these Spaniards' titles than is absolutely necessary."

"But Costello is an Irish name," said Gerald.

"Is it? You ought to know. Well Costelyo is Spanish; and now, my dear boy, I must positively turn you out."

Gerald went straight home without returning to the office.

He unlocked his desk, and took from it the two results of his first essay in detective craft. Silently he laid them side by side and scrutinized each closely in turn. The pale, set face of the beautiful dead, as reproduced by the photographer's art, told him nothing. He strove to trace some resemblance, to awaken some memory, by long gazing at the passionless features, but it was in vain. Then he turned to the illuminated shield. Every line was familiar to him, and a glance sufficed. It was identical in all respects with the arms on the seal. Of this he had been already convinced, and his recollection had not betrayed him. Then he placed the two – the piteous photograph and the proud blazonry – in his pocketbook, and left the room. The same evening he took his place on the Sacramento train en route for Marysville.

When Gerald reached San Luis, the postoffice address of the Ugarte ranch, a disappointment awaited him. Evening was falling, and inquiry elicited the fact that Don Vincenza's residence was still twelve miles distant. Ffrench, after his drive of eighteen miles over the dusty road from Marysville, was little inclined to go further, so he put up his horse at a livery stable, resolved to make the best of such accommodations as San Luis afforded.

The face of the man who took the reins when Ffrench alighted seemed familiar. The young fellow looked closer at him, and it was evident the recognition was mutual, for the stableman accosted him by name, and in the broad, familiar dialect of western Leinster.

"May I niver ate another bit if it isn't Masther Gerald Ffrench!" he said. "Well, well, well, but it's good for sore eyes to see ye. Come out here, Steve, an' take the team. Jump down, Masther Gerald, an' stretch yer legs a bit. It's kilt ye are entirely."

A swarthy little Mexican appeared, and led the tired horses into the stable. Then the young journalist took a good look at the man who seemed to know him so well, and endeavored, as the phrase goes, to "place him."

"Ye don't mind me, yer honor, an' how wud ye? But I mind yersilf well. Sure it's often I've druv ye and Mr. Edward too. I used to wurruk for Mr. Ross of Mullinger. I was Denny the postboy – Denis Driscoll, yer honor; sure ye must know me?"

"Oh yes, to be sure – I remember," said Gerald, as recollection slowly dawned upon him. "But who'd have thought of finding you in a place like this? I didn't even know you'd left Ross's stables."

"Six or siven months ago, yer honor."

"And have you been here ever since? I hope you are doing well," said Gerald.

"Iver since, sor, an' doin' finely, wid the blessin' o' God. I own that place," pointing to the stable, "an' four as good turnouts as ye'd ax to sit behind."

"I'm glad of it," said Gerald heartily. "I like to hear of the boys from the old neighborhood doing well."

"Won't ye step inside, sor, an' thry a drop of something? Ye must be choked intirely wid the dust."

"I don't care if I do," answered Gerald. "I feel pretty much as if I'd swallowed a limekiln."

A minute later the two were seated in Denny's own particular room, where Gerald washed the dust from his throat with some capital bottled beer, while his host paid attention to a large demijohn which contained, as he informed the journalist in an impressive whisper, "close on to a gallon of the real ould stuff."

Their conversation extended far into the night; but long before they separated Gerald induced Denny to despatch his Mexican helper, on a good mustang, to the Ugarte ranch, bearing to Senor Vincenza Mr. Ffrench's card, on which were penciled the words: "Please come over to San Luis as soon as possible. Most important business."

For the tale told by the ex-postboy, his change of residence and present prosperity, seemed to throw a curious light on the Drim churchyard mystery.

Senor Vincenza appeared the following morning just as Gerald had finished breakfast. The ranchero remembered the representative of the Evening Mail and greeted him cordially, expressing his surprise at Gerald's presence in that part of the country. The Spaniard evidently imagined that this unexpected visit had some bearing on the recently decided lawsuit, but the other's first words dispelled the illusion.

"Senor Vincenza," Ffrench said, "I have heard a very strange story about your sister, and I have come to ask you for an explanation of it."

The young Spaniard changed color and looked uneasily at the journalist.

"What do you mean?" he asked. "I do not understand you. My sister is in Europe."

"Yes," answered Gerald, "she is in Europe – in Ireland. She fills a nameless grave in Drim churchyard."

Vincenza leaped to his feet, and the cigarette he had lighted dropped from his fingers. They were in Gerald's room at the hotel, and the young man had placed his visitor so that the table was between them. He suspected that he might have to deal with a desperate man. Vincenza leaned over the narrow table, and his breath blew hot in Ffrench's face as he hissed, "Carambo! What do you mean? How much do you know?"

"I know everything. I know how she died in the carriage on your way from Mullingar; how you purchased a coffin and bribed the undertaker to silence; how you laid her, in the dead of night, among the weeds in the graveyard; how you cut her name from the chatelaine bag, and did all in your power to hide her identity, even carrying off with you the postboy who drove you and aided you to place her where she was found. Do you recognize that photograph? Have you ever seen that coat-of-arms before?" and Ffrench drew the two cards from his pocket and offered them to Vincenza.

The Spaniard brushed them impatiently aside and crouched for a moment as if to spring. Gerald never took his eyes off him, and presently the other straightened up, and, sinking into the chair behind him, attempted to roll a cigarette. But his hand trembled, and half the tobacco was spilled on the floor.

"You know a great deal, Mr. Gerald Ffrench. Do you accuse me of my sister's murder?"

"No," answered Gerald. "She died from natural causes. But I do accuse you of fraudulently withholding this property from its rightful owners, and of acting on a power of attorney which has been cancelled by the death of the giver."

There was a moment's silence, broken only by a muttered oath from Vincenza as he threw the unfinished cigarette to the ground, and began to roll another, this time with better success. It was not till it was fairly alight that he spoke again.

Listen to me, young man," he said, "and then judge me as you hope to be judged hereafter – with mercy. My sister was very dear to me; I loved her, O God, how I loved her!" His voice broke, and Gerald, recalling certain details of Denny's narrative, felt that the Spaniard was speaking the truth. It was nearly a minute before Vincenza recovered his self-command and resumed.

"Yes, we were very dear to each other; brought up as brother and sister, how could we fail to be? But her father never liked me, and he placed restrictions upon the fortune he left her so that it could never come to me. My mother – our mother – had died some years before. Well, Catalina was wealthy; I was a pauper, but that made no difference while she lived. We were as happy and fond a brother and sister as the sun ever shone upon. When she came of age she executed the power of attorney that gave me the charge of her estate. She was anxious to spend a few years in Europe. I was to take her over, and after we had traveled a little she was to go to a convent in France and spend some time there while I returned home. But she was one of the old Costellos, and she was anxious to visit the ancient home of her race. That was what brought us to Ireland."

"I thought the Costello family was extinct," said Gerald.

"The European branch has been extinct since 1813, when Don Lopez Costello fell at Vittoria; but the younger branch, which settled in Mexico towards the end of the eighteenth century, survived until a few months ago – until Catalina's death, in fact, for she was the last of the Costellos."

"I see," said Gerald; "go on."

"She was very proud of the name, poor Catalina, and she made me promise in case anything happened to her while we were abroad that she should be laid in the ancient grave of her race – in the churchyard of Drim. She had a weak heart, and she knew that she might die suddenly. I promised. And it was on our way to the spot she was so anxious to visit that death claimed her, only a few miles from the place where her ancestors had lived in the old days, and where all that remains of them has long mouldered to dust. So you see, Mr. Ffrench, that I had no choice but to lay her there."

"That is not the point," said Gerald; "why this secrecy? Why this flight? Dr. Lynn, I am sure, would have enabled you to obey your sister's request in the full light of day; you need not have thrown her coffin on the ground and left to strangers the task of doing for the poor girl the last duties of civilization." Gerald spoke with indignant heat, for this looked to him like the cruellest desertion.

"I know how it must seem to you," said Vincenza, "and I have no excuse to offer for my conduct but this. My sister's death would have given all she possessed to people whom she disliked. It would have thrown me, whom she loved, penniless on the world. I acted as if she were still living, and as I am sure she would have wished me to act; no defence, I know, in your eyes, but consider the temptation."

"And did you not realize that all this must come out some day?" asked Ffrench.

"Yes, but not for several years. Indeed, I cannot imagine how it is that you have stumbled on the truth."

And Gerald, remembering the extraordinary chain of circumstances which had led him to the root of the mystery, could not but acknowledge that, humanly speaking, Vincenza's confidence was justified.

"And now you have found this out, what use do you intend to make of it?" asked the Spaniard after a pause.

"I shall publish the whole story as soon as I return to San Francisco," answered Gerald promptly.

"So for a few hundred dollars, which is all that you can possibly get out of it, you will make a beggar of me."

"Right is right," said the young Irishman. "This property does not belong to you."

"Will you hold your tongue – or your pen – for fifty thousand dollars?" asked the Spaniard eagerly.

"No, nor for every dollar you have in the world. I don't approve your practice and I won't share your plunder. I am sorry for you personally, but I can't help that. I won't oust you. I will make such use of the story as any newspaper man would make, and so I give you fair warning. You may save yourself if you can."

"Then you do not intend to communicate with the heirs?" began Vincenza eagerly.

"I neither know nor care who they are," interrupted Gerald. "I am not a detective, save in the way of my profession, and I shall certainly not tell what I have discovered to any individual till I give it to the press."

"And that will be?" asked the Spaniard.

"As soon as I return to San Francisco," answered Ffrench. "It may appear in a week or ten days."

"Thank you, senor; good morning," said Vincenza, rising and leaving the room.

Three days later Senor Miguel Vincenza sailed on the outgoing Pacific mail steamer bound for Japan and China. He probably took a considerable sum of money with him, for the heirs of Catalina Costello y Ugarte found the affairs of the deceased in a very tangled state, and the ranch was mortgaged for nearly half its value.

Gerald Ffrench's story occupied four pages of the next issue of the Golden Fleece, and was widely copied and commented on over two continents. Larry, the groom at Ballyvire, read the account in his favorite Westmeath Sentinel, and as he laid the paper down exclaimed in wonder –

"Begob, he found her!"

Lady Betty's Indiscretion

"Horry! I am sick to death of it!"

There was a servant in the room gathering the tea-cups; but Lady Betty Stafford, having been brought up in the purple, was not to be deterred from speaking her mind by a servant. Her cousin was either more prudent or less vivacious; he did not answer on the instant, but stood looking through one of the windows at the leafless trees and slow-dropping rain in the Mall, and only turned when Lady Betty pettishly repeated her statement.

"Had a bad time?" he then vouchsafed, dropping into a chair near her, and looking first at her, in a good-natured way, and then at his boots, which he seemed to approve.

"Horrid!" she replied.

"Many people here?"

"Hordes of them! Whole tribes!" she exclaimed. She was a little lady, plump and pretty, with a pale, clear complexion, and bright eyes. "I am bored beyond belief. And – and I have not seen Stafford since morning," she added.

"Cabinet council?"

"Yes!" she answered viciously. "A cabinet council, and a privy council, and a board of trade, and a board of green cloth, and all the other boards! Horry, I am sick to death of it! What is the use of it all?"

"Country go to the dogs!" he said oracularly, still admiring his boots

"Let it!" she retorted, not relenting a whit. " I wish it would; I wish the dogs joy of it!"

He made an extraordinary effort at diffuseness. "I thought," he said, "that you were becoming political, Betty. Going to write something, and all that."

"Rubbish! But here is Mr. Atley. Mr. Atley, will you have a cup of tea," she continued, speaking to the newcomer. "There will be some here presently. Where is Mr. Stafford?"

"Mr. Stafford will take a cup of tea in the library, Lady Betty," replied the secretary. "He asked me to bring it to him. He is copying an important paper."

Sir Horace forsook his boots, and in a fit of momentary interest asked, "They have come to terms?"

The secretary nodded. Lady Betty said "Pshaw!" A man brought in the fresh teapot. The next moment Mr. Stafford himself came quickly into the room, an open telegram in his hand.

He nodded pleasantly to his wife and her cousin. But his thin, dark face wore – it generally did – a preoccupied look. Country people to whom he was pointed out in the streets called him, according to their political leanings, either insignificant, or a prig, or a "dry sort;" or sometimes said, "How young he is!" But those whose fate it was to face the Minister in the House knew that there was something in him more to be feared even than his imperturability, his honesty, or his precision – and that was a certain sudden warmth, which was apt to carry away the House at unexpected times. On one of these occasions, it was rumored, Lady Betty Champion had seen him, and fallen in love with him. Why he had thrown the handkerchief to her – well that was another matter; and whether the apparently incongruous match would answer – that, too, remained to be seen.

"More telegrams?" she cried now. "It rains telegrams! how I hate them!"

"Why?" he said. "Why should you?" He really wondered.

She made a face at him. "Here is your tea," she said abruptly.

"Thank you; you are very good," he replied. He took the cup and set it down absently. "Atley," he continued, speaking to the secretary, "you have not corrected the report of my speech at the Club, have you? No, I know you have had no time. Will you run your eye over it presently, and see if it is all right, and send it to the Times – I do not think I need see it – by eleven o'clock at latest. The editor," he added, tapping the pink paper in his hand, "seemed to doubt us. I have to go to Fitzgerald's now, so you must copy Lord Pilgrimstone's terms, too, please. I had meant to do it myself, but I shall be with you before you have finished."

"What are the terms?" Lady Betty asked. "Lord Pilgrimstone has not agreed to – "

"To permit me to communicate them?" he replied, with a grave smile. "No. So you must pardon me, my dear, I have passed my word for absolute secrecy. And, indeed, it is as important to me as to Pilgrimstone that they should not be divulged."

"They are sure to leak out," she retorted. "They always do."

"Well, it will not be through me, I hope."

She stamped her foot on the carpet. "I should like to get them, and send them to the Times!" she exclaimed, her eyes flashing – he was so provoking! "And let all the world know them! I should!"

He looked his astonishment, while the other two laughed softly, partly to avoid embarrassment, perhaps. My Lady often said these things, and no one took them seriously.

"You had better play the secretary for once, Lady Betty," said Atley, who was related to his chief. "You will then be able to satisfy your curiosity. Shall I resign pro tem?"

She looked eagerly at her husband for the third part of a second – looked for assent, perhaps. But she read no playfulness in his face, and her own fell. He was thinking about other things. "No," she said, almost sullenly, dropping her eyes to the carpet; "I should not spell well enough."

Soon after that they dispersed, this being Wednesday, Mr. Stafford's day for dining out. Everyone knows that Ministers dine only twice a week in session – on Wednesday and Sunday; and Sunday is often sacred to the children where there are any, lest they should grow up and not know their father by sight. Lady Betty came into the library at a quarter to eight, and found her husband still at his desk, a pile of papers before him waiting for his signature. As a fact, he had only just sat down, displacing his secretary, who had gone upstairs to dress.

"Stafford!" she said.

She did not seem quite at her ease, but his mind was troubled, and he failed to notice this. "Yes, my dear," he answered politely, shuffling the papers before him into a heap. He knew he was late, and he could see that she was dressed. "Yes, I am going upstairs this minute. I have not forgotten."

"It is not that," she said, leaning with one hand on the table; "I only want to ask you – "

"My dear, you really must tell it to me in the carriage." He was on his feet already, making some hasty preparations. "Where are we to dine? At the Duke's? Then we shall have nearly a mile to drive. Will not that do for you?" He was working hard while he spoke. There was a great oak post-box within reach, and another box for letters which were to be delivered by hand, and he was thrusting a handful of notes into each of these. Other packets he swept into different drawers of the table. Still standing, he stooped and signed his name to half a dozen letters, which he left open on the blotting-pad. "Atley will see to these when he is dressed," he murmured. "Would you oblige me by locking the drawers, my dear – it will save me a minute – and giving me the keys when I come down?"

He was off then, two or three papers in his hand, and almost ran upstairs. Lady Betty stood a moment on the spot on which he had left her, looking in an odd way, just as if it were new to her, round the grave, spacious room, with its somber Spanish-leather-covered furniture, its ponderous writing-tables and shelves of books, its three lofty curtained windows. When her eyes at last came back to the lamp, and dwelt on it, they were very bright, and her face was flushed. Her foot could be heard tapping on the carpet. Presently she remembered herself and fell to work, vehemently slamming such drawers as were open, and locking them.

The private secretary found her doing this when he came in. She muttered something – still stooping with her face over the drawers – and almost immediately went out. He looked after her, partly because there was something odd in her manner – she kept her face averted; and partly because she was wearing a new and striking gown, and he admired her; and he noticed, as she passed through the doorway, that she had some papers held down by her side. But, of course, he thought nothing of this.

He was hopelessly late for his own dinner-party, and only stayed a moment to slip the letters just signed into envelopes prepared for them. Then he made hastily for the door, opened it, and came into abrupt collision with Sir Horace, who was strolling in.

"Beg pardon!" said that gentleman, with irritating placidity. "Late for dinner?"

"Rather!" cried the secretary, trying to get round him.

"Well," drawled the other, "which is the hand-box, old fellow?"

"It has just been cleared. Here, give it me. The messengers is in the hall now."

And Atley snatched the letter from his companion, the two going out into the hall together. Marcus, the butler, a couple of tall footmen, and the messenger were sorting letters at the table. "Here, Marcus," said the secretary, pitching his letter on the slab, "let that go with the others. And is my hansom here?"

In another minute he was speeding one way, and the Staffords in their brougham another, while Sir Horace walked at his leisure down to his club. The Minister and his wife drove along in silence, for he forgot to ask her what she wanted; and, strange to say, Lady Betty forgot to tell him. At the party she made quite a sensation; never had she seemed more recklessly gay, more piquant, more audaciously witty, than she showed herself this evening. There were illustrious personages present, but they paled beside her. The Duke, with whom she was a great favorite, laughed at her sallies until he could laugh no more; and even her husband, her very husband, forgot for a time the country and the crisis, and listened, half-proud and half-afraid. But she was not aware of this; she could not see his face where she was sitting. To all seeming, she never looked that way. She was quite a model society wife.

Mr. Stafford himself was an early riser. It was his habit to be up by six; to make his own coffee over a spirit lamp, and then not only to get through much work in his dressing-room, but to take his daily ride also before breakfast. On the morning after the Duke's party, however, he lay later than usual; and as there was more business to be done – owing to the crisis – the canter in the Park had to be omitted. He was still among his papers – though momentarily awaiting the breakfast-gong, when a hansom cab driven at full speed stopped at the door. He glanced up wearily as he heard the doors of the cab flung open with a crash. There had been a time when the stir and bustle of such arrivals had been sweet to him – not so sweet as to some, for he had never been deeply in love with the parade of office – but sweeter than to-day, when they were no more to him than the creaking of the mill to the camel that turns it blindfold and in darkness.

Naturally he was thinking of Lord Pilgrimstone this morning, and guessed, before he opened the note which the servant brought in to him, who was its writer. But its contents had, nevertheless, an electrical effect upon him. His brow reddened. With a quite unusual display of emotion he sprang to his feet, crushing the fragment of paper in his fingers. "Who brought this?" he asked sharply. "Who brought it?" he repeated, before the servant could explain.

The man had never seen him so moved. "Mr. Scratchley, sir," he answered.

"Ha! Then, show him into the library," was the quick reply. And while the servant went to do his bidding, the Minister hastily changed his dressing-gown for a coat, and ran down a private staircase, reaching the room he had mentioned by one door as Mr. Scratchley, Lord Pilgrim-stone's secretary, entered in through another.

By that time he had regained his composure, and looked much as usual. Still, when he held up the crumpled note, there was a brusqueness in the gesture which would have surprised his ordinary acquaintances, and did remind Mr. Scratchley of certain "warm nights" in the House. "You know the contents of this, Mr. Scratchley?" he said without prelude, and in a tone which matched his gesture.

The visitor bowed. He was a grave middle-aged man, who seemed oppressed and burdened by the load of cares and responsibilities which his smiling chief carried so jauntily. People said that he was the proper complement of Lord Pilgrimstone, as the more volatile Atley was of his leader.

"And you are aware," continued Mr. Stafford, still more harshly, "that Lord Pilgrimstone gives yesterday's agreement to the winds?"

"I have never seen his lordship so deeply moved," replied the discreet one.

"He says: 'Our former negotiation was ruined by premature talk, but this last disclosure can only be referred to treachery or gross carelessness.' What does this mean? I know of no disclosure, Mr. Scratchley. I must have an explanation, and you, I presume, are here to give me one."

For a moment the other seemed taken aback. "You have not seen the Times?" he murmured.

"This morning's? No. But it is here."

He snatched it, as he spoke, from a table at his elbow, and unfolded it. The secretary approached and pointed to the head of a column – the most conspicuous, the column most readily to be found in the paper. "They are crying it at every street corner I passed," he added apologetically. "There is nothing to be heard in St. James's Street and Pall Mall but 'Detailed Programme of the Coalition.' The other dailies are striking off second editions to contain it!"

Mr. Stafford's eyes were riveted to the paper, and there was a long pause, a pause on his part of dismay and consternation. He could scarcely – to repeat a common phrase – believe his eyes. "It seems," he muttered at length, "it seems fairly accurate – a tolerably precise account, indeed."

"It is a verbatim copy," said the secretary drily. "The question is, who furnished it. Lord Pilgrimstone, I am authorized to say, has not permitted his note of the agreement to pass out of his possession – even up to the present moment."

"And so he concludes," the Minister said thoughtfully – "it is a fair inference enough, perhaps – that the Times must have procured its information from my note?"

"No!" the secretary objected sharply and forcibly. "It is not a matter of inference, Mr. Stafford. I am directed to say that. I have inquired, early as it is, at the Times office, and learned that the copy printed came directly from the hands of your messenger."

"Of my messenger!" Mr. Stafford cried, thunderstruck. "You are sure of that?"

"I am sure that the sub-editor says so."

And again there was silence. "This must be looked into," said Mr. Stafford at length, controlling himself by an effort. "For the present, I agree with Lord Pilgrimstone, that it alters the position – and perhaps finally."

"Lord Pilgrimstone will be damaged in the eyes of a large section of his supporters – seriously damaged," said Mr. Scratchley, shaking his head, and frowning.

"Possibly. From every point of view the thing is to be deplored. But I will call on Lord Pilgrimstone," continued the Minister, "after lunch. Will you tell him so?"

A curious embarrassment showed itself in the secretary's manner. He twisted his hat in his hands, and looked suddenly sick and sad – as if he were about to join in the groan at a prayer-meeting. "Lord Pilgrimstone," he said, in a voice he vainly strove to render commonplace, "is going to Sandown Spring Meeting today."

The tone was really so lugubrious – to say nothing of a shake of the head with which he could not help accompanying the statement – that a faint smile played on Mr. Stafford's lip. "Then I must take the next possible opportunity. I will see him tomorrow."

Mr. Scratchley assented to that, and bowed himself out, after another word or two, looking more gloomy and careworn than usual. The interview had not been altogether to his mind. He wished now that he had spoken more roundly to Mr. Stafford; perhaps even asked for a categorical denial of the charge. But the Minister's manner had overawed him. He had found it impossible to put the question. And then the pitiful degrading confession he had had to make for Lord Pilgrimstone! That had put the coping-stone to his dissatisfaction.

"Oh!" sighed Mr. Scratchley, as he stepped into his cab. "Oh, that men so great should stoop to things so little!"

It did not occur to him that there is a condition of things even more sad: when little men meddle with great things.

Meanwhile Mr. Stafford, left alone, stood at the window deep in unpleasant thoughts, from which the entrance of the butler sent to summon him to breakfast first aroused him. "Stay a moment, Marcus!" he said, turning with a sigh, as the man was leaving the room after doing his errand. "I want to ask you a question. Did you make up the messenger's bag last evening?"

"Yes, sir."

"Did you notice a letter addressed to the Times office?"

The servant had prepared himself to cogitate. But he found it unnecessary. "Yes, sir," he replied smartly, "Two."

"Two?" repeated Mr Stafford, dismay in his tone, though this was just what he had reason to expect.

"Yes, sir. There was one I took from the band-box, and one Mr. Atley gave me in the hall at the last moment," explained the butler.

"Ha! Thank you, Marcus. Then ask Mr. Atley if he will kindly come to me. No doubt he will be able to tell me what I want to know."

The words were commonplace, but the speaker's anxiety was so evident that Marcus when he delivered the message – which he did with all haste – added a word or two of warning. "It is about a letter to the Times, sir, I think. Mr. Stafford seemed a good deal put out," he said, confidentially.

"Indeed?" Atley replied. "I will go down." And he started at once. But before he reached the library he met someone. Lady Betty looked out of the breakfast-room, and saw him descending the stairs with the butler behind him.

"Where is Mr. Stafford, Marcus?" she asked impatiently, as she stood with her hand on the door. "Good morning, Mr. Atley," she added, her eyes descending to him. "Where is my husband? The coffee is getting quite cold."

"He has just sent to ask me to come to him," Atley answered. "Marcus tells me there is something in the Times which has annoyed him, Lady Betty; I will send him up as quickly as I can."

But Lady Betty had not stayed to receive this last assurance. She had drawn back and shut the door smartly; yet not so quickly but that the private secretary had seen her change color. "Umph!" he ejaculated to himself – the lady was not much given to blushing as a rule – "I wonder what is wrong with HER this morning. She is not generally rude to me."

It was not long before he got some light on the matter. "Come here, Atley," said his employer, the moment he entered the library. "Look at this!"

The secretary took the Times, folded back at the important column, and read the letter. Meanwhile the Minister read the secretary. He saw surprise and consternation on his face, but no trace of guilt. Then he told him what Marcus said about the two letters which had gone the previous evening from the house addressed to the Times office. "One," he said, "contained the notes of my speech. The other – "

"The other – " replied the secretary, thinking while he spoke, "was given to me at the last moment by Sir Horace. I threw it to Marcus in the hall."

"Ah!" said his chief, trying very hard to express nothing by the exclamation, but not quite succeeding. "Did you see that that letter was addressed to the editor of the Times?"

The secretary reddened, and betrayed sudden confusion. "I did," he said hurriedly. "I saw so much of the address as I threw the letter on the slab – though I thought nothing of it at the time."

Mr. Stafford looked at him fixedly. "Come," he said, "this is a grave matter, Atley. You noticed, I can see, the handwriting. Was it Sir Horace's?"

"No," replied the secretary.

"Whose was it?"

"I think – I think, Mr. Stafford – that it was Lady Betty's. But I should be sorry, having seen it only for a moment – so say for certain."

"Lady Betty's?"

Mr. Stafford repeated the exclamation three times, in pure surprise, in anger, a third time in trembling. In this last stage he walked away to the window, and turning his back on his companion looked out. He recalled at once his wife's petulant exclamation of yesterday, the foolish desire expressed, as he had supposed in jest. Had she really been in earnest? And had she carried out her threat? Had she – his wife – done this thing so compromising to his honor, so mischievous to the country, so mad, reckless, wicked? Impossible. It was impossible. And yet – and yet Atley was a man to be trusted, a gentleman, his own relation! And Atley's eye was not likely to be deceived in a matter of handwriting. That Atley had made up his mind he could see.

The statesman turned from the window, and walked to and fro, his agitation betrayed by his step. The third time he passed in front of his secretary – who had riveted his eyes to the Times and appeared to be reading the money article – he stopped. "If this be true – mind I say if, Atley – " he cried, jerkily, "what was my wife's motive? I am in the dark, blindfolded! Help me! Tell me what has been passing round me that I have not seen. You would not have my wife – a spy?"

"No! no! no!" cried the other, as he dropped the paper, his vehemence and his working features showing that he felt the pathos of the appeal. "It is not that. Lady Betty is jealous, if I may venture to judge, of your devotion to politics. She sees little of you. You are wrapped up in public affairs and matters of state. She feels herself neglected and set aside. And she has been married no more than a year."

"But she has her society," objected the Minister, compelling himself to speak calmly, "and her cousin, and – and many other things."

"For which she does not care," returned the secretary.

It was a simple answer, but something in it touched a tender place. Mr. Stafford winced and cast a queer startled look at the speaker. Before he could reply, however – if he intended to reply – a knock came at the door and Marcus put in his head. "My lady is waiting breakfast, sir," he suggested timidly. What could a poor butler do between an impatient mistress and an obdurate master?

"I will come," said Mr. Stafford hastily. "I will come at once. For this matter, Atley," he continued when the door was closed again, "let it rest for the present where it is. I am aware I can depend upon your – " he paused, seeking a word – "your discretion. One thing is certain, however. There is an end of the arrangement made yesterday. Probably the Queen will send for Templeton. I shall see Lord Pilgrimstone tomorrow, but probably that will be the end of it."

Atley went away marveling at his coolness, trying to retrace the short steps of their conversation, and so to discern how far the Minister had gone with him, and where he had turned off upon a resolution of his own. He failed to see the clue, however, and marveled still more as the day went on and others succeeded it, days of political crisis. Out of doors the world, or that little jot of it which has its center at Westminster, was in confusion. The newspapers, morning or evening, found ready sale, and had no need of recourse to murder-panics, or prurient discussions. The Coalition scandal, the resignation of Ministers, the sending for Lord This and Mr. That, the certainty of a dissolution, provided matter enough. In all this Atley found nothing to wonder at. He had seen it all before. That which did cause him surprise was the calm – the unnatural calm as it seemed to him – which prevailed in the house in Carlton Terrace. For a day or two, indeed, there was much going to and fro, much closeting and button-holing; for rather longer the secretary read anxiety and apprehension in one countenance – Lady Betty's. But things settled down. The knocker presently found peace, such comparative peace as falls to knockers in Carlton Terrace. Lady Betty's brow grew clear as her eye found no reflection of its anxiety in Mr. Stafford's face. In a word the secretary failed to discern the faintest sign of domestic trouble.

The late Minister, indeed, was taking things with wonderful coolness. Lord Pilgrimstone had failed to taunt him, and the triumph of old foes had failed to goad him into a last effort. Apparently it had occurred to him that the country might for a time exist without him. He was standing aside with a shade on his face, and there were rumors that he would take a long holiday.

A week saw all these things happen. And then, one day as Atley sat writing in the library – Mr. Stafford being out – Lady Betty came into the room for something. Rising to find her what she wanted, he was holding the door open for her to pass out, when she paused.

"Shut the door, Mr. Atley," she said, pointing to it. "I want to ask you a question."

"Pray do, Lady Betty," he answered.

"It is this," she said, meeting his eyes boldly – and a brighter, a more dainty little creature than she looked then had seldom tempted man. "Mr. Stafford's resignation – had it anything, Mr. Atley, to do with – " her face colored a very little – "something that was in the Times this day week?"

His own cheek colored violently enough. "If ever," he was saying to himself, "I meddle or mar between husband and wife again, may I – " But aloud he answered quietly, "Something perhaps." The question was sudden. Her eyes were on his face. He found it impossible to prevaricate.

"My husband has never spoken to me about it," she replied, breathing quickly.

He bowed, having no words adapted to the situation. But he repeated his resolution (as above) more furiously.

"He has never appeared even aware of it," she persisted. "Are you sure that he saw it?"

He wondered at her innocence or her audacity. That such a baby should do so much mischief. The thought irritated him. "It was impossible that he should not see it, Lady Betty," he said, with a touch of asperity. "Quite impossible!"

"Ah," she replied with a faint sigh. "Well, he has never spoken to me about it. And you think it had really something to do with his resignation, Mr. Atley?"

"Most certainly," he said. He was not inclined to spare her this time.

She nodded thoughtfully, and then with a quiet "Thank you," went out.

"Well," muttered the secretary to himself when the door was fairly shut behind her, "she is – upon my word she is a fool! And he" – appealing to the inkstand – "he has never said a word to her about it. He is a new Don Quixote! a second Job, new Sir Isaac Newton! I do not know what to call him."

It was Sir Horace, however, who precipitated the catastrophe. He happened to come in about tea-time that afternoon, before, in fact, my lady had had an opportunity of seeing her husband. He found her alone and in a brown study, a thing most unusual with her and portending something. He watched her for a time in silence, seemed to draw courage from a still longer inspection of his boots, and then said, "So the cart is clean over,

Betty?"

She nodded.

"Driver much hurt?"

"Do you mean, does Stafford mind it?" she replied impatiently.

He nodded.

"Well, I do not know. It is hard to say."

"Think so?" he persisted.

"Good gracious, Horry!" my lady retorted, losing patience. "I say I do not know, and you say 'Think so!' If you want to learn so particularly, ask him yourself. Here he is!"

Mr. Stafford had just entered the room. Perhaps she really wished to satisfy herself as to the state of his feelings. Perhaps she only desired in her irritation to put her cousin in a corner. At any rate she coolly turned to her husband and said, "Here is Horace wishing to know if you mind being turned out much?"

Mr. Stafford's face flushed a little at the home-thrust which no one else would have dared to deal him. But he showed no displeasure. "Well, not so much as I should have thought," he answered frankly, pausing to weigh a lump of sugar, and, as it seemed, his feelings. "There are compensations, you know."

"Pity all the same those terms came out," grunted Sir Horace.

"It was."

"Stafford!" Lady Betty struck in on a sudden, speaking fast and eagerly, "is it true, I want to ask you, it is true that that led you to resign?"

343